Lagan
Love

Peter Murphy

D0556839

**fiction
studio
books**

This is a work of fiction. Names, characters, places, and incidents either are the product of the author's imagination or are used fictitiously. Any resemblance to actual events, locales, organizations, or persons living or dead, is entirely coincidental and beyond the intent of either the author or the publisher.

The Fiction Studio
P.O. Box 4613
Stamford, CT 06907

Copyright © 2011 by Peter Damien Murphy

Jacket design by Barbara Aronica Buck

ISBN-13: 978-1-936558-12-4

Visit our website at www.fictionstudiobooks.com

First Fiction Studio Printing: June 2011
Publication Date: June 7, 2011

Printed in the United States of America

About the Author

Peter Damien Murphy grew up in Dublin and now lives in Toronto, Canada. *Lagan Love* is his first novel.

For:
Danny and Willie,
Jimmy and Joe McPeak,
Emanuel and Shuggie Murray,
Paddy and Tommy,
and of course, Jimmy Neil.

Acknowledgments

The Poem, "On Raglan Road," by Patrick Kavanagh is reprinted from *Collected Poems*, edited by Antoinette Quinn (Allen Lane, 2004), by kind permission of the Trustees of the Estate of the late Katherine B. Kavanagh, through the Jonathan Williams Literary Agency.

The Poem, "The Blackbird of Derrycairn," by Austin Clarke is reprinted from *Austin Clarke: Collected Poems* edited by R. Dardis Clarke and published by Carcanet/The Bridge Press (2008), by kind permission of R. Dardis Clarke, 17 Oscar Square, Dublin 8.

The copyright for the lyrics of "Jarama Valley," as written by Alex McDade, and first published in *The Book of the XV International Brigade,* are unclaimed, but I wish to acknowledge the author of the song I learned from the singing of Scots corner. I also acknowledge using excerpts from "The Land of Heart's Desire" by William Butler Yeats, free of copyright since 2009. Yeats will always be a towering figure on the Irish landscape.

The excerpt from "What I Learned from Caesar," by Guy Vanderhaeghe is used by permission of McClelland & Stewart and The Cooke Agency Inc.

I am grateful and indebted to Lou Aronica of the Fiction Studio who has been a great friend to *Lagan Love*, offering editorial guidance and encouragement throughout.

Also, Guy Vanderhaeghe, Canada's greatest writer, who encouraged me when others didn't and, of course, Eduarda, for keeping faith.

My Lagan Love

Where Lagan stream sings lullaby there grows a lily fair.
The twilight gleam is in her eye; the night is on her hair.
And like a lovesick lenanshee, she hath my heart in thrall;
Nor life I owe, nor liberty, for Love is Lord of all.

And often when the beetle's horn hath lulled the eve to sleep,
I steal unto her shieling lorn, and thro' the dooring peep.
There on the crickets' singing stone she spares the bogwood fire,
And hums in sad, sweet undertone the song of heart's desire.

Her welcome like her love for me is from deep within.
Her warm kiss is felicity that knows no taint of sin.
And when I set my foot to go, 'tis leaving love and light
To feel the wind of longing blow from out of darkest night.

(Translated from the Irish by Joseph Campbell)

Chapter 1

The dawn sprinkled the suburbs with golden promise that paled in the older parts of town, down streets broad and narrow to the docklands where everything was just plain and ordinary. Another brave new world beckoned, but Dublin was dubious – too often hope had been trampled down by foreign armies or strangled in dark alleys by the shadows of avarice and graft. Dubliners would rise to the inevitability of it all. They had risen up before and shaken off the Danes and Normans and then the British: only that took forever. No self-respecting Jackeen could consider putting faith in hope, even as European money rebuilt the roads and opened the whole country to progress.

At the mouth of the Liffey – the river that dissected the city in so many ways, the Pigeon House was encircled by gulls. More dangled above Dollymount where coral skies reflected puddled sands, reluctant to land while a black dog barked and gamboled around a woman who left imprints on the wet sand until the tide reached up and wiped them away. "Go back." Her voice like a Matins bell, she stood and faced the sea. The dog barked and plunged into the surf, its black coat like latex as it swam until she could see it no more.

On the Northside, someone whistled to the dawn. Dorset Street rose early; it had a proud heritage. O'Casey, Kearney and more than one Sheridan had all been born there, back when the

English owned the place, before they fled and Gombeens bought it up for a song: scruffy little landlords with no love for the place, slithering around for their rent, heedless to damp and disrepair. Some of the houses had given up and crumbled in on top of themselves. When you whistled on Dorset Street, you had to do it with bravado. Most people just prayed for better days or the occasional cause for celebration in the pub on the corner where there was always time for that.

Brendan Behan smirked from his place of prominence on the wall. He had faded and his face had been torn and glued back together. There were pin holes in the frayed corners, but he suited the mildewed wallpaper. Sinead shivered as remorse knelt by the side of the bed. *Hail Mary*: the Mother of God would understand. She'd be shocked too but she'd forgive, no matter how bad they were. She was a mother after all.

There was no response, other than the whistler, so she rose and scampered after her clothes, reaching with one arm with the other folded to shield her from the single eye that followed her around the room: James Joyce squinted from his self-imposed exile. He didn't look happy about sharing a room with Behan.

She'd have to call her mother, to let her know that she was all right. She'd tell her she was studying with a friend and had fallen asleep. She couldn't tell her about Aidan.

Her head was spinning and her stomach was delicate, but she had to get going. She'd sort it all out later. Right now, she needed to sneak out, as quietly as she could, but it was too late; he'd woken. She turned away and wriggled into her clothes as he fingered his hair away from his face and scratched his stubbled chin.

"You're sneakin' off then?"

"Yeah, I've class this morning."

"Better late than never I suppose," he muttered as she searched for her shoes.

"I didn't hear that."

"I said 'that's too bad.' I was goin' to take you somewhere nice for breakfast."

"Ya, that's too bad, but I gotta run. I had a great time – you know."

"That's it – 'I had a great time.'" He smiled and sat up reaching for a small cigar.

"Feck-off, I don't want a row; I just want to get to my lecture."

"Off you go then, you're probably scared anyway."

Sinead froze as she slid into her shoes. "What the hell would I be scared of – falling head-over-heels for some drunken poet?"

"Well, in that case, why don't we go?"

"I can't, Aidan." But she lingered. Her lecture wasn't for a few hours. She'd hoped to go home and shower. She needed to get a change of clothes, too. She felt a little cold and damp, like a fish.

"Just a quick cup of tea then?"

"I'll be late."

"Ah, sure what'll ya miss?"

"C'mon," he beckoned from the taxi. "Let's go to Bewley's and then you'll be right beside Trinity. Maybe I could even go in with ya and see what all this business stuff is about. I could even give my perspective – ya know, as a poet an' all."

She squirmed as she settled low in the back seat. *This was what you get for getting drunk and . . .*

She couldn't even finish the thought. It was the first time she'd slept with him – something she wasn't so sure about anymore. But it was all right to let her hair down once in a while and besides, if she didn't have a few drinks, she'd never find the courage to even talk with a man.

Mary would understand, both of them.

She did, however, look around before she got out and hurried him into the cafe where boilers and kettles hissed beneath the bins of wrinkled teas and coffee beans from everywhere the old merchants had traded, back when Dublin was in the Empire, when the British ruled the world.

Aidan toyed with the linen napkin, spreading it and folding it neatly again. "Can ya believe it, this is my first time in here, I mean, I walk past it all the time."

"That's nice," she muttered as she ordered Earl Grey.

"And what type of tea would you like?" the waitress smiled at him.

"Milk and three spoons of sugar, please, darlin'." he winked. "What's wrong?" he added as she left.

"They bring the milk and sugar to you."

"So why's she askin' then?"

"Never mind."

"I suppose you think you're so superior?"

"Only to some."

She waited for things to go wrong – they always did. She'd no idea how to talk to him now that they were sober. She should try being a little nicer though; he wasn't that bad after all. "Tell me, what are you writing these days?"

"I'm working on another anthology, ya know? With the Twilight Press, too."

She smiled as the waitress set their teas on the table, but he frowned at the empty cup before him.

"Is there anything wrong?" the waitress asked with professed concern.

"No, that's great now," he was smiling again, "and don't worry, I can pour it myself."

After he filled his cup, he took a white sugar cube with the tiny silver tongs and dipped it slowly, letting the tea spread like cancer. He did it five more times before pocketing the tongs.

"So what's that you're havin' – somethin' foreign?"

"Drinking Earl Grey in Bewley's is as Dublin as it gets."

"Only for posers from the Southside."

"Actually, the original owners were Quakers. They wanted to make sure everyone in Dublin could enjoy a nice cup of tea, no matter if they were rich or poor."

"Quakers? Weren't they the fuckers who gave soup to anyone who gave up the Old Religion during the famine? They think we'd sell our souls for a bowl of soup."

"Feck-off, Greeley, you'd sell yours for a pint."

"At least we're still Dubliners on the Northside, ya know, not like fuckin' Southsiders.

"Feck-off Greeley or I'll call the Guards and have you deported."

"Call them. Culchies are afraid to cross the river.

"So?" He asked as he stubbed his cigar in the clean white ashtray. "Why's it that we're an item then?"

"Is that what we are?"

"I hope so, otherwise, you'd just be usin' me 'cos I'm about to become famous an' all."

"Go an' feck yourself."

"I would, but I'm all fucked-out."

"I thought you'd be used to that, what with all your fans and all."

"Ah, c'mon, Sinead, I'm a poet; I need passion in my life."

"Are you saying that being with me inspires you?"

"No. But I'd like to give things a chance between us."

"Sorry Aidan. I have to run."

"Okay, then, but when are you goin' to let me see you again?"

"And why would you want to do that?"

"Because you're not as much of a bitch as you pretend."

"Fuck you, too, Greeley."

"That's the way it is with men," she muttered as she steered her way through the crowd. "As soon as you did it with them, they lose all respect for you." It never would have worked out: she should have known better. She cut across Duke Street, to Graham O'Sullivan's, to read the paper over coffee. Maybe she'd get a chance to talk with that really good-looking guy who worked there. Maybe he'd even notice her this time. She flicked her hair away from her face and marched on. She called her mother from a payphone along the way.

On the Southside, where Rathmines Road stretched toward the mountains, Janice sat in her window. Her reflection was pale and grimy. She had only been able to clean the inside of the windows, but she could live with that. She had to: she had made her bed and, as the night prowled, she was reluctant to lie in it. She had never been so alone before. There had been a fight on the street. It wasn't what she was used to. She couldn't think of any part of Toronto that was so unsettling, but she had never been around Queen and Sherbourne at night, one of the places her mother didn't approve of. She didn't approve of her moving to Ireland, either, even if it was to study at Trinity.

'Are you sure about this?' her mother had inquired with restrained insistence.

'Mother, I have told you several times. It is what I want to do.'

'I certainly hope so. Your father worked very hard to put that money aside for you. It cost us our marriage, you know? But I am sure you are old enough now to do as you will.'

'Mother, I am twenty-two years of age.'

'Don't be silly, you will always be my child, even when you are being headstrong and rash.'

Janice got that from her father, along with a fund. It was all that was left of him. Her mother expunged the rest, except the insurance money; she felt entitled to that. She had been his wife, even after his attentions had strayed. Yet, he had left money for Janice to spend on her education, but he had stipulated that she take her Master's Degree abroad. Janice had chosen Ireland because she thought that would please him. He was French Canadian, but she knew he would get the point.

'But why Ireland?' her mother's family asked in unified indignation. They couldn't understand why anyone would want to leave Canada. 'They kill each other for religion over there.'

'I will be fine. I am going to Dublin.'

'Is that in the North or the South?'

'It's in the east, actually.'

But it wasn't what she had expected. It was far more tired and dirty. She hoped it would be Georgian-like with bonneted ladies strolling on the arms of military gentlemen, as dark horses strained, as buskers fiddled for farthings and hawkers and street urchins littered the back drop.

A sudden breeze fluttered through her curtains. She wrapped herself in her robe and went to shower before the hot water was gone.

Pot-bellied lampposts, bulging windows, wide stone steps and recessed doors crowned by fanlights, dirty and dusty between wooden spars whose years of paint had wrinkled and crinkled. When she got to the coffee shop, she would sketch them in her journal. And St. Ann's Church, a microcosm of the past, a confusion of Romanesque between the solid keep of the beleaguered and stiff tower of the Enlightenment, wrapped in solid grey stones, but the doors were a dull red. Her sketches were like that, too, a confusion of styles pulling her in different directions.

Dawson Street was no longer the elegant enclave of the Protestant Ascendancy and now housed musty offices of aging public notaries with old school ties to Belvedere and King's Hospital: dusty old places with large grimy windows looking across at the rude intrusion of dull little cubicles aspiring to be offices. Near the coffee shop, buses bustled around the corner, swaying from side to side, hock-deep amongst impatient cars, diesel engines growling and belching clouds of thick black smoke as a phalanx of people crossed against the lights. But Janice waited for the little green man to mutely say: 'Walk now!'

"Oh! Look, there's that Canadian. You gotta watch."

"How long does it take to cross a feckin' street?"

"Forever, she keeps looking the wrong way."

Janice hesitated as the lights changed again, afraid to step in the surging river that went past regardless of signals and right-of-way. She waited for a large enough crowd to force passage to the other side. And, as she waited, she could see her classmates watching through the window.

Sinead lingered by the counter. She thought about asking about him, but she couldn't do that in front of the others. And besides, she probably looked like shite, she certainly felt like it but a few coffees would clear her head.

"Here," she called after the young woman who'd just served her. "Give me another coffee, please. I just saw my friend across the street." She waited by the counter for as long as she could. He might be in the back somewhere, piling up heavy boxes or something.

The young woman brought the coffee and the girls' voices grew louder. "She is such a . . ."

"Difference?" Sinead bustled past them to an empty table. "Give her a chance, will you? She's probably feeling really lost."

"That one would get lost in her own wardrobe."

"And she goes around like she's so much better than the rest of us."

"And why's she always writing things?"

"She probably keeps a diary."

Sinead usually sat with them and they made no secret of their feelings toward Janice so she found a clean table as the others gathered their things to leave, giggling and laughing as they went.

"What's so funny?" Janice asked as she squeezed through.

"You never know. One of them might have sneezed. How are things?"

"Very good, thank you. But I don't think I can get used to crossing streets here, you drive on the wrong side of the road and no one obeys the signals."

"They are more like suggestions. The trick is numbers: if there are enough of you, you can cross, if not, you've to wait."

"In Toronto, you would be charged with jay-walking."

They smiled at each other as they searched for something else to say. Sinead fidgeted with the corner of a page before folding the paper and pushing it to one side. "You're probably just feeling a little homesick. I know I'd be. But don't worry, in a few weeks, it will all be fine."

Janice sipped her coffee as her eyes grew moist. She was so glad to have someone to reach out to. She had cried herself to sleep for weeks. She could be brave through the day but tossed and turned at night counting wooly doubts as strange noises prowled until scattered by bawdy laughter lingering in the embrace of boozy sentimentality. But they dispersed, too, and wandered home to damp flats and dingy houses, straggling off in clusters and couples, a part of something and not alone like her.

But this morning, it was more than that. She was shaken by the fight. She had watched from behind her curtains as the gangs met. The night had filled with curses and the sounds of breaking bottles until police cars added lights and sirens to the frenzy.

"Were you hurt?"

"Well . . . not really. But I'm not used to things like this."

As her eyes began to well up, Sinead reached across and took her hand. "Well, then, you're going to have to go back and that's a pity as I just met you. It'll be all right, you'll see. I was just reading a new report that says we're starting to see a rise in foreign investment. That's great news."

"Is it?"

"Don't dwell on what's wrong with the world. It'll end up driving you mad. Then you'll go and kill yourself and that'll be a real tragedy."

"Why?"

"I've nothing stylish to wear to a classy funeral."

It did bring a brief smile to Janice's face before the next shadow flitted by. "Why is there so much violence here?"

Sinead thought about something funny to say, but she couldn't find anything fitting. "Poverty, despair and too much drink but that's all going to change. Soon, we'll see all kinds of opportunities, and we won't have to emigrate anymore. I don't know if that means anything to you, but for us, it's a huge change. So! How are you settling in?"

Aidan walked in the Green and kicked little stones by the pond. When one splashed into the water, the ducks and geese rushed over, in case it was bread. They were always hungry: enough to move Billy Cullen to remark: 'Feeding the ducks is an art, I declare, to see that each duck gets no more than his share.'

The thought of Billy always made him smile; despite all the shite that life threw at him.

'I was a little down,' Billy had once confided in him, a few years back, before Aidan got published. He hung around Grogan's then, trying to get noticed by those who'd known Kavanagh and Behan, people like John Jordan and Paddy O'Brian. He was hoping they might accept him, too.

'So I decided to end it all. I had a bottle of Spanish wine, and I put on some tango music: I wanted to create a bit of show, you know, to make a grand exit and all.

'Well! I'd almost finished the bottle, and I'd been dancing up a storm and all of a sudden, the fella downstairs is banging on the ceiling. "Jazus Billy," he shouts up. "What the fuck are you doing up there? My ceiling is after falling down."

'Anyway, by the time I'd finished helping him clean up, I didn't feel like ending it any more so here I am, by God's grace, to enjoy another day of misery and shite, and how are things with yourself?'

Ah fuck it. There's that old bitch again.

He'd never spoken to her, but she always stopped and stared at him. She usually wandered near Moore Street: the women in the markets had told him she went crazy and pushed her fella off Howth Head as he nodded to the barman, to bring another round. He didn't want to cause an interruption; he was getting it straight from those in the know. 'An' why the fuck would she do somethin' like that?'

'Ah, Sweet Jesus, it's as plain as the nose on your face. She did it for love.'

'I heard that he was seeing someone else.'

'I heard that she got off Scot clean.'

'Ah, not really, she was up in Portrane for years; and not sunning herself on the beach. She was in the hospital, ya know?'

They looked like the three monkeys as they reached out for their drinks. 'God bless you, Aidan Greeley. You're a true Bard of the People.'

She passed as the bells chimed: quarter past ten. Grogan's would be open soon. He could start ambling over, slowly. He didn't like being the first – that smacked of desperation, but it would be quiet and he could spread his notes on the bar, bits and pieces of paper scratched out and rewritten with a different word here or a new line there – so many possibilities hanging on delicate threads. But there was something beautiful in there if he could just reorganise it, if he could just find that pattern that was not a pattern at all.

His mind was a mess of disorganised verses piled on top of each other. Some were orphans and would wither, but others lingered defiantly, like stones in his shoes. They were the ones he found the time to polish. But even some of them were destined to irrelevance. He sipped his first with trepidation and lit another cigar. He'd start in a minute, after he had his smoke, after his first pint. By then, everything would settle down.

"Everything worth reading's been written," someone muttered as they sat beside him. Aidan covered his papers and raised his glass, swallowing a mouthful. There was no malice behind it, just the usual banter. Jimmy Neil could bite much harder than that. "Tommy, give us a couple of pints."

Jimmy lit a foul smelling cigarette and stared at Aidan who stared at his yellowed reflection between the rows of bottles behind the bar. His latest anthology had been well received – even 'The Irish Times' had reviewed it. He flicked his ash and blew smoke through his nose as Tommy placed the fresh pints before them and smiled until he could think of the right thing to say. "Aidan, I saw the review in the 'Times.' You're moving in elevated circles."

Gwen was right! He was getting noticed, but it felt hollow. He'd cut out the article and put it in his pocket. He wanted to take it out and read it again.

"He's still a gutter-snipe."

"Fuck-off, Jimmy."

The phone jangled loudly and Tommy was glad of the intrusion. The lads were a bit cranky this morning, it was best to leave them alone for a while. "Hello, Castle Lounge. Sure! Mrs. Fitzwilliams. I'll get him for you right now." He beckoned with the phone and busied himself slicing lemons.

"So," Jimmy smirked as Aidan returned, "getting calls from Horse-Protestants now? Some fuckin' workin' class hero."

"She's my fuckin' editor, ya gobshite."

"What the fuck do you need an editor for? Can't Catholic's spell?"

Aidan might have reacted, but Jimmy was an Atheist. "Tommy, give us two more and then I got to go."

"She has you on a short leash?"

He lingered over his pint for a while. He didn't want Jimmy to think he was at her beck and call.

Gwen's shoulder-length hair was carefully turned in at the ends. She wore a pearl necklace that flickered in the light as she moved. Her eyes were green and her lips were narrow but opened when he pressed against them. Her cheekbones were high and smooth, like Belleek china. Her hotel room was warm and smelled of woman, fragrances and scents that aroused his passions and his curiosities. She rose to greet him and her brocade robe opened revealing her scalloped lace bra, a short black mini slip and black silk stockings.

She smiled crookedly: their times together were so contrived.

She held his face for a moment. Her breath smelled of gin and her lips were warm as her hands fluttered, stripping him without ceremony. She pushed him back on her wide bed and mounted him without disrobing.

He liked watching her body coil and thrust as her breasts brushed against him and her mouth puckered, emitting a stream of oh, oh, ohs. He always knew when she was about to climax. She would lean back and run her hands through her hair, moaning loudly as her eyes rolled back into her head. And then, with sudden awareness, she would lean forward and grasp her breasts, staring into his eyes as she bit her lower lip. She would begin to nod knowingly at him in time to her writhing hips. She would moan, louder than before, and freeze, nodding at him with staccato conviction.

"Yes, yes, yessssssss!" She collapsed and slithered up his chest until their lips met. She inhaled urgently with her eyes closed so he couldn't see into her soul, but he didn't notice as he held her and stared at the ceiling.

There was a time when they lay together and his mind wandered through fields of words ripe for picking. But now as he reached for them, they scattered like crows across the closing window of the sky, denouncing their love with a raucousness that would follow him back into the streets, dogging him as he stepped around puddles.

"Oh my God," she exhaled as they lay back, sharing one of his cigars. "You make me feel so good. I don't know how I would manage without you."

"Isn't the old man enough for ya?"

She wished he hadn't said that. It would have shattered the mood if they were like other lovers. But it did shred the veils she had draped around the room, and now it looked a little dowdy. The wallpaper had a damp stain in the corner and his breath was tinged with stout, even the taste of his cigar couldn't mask that. But that was the way Fate had decreed it. She got into the ridiculous costumes their trysting demanded and played the part so well. She could inspire him with her passion and hunger; she had done it often enough. She could even seem grateful as she doled out his rewards – Fame, Adulation, Relevance and Influence, such easy favours to bestow.

"So why don't ya leave him?"

"Leave him? Then what? Set up house with a penniless poet?" She laughed a bitter twisted laugh that hung in the air. "Aidan, darling, we have a very good arrangement; let's not do anything to mess it up."

He took her in his arms as he nuzzled her until she seemed to sleep.

But she was awake.

Their covenant demanded True Love, something he was incapable of. Without that, she had little command over him. But there were ways: the Laws of Fate were pervious. There was always a chink. She would just have to find it and force her hand inside and squeeze his heart. He could decide how long she squeezed.

He stayed awake, too. He had to get away, but she wouldn't allow it. She published his work and pulled the strings to get him noticed. She promised to make him famous if he promised to keep her sated. It was a price he'd been happy to pay. But now that lust had evaporated, it was just a little sordid. It made him feel servile. He wanted to move, but even as he stirred, she murmured and held him.

"Promise me that you will never leave me. After all, we have just begun to shake the world. The article in the 'Times' was just the beginning."

"I know darlin' an' listen, I'd never fuckin' dream of leavin' you."

"Forsaking all others?" she whispered without opening her eyes.

"Ah, now, you're married; you shouldn't be askin' me things like that." He pulled himself away and sat on the edge of the bed.

"Aidan. A good poet would know better than to risk a woman's scorn."

She watched with some trepidation. She couldn't afford rejection. She feared that more than anything, fading into memory; like an old photograph. "Do you need money, darling?"

"Nay."

"Well, there's money on the dresser, take it if you want it."

He reconsidered and slid it into his pocket with a dexterity he'd learned on the street.

As the door closed behind him, she rose and walked to the mirror. She would find a way. If she couldn't gain his heart, someone else might, someone who might mean more to him. Then she would find a way to tear that someone from him and leave him to bleed to death in the gutter.

The old green Jaguar was parked outside of the Laragh Hotel when she got off the bus. Maurice was inside fortifying himself with whiskey, but Gwen didn't chide him for that. It was part of their deal: they would never intrude on each other.

"Bridey, darling," he greeted her as she stepped inside, "will you have a little sherry?"

"Actually, darling, make it a whiskey, a big one."

His face was owlish, but he smiled as only a cuckold can. "Did you sort out everything in the city?"

"Yes, darling. Thanks for asking."

"And did you deal with that damn dog?"

"Oh, darling, he wasn't so bad. He didn't mean to upset the sheep."

"And the cattle, even the horses were skittish around him. Damn hound of Hell if you ask me."

I never could stand your side of the family, Maurice smiled to himself. "Well, you look damn fine, Bridey, if I may say so. Let's have another drink?"

"Oh, darling, let's make it an early night. I am exhausted." She looked at her reflection in the mirror behind the bar. No one else would notice, but she was starting to wither a little. Maurice certainly wouldn't; he was lost in his own thoughts.

Chapter 2

"What's his problem?"

"He came home last night with his head full of nonsense."

Her father had stormed out as she came down the stairs. He hadn't even said 'Good Morning.' She poured herself a cup of tea and waited as her mother fidgeted in her gaze.

"Ah, it's nothing – just some gossip about the curate in Joe and Nuala's parish – the one that left a few weeks back."

Sinead remembered him: a lonesome man in his early thirties, one of those modern priests who held folk masses and all. Only he always looked like he'd taken his vows for the sake of his mother and now the reality of it all was pressing down on him. "He always gave me the creeps."

"May God forgive you for saying such a thing." But her mother wasn't too upset – Sinead really was a good daughter – a bit headstrong sometimes, she got that from her father, but she had her heart. If only her father hadn't talked her into going to Trinity. He had planted the seed early, too. When she was younger, he used to take her right inside, and she'd come home like she's seen the wonders of the world.

And ever since she had started to go there, all she talked about now was Mary Robinson this and Mary Robinson that. It was sure to end badly.

"Since when did Da care about anything that happened in the Church?"

"That's just what I was thinking, too. The devil himself must have a hold of his ear."

"I wouldn't worry about it; they'll fall out in a few days. Anyway, it's getting late and I better run."

Sinead didn't want to be rude, but she could tell her mother was in one of those moods. She didn't even finish her tea or read the paper. She might get the chance in the coffee shop. Janice would be waiting for her, but Sinead didn't mind. If only she didn't have so much to say, usually about herself.

Some mornings Janice had to wait, but she didn't mind – it gave her time with her journal. She added notes about details she would paint and besides, when she reread it, everything sounded so much more exciting and not at all lonely.

Dublin, September, Nineteen-Eighty Seven.

Bustling toward a time when it is no longer a provincial capital. It will never be London, but it has its own place in history. Great people lived here: Joyce, Swift, George Bernard Shaw and Samuel Beckett. I am absorbed by the millennium of life that whispers about memories and aspirations, marching bravely toward an odyssey of renewal. Sadly, it may be the end of the Celtic Twilight, yet it welcomes me. I feel that I am supposed to be here. The Irish and in particular, Dubliners, are not at all surprised that someone would move halfway around the world to live among them. They have charm and a gentle disposition toward life and conceal untamed passions in their pagan souls.

She carried it everywhere she went. As a teenager, she kept two, one her mother could easily find and one that was private. That was when she started calling it a journal. She also wrote many letters through the first few weeks, reaching out to what was familiar, letters to eccentric old aunts, covens of cousins and liver-spotted grand-dames whose relationship to the family was vague. She wrote to assure them she was doing well, but she couldn't convince her mother who had predicted she'd be home in a few months: 'Remember, Dear, it is a very Catholic country, they do not think as we do. They are not enlightened.'

'Father was a Catholic.'

'He was, but he gave it up.'

'Can you give it up?'

'Not entirely.'

"Good morning Sinead. I have to tell you about a dream I had last night of the border collie we had on the farm near Picton. I spent my summer holidays there and the dog would follow me everywhere. It was so nice – I never got lonely. Anyway, it had a mottled face, like a Taijitu, and would run off and then sit waiting with its red tongue hanging from the side of its mouth. What do you think it means?"

Janice leaned forward, but Sinead just smiled without looking up. "I think it means you miss your dog."

"Really? I think I'm being led to a new Fate."

"Maybe, but does Fate have time to deal with each one of us individually?"

"Sinead! Why do you read all of those stories? It's just news, none of it matters."

Sinead looked up before she could mask her frustration. She'd been reading about a European development agency and Ronan was still busy at the counter. In time, he'd come out and clear tables.

"They matter because we've had centuries of nothing. Everything we had was taken, and now we've a chance to build a future." She closed her paper with a resigned sigh and sipped her coffee. "So, tell me something again. Why are you here?"

"For the coffee," Janice struggled to contain her loneliness.

"Don't you have coffee in Canada?"

"We have Tim Horton's! It's a Canadian institution." And even as she spoke, tears welled up.

"What's the matter?"

"Oh, Sinead, I'm so homesick this morning."

Ronan was coming out to clear the tables; Sinead had to create a diversion.

"C'mon, Janice, you can't be crying like this in the middle of the morning."

"Sinead, I'm serious. I miss my father and came halfway around the world just to get away from mother and. . ."

She never finished and dashed for the toilets.

"Is everything okay?" he asked as he took their old cups away.

Sinead flustered in his smile. "Everything's fine."

"Are you sure? She seemed very upset."

Oh shit, he's going to think I'm heartless. "Actually, it's a woman's thing, you know?" *Ah, feck it. Why did I have to say that?*

"Good. I was afraid I might have poisoned her."

"She's fine. Could you get us more coffee?"

"Thanks, but shouldn't we be heading to class?"

"We have plenty of time."

"Really?"

"Really, so tell me, besides studying history, what else do you do?"

"I really want to become a painter."

"Are you any good?"

"I think so. I have painted since I can remember." She hesitated as Sinead smiled and turned to a new page.

"I know very little about painting except I do like lots of colour."

"So do I, colour is like a language to me," Janice beamed; they probably had so much in common. She paused to read Sinead's reaction; she wanted to seem ethereal, but Sinead had her head down so Janice stopped and wandered off into her own thoughts, back to her bedroom in that nice house, just off Don Mills Road, where life had been so much easier. Where she used to stand and look at the nascent canvas.

Her father always said there was still something from before, something that was all but obscured by the 'buzz-whuzz.' She wanted to capture it in her brush strokes – if for no other reason than to keep a part of him alive.

When he died, her secret painting flourished. Coloured curves gave way to probing angles and the canvas had depth and sometimes her brush strokes caressed desires she could not articulate. That raised a flutter of embarrassment in the bottom of her stomach. It was something she could no longer discuss with anyone. She looked like she might cry again, but Sinead noticed in time.

"Listen to me. I don't know you very well, but I think you're one of those people you read about, you know, who suffer all kinds of doubts and obstacles before they succeed."

"You really think so?"

"Of course, I do. You're just afraid and that's normal. I think what you're trying to do is very brave; you know, to leave home and try to do it on your own. I'm not sure I'd be able to do that."

"Do you really mean that?"

"Of course, I do and what's more, I think you'll become a great success. And now I think we better get to class."

They chatted all the way under the arch to the soft green space inside where everyone scattered to classrooms and libraries, sheltered from the ghosts of the savage years when the British imposed their civility. It was an old hallowed place where the selected few could consider the greater questions that were wisped away by the hustle and bustle of the day-to-day city. But sometimes, their ruminations spilled out into the streets, causing ripples as Trinity looked on with academic dispassion, even on Gratton's Parliament and the dirty Act of Union.

That evening, Janice painted with renewed passion and painted those things her dreams spoke of. She painted blue-white snow-covered landscapes where Voyageurs wandered in search of warmth and shelter, leaving only footsteps in the snow: footsteps that would fade as bitter winds came from the north and remade everything undisturbed. "Mon pays ce n'est pas un pays, c'est l'hiver," she hummed to herself as she paused. It had been her father's favourite song:

> *"Mon jardin ce n'est pas un jardin, c'est la plaine*
> *"Mon chemin ce n'est pas un chemin, c'est la neige.*
> *"Mon pays ce n'est pas un pays, c'est l'hiver."*

Her father left Quebec when the rumblings of separation incited the Anglo-exodus. He followed for a chance at a future and kept his old identity hidden to all but Janice.

Her mother's people had settled the Ohio valley but came north with the Empire Loyalists, fleeing the madness of revolution and retribution. They celebrated their 'Britishness' with an understated defiance, like they were clinging onto something the wind might take away. It meant little in Janice's time of growing up, but it meant something before. Her grandmother had been a 'Daughter of the Empire' and had photographs from those days.

But times change, even in Ontario, and old ways and old ideas were cast aside and, for the most part, forgotten. But there were some rumblings when her mother married Michael Tremblay.

'Michelle Tram-blai' was how her father would say it when he wanted to vex her Mother.

'Damn Frenchie,' was the chorus from assorted uncles and aunts. 'He's a papist, too.'

"I'm even starting to miss hockey!" Janice said a few days later. Her father had been a 'Habs' fan.

She really didn't like hockey, but she did like the reaction it brought out in her father. It spoke of the spirit that had braved winter in the wilderness – a spirit that was now hard to find. When the playoffs were on, he would sit in front of the television, night after night drinking 'Brador' which she'd fetch from the fridge, cradling the short stubby bottle as the coldness made her skin tingle.

"One Christmas, I bought him a Montreal sweater and he wore it every time he watched a game."

It was another secret bond between then. She liked to remember him when she spoke with Sinead; it helped to keep him alive, like he was still back in Toronto, where she could go and see him – anytime she wanted to. But she brought the sweater and wore it when she was alone.

"We play hockey here, too," Sinead smiled. "Only we play on grass. It's great fun; we get to run around whacking each other. We're playing on Saturday. C'mon out and watch and we can go out after. We might even find ourselves a few fellas."

"Will we need sticks for that?"

"It won't hurt to bring them along."

"Are you sure, Bridey?" Maurice asked as they stopped in front of the Shelbourne Hotel. It was Saturday morning and traffic was light. He had made good time.

"No, darling. I will be fine. You know what these things are like. It will be the usual crowd of pretensions expressing the same opinions in different words." She reached for the door handle but paused. "Oh Christ!"

"What's the matter?"

"Oh, it is nothing darling. I am just going to wait until that old woman passes."

She wore a tweedy Princess-line coat and her umbrella looked like Mary Poppins'. Her hat was adorned with freshly plucked flowers. "Humph. I think she's harmless, Bridey."

"Perhaps, but this is the third time I have seen her in the last few weeks."

He smiled as she stepped from the car. He would never intrude. They were man and wife in public: he was more of a man's man. He had hoped to remain a bachelor but succumbed to pressure from his mother. She had known about him and 'Pimples.' But it wasn't one of those things people discussed, certainly not people like them. Gwen had accepted it from the outset and smiled from his arm when society called. She was passionate; he had known her since she was a child. She thrived among artists and that was very good for business. How she satisfied her passions was not his concern, as long as she was discrete. One didn't want a scandal, after all.

"See you tomorrow, Darling." Gwen mewled through the open window. "And go straight home,"

After she had settled into her room, she phoned and left another message with the bar staff and headed to Bewley's.

When Janice finished shopping she stopped for cappuccino and a bagel, tucked her bags beneath the table and opened the wonderful book of poems she'd read about it in the 'Times.' The words spoke to things that echoed in her loneliness. They spoke of rebirth and finding the way to the very heart of the Fates and of love and hate as if they were interchangeable. They spoke of ancient forces that moved through the modern world preying upon the unsuspecting. They spoke of alienation in the middle of a crowded family and they spoke of the aloneness of truth. She finished her coffee and bagel as she studied the book jacket cover. He was very handsome in a damp, casual way, not at all what she had imagined. His words suggested he'd be more refined.

As she rose to leave, an elegant woman was watching her but quickly looked away. Janice smiled, but the woman never looked back.

"That's Dublin Castle," Sinead explained as they walked home from her game. "It used to be a dreadful place when the Brits were here, lots of torturing and bribery and all the other skullduggery they used to get up to."

"You're not very fond of the British, are you?"

"Personally, I don't mind them, but they're very full of themselves. They say they were just spreading civilization and all, but they were just stealing whatever they could get their hands on. We used to hate them and all they stood for. We blamed them for everything that went wrong, and some of the time we were right. They did everything they could to destroy us, claiming we were some type of sub-species. But things have changed since we joined the Common Market. We're becoming a part of a New Europe now."

Janice's British side was miffed. "How's that going?"

"It's going great, but we still have a lot of changing to do. When the Brits left, we got stuck in the way they used to do things. There was poverty everywhere, and the only escape was to leave the country." Sinead paused as a chorus of bells rang from every spire and steeple:

"The Angelus of change

"Peeling over tenements,

"Miasmas of neglect,

"The legacy of absentee Landlords

"And Gombeen men."

"Did you write that?"

"Are you kidding me? That was written by some drunken lout who passes himself off as a poet."

"I liked the way he used the Angelus though. Is he religious?"

"No one in Ireland is really religious. We all pretend to be, but we're still pagans at heart. We've just learned to mask it so the rest of the world stops bothering us."

"I think you're all a little paranoid, eh?"

"Not really. It's just that we haven't had a moment of peace in fifteen-hundred years."

"Who do you hate more, the British or the drunken lout who passes himself off as a poet?"

"Like I said, Janice, things have changed. There's no time for brooding over old hurts. A girl just has to move on. Besides, that's my bus stop, over there. Will you be all right from here? I wouldn't want you to get lost, you know. You might fall into bad company and I'd never forgive myself if anything happened."

"Go on. I'll be fine. See you on Monday."

Sinead waved from the bus. She had wanted to invite Janice home for dinner, but she had no idea what would be waiting for her. She blew a kiss as the wind rippled up from the river, whipping brown and yellow leafs from the trees along the quays where a new building struggled out of the ground, devouring Wood Quay as it rose. Even Mary couldn't stop it.

Janice was feeling a little adventurous, like something was calling to her; daring her to step out of all that she had been. She wanted to walk, but it was becoming a little scarier with every step she took. Dublin was a wild beast. It wasn't malicious, just unpredictable: you never knew what might be prowling around.

He loitered, just beyond a pool of light, looking more disheveled than his book-jacket photo. He lit a small cigar, holding the flaming match long enough to cast a flickering light across his face as the sulfured air reached her. She wanted to say something casual, but she couldn't think of anything. The 'Times' said he was 'a voice for his times' and 'a rapidly maturing talent worthy of praise'. She didn't dare speak to him; it would just come out all wrong. Instead, she cast a long cool glance that would suggest mild interest. She had practiced that 'look' as a teenager, only then it made her look constipated. But, at the moment when she would hold his eyes and send a little arrow to his heart, he smirked and she was destined to walk on into the night.

"What time is it?" he asked after her.

She turned and saw the wall clock above his head. "It's eight thirty."

"What?"

"Half past eight."

"That's almost past my bed time."

"Not mine, I'm out for a stroll." She continued to walk, hoping he would follow.

"So where are we goin' then?"

He looked so cute despite his posturing, shyly playing the tit-for-tat game that boys and girls had played for ever. She could see he was interested, but she feigned a moment of disdain.

"You're very sure of yourself."

"Don't ya know me – I'm Aidan Greeley. Perhaps you've heard of me?"

Janice tried not to smile. She demurred with what she hoped looked like tired resignation, but she stepped in time to his loping gait.

He played along, too, and insisted she let him buy her a drink to make up for his lack of manners. She resisted for as long as she dared, afraid he might give up and wander back into the night. But he could read mixed signals and soon they were seated at the bar of a little pub, full of noisy banter and the smoke of a hundred cigarettes glowing between red lips, smoldering between brown fingers chatting on the air or growing grey as they lay forgotten in ashtrays. It was the type of place that should have made her feel like an outsider, but he wrapped her in his charm, apart from the muffled crowd and their beery good humour. He smoked one small cigar after another and when he offered her one, she decided what the hell, and as her head began to spin, he began to tell her about himself as he nodded to the barman, who quickly obliged.

He was born in the middle of a large family, in the poorer streets of the Northside, "not far from the docks," he stressed and watched her face, leaning toward her like he was sharing a secret. "My Da was a strict man, ya know? He worked at the docks – it was his life. He felt that unloadin' ships made him a part of the whole world. 'Did a boat from Algiers today an' tomorrow we've one from Singapore' he'd say an' stick his chest out – like it made him important or somethin'.

"He'd go to the pub every night an' if we needed anythin' – that's where we saw him. But he was good enough and we never really went without – at least we ate an' had shoes."

"I thought everyone in Ireland grew up barefooted and wrapped in rags." She dipped her lips to her second drink so he wouldn't see her smile, but when she reached out to place her glass on the bar, she leaned closer to him, almost tipping her stool and spilling into his lap.

"Only those with literary pretensions and smeared with ashes from the fireplace, ya know?" He'd almost reached to steady her.

"You seem to have done well enough."

He was not the type of man she would have considered, but he had a look in his eyes, a look she had often seen in her father's.

"I suppose. My Ma did everythin' for us while she could an' she had nine children. She would've had a tenth, but they both died." It all seemed so normal and everyday; like he was inured. She made sympathetic sounds and leaned a little more when he turned to try to get the barman's attention.

When he turned back, he noticed and smiled before he continued. "Then we all grew up an' went our separate ways. One of my brothers joined the Merchant Navy an' sailed the world. Another joined the British Army an' died in the Falklands War. I never got over that. I mean its bad enough fightin' for the Brits but to die over a bunch of scraggy islands in the middle of nowhere – it makes no sense."

Janice leaned back and gazed at him. He was a little crude and vulgar and his spoken word was rough, much rougher than the raw voice of his poetry. But he had deep dark eyes and his lips were full and sensual.

He'd tried to finish school when he wasn't before the courts for petty larceny. His trail was filled with twists and turns as though Fate defied him at every corner, but he persevered with a good-humoured defiance. He had more life in him than any man she'd met, and as she thought that, she considered the idea of him and her and that was so out of character for her.

He moved his seat closer to allow someone to squeeze by and his hands brushed her knee. And when they leaned toward each other they were almost face-to-face. "Tell me about yourself."

And Janice began to talk of all that was safe in her life – all that was Canadian. She told him of her father and how she missed him but never mentioned that he was dead. It wasn't something she was ready to share with him.

"You're not one of those spoiled little princesses, are you?"

She was surprised and a little angry so she told him about Robert and how she could go back anytime.

"Do ya really think he'll wait for ya?"

"I beg your pardon?"

"Ah, don't get all prissy on me, I didn't mean anything. It's just that you sound like you're a bit fascinated by yourself."

That was enough for Janice. She stood up, wanting to slap his face, but instead, she walked out as the warm mists of their intimacy shriveled. It was a damp night, but she hardly felt it. He was rude and vulgar, and he'd no right to talk to her like that, not when she was about to consider him.

As she walked the cobblestone street, her heels clattered the rhythm of her rage. The night was clearing, and with the cold breath of the city on her flushed cheeks, her anger started to ebb. And, as her anger ebbed, she began to realise she was alone again, on a dark street, in a strange city, late at night.

But he'd followed along behind her, calling out: "Slow down, you're all alone out here, an' it might not be safe!"

He was right. Her choice was obvious — *I can have this rude man walk me to my door and then I can wish him a good night and I will never, ever, buy his books again.*

As they turned along the bank of the Grand Canal, he was close enough to reassure her and far enough to make it obvious that they were not together. He began to talk again and his voice was different. It was like he was struggling to explain something, something that was difficult for him to say. He spoke of how open he was with people and how that sometimes caused him problems.

"It happens a lot with women," he told her and, despite herself, she softened.

"I get flustered, ya know, an' I say the wrong things, but it's only because I'm stunned by beauty. I can't help myself, I just get all defensive an' all. It's a Dublin thing, ya know, like a virus."

She wasn't going to forgive him so easily, but he was seeing her home. "Are you saying I am Mary of the Plagues?"

"Who?"

"A queen of Scotland and England for a while, but you probably know her as Bloody Mary."

"Ah," he hid his confusion behind a flaring match as he coaxed his cigar. "Ya know," he smiled as he emerged from the smoke, "you remind me of how my mother must have been — ya know, before she got married an' started having children an' all."

"Aidan that is almost oedipal."

He hunched his shoulders like he was in need of comfort, but he recovered quickly.

"So you're studyin' in Trinity, an' you're Canadian, an' you're very pretty."

"Pretty? Is that the best you can do?"

"Well, see that's the thing, ya know, some people say that beauty is only skin deep."

"Is that a problem for men?"

"Well, I don't speak for all men, ya know. I only speak for me."

"I thought you were supposed to be the voice of your times."

"So you lied."

"When?"

"You knew who I was."

"So recite something for me."

He knelt on the cold damp street and held her hands as he spoke into her eyes:

"An' when beauty walks on narrow streets

"It reaches in through narrow doors an' dirty windows.

"It lights up the dingy rooms where poets gather to offer praise."

She gazed at him for a moment, until a breeze ruffled the surface of the dark waters of the canal. "You could charm the pants off a girl."

He almost looked shocked for a moment.

"What?" Janice pleaded, "What did I say?"

"Oh, it's nothin'; it's just that we're not used to such talk here in Dublin."

"Oh! Right! It might interest you to know I have been around the university crowd for ..."

"Ah! The University crowd – a bunch of posing Southsiders, not like in the old days when Swift and Emmet went there and

Henry Gratton and, the best of them all, Theobald Wolfe Tone – the one who tried to unite us under the one banner."

"You sound like a ragged-trousered poet."

"What? Don't you have classes in Canada or do you all pretend to be in the middle?"

"It's not that, it's just an odd time to bring it up."

"I'm proud of my class. We're the heart an' soul of this city."

"Is that why you're all so defiant?" Janice was cautious; it was a powerful undercurrent in Dublin and it drove its people to live in defiance like their whole lives were revolution against oppressions. It drove others to live lives of indolence, but it drove him to write, it said so in the 'Times.'

"What choice do we have?"

They stopped at the stairs to her flat. She stepped on the first step so she could look directly into his eyes. She was feeling playful, but she couldn't invite him in. She thought about it, about her empty bed that overlooked the street where the fight had been, but it wasn't right, not yet.

He kissed her on the cheek and smiled. "Goodnight to you now, you'll be fine from here? I'll drop by in the mornin', if you like."

"Goodnight, Aidan."

She closed the door and listened.

On the street outside, his footfalls faded in the ancient silence and a shadow moved between the pools of light. It paused to look up at her window and smiled.

Chapter 3

Janice tossed and turned and her breath misted as a cold hand reached her face. It stroked her cheek and traced the edge of her lips. She murmured but didn't wake as something stretched out beside her and when it exhaled, soothing colours swirled around her heart. All that had been ambiguous took shapes that were new and wondrous and filled her with heady disregard for all that constrained her. But when her visitor inhaled, it drew out particles of her vitality. And, each time it inhaled, it did so with more urgency.

Janice floated on the surge and ebb that rose a little higher until she could take no more.

The night visitor laid her gently back and stood over her for a moment.

Janice opened her eyes as it began to fade.

"Wait," she called into the darkness.

Someone was banging on the door as she fumbled into her robe and teased her hair from her flushed face. Aidan was standing there as if he'd never left. He'd come to see if she was okay, and, as it was 'a nice Sunday, a bit cold, but sunny for the beginnin' of October,' he was wondering if they could take a walk, 'to see the sights an' take the air?' He handed her a bunch of wild flowers in a scrawny sprig of heather. She tried not to laugh, and he saw the struggle in her face. "Do ya not like them?"

"No! Of course, I do." Janice gingerly handled the clump of earth attached to the roots. "I'll just put these in water."

"I'll wait out here," he offset the awkward silence. He was being cute and shy so she tried to arrange herself accordingly. But as she stopped by the mirror, her dream followed. She dismissed it with a smile; it was only a dream, strange and disturbing, but still a dream. Her reflection grinned back: a familiar face that knew everything about her. She'd been alone too long, cloistered in her refuge, but maybe that was about to change. "Would you like some coffee?" she asked from her window.

"No, I'm fine, but you go ahead."

"Tea?"

"No, I'm fine, really."

He sat on the railing with his back to her window, his foot resting on the boot scrapper and smoked a small cigar. He was excited and, though he'd never admit it, nervous.

I could really like her. I mean she listens and there's no slaggin' or bullshit with her and she seems to like me for who I really am?

A drunken fornicator?

I prefer to think of myself as a poet.

He whistled to drown out that voice – the one that rose whenever the sun was about to shine.

Janice dressed hurriedly but made sure what she wore was perfect. She was doing fine until she got to the shoes. *Is it going to be a long walk? Should I wear running shoes?*

And, after she had changed her shoes, she had to start again as he began to whistle.

They stopped for a moment where Portobello Bridge humpbacked over the canal that dwindled now between over-grown banks and the flotsam and jetsam of the city. She had sat by the lock one free afternoon, sketching as a swan passed in full sail, past the mediocre ducks and clustering geese that came south for the winter and made an awful noise when disturbed.

"The belfries bid their matins

"Soft as the day begins

"Soothing Saints and Sinners

"Coming home from Saturday night."

"I love that poem. It catches the mood of the city so well."

"Are you an expert on Dublin now?"

She wasn't sure if he was joking and brushed her hair behind one ear. "Well, I've been here for almost two months and, besides, I appreciate good poetry and good poets." She bumped her shoulder against him and let her hand brush the back of his. She was excited and nervous. She'd never behaved this way before. He could feel it, too, and it wasn't what he was expecting. "Thanks, Janice. It means somethin' that you like it."

He turned toward her, to take her in his arms, but it was far too soon.

He stood in limbo until someone moved in the corner of his eye, singing tunelessly and trying to touch the end of his dropping cigarette with the sputtering flame of a match. He tried a few more times as they approached.

"Ya know," Aidan continued as he reached for his pocket, "We're the last bastion of the Celts, a people unto ourselves – always fightin' change but never conformin' to it." He wanted to sound knowledgeable; she was going to Trinity after all.

She smiled as she noticed him blush. "Freud had an interesting view on the Irish."

He wasn't sure what she meant, but he was sure it had something to do with sex so he decided to play cool. "Isn't he dead? Anyway, as I was sayin'," he wanted to stay on more familiar ground, "we had to learn to live outside the laws the British imposed. And now we've our own talkin' shop in Leinster House – we ignore their laws, too." He stopped and cupped a flaming match in his hands. The swaying man struggled to aim his dropping cigarette. "God bless you. And your missus, too," he added after noticing Janice. "It's great to see young people still getting up for Mass."

She looked on disdainfully as the man puffed his cigarette and shook hands with Aidan before swaying off. "And I thought this was still a very pious country." She meant it in jest, but his eyes hardened a little.

"I suppose you think we're still priest-ridden peasants."

"Not that so much as, well, there are a lot of religious references everywhere and the church does seem to have a stake in everything."

"Well," he paused to consider what he said. "That was the way things were, but it's all changin' now that everyone is findin' out about what the priests and nuns were really up to – all the scandals, ya know? They've been buggerin' us for years and no one would do anythin'. The Guards look the other way and no politician has the balls to go up against the Church."

"That man was in a sorry state," she said to end the new silence.

Aidan paused before he answered. "Are you against a man havin' a drink or what?"

"No, not at all, but you have to admit he was in an awful state."

"Brendan said 'to get enough to eat was an achievement but to get drunk was a victory.'"

"I was never a fan of Behan, I preferred Joyce or Yeats."

"And what do you think about Beckett an' Synge an' O'Casey?"

She smiled; she knew the litany so well. Dubliners were proud of their literary legacy. It was collective, a feeling of shared achievement, though most of those writers had been outcasts in their own time, in their own city. But she knew enough to let it pass.

The walked by the canal, single-file, along the towpath where horses had strained hauling sluggish barges over slow moving water as perch darted through stems of lily pads in constant dread of prowling pike.

"Back that way, there's a monument to Patrick Kavanagh."

Janice had visited the bench that commemorated the dead poet: a place to reflect on a dissolute life that left poems of such simplistic beauty.

Aidan spoke of Kavanagh like he knew him, and like half of Dublin, he was familiar with the small details of the ex-farmer's life.

"Ya know," he lilted in that way the Irish relay the delight they take in their own stories. "Paddy himself said that he was a poor farmer who dabbled in verse an' became ensnared."

Janice didn't want to talk about the host of poetic ghosts that hovered over Dublin; she wanted to talk about him. She wanted him to tell her about his own writings and feelings, and she wanted to know how he felt about her. And as they searched for the things they could have in common, they walked and talked right through the confusion of streets behind Portobello House.

"It used to be a hotel when people traveled by canal. Then it became a nursin' home. Jack Yeats lived there for a while. Do you know of him?"

"No, but I'm not in the habit of meeting men in nursing homes."

"What?"

"Nothing, Aidan, I'm joking. Don't women joke in this country?"

"They make me laugh."

They walked and talked as the city rose, un-entwined, but on occasion, her hand brushed the back of his, or she miss-stepped enough to gently brush against his arm and once, in a cobblestone lane, she almost stumbled. He held her until she was steady, and when he let go, his hands traced to the tips of her fingers. They smiled at each other by Christchurch Place where they could see all the way down to the Liffey, under the arch and along what was left of Winetavern Street, hoarded now as the digging continued, right down to the bones of the old city.

Across the river, the Four Courts stood proud, looking down to the Custom's House – monuments to the British days. But the Northside was decayed. Buildings leaned against each other and roofs sagged under the weight of history. Tradesman's shops and dwellings combined; they'd never been fashionable and now housed the rag-tag clothing factories where girls from the 'flats' earned a few shillings stitching and sewing.

It was where he liked to prowl, along Capel Street, and Henry Street, in search of the old Dublin that flourished in the markets off Moore Street where hawkers sang the same old songs. And around East Arran Street where men loitered to unload fruit-trucks for ready cash that never made it past the pubs that stood like toll collectors on the corners. His commentary wafted out behind him, but they wouldn't walk that way today; he'd something else to show her.

"Up this way is the Coombe where Dutch, French an' Spanish tradespeople flocked when Dublin was the place to be, ya know, when the gentry spent a part of their season here, before Gratton's Parliament was sold out."

She looked at fruit rotting in the gutters as the wind played catch with plastic bags and the discarded pages of yesterday's news.

"This is where we lived when the British owned the place. This is where they kept us, the tinkers an' tailors an' candlestick-makers, all crammed in here out of sight an' out of mind. This is the real Dublin. Not like where you go to school – that's where Horse-Protestants liked to parade."

"I take it you're not very fond of them?" she asked to change the mood, before his intensity gave way to brooding.

"Most of them were nothin' more than brigands an' bastards. They jacked the rent to pay for their idle lifestyles an' when the famine came, we starved while they went on as if nothin' happened.

Ya know, the famine was a load of bullshit; the country was producin' more food than it needed. Only that food didn't belong to us. We grew it, on our own land too, but we had to pay it as rent. We had to subsist on potatoes an' when they failed, we were fucked.

"Of course, that worked in their favour, too. After we all started to leave, they were able to clear the land. They wanted us out an' they nearly succeeded. In eighteen-forty, there were eight million of us an' by nineteen-twenty, there was less than two."

It wasn't what she wanted to talk about, but she couldn't be rude. It was a local holocaust with its own legion of deniers: she had to be sympathetic. "Not that many died during the famine, did they?"

"No one has a clue. We didn't rate high enough for them to keep track of it all. They used to say we were vermin."

"And what happened to the rest?"

"Emigrated to Canada and America mostly. Others were sent to Australia as criminals."

"For rebelling?"

"Sometimes, but most were sent for takin' fish out of the gentry's rivers. They owned everythin'. The Penal Laws let them take whatever they wanted."

"The Penal Laws?" She wanted him to know that she was fascinated. She was but at something else. He reminded her of Pablo Neruda: her father had kept a book of his poems from his student days, though Aidan was far more handsome.

"Ya, they were laws that meant the Irish had no right to anythin'. They couldn't own anythin' an' if they did, it could be bought off them at a price decided by a Protestant. I guess it was a plan to turn everybody over to the New Religion."

"And how did the Irish survive?" Janice was enthralled, not by what he said but by how he spoke. He was tall and, when his convictions got the better of him, intimidating. But she felt safe beside him as he guided her through his streets.

"Every generation rose up to rid ourselves of them. That's why they fear us so much – because we won't lie down."

"I thought the Irish were belligerent and loved to fight."

He stopped and eyed her coolly as he lit another cigar.

"We don't really. It's just that for the last millennium, we've had no choice."

"In Canada, we see Ireland as a very sectarian place because of Northern Ireland."

"That's a load-a-shite, really. That was imposed by the British – ya know – the divide an' conquer thing they do everywhere. It's just that we've very strong feelings about injustices. We know what it feels like at the bottom."

They drifted in silence for a while as she wandered in her own mind. She was miles away, in Paris.

She would live there when she became famous. She might even let him move with her. He could sit in cafes penning ballads of Revolution while she painted in the garret above. In the evening, she would come down in a red dress and they would tango in the street. "Tell me," she asked as she linked his arm, "how did you become a writer."

"Well, after my Ma died, it was hard for me in school an' all. But I liked the readin' an' writin' parts. I didn't care for the other stuff, 'cept maybe history. There was loads of stuff about Romans an' Greeks an' people that liked good poetry and treated poets the way Bards were treated. An' I couldn't see myself bein' very happy doin' anythin' else so I started to tell everyone that I was a poet. An' then I went off to write all my poetry before anyone could come askin' to hear them.

"Then, one day, I showed them to my teacher an' she loved them. She said that she'd give them to a friend of hers who knew someone who might print them in a magazine. That was around the time I got wounded – for Ireland."

"Wounded?"

"Yes, darlin', fightin' for Ireland, ya know – with the boys!"

Janice didn't want to know. 'The boys' was a euphemism for the IRA, as well as criminal activists who pursued more personally rewarding ideals.

They passed along Francis Street with gaps here and there, where a house had fallen, leaving an imprint on its neighbour: the jagged edges of collapsed roofs, the fossils of rooms, walls, stairs and a diversity of distorted fixtures, all gone but for the fluttering of old wallpaper.

And, as they walked, she noticed the music in his voice. He offered words like each one was a treasure that had been selected from the rubble and jumble for her alone. He was very handsome and, she decided, was quite well kept. His eyes were deep and calm but ruffled now and then by stirred emotions.

And, as he continued to tell her the history of his city, she didn't tell him she was doing research at the history department. It wouldn't have mattered, the history he spoke of was a living story unlike anything she'd read. It was as if the past still hovered, infecting him with resentment and pathos. It seemed to leave impressions on the air; pleading to be captured before all memory of it was lost.

He stopped every now and then to point to buildings and tell the stories they'd hidden from change and progress – "a thousand years of struggle and strife," he called it. "On this corner, Robert Emmet was hung, drawn an' quartered – the mercy of British Justice an' all that fair-play shite they're always goin' on about."

It was something he had to talk about, like family history that shaped them all individually and collectively. But he wanted to soften it, to show other emotions, so he talked of characters whose memory would never fade, those that stood out and made life a bit more colourful. She wished she'd brought a sketchpad: there was so much to remember.

He waved his hand to clear it all and told her how the city had grown from its Viking past of wooden huts that huddled by the river.

"Dubh Linn," he emphasized, "the Dark Pool. But the Gaels used to call it Baile Atha Cliath, the town of the hurdled fords. That was before the Normans came and took the whole place from us."

In her mind, Janice could see Vikings and Normans building walls and keeps to fend off the wildness so they could sleep in peace in the strange land of a feral people. But somewhere along the way, the Irish had crept back in and re-established themselves – but they always had to struggle.

"It's tough growin' up in places like this, especially without a mother around. You end up gettin' very hard an' bitter. That's why I started to write, ya know; to get some of those feelings out. That an' the fact that it's somethin' to do over a couple quiet pints of Guinness, ya know?" He laughed as he motioned with his head toward the low door of an old pub.

Sometimes, it took a while for someone to answer.

"Morning," Sinead offered cheerfully. "Can I speak with Janice?"

"I don't think she's in right now. Would you like me to check?"

"If you wouldn't mind."

The phone rattled, the knocking went unanswered, the footsteps returned and the phone rattled again. "There's no answer. I'm sure I heard her talking to a man outside."

"Really, what did he look like?"

"I didn't see him, but he smoked cigars."

"Is everything all right there, Sinead?" her mother called from the kitchen. Her father shuffled by in his Sunday suit, heading for the pub. "Do you need a few quid?" It was the first time he'd spoken in days. Things were still tense.

"No, thanks anyway, Da, I'm fine."

"Take it while he's offering, he's only going to spend it in the pub."

"Would you begrudge me a day of rest?"

"Ya had all of yesterday to rest. You should get yourself to Mass if you can still remember where the church is."

"Sure how can I miss it? It's where all the children have sore arses."

"Well, God forgive you. How dare you say such a thing in this house?"

"Can't I speak the truth in my own house?"

Her father picked up his paper and rolled it tight, but her mother couldn't contain herself. "Why are you happy to believe lies against anything that's proper and decent?"

"There's nothing decent about what that little fucker did and if the bishop hadn't hidden him . . ." He slapped the rolled-up paper against his palm.

The whole parish was awash with rumours. Even the Parish Priest heard them. He covered it in his sermon too, about the evils of idle gossip – 'An evil arrow that can penetrate the armour of a life of good deeds'. Her mother made a point of repeating it every chance she got. "That's enough about it now. We're in my house and I'll not hear another word about it.

Her father stammered. "Your house? And who spent their whole lives slaving to pay for it? This is my house, too, woman or am I mistaken?"

"Your house? If you spent some time here instead of down in the pub . . . "

But her father excused himself to get his coat.

She got off the bus at Stephen's Green and hurried past the hoarding toward Grafton Street.

She cut through Johnson Court, to the jewelry shop where she sometimes liked to pause to look at the rings in the windows. She liked to pick an engagement ring from the display and imagine the man who would give it to her. She wasn't too sure what he looked like, he changed so often, but that really didn't matter.

Lately, he looked a lot like Ronan, only he'd be far more interested. He'd notice her right away and fall head over heels in love with her, right from the beginning.

She stepped between the open gates to the peace and quiet of Saint Teresa's and let the door close softly behind her. There was a Mass in progress, something she didn't want to disturb and something she didn't want to be part of. She moved softly to where shadowy figures sought direct audiences with the ornate ceilings and the lower deities that lingered in the niches along the wall.

"I don't want to let this become an issue between me and Janice," she whispered, the swish-whish of her lips joining the muted chorus around her. "I guess I still have a bit of a soft spot for Aidan, but that's over now . . ."

Her meditations were interrupted by the hissing penitent two pews over: almost prostrate, deep in solitary anguish, beating his chest as his eyes rolled to the roof, oblivious to the tinkling of bells and the drone of responses, alone and apart from the common communion. Sinead recognized the coat, old and tweedy with a high collar that almost hid his face. *Now what does Gerry Morrison have to be so contrite about?*

She raised her hands before her face like she was deep in her own prayers. She could peep through her fingers without being noticed. Gerry's lips were moving in time with the shuffling of beads as his head rose to the roof and back down to his chest.

Each time his head came down, Gerry thumped his chest as if to drive his demons out.

Sinead smiled a knowing little smile: old people were like that. The older they got, the more time they spent regretting the past. She'd seen it in her grandfather, a violent drunken lout who beat all shreds of life out of his wife until she gave up and died. Alone in the

world, the old man turned to public acts of contrition and impos-
ing his new-found piety on all around him. *I never figured Gerry to be
like that.*

She sidled out as the Mass rose to praise God while Gerry
contorted himself some more.

Grogan's was abuzz and she had to fight her way to the bar.

"How are ya, Tommy, have you seen Aidan this morning?"

"No. Mister Greeley hasn't graced us with his presence as yet.
Perhaps he's attending Mass."

"Ya, right! I never thought of that. Give me a pint of lager."

She was jostled as she raised her drink and some of her beer
sloshed on the floor. Sunday mornings in Grogan's were like that, a
bustle of gaiety crammed into a brief hour and half, barely enough
time to rekindle the warm embers of Saturday night, still in the
netherworld of half-drunkenness and when the pub shut, most of
them would go home and sleep the afternoon away. Sinead moved
away from the bar, to be alone with her thoughts and to seem nonchalant. If Janice and Aidan showed up, she'd look like she'd just
dropped in for a drink, like nothing had happened.

"How are ya, Sinead?"

"Ah! How are ya, Gerry?"

"Can I join you?"

Sinead found two stools as Gerry got his drink. He looked
different now, lined by ages and cares but not as twisted. "So? Are
you well?"

"I'm a bit delicate, you know? We'd a bit of a session last night,
and now we've to pay for our sins. He lit a small Woodbine and took
a long swig of his stout.

Janice hated drinking at midday. She wanted to leave but
sensed he'd rather stay. He was telling another story about when he
read his work at the home of some literary 'big-wigs.'

"The house was massive, I would've gotten lost in it but my publisher was there. She got me a drink an' started to introduce me to everyone." He watched her face for a moment; he wanted to make the right impression. "She knows a lot of people, ya know, an' goes to all kinds of artsy parties. Maybe I should bring you to the next one."

"And why would you do that?"

"Because I'd love to show those Southside posers, ya know, showin' up with the best lookin' woman they've ever seen."

"Oh, Aidan, was that a compliment?"

It was a bit awkward. He wanted to be more aloof, but he also wanted to make the right impression, she was Canadian and all, and she went to Trinity, and she was beautiful. "Of course it was. I'm a poet, ya know, it's my job to pass comment on beauty an' all."

They were cozy, but the pub was shutting for the dreaded holy-hour and they were ushered out onto the sunny sidewalk. She stood back to watch him as he lit another cigar. He smoked so many that he looked incomplete without one.

"Let's be off then," he smiled back. "Let me show ya where so many of us died for Ireland."

There is that sense of oneness again, she thought to herself but said nothing. She knew where they were going. She had visited Kilmainham Gaol before, wrapped in its brooding walls lest the ghosts it housed should break free and point accusing fingers at those who used the reins of power to drive the horses of personal ambition. It was a sad place where the residue of human suffering lingered – it had no place else to go. He, of course, knew someone who allowed them in to walk unguided.

"I write a lot of my stuff here, ya know? It sort of inspires me." And even in the sunshine, Janice could imagine him sitting in a dark haunted cell writing vitriolic lines by flickering candlelight while his dark hair framed his white face against the shadows.

"This is the original part," he explained as they walked down a dank corridor, past innumerable cells; mildew stained recesses where the Irish had been interned for defying their British masters.

"Back then, democracy was reserved for those of the New Faith. The Catholic Irish had lost their say in their own affairs an' any effort they made to regain it was met with brutal an' dissuadin' violence. Any call for change was charged as sedition, but we wouldn't bow down."

His voice evoked the ghosts of those who had paid that price and died horribly. They hovered in the shadows muttering vengeance, but he didn't appear to be affected as he walked and talked. He was at home with the living and the dead.

"Oh Look!" Janice turned and held her index finger to his face. "It's a ladybug."

"It'll bring ya luck."

"Perhaps it will lead me out of here."

They walked back into the light, but even in the warmth of the early afternoon, the lingering cold seeped from the limestone walls along with the echoes of despair.

"This is where they executed the leaders of Nineteen-Sixteen. They were brought out here an' shot to death, even James Connolly. He wasn't able to stand because of the wounds he'd suffered in the battle so they brought him out tied to a chair – an' then they shot him – the cowardly fuckin' bastards!"

His words lingered like thunder. The walls and all of the sad history they guarded were closing in around her. She needed to get out into open space, away from the past and away from all of its sad memories.

"We can walk by the river for a while," he offered, sensing her mood. "It'll be nice in the sun an' we can talk about you for a while. Tell me, what kinda painter are you? Do you paint scenes or people? It's a bit like writin' poems, I suppose. I mean when I . . ."

But Janice interrupted him. She wanted to tell him about her painting. She wanted him to listen to her, and she wanted him to see the artist inside of her.

"I paint images of the things that move me. Sometimes, I paint scenes. Sometimes, they are real places, places I have been to, places that have reached inside of me. Other times, I paint images of how I would like places to be. I suppose I paint so that I can say something about the way I see the world. Does that make any sense?"

"Of course it does; sure aren't we both artists? Sure we can both understand each other."

Janice moved a little closer and took his hand in hers and they walked until the sun settled low behind them, casting long shadows as they passed along the quays. The evening cooled and the river rippled, but she was warm inside.

They were both artists. Perhaps, when the time was right, they could become more.

Chapter 4

They huddled together as the crowd reeled around them. The night was getting blurred as voices mingled with the dense smoke. She was beginning to believe, as the man she read about in the 'Times' smiled and encouraged her, that she could become an artist.

"People are sheep an' they flock an' follow anything. But artists trust in Fate an' understand that even their own lives must come second." He looked pensive for a moment and then smiled at her again. "But we know it's worth it."

"We?" She casually brushed the back of his hand.

He smiled but didn't look at her face. "Sure of course. You just need to meet the right people, ya know?"

"And where would I meet them?" She sat a little straighter, pushing her breasts out between them. He smiled again and looked into her eyes. "Don't worry about that, I know everybody who's anybody."

They left the bar wrapped in a cocoon that was impervious to doubts and the jealous whispers of the begrudging streets. They were free to follow as Fate beckoned and they were warm together, hips bumping as they walked.

"So? What's the story with the guy in Canada?" It might have been impertinent if they weren't so entwined, if she was still in love with Robert.

"Robert and I are over. I thought I had mentioned it." She paused to tilt her head, leaning in front of him for effect so her hair would fall across her face, but the cobblestones were damp, and her shoes were hard and she was a little drunk.

"No." He caught her and helped her steady herself. "I think I would've remembered that."

"But you came to see me anyway?"

"Ah now, I's just bein' friendly."

"Is that what you're being?"

"Well, it was at first. Only now it's somethin' else?"

"And what would that be?"

"Listen, Janice, I don't want to say the wrong thing or anythin' like that, but I really like you. I get this feelin' when I'm around you that I've never felt before."

"Oh and what would that be?"

"I don't know an' I don't want to fuck it up by doin' or sayin' the wrong thing. I have a feelin' about you. I think that you're goin' somewhere big, I can see it, an' I want to get to know you before you leave." He was much closer now, waiting on a sign. "Unless you don't think it would be right."

"Wow, Aidan. That almost sounded like you were sharing your feelings."

The lights of passing cars flashed in his eyes, and his breathing was more deliberate. "I do have feelin's an' I do express them. People like my feelin's. People even buy an' read them."

He was right; she had been glib so she snuggled in under his arm. "I know, Aidan, and I know the courage it takes to do that, to put everything out there in front of everybody."

"Ah sure, it's not that big a deal. What you do is much harder. You deal with details. I just evoke images, but you actually go the bother of layin' them out. I could never do that."

"If I didn't know better . . ." She never got to finish. He leaned in and gently touched his lips to hers. It was barely a flutter, but it caused her to tremble. She wasn't so subtle and kissed him with the passion of loneliness. "And you? Surely, you are seeing someone?"

"No, I'm not." He almost hesitated. "I'm single an' gettin' over a broken heart. My last girlfriend walked out on me. I guess I was too common or somethin'."

"I find that very hard to believe. Are you telling me there is no mysterious lady somewhere in your life?"

"Well, here you are then. I suppose I should say goodnight to you now?"

They lingered in awkward silence, each waiting on a sign from the other as their breath mingled in the cool space between them. His lips were full and trembled and his voice was husky. His breath was warm against her face. He pressed against her, and as his lips parted, hers did, too. A soft moan escaped from her emptiness. She felt betrayed but opened the door and tilted her head to one side, masking shyness. "So? Would you like to come in?"

He nodded and followed, still holding hands as she closed the door with her heel. In the cold darkness of her room, streetlights fell like mystical pools. He crossed his arms in front of her and wrapped her in warmth that she had missed. She wanted more and nothing more.

They swayed for a while, tingling at each other's touch. His lips traced her ear and down her neck to her shoulder that was bared: her sweater had slipped or had been pulled. She arched back as he pushed forward and, without letting go, walked into her bedroom.

"You're being very brazen." Janice said trying to straighten her clothes and her hair.

"I am," he agreed, "but I don't have much choice. You're after makin' me fall in love with ya."

"That might work on Irish girls but . . ."

He pinned her arms to her sides, drawing her closer to his face. "Can I take ya to your bed?"

A thousand words buzzed, words like 'modesty' and 'propriety.' Words her mother would have used, but they were drowned out by words like 'passion' and 'pleasure.' She might have hesitated and drawn back. The old Janice would but that was before the night visitor came. She'd been alone too many nights listening to her neighbours making sounds that made her cry. She wanted abandon even for a few hours without question of moral or right. The old Janice would've wanted indication that this would be meaningful. She wouldn't give herself cheaply.

But that was the old Janice who'd sat alone while life went without her. That Janice would grow cold and withered, shriveled and wrinkled in her dull little room, surrounded by paintings of places and things she never dared to be part of. The new Janice would reach out and take what life offered. The new Janice threw her arms around him.

He peeled her sweater over her head and her hair tumbled around her shoulders. He stopped for a moment to hold her at arm's length, his breathing cool on her breast. She was embarrassed and emboldened, and pulled back and placed her hands on her hips and carefully wriggled, like an Egyptian, pushing her jeans past the curve of her hips. She leaned forward and smiled: "Do you like what you see?"

He agreed in a husky voice that might be afraid. "But I want to see all of ya."

The new Janice dropped her jeans and began to unbutton his shirt, running her fingers along exposed skin. He groaned as her hand crossed his belly freeing his shirttails and revealing his waist. She hesitated so he pushed her back on the bed and kissed her face while reaching between her legs. Her impulse was to resist, involuntary but innate, so he gently pried her thighs apart.

She lay on her back, unable to resist as his lips whispered between her breasts. She arched toward his mouth while thrusting against his hand, but he was in no hurry. He bared her breasts and took her nipples between his lips. His other hand traced upward between her legs, lingering for a moment when it reached her belly, and then plunging down between her skin and the softness of her panties, stripping them away.

He traced along the inside of her thighs and swung his body down until his head was beside his hand, searching with his tongue. His finger rested for a moment before gently sliding inside. She forgot herself and wrapped her legs around his head, bucking against him until he pushed her back and lay against her heaving belly.

As the waves subsided, she contemplated being in love with him or at the very least – in lust. She nestled into him and fought the warm sleep rising. She had to stay awake; she had to prove herself to him. She let her hand drift along the edge of him and across his hip until she held him. And, as she held him, he began to writhe against her. She leaned over and climbed on top.

She knew Robert loved when they did it like that. Aidan was no different except it hurt at first and, as she eased him in, he grew impatient and threw his hips to meet her. She felt he might tear her apart and gripped his hair, but he bucked wilder until they both collapsed in a frenzy of spasms and profanities.

As she rolled to one side, she remembered they hadn't bothered with contraception.

"I'm losing my mind," she whispered to the Irish poet in her bed, breathing deeper as he drifted away. "And you're after stealing my heart." She wanted to look into his eyes, but he'd turned on his side and was sleeping. It didn't matter; she was satisfied for the first time in months and drifted off serenely.

She walked in moonlight, overlooking a sullen sea with white-tipped waves breaking incessantly on the rocks and seawall. The cliffs towered, but it was bravado; piece by piece, they'd be torn down and ground into sand. Nothing could withstand the sea. It was coming to claim its prize: it would cover all of the land and return everything to the beginning.

Seagulls squalled, unsettled by her presence, banking and riding, making raucous noises. She followed a path animals made out into the mists. She could see a few yards in front of her, and with each step, she could see new shapes and she could tell what they might be – lichened rocks and stunted shrubs rising out of wind-blown grasses and a woman wearing a shawl around her face and shoulders. She faced the sea and, as Janice approached, turned and looked at her from a far and then, without moving, was in front of her. Her lips were a pale lime colour shaped like ripples on small waves in sheltered coves. Her eyes a green or blue, a colour you might see when the tide turns. Her hair frosted like dried brine.

Janice stood outside of herself, outside of her dream, a curious bystander and none of it felt strange: the cliff walk at night and the ageless woman wrapped in shrouds of sea-mist and long tresses of her own hair.

"Why have you come to the edge of the world?"

"I am looking for Truth and Love."

The woman laughed like a bell: "You will not find them in this world." She held Janice in her gaze like she was measuring her.

When she woke, he was gone. She stretched out where he and she had been, touching sheets that were still warm. She would stay in bed forever, but the day called. "Janice? You never showed up today. Is everything okay?"

"Yes, Sinead, everything's fine. Sorry, I should've called. I met someone."

"Oh! And does he have a name?" It could still be someone else; he wasn't the only one in Dublin that smoked cigars.

"Aidan Greeley."

"The poet, Aidan Greeley?"

"Yes, the very same."

"I hope you know what you're getting yourself into."

"Why, do you know him?"

"Aidan Greeley was the drunken lout I told you about."

"Oh, my God, Sinead, it never occurred to me."

Sinead bit her lip; it was a bitter twist of fate. She blew her fringe away from her eyes. "Anyway, good for you, and I'll see you later."

"Sinead, wait, let's talk about this. I am sorry. I will stop seeing him, of course. I couldn't possibly. . ."

"Don't do it on my account." After all, they had never really been an item. "Don't worry. I'm over him."

"But I can't go on seeing him now."

"Why wouldn't you?"

"Well because we are friends, Sinead, and friends wouldn't . . . "

"Listen to me Janice; I'm serious. It didn't work out between us, but that might have been partiality my fault."

"Well, only if you're sure you're okay with it."

"I am, but are you sure you know what you're getting yourself into?" She wished she hadn't said that, it sounded so shrill.

"Oh, Sinead, that's so sweet of you but I'm just passing through, remember?"

"Ah, sure then you'll be fine." Sinead repeated her goodbyes and hung up the phone.

Ah, sure how could she've known? Don't get all feckin' spiteful now.

"Is everything all right there, Sinead?" her mother called from the steaming kitchen. "You've a very dark face on."

"I'm just tired, Ma, I'm going upstairs to lie down until dinner is ready."

"Good for you. I'll call you when your father comes home. He's still driving me mad, girl. I don't know what to do. Those feckless bastards down in the pub are filling his head with nonsense."

But Sinead hardly heard her as she dashed up the stairs and threw herself across her bed. She wasn't crying for Aidan: she was crying for herself. She didn't have time for love and all that right now.

Janice stopped by the mirror and let the shower run until it was hot. Her hair was a mess and her lips were swollen, but she looked good. Other times, when she was with Robert, when she rushed to the bathroom, she looked guilty; like they had just done something strange. But everything was different now. She had become a woman of muted power that men would sense her long before they saw her. And when they looked at her, their hearts would melt and become hers forever. They would follow in her wake, like wraiths, moaning and groaning for what they could never possess. She would lure them to the doom that was Lust and wouldn't be concerned; she would just toss her hair out and walk on.

But her reflection looked a little dubious. She looked tired and messy; her hair was contorted and she had goose-bumps on her arms.

That's what my dreams are trying to tell me, she tried to remind herself, but she wasn't sure she heard. She was busy examining her face in the fogging mirror. She was pale, even for Don Mills, but it worked: it made her look vulnerable. Her eyes were darker, too. And there was something else; they sparkled with a secret. She had tasted something last night: she had sipped from the chalice of power.

She traced her reflection in the steamed mirror, standing on her tiptoes, reaching forward until she teetered. If she squinted, she could almost see it. It was a little distorted and not in a Picasso way. It was more like something Dali might do.

What do you think? she asked her subject in the billowing mist, but her reflection didn't answer. She pulled the curtain back and stepped into the shower.

Damn it to Hell! Why does this always happen to me? But the show-erhead responded with more cold water.

She shivered into the folds of her robe, but her reflection was smiling again: the smile she remembered from home movies, standing on the deck knock-kneed and shivering even though the lake had looked warm in the hot summer sunshine. *You've come a long way, baby.*

Please, let's not speak in clichés. Her reflection smiled again and left to get dressed.

He had left a note to meet him in Grogan's. She understood the significance: 'Grogan's is where I grew up. It's the closest thing I've had to a real home, at least since my mother died.'

So this is it, I get to meet the family. I must make a good impression. What would complement my Just-had-good-sex-but-I'm-still-horny smile? Perhaps something in red, with black pants — no, a short black skirt. She wanted to leave an impression on his soul, as well as his body.

For a while, she would become a fixture on his arm, and in time, the world would know her for her own work. After that, Fate would decide if she stayed or went, but first, she had to look the part.

She paraded back and forth in front of the long mirror that leaned against the wall. It offered that nice perspective, sloping away. She could turn and see most of her back, right down to her long slender calves. *Was it really fair to Sinead?* She said it was okay, but her reflection wasn't listening. She was posing in her black underwear. *And what was it you were saying about clichés? We could try the red set.*

It was perfection. Her skin looked like alabaster, her lips like wine and her hair like storm-clouds. She shimmed into her short skirt and, corseted in her red shirt, checked herself one more time. *Dark and dangerous, like a child of the night*, she offered her passing reflection as she left.

Be careful, you don't know what else wanders in these nights, in this ancient city, in this strange land, her likeness tried to warn her but she had closed the door and was walking the moonlit street. Her heels clattered quickly past the shaded bench where a shadow flitted and was gone.

By the time she arrived in Grogan's, he was standing by the bar. Her shirt was tight and her skirt was, perhaps, a bit short, but what the hell. She opened her leather jacket slowly. Her top three buttons were undone. She wanted to push her breasts forward, but she was losing her nerve. Most of the men in the bar had turned. They almost formed a circle around her but kept their distance and opened like a path before her.

She grew a little shy as they eddied back to their smoking and swearing as she passed. She smiled with as much assurance as she could muster and reached forward and kissed his lips as he ordered drinks and steered them to a small table in the corner. As Janice sat, she was careful to let her skirt ride up a little. His eyes followed her hips and she felt warm in his gaze. She reached out across the table; she wanted to be close to him again.

He leaned back and looked at her for a moment with that glazed look men get, but he was calm. "I was thinkin' about you all day, an' I was thinkin' that maybe I'd write a poem about you or somethin'."

The 'something' sounded appealing but, after her lust was sated, love poems would make the whole thing perfect. She would paint him of course; it would be a part of her Dublin period, a blue period when the seeds were sown. He'd be world renowned by then, too. It was all so good that she almost shivered.

"Are you cold?"

"No, of course not," but she did lean forward and push her breasts together.

"Maybe," he smiled at her adjustment, "we could collaborate, ya know? I could talk with some people I know, and we could do one of those fancy books with paintin's and poems together. I think that would be fuckin' brilliant, don't you? I mean it wouldn't be hard now that everybody is talkin' about my poems already."

That raised a flutter inside of her. They could share lives for a while; not a happy-ever-after thing, they were far too bohemian for that. But they could spend some time together. He could even meet her in the coffee shop for everyone to see. She almost frowned when she thought about her, but as she had said, Sinead was okay with this. She knew Janice was an artist, someone who couldn't be expected to paint between the lines.

In time, they would part and she'd go back to Canada, but not to Robert, he would be married by then, and she'd have a signed copy of 'Poems for a Woman' or some such title. Perhaps, she'd leave it on her bedside table, when Leonard Cohen spent the night.

New Love, her old-self reminded her, *is such a heady mix, potent and likely to cause missteps.*

I don't care. I feel alive and free. I feel like I've never felt before.

Christ! Get a grip; after all, he's not the first!

But this will be delicious, he's a poet and I'm a painter. It's all so terribly un-Toronto of me.

It is amazing how a good fuck can change your mind, she reminded herself in a tone that might have been borrowed from Sinead.

He was still talking about himself, and as long as she looked into his eyes and nodded during the brief pauses, he'd continue. He was very happy with himself; he might be invited to read his work as part of some Irish cultural exchange. He was Dublin's street poet, and he was in demand right now. He ordered her another Scotch, and she took another of his cigars. Both tasted foul in her mouth, but she wanted to look the part, the mysterious woman with the handsome poet.

She must have been doing it right because every man who wrestled his way past looked her up and down. Janice loved the feeling and tingled between her crossed legs as the whiskey surged, dispelling caution and daring her, with every sip, to take yet another step out and away from everything she had been.

And, when he lit her cigar, he held the match before her face, looking into her eyes. As he drew his hand away, he let the back of his fingers trace along her cheek. The burning match was far too close, but it added to her excitement. He'd moved to the seat beside her and discreetly took her hand in his. He was being demonstrative, something Janice knew was unusual for him.

"So are you gonna be the one to catch the great Greeley?" someone called from the bar where a line of men sat in a row, turning every once in a while to look her over.

"She's far too good for the likes of him."

"Maybe she's one of those people that do studies on endangered species."

"Would ya ever go and fuck yourselves," Aidan softly dropped her hand and reached for his pint.

"Ah! C'mon now, Aidan. Aren't ya goin' to introduce us to the young lady?"

"Janice, these are the lads. Lads, this is Janice."

A few of them flocked around the table to introduce themselves, to get closer to her, and Janice smiled as she looked each one in the eye as they shook hands. For all their bravado, they were really very shy.

"So you're from Canada, then," one of them remarked as if that explained something that had mystified them all. "And what are you doing in Ireland?"

"In Trinity, Jazus, Greeley, this one's a cut above."

"Would ya ever go and fuck-off now and give us some peace and privacy."

"C'mon on now, lads," Paddy called from behind the bar, "leave the young love birds alone."

Aidan squirmed. He didn't want this attention.

"Are those your friends?"

"Some of them."

"They seem nice."

"Trust me, they're not!"

By the end of the evening, Janice had difficulty keeping her poise as they walked to her place. She was carefree and exhilarated by the promise of intimacy, something that could never be broken by wind nor rain. She tried to brush against him as often as she could, to feel his body against hers, to touch, as if by accident, some part of him, but she was in danger of falling over. Her jacket was open and her shirt undone to the fourth button. *My true self emerges*, she laughed to herself. He laughed, too, and she wondered if her mind was open to him. She really didn't care. She was becoming something she had read about and never tried before.

"Aidan, you're not brooding. In fact, you almost seem happy. Are you sure you're a poet?"

"Ya know that I think you're havin' an effect on me."

"Oh, Aidan, are you suggesting you've found everlasting love with me?"

"Nay, I just feel that you and I could stay in the here and now for a while and never have to worry about all the other shite."

"But what about when we get old and wrinkled?"

"Then we'll just have to have a few extra drinks so we don't notice so much."

"Aidan, you've given this a lot of thought."

"Like I said, Janice, I think you're havin' an effect on me. So, wanna do it again?"

"Do what?"

"You know, doin' it."

"Not until you say it."

"Janice, darlin', would you like to make love with me?"

"Nay, I just want to have sex."

"Fair enough, I can do that, too.

As soon as her door closed, she tore at his clothes and searched in the darkness with her mouth as they fumbled and stumbled into her room. He forced her to the floor, turning her until she was on all fours. He didn't stop to take her clothes off so she knelt there in her open shirt with her leather jacket hanging from one shoulder and her short skirt, now like a belt, around her waist. He pulled her panties down to her knees and pushed inside, forcing his way, almost to her belly. He shifted a few times until he found a rhythm they could both move to. His fingers bit into the whitening flesh around her hips until she wanted to cry out but she couldn't. She could hardly make a sound, surging higher and higher until she came with total abandon: her hair tossed all around. As she reached to brush it back, she crumpled to the floor.

He was staring at the wall and rose to look closer. He turned on her desk light and stood naked in the middle of her room staring at her painting, the one of the naked Polynesian girl with the lily held in front of her – her first effort at erotic art. It was trite and predictable, but she still loved it for the colours she chose.

He looked great, too, as the light glistened on his long, lean body. His chest was heaving, rippling the shadows that fell below his waist, like he was steeping out of the sea.

"Who painted that?"

"I did."

"It's brilliant."

"No, it isn't."

"It feckin' well is."

She rose and wrapped her arms around him and laid her head against his chest that shivered when the leather touched his skin. But he held her tight and gently stroked her hair. "You should go for it."

"For what?"

"You should give up the studyin' and just work on your paintin'."

"Oh, Aidan, you're so cute. You'd say anything after sex."

"True, true, but what I said is also true."

"Aidan, I just dabble."

"You just have to meet the right people. I know someone who knows everythin' about art an' all. I'm goin' to talk with her about you."

She shed her clothes and pulled him to her bed, snuggling as close as she could. He liked her painting, and he made her feel so good. Sure, he talked too much, but all Dubliners did that. And there was something else; she could be someone new with him. She had lived a life of insipid water-coloured love, but now she was free to explore the full richness of passion: wanton and more fulfilling than anything she'd felt before. But was it Love or Lust or did any of that matter anymore?

Love, lust, love, lust, love, lust and with the ticking of his heart, she fell asleep upon his chest.

But Aidan couldn't sleep, he wanted to turn on his side, but he didn't want to move her head. He was thinking of Gwen. It was a growing ache inside of him. It had been so exciting at first, being with a woman who took control – of everything. But it had changed. He'd begun to feel like a big dog on a short leash. He'd begun to feel like he was needy.

But the worst part is that it's hurtin' my writin'. I suppose its guilt – fuckin' a married woman an' all. I gotta end it. I mean now that I really like Janice an' all.

And, as he lay there, with Janice sleeping beside him, her warmth and scent reaching toward him, he began to see a way. He'd let Gwen see him with Janice. She'd see them together and she'd understand. It just wasn't fair to Maurice; it wasn't even fair to

Gwen and besides, Gwen would want to help Janice, he just had to handle it carefully.

Sinead couldn't sleep, either. Her father came home late, creaking up the stairs to the spare room. She couldn't get involved, for a lot of reasons. She'd so much school work, and she needed to have a bit of her life alone; after all, she did deserve that.

But that wasn't the real reason. She just didn't know what to tell them.

Things weren't supposed to be like that anymore. She'd heard all the stories the old people used to whisper about, but that was before. Things were different now. Whatever happened would be dealt with behind closed doors, without fuss nor bother, she was sure of it.

Chapter 5

"I want ya to meet some friends of mine."

He'd made coffee and made himself at home. The room was heavy with smoke and his book lay open on the counter and another in the bathroom. He'd spread himself about, but she didn't mind too much. She hated being alone, tossing and turning in her empty bed. When he came over, she slept soundly, reassured by his breathing. On occasion, he snored and she would pat him like a great big dog. But he left parts of himself everywhere and never lowered the toilet seat. He re-filled his cup, overfilling it and leaving a brown ring.

"More bar friends?" She squeezed into the tight galley.

"Have you got somethin' against the lads?"

"No," she reassured him as she poured coffee. "I like your friends, they're very real."

"What's that supposed to mean?"

"So who are these friends?" she raised her cup and peeped through her hair.

"The Fitzwilliams of Glendalough. They know everyone on the Arts Council an' the National Gallery." He paused to crack a match. "They've a place out in Wicklow, ya know, a big country manor with trees and they even have their own lake. They've invited us out for lunch."

"Oh, Aidan, I'm still just dabbling. Why would they want to meet with me?" She peered through her hair and got the response she wanted. He reached forward and pulled her to his chest, stroking hair away from her face. "I told them you're great."

She spent a moment in the warmth of his flattery, but he had to leave. He blew a kiss when he got to the garden gate.

She stretched out on her settee; he would be gone all day. She didn't mind. It gave her time to sort a few things out. It had been a whirlwind: going from being alone to almost living with a man she hardly knew. It was great spending the nights with him, but sometimes, she needed a little break from him and the her that she became around him. It was going to be a struggle to be a free spirit. She would have to wriggle out of all that once constrained her, even her own views; at least, the narrow ones.

"Scattered showers in the morning," the radio warned, "giving way to periods of sunshine and the rain will move off by Saturday in time for everyone to get all dressed up for Halloween."

"Is this car stolen?" she asked of the old rusty Audi with the crumpled fender – but the light still worked!

"Nay, I got it from Flanner."

"Did he steal it?"

"Probably, but nobody's gonna come lookin' for it."

"Does he know you have it?"

"In a way."

"What does that mean?"

"He's in the Joy at the minute, he won't mind."

"Is that some kind of drug-enhanced state?"

"The Joy, ya know? Mountjoy Jail."

"Why he is there?"

"Stealin' cars."

The Audi hesitated and farted a dense black cloud. It shuddered a few times and sputtered. He smiled as he struggled with the gears. Grinding noises rumbled through the floor. Billowing black farts hung in the air behind them. *Fuck Flanner anyway. I should've known better than to borrow anythin' of his.* He couldn't find second and jumping to third was a bitch with the dodgy clutch. He didn't have time for her questions as the car lurched away from the traffic lights with a funeral of impatience behind.

"Janice, everything's goin' to be fine an' don't worry I told them what to expect."

"Oh, really, and what are they expecting?"

"A real artist who doesn't give a shite what the rest of the world thinks."

She slumped back in sullen silence. He wasn't sure how to deal with her so he continued to talk while they drove past Templeogue, to the new bridge. He'd been there often, walking along the banks of the doddering river, up to the rotting weir beneath the old stone bridge where Austin Clarke's house stood before the street was widened.

"I heard about him so I used to walk back an' forth until he came out to stand on the bridge with an old black hat an' a cane an' stare into the river for hours."

He looked sad as he pointed to where the house had stood before the future brushed it aside, sad enough to defuse her.

"Did you ever talk with him?" She smiled to encourage him.

"Nay, I knew he was a poet, an' I knew that he was makin' his poetry so I thought that I'd better not disturb him:

Stop, stop and listen for the bough top
Is whistling and the sun is brighter
Than God's own shadow in the cup now!
Forget the hour-bell. Mournful matins
Will sound, Patric, as well at nightfall.

Faintly through mist of broken water
Fionn heard my melody in Norway.
He found the forest track, he brought back
This beak to gild the branch and tell, there,
Why men must welcome in the daylight.

He loved the breeze that warns the black grouse,
The shouts of gillies in the morning
When packs are counted and the swans cloud
Loch Erne, but more than all those voices
My throat rejoicing from the hawthorn.

In little cells behind a cashel,
Patric, no handbell gives a glad sound.
But knowledge is found among the branches.
Listen! That song that shakes my feathers
Will thong the leather of your satchels.

They rumbled along the suburbanism of Ballyroan Road, up to Ballyboden where houses gave way to open fields stretched like patchwork toward the solid wall of fir and pine that stood in straight rows, an exaggerated green in the yellowing landscape. The old Audi rattled and groaned as they crossed the shoulders of the mountain and turned sharply in the shadow of the Hell Fire Club.

"That," he pointed with his cigar, "is where the gentry liked to debauch, playin' cards an' deflowerin' local girls. They say the Devil himself used to drop by an' play for their souls. He might even be around tonight; maybe we can drop in on the way home."

"You don't really believe all that?"

"Of course I do: the Devil himself was a Horse-Protestant."

"Aidan. Perhaps I never mentioned it, but I'm a Protestant."

"But you don't have a horse? Do ya? That's the issue, ya know. It's the symbol of our Overlords, ridin' around like they're better than the rest of us: a spotty bunch of fuckin' fops if ever there was."

She studied the broken shell of the hunting lodge as they passed. "I think you should be grateful to the English, they built this country and made it civil."

"I suppose you've a point. This road was built when they wanted to civilise the Wicklow Chieftains: fuckers like Charles Coote who slaughtered Irish children and laughed it off sayin' 'nits would grow to be lice.'"

"It offers a great view, but it looks like it was made by wandering livestock."

He lit a cigar and smiled. He was beginning to know her moods, and after a glance in her direction to let her know that he would give her time and space, he rummaged through the disorderly pile of tapes that littered the floor until he found one he liked. "A bit of Planxty – to shorten the road," and the car filled with honeyed sounds: uillean pipes hopping and popping, swarming twangs of reverberating strings and the steady rattle of the bodhran. She smiled and started to tap her knees in time, almost a different person now.

He didn't understand but most of the time, it didn't matter. They were still in that forgiving time when even their flaws were quaint. But there were times when she could be such a pain in the ass. He smiled over at her, but she looked away. *Ah fuck it, why's everything so fuckin' complicated?*

Because you make it complicated. You can't go around shaggin' every girl ya meet. And besides, you're the one who's bringin' them together.

I'm just tryin' to do somethin' nice for Janice, ya know, to get her noticed.

She is gonna to get noticed all right. Gwen's gonna notice her real fast. What the fuck were you thinkin'?

It's goin' to be fine. After Janice sees me with Gwen, she's gonna realise that important people take me seriously. She'll know that I'm not just some wanker tryin' to pass myself off as somethin' I'm not.

He had to get out of his head, dark voices were stirring, voices that often woke him in the early morning when he was delicate from drinking and called him out for his sins. But his life had a way of working out. He lit another cigar, ignoring Janice's exaggerated cough, and tapped his fingers on the wheel. The road rolled past the masts at Kippure that touched the lowest clouds and when it seemed the car could give no more, they plunged down the other side.

A long narrow valley yawned before them, cut by the sword of a giant who lumbered by when the ice was retreating. A place where the past huddled from the winds of change: well-ordered, rich and green and free of stones and weeds, an outpost of Anglo-Irish civility, once the domain of the O'Byrne's: a savage tribe that came down from the mountains to menace Dublin in times past. They were outside the Pale. They passed neat hedges around well-tilled fields, scored now by long straight furrows, like scratches on skin, and pastures sprinkled with black and white cows and a few nut-brown horses that shied away as they rumbled past. The house was at the end of a long sloping driveway, fortress-square with large windows looking down in lacey vigilance on the activities of the village.

"What's Gwen like?" she asked as they pulled into the driveway.

"She's a bit older now, probably thirty-five – but still a fine thing. You'd imagine her in jodhpurs and ridin' boots and nothin' else, 'cept maybe a leather corset – ya know the ones that stop below yer tits?"

He was nervous behind the coarseness, but she decided to go along with it for now: "And of course, a studded black leather collar and a ridin' crop."

"Whatever turns ya on, darlin'?"

The windows watched from grey walls with large corner stones, bearded with lichen and fossils of long-dead ivy reaching to the grey slate roof and around a bright blue door – a duck egg colour that beckoned as the car slid on the loose gravel, coming to a halt at the foot of a wide stone staircase that rose four steps. The railings tangled with wild roses and shrubs that should be pruned, book-ended by large urns on which faces of river Gods collected dirt and mosses in the grooves around their noses and eyes but smiled regardless. Janice fidgeted with her sketchpad, but that would be too contrived.

Between stone pheasants with red eyes, a whimsical splash of colour against rain-stained grey unruffled plumage, the door swung in as a tall woman emerged.

"Welcome, darlings. Please, come in," Gwen kissed the air on either side of her cheeks and Janice froze for a moment, between two worlds. "Aidan, you have landed a wonderful catch, be careful you don't lose this one." Gwen smiled, but her eyes narrowed. "Gwen Fitzwilliams, darling, it is delightful to meet you."

"Janice Tremblay, and please, have we ever met before?"

"I don't think so, darling. I would never forget a pretty face like yours. However, I am often near the College. Perhaps you noticed me on the street, or in an art gallery. I prowl them for new art, and artists."

Janice shivered and fumbled among her swirling emotions. "What a beautiful home. I hardly dared to believe such places still existed."

"So pretty and so well spoken," Gwen winked at Aidan.

They stood in perfect light from the wide fanlight. A broad stairway led to a landing above paintings squeezed in, not by style or subject but by size. A Flemish barge glided between a bulbous man on a ponderous horse rousing men to war and a fishing village somewhere warm and bright.

"It is so terribly disorganized. Maurice calls it my stamp collection." She took Janice by the arm and swept into the dining room. "We will have lunch at the small table, by the window."

"What beautiful furniture you have."

"French, darling, early seventeenth century, it has been in my family for years."

She didn't know what else to say and looked to Aidan whose shoulders were hunched.

"We had stuff just like it."

"Really, Aidan, and where is it now?"

"We burnt it durin' the winter of sixty-three."

Janice wanted to calm his hackles, but Gwen stepped between them. "Janice!" She pointed to a seat across from Aidan. "Boy, girl, boy, girl. Now we are set. Maurice? Maurice darling, we are waiting."

"I was just getting a nice claret for our international visitor."

He shook hands with Janice as he might shake hands with a horse-trader and struggled with the corkscrew. "Ah!" he sampled the freed bouquet, "now we can eat."

Beside the generous slices of cold ham and diced hard-boiled eggs, two shriveled radishes straddled green scallions on a blue willow pattern. Gwen watched her for a moment. "The radishes and scallions are from the garden and the eggs are mine, too. The ham was once called Wendy. She had a terrible, squinting, disposition. I must say, she is much more pleasant with some hot mustard."

"That damn pig will probably give us all heartburn." Maurice chewed nosily between large gulps of the delicate wine. Gwen turned her smile on him. Something was brewing inside of him, but he was enjoying himself so she carried the conversation, inquiring politely of her guests and admonishing Maurice for slurping and occasional farts.

"Maurice, darling, are you sure the pig is dead? And, Janice, Aidan tells me you are a fine painter. He has urged me to look at your work." For a moment, her eyes grew soft, reaching across like a soothing hand.

"Well, thank you, but Aidan is being kind, I just dabble." She felt exposed but Maurice came to her rescue as he gurgled. "My dear young lady, the bard, apparently, has many fine attributes, but I have never known kindness to be one of them."

"Now, Maurice, Janice is being modest." Gwen smiled a measured smile. "Perhaps you can show me some of your work. I have friends in the business and they are always on the look-out for talent."

"C'mon Janice, you've four or five pieces that are great. I've seen them."

"Oh! The bard is becoming an expert on artists now?"

"Maurice! Be so kind as to pour some wine before you guzzle it all and Aidan, what are you writing these days?"

"I've a few new pieces that I'm very happy with but not enough for a collection, not yet."

Maurice spluttered again. "Listen here, Aidan. Bridey and I were wondering when you are going to commit your next anthology to us."

"Darling, we are having lunch! Can it not wait?"

"Bridey, the young bugger has not replied to any of my previous inquiries."

"I was thinkin' of tryin' a bigger press."

Maurice's eyes began to bulge as he drained his claret and refilled their glasses. "A bigger press, humph! And what is wrong with the one that has stood by you all these years when no one bought your bloody poetry?"

"Maurice, please! Let us enjoy lunch and then you can discuss these things without upsetting our guest."

"I do beg your pardon," Maurice gushed as he refilled Janice's glass. "That was very boorish of me."

They tiptoed through the rest of lunch until Maurice excused himself.

"Please, ignore him, darlings. He always gets cranky when we don't have lunch at twelve, he will be fine after his walk."The sunlight streamed through large windowpanes, drawing squares across the table and in the sunbeams, cigar smoke meandered, reaching toward Janice, reaching toward Gwen. "Oh! Here he comes, let's all try to be pleasant?" She glanced at Aidan who grumbled but agreed.

"Up for a spot of shooting, Bard?" Maurice beamed from the doorway, wearing a tweedy deerstalker and a coarse Squire's jacket.

"Jazus, I love shootin' things?"

"Me, too, especially cuckoos, hate those blighters!"

"Isn't it a bit late for cuckoos, darling?"

"That's the thing Bridey; they show up when you least expect them." He followed Aidan across the lawn, loading his shotgun as he went.

"Darling, let's take a stroll toward the monastery. We can chat while the boys are off shooting."

"Will they kill anything?"

"I doubt it, darling. After a bottle of wine Maurice will make more noise than an elephant."

Janice stepped carefully around her lingering trepidations, falling in time as they strolled the stone driveway.

"I must apologise for Maurice. He gets frustrated with Aidan, who can be such an ingrate. He assumes that everything happens by the unseen hand of Fate. He has no idea how much effort it took to have his verse noticed." She laughed again, a clear ringing laugh like a silver ball against filigreed gold. "We have friends who know the right people. When we find young artists, we set them on their way. Perhaps, we might find someone to take interest in your work."

Janice blushed. She didn't want to seem too eager! She needed to say something casual, like she just wanted them to be friends. "Why does Maurice call you Bridey?"

"My father insisted on Gwyneth. He was very British. He was educated there so he saw Ireland as Lilliput. My mother insisted on Bridget, but my father couldn't accept that. Their compromise was 'Bridey.' My father agreed it had horsy connotations and could pass for a nickname. People can be so odd, don't you think? But then again, we are an oddity. The English dismiss us as Irish and the Irish suspect our Englishness. It does have its advantages though; we are a go-between. Perhaps that is why we are best suited to promoting the arts."

"Aidan tells me that you own the Twilight Press?"

"Yes, Maurice bought it for me. He knows how important the arts are but he is not a fool. He expects to make some money from it. We are not mercenary: we do it for the sake of art, but it is a business. After all, these young artists couldn't survive if we did not help." She paused to look at Janice. "But enough about me; tell me what such a young and gifted person is doing in Ireland of all places?"

"I am reading History at Trinity."

"Well, Ireland is an excellent choice for research."

"Yes, it is," Janice continued hesitantly. "Sometimes, I feel like the past is still here." She looked sideways to see if Gwen reacted.

"I know exactly what you mean, darling." Gwen linked arms as if they were friends. "Ireland is a very old place and much of it remained rustic and undisturbed. I believe that has allowed the old ways to linger here. Poets and Artists are aware, but even ordinary people sense it, too. The Irish can be such a superstitious lot sometimes, but there are times when I would defy anyone to dispel the feelings one gets near the old places.

"Here," she pointed through the bare trees, to the slender tower standing over the bones of the old monastery, "one feels one is walking between the worlds. The Christians were aware of this and built their churches on sites that were sacred to the older beliefs. They were afraid of their power and tried to smother them with rituals and rites, but sometimes, especially at night, I don't think that they succeeded."

They paused for a moment to consider the view: the tower beside the squat stone church and the scattered stones of long forgotten graves. It was where Saint Kevin fought his monster, and English soldiers had scorched the place as marauding forces do.

"There are things that cannot be explained outside of mythology; things that are wondrous and, sometimes, disturbing. I firmly believe that the old spirits can still reach out, only we can't hear them so well anymore. Artists can, darling, artists like you and Aidan. Perhaps that is what drew you together."

Janice stared at the old stone tower and the bones of churches and dark cells where monks lived and worked away from distraction. There were so many things lingering and she wanted to lighten the mood. "Or perhaps I am his succubus."

"Oh don't be silly. You are the best thing that has ever happened to Aidan. He speaks of you in the highest terms. I am beginning to think he might be falling in love with you."

Janice couldn't decide if it was a statement or a question. "Does Aidan really fall in love? He strikes me as someone who wanders through life as a commentator and not someone who really commits."

"Janice, Aidan is looking for someone to move him from the shabby world he squanders in. He knows that only men who have been significantly moved are capable of really expressing true feelings. Women have the power to truly inspire men. We can turn them from the baseness they would wallow in."

Janice couldn't shake the feeling that Gwen could see right into her heart.

"That is why we have been demonized. That was why the ancients created the myth of the succubus: a beautiful woman who could seduce monks away from meditation, such nonsense."

Janice shivered again as she listened, even though the sun was high and the wind abated, even though she walked in daylight.

"I am sorry, darling, you are getting cold as I ramble on about silliness, forgive me. I have spent too much time in our little backward valley. I will be imagining that I see leprechauns and banshees next."

They linked arms again as they turned toward the house. "My dear, you are trembling. I think that you are not quite used to our Irish weather yet. Let us go back to the house." She put her arm around Janice and pulled her into her warm tweedy bosom. The end of a silk scarf fluttered against her cheek. "Let us go back and enjoy a pot of tea until the men return."

As the kettle whistled, their peace was shattered: Aidan staggered through the door.

"Jazus, he fuckin' shot me!"

And before there was time for further explanation Maurice padded in, almost breathless. "Bridey darling," he paused to catch his breath. "We have had a spot of bother. I am afraid that I shot the Bard in the bottom. Good thing that I was over fifty paces away."

Gwen smiled, but her brows furrowed. "It was good of you to count them, now go and get the first-aid."

"Will he be all right?" Janice held Aidan's hand and helped him onto the table.

"Oh, he will be fine, darling. It's not the first time Maurice has shot him. That's how we met. It really is a funny story. We were at the theater one night – at the 'Gate.'"

"Are you gonna fix my arse or talk about some fuckin' play?"

"Hush Aidan, you are being dramatic. Anyway, it was a new work by an Icelandic writer."

Gwen leaned forward to inspect the damage. "And, when we got back to the car, Maurice noticed a group of young men breaking shop windows. He let me into my seat and, as he walked by the back of the car, retrieved the shotgun from the trunk. 'Be off or I will shoot.' He ordered and they all ran but one.

　　"'Shoot my fucking arse!' this one young man said, and to make matters even more hilarious, he dropped his pants."

　　"How was I to know the fuckin' bollocks was carryin' a real gun?"

　　"Now, Aidan, please! Of course, we didn't wait for the police to come snooping around so we brought him back here and nursed him back to health. Then we found out how talented he was, and we simply fell in love with him."

　　"Will you two ever shut-the-fuck-up and fix my arse."

　　"Now, Aidan, we have been through this before, relax and Gwen will make it all better," she glared at the contrite Maurice.

　　"I brought the repair pack, just as you asked, Bridey."

　　He almost bowed as he retreated to his study where hung the heads of things that had been shot – a great many dead animals, including the tiger's head he had bought the last time he was in London. He emptied the coal scuttle onto the smoldering fire, poked it a few times with the long black poker and poured himself a stiff drink. He settled behind his great oak desk. He was quite content.

　　"Aidan! You really are a big baby. It is barely a scratch, just a few pellets right under the skin. I will have them out in no time. I'll kiss your bottom afterward or would you prefer to have Janice do that?"

　　"Ya can both fuckin' do it if you like?"

　　"I won't stay for this part," Janice offered as her stomach began to churn, "I don't do shootings very well."

　　She strolled into the large hall that was darkening as the day sank behind the mountains. Framed faces watched her cross the tiled floor as her shoes made a racket that echoed, unnerving her a little more. She almost wished they hadn't come, but Maurice emerged and beckoned to her.

"Come my dear, I have a warm fire and a tumbler of the finest malt. Come and we can have a quiet chat in peace."

"What a perfect room," Janice agreed as she sipped delicate whiskey by the fire, as her beaming host fussed until she was comfortably cushioned in an old Queen Anne chair.

"It is my refuge." He spoke into the hissing anger of burning coals as red and yellow light flickered on his ruddy face. "But damn it all, young lady, I have earned it. It was something I learned as a young boy, you know. We had to reach out and take what opportunity offered before the next chap came along and took it."

He was really talking to himself. It was a part of his ritual, to sit by the fire as the evenings grew longer and think back to sunnier days when he had promised 'Pimples' that they would step out together and let the world see them for what they really were.

"Sometimes, life demands a leap of faith and believe me, it is quick to deal with cowards."

Janice drained her glass, hoping her movement would remind him of her presence.

Maurice refilled it, from a distance. He had lost his nerve when he realised he couldn't bring that shame home with him. He never did go to the edge of their lover's leap. Not that 'Pimples' jumped, either, he reminded himself as he absentmindedly topped up their glasses again.

But he never dared to love again and now his life was hollow; a fate he wanted to warn her about. "Remember, my dear. Always reach out and take what life offers. You may not get the same chance twice."

His face was distorted by the blazing coals, a light that flickered on the walls behind him, dancing with the shiny inlays of a thousand books and the glassy eyes of antelopes and elands, leopards and tigers and the placid face of a water buffalo. A browned cricket bat leaned against the book shelves in case any of them came back to life.

Old faces peered down through dark oily windows. The fire was far too big. It was getting hot and hazy. None of it made sense: Maurice and Gwen, shootings and night-visitors all jumbled in Janice's scotched mind, along with Aidan and the confusion he brought. As sprightly flames danced on the walls, she saw herself and Aidan tango, a devilish dance along the path to Hell, but she had to agree, it was far better than being alone.

As Gwen removed the last pellets, her hands were still shaking. She couldn't be mad at Aidan, he was just playing his part, but it was difficult.

"So?" he asked as he carefully tucked his shirt back into his pants. "What do you think of Janice?"

"I like her. I think she might up for the challenge of loving you."

"So you don't mind then. I gotta tell you, I was a bit worried. I thought you'd hate her."

"Really?"

"It's better this way, ya know, to keep up appearances an' all."

"Is that what you are doing?"

"Of course, it is. You don't think that I love her more than you? C'mon, I'd never let anythin' come between us. It's only that you and I can't be seen together. This way, nobody will guess."

He looked at her as he waited for her response. It was plausible.

"You are right, darling." She spoke with more conviction than he expected.

"Gimme a kiss then, will ya?"

"Later, darling, let's remember to keep up appearances, like you said. And, I suppose you will have to stay the night now. I will put you in separate rooms – it would be more appropriate, anyway."

Chapter 6

They were all tipsy by the time they sat down to a dinner of Cornish hens in wild herb sauce; crisp, roasted potatoes and seared parsnips with glazed carrots. Gwen placed it on the harvest table and hovered nearby as Janice took the seat beside Aidan and arranged his cushions. But he couldn't find a comfortable position and grumbled until Gwen chided him: "Aidan! Let us eat in peace without moaning and groaning like a Beanshee."

"More wine, Janice?" Maurice struggled to hide his smile.

Janice nodded as the strange day swirled around her, but Gwen seemed at ease with it all: Maurice's smoking gun and Aidan's shredded bottom. She had bandaged him and found another pair of pants. "There, shall we begin."

"Bridey, this sauce is to die for." Maurice hummed as he poured a modest Burgundy that had impressed him with its simplicity. "They call it a 'Village' wine, but it has quality and yet, a simple, earthy flavour."

"You seem content, darling. It is the meal, of course, and the company. Or have you had another visit from Good Fortune?"

"Yes indeed, Bridey. My horses did rather well." He kissed her hand as he burped. "A good wine for a good day," he toasted.

Janice was effusive with her compliments and even took a little more. That seemed to please Gwen, but she refused help when she rose to clear the table. "I can manage my own kitchen, and besides,

I am sure you will want to start getting ready. I left out a shawl; it might get cold later on."

"Thank you, Gwen. That was very thoughtful."

"I am afraid it is bright red, darling, but it is Hallowe'en, after all."

As they rose, Maurice cajoled Aidan in to joining him to smooth over recent events. He offered a Cuban, too. He kept them on his desk though he rarely smoked. "Now, Aidan," he paused as he refilled his glass. "We have business issues that gentlemen should discuss alone."

"Thanks for callin' me a gentleman an' all, but I'm not sure I want to talk to you about my business."

"I will pay your advance, right now."

"Everybody's sayin' that I should try somewhere bigger, ya know?" Aidan puffed on his Cuban looking shrewd, but his eyes widened as Maurice counted out crisp bank notes. "It's not just about the money, ya know?"

Maurice continued to count, adding to the pile that was beginning to tip the scales.

Ah fuck it! Aidan's resolve melted. He'd just do one more book. He had enough to keep them happy, and besides, there was Janice to think about. In fact, he was really doing it for her so he stuffed the money into his pocket. "Ah, the fatted calf."

"Young man, you may be prodigal, but you are no son of mine."

"Are ya sure 'bout that? Ya never know?"

"Believe me," Maurice chuckled as he refilled their glasses. "I would know."

The moon was smiling like it knew what the night might bring. The rain held off so the souls of the restless could wander in relative comfort. The past misted up and all that was forgotten moved just beyond the range of perception. The veneer the Christians had smeared was very thin. They piled into the brown leather seats, giggling like witches in the dashboard light as they careened down the driveway. Except Aidan, who complained loudly, but the road just got worse. Gwen glanced at Maurice, whose eyes were darting back and forth, looking for potholes. "Maurice, darling, perhaps it is time to have someone look at the springs?"

"Nonsense, Bridey, this car is in mint condition."

"Will my bleedin' all over the seat lower the value?" Aidan was in a much better mood, like all was forgiven, even as he winced a bit. Gwen turned and winked at Janice. "Oh, Aidan, don't be such a baby and try not to bleed on the rug; it is a 'Foxford.'"

"Bridey," Maurice exclaimed with both hands clasped to his face as the car rolled on without him and found a less bumpy road. "I saw that damn fox again. It sat just beyond my range, and it laughed. We should rouse the hunt before the winter comes."

"Oh darling, I am too old for traipsing around the countryside."

"Nonsense, Bridey, you are still a goddess of the hunt."

"Darling, remember our guests. They might not view the hunt so favourably."

"I told you," Aidan whispered, "ridin' boots an' jodhpurs."

Gwen turned in her seat. "I admit it; I loved the pageantry, the ballyhoo of hounds and horns and the thunder of hooves. But most of all, I loved the pursuit."

"Studded leather collar an' a ridin' crop," Aidan whispered again and Janice had to stifle a giggle, but Gwen didn't seem to notice. She just smiled at Maurice as they prowled down the street and came to a squeaking halt outside the pub where children passed in costume. Maurice pleaded as he struggled from the car, startling the smaller ones, "Take my pitiful soul, but leave my money." They wheeled and closed as he flustered waist-deep among them, fumbling with his pocket change, trying to distribute it fairly. They giggled as they pocketed his coins and held their hands up for more but the smallest one, lost in the jostling, let go her brother's hand and walked toward Janice. She was dressed as a fairy with a long wand with a tinfoil star. Janice knelt before her and looked into her eyes. "You must be a real fairy."

But the child's face was like a stone cherub, greyish in the streetlights, as she spoke through missing teeth. "If I was real, what would you wish for?"

"To be happy. Could you make that come true?"

"I'm only seven," the fairy hesitated. Her face was ashen, but her eyes grew wide as Janice handed over shiny coins. She stared at her palm until her brother grabbed her by the arm, tugging her as they ran off into the moonlight of All Souls evening: a potent time when the old ways ruled. At the edge of the village they moved in shadows, free from the constraints life placed on them, free to behave as their ancestors had done for eons.

The men stood at the bar while the ladies sat by the peat fire in musty old armchairs.

"This is where we mingle with the locals," Gwen smiled, but Janice could only nod as the day swirled around her like a pack of cards. She clasped the red shawl as Gwen leaned back with her drink on the armrest. "It allows Maurice to keep an ear to the ground. He is very clever, you know?"

Janice's arm slipped as she turned to look at Maurice's ruddy face and rheumy blue eyes. *If he's clever, he knows to hide it well.*

The pub was where villagers gathered in the evenings to talk about the weather, the price of livestock and, when all matters of local interest had been exhausted, the troubling news from the greater world outside; whispers of mountains of beef and butter and lakes of wine but Irish farmers, though they wouldn't admit it, had done very well by Europe. On the mantle, a Child of Prague lingered in the shadow of a Sacred Heart and a clutter of dusty old sepias in tarnished frames. The villagers, too, were a collection of oddities, and as others arrived, Gwen had a story or piece of gossip to tell. "The farmer with the limp broke his leg while fornicating with a pony. I am not sure who was doing what."

Janice struggled to keep a straight face as another newcomer offered his greetings.

"Maurice bought a horse from him," Gwen whispered as the small, constricted man took his place by the bar. "The damn nag was nearly blind."

"How's that horse of yours, Squire?" someone inquired with a wink to his friends, but Maurice was ready for the thrust and parry of it all. "A most remarkable beast," he smiled. "It turned out that she cannot see very well. However, she has no idea how far she has walked and will pull a cart all day. I sold her for a handsome profit."

The small, constricted man might have choked on his drink, but Aidan joined in: "The luck of the Horse-Protestants."

"Horse-Protestant be damned," Maurice chuckled, "I am as Irish as the rest of you, but I don't get to blame someone whenever things don't go my way."

"When do things ever go wrong for you? Ya get stuck with a blind horse an' still make a profit; it's no wonder Ireland's impoverished with the likes of you suckin' the fuckin' fat off the land."

"Well, that is rich. Who would know more about the fat of the land than a poet?" Maurice was a little glazed. The wine and port, and now the whiskey, were beginning to take their toll, but he seemed to enjoy the banter, though he would never admit it.

"Maurice views Aidan as the son we never had and they squabble like family," Gwen was smiling, but her voice wavered. Janice wanted to pry but couldn't, that would be far too rude. The men at the bar were getting boisterous: Maurice insisted on buying them a drink 'from the sale of the horse.' Earlier, he had also insisted that Janice and Aidan spend the night, given Aidan's condition. Gwen had smiled at him, like it was his idea. 'Yes, do stay,' she had agreed. 'We can go to the village and have drinks with the locals. Maurice insists. He loves company. He avoids solitary drunkenness.'

'I only drink socially. No time for all of that brooding stuff. That's for poets and agitators.'

"Do you ever have trouble with them?" Janice asked, as she looked at the crowd at the bar. Her mind was edged with grainy images of rowdy youth fighting street battles with shielded and helmeted soldiers, of shadowy men in ski masks carrying rifles and duffle bags of explosives, and pubs exploding, scattering mangled limbs in red mists of broken glass through clouds of thick black smoke.

"Not with the locals, darling, they come to us for advice with official matters. Maurice has a way of dealing with officialdom: he is not afraid to put them in their place. The last time we were audited, he took the taxman out shooting."

"He didn't?"

"Of course not, we are not murderers but he did have a slight accident. Apparently, his gun had a tricky trigger and discharged, accidentally, of course, and shot the heel off the tax-man's boot."

"That was fortunate." Janice tried to sound indifferent, like it was all so understandable.

"Not really, Maurice is a damn fine shot."

"And the tax-man?"

"His wounds were psychological and very easy to cure with whiskey. He stayed a few days to review our books and found everything in order. He still visits; they go rabbit hunting, but he now insists that Maurice takes the lead."

Janice sat back and stared into the fire where flames and shadows danced like pagans. Gwen had such poise but was also so relaxed, like she was comfortable sharing the details of her life with a stranger.

"Yes, darling, Maurice's family was very good during the famine and the troubles that followed. They shared what they had and almost became impoverished. Parnell was a family friend." She waited for the name to register. "But you are a Canadian; you know what it is like to live in the colonies."

"Well," Janice hesitated. She could almost hear Aidan's accusations in her mind – 'the Anglo-Irish brigands who stole the land and kept our people captive for a millennium.' She remembered her father's family, in the Gatineau. When the Separation Issue rose, it dredged up old resentments from the dank cellars of history where terrible thing were done in the name of the King. "Actually, I am part French on my father's side."

"What a coincidence, darling, so is Maurice. Some good things did come out of France, but the place has become unbearably Gaulish don't you think?"

"Well, I am proud to be part French."

Gwen smiled. It had been so long since she had sat with someone she could be young with again.

"So! Darling, tell me. Why did you leave Canada?"

'But why Ireland?' her mother asked as they strolled through Mount Pleasant Cemetery. The spring was struggling up through mounds of crusted snow thick in the shadows of headstones and brittle like lace in the shade of stark naked trees under brilliant blue skies. It was an annual pilgrimage; her mother's favourite aunt was buried there. 'Why not somewhere closer, like Kingston or Ottawa? You could even consider Montreal if you must travel.'

Janice watched a squirrel dart across the road where black hearses purred in deference to the deceased. The high-rises on the other side of Yonge Street, across the subway tracks that rose from the ground just north of Saint Clair Avenue, glistened with lights even though the afternoon was bright and crisp. She could never live like that, compressed in tiny slabs. She didn't want to discuss it. She had made her mind up; it was what she was going to do despite what her mother might say.

'I need to go there, Mother. It is an opportunity that I would regret for the rest of my life, and besides, it's only for a few years and I can come home during the holidays.' The silos at Merton frowned over the scant tips of the trees. She tilted her head for an answer, but her mother had already shut her out. She smiled at the face of unspoken rebuke, that look that her father called 'the face of stone'.

She stood over the grave of Elizabeth Wray, who died in the year of nineteen-hundred and nineteen, the year of the great influenza, dead before life started.

Abiding now where Angels dwell
Far from sorrow and pain
Fairest child, sweetest girl
Life's loss is Heaven's gain.

Her mother grew impatient and folded her arms as she waited, but Janice didn't care anymore. There was nothing she could say, and besides, she had been accepted. But her mother wouldn't give up so easily. 'I can't think what your father would say.'

'It is a very famous university and I am very lucky, you should be proud of me.'

'Of course I am dear, but you will be so far away from Robert and me. Perhaps, he might not wait.'

The grey stone stood so forlorn in the deep snow, forgotten now by all but the most curious.

'Robert knows it's something I really should do. We have discussed it and he agrees.'

Robert had taken the news rather well. He knew their time together was ending. He almost seemed relieved, like she had removed a problem he didn't know how to deal with.

'Robert is just being kind, my dear. He is a good man, and after you are married, I am sure he will support you in whatever it is you want to indulge in. Don't risk throwing everything away.'

They left the cemetery in silence as the subway rumbled and passing cars swished through slush. They would meet Robert at Fran's – he loved their apple pie with cheese, it was his favourite treat. It had been for years. *How terribly boring*, Janice thought for the thousandth time.

"I had to get away," she finally answered. "I need to be alone with my painting."

"Of course, darling, I understand."

"I couldn't just move to Europe; my mother would never have understood so I go to school here."

Gwen raised her glass and casually rested her hand on Janice's knee; it was refreshingly cool against the heat of the fire. "What is it that you want to do?"

"I suppose that I'm not ready to call myself an artist. I'm not sure if I am good enough." She lowered her head, staring through her glass to the turf fire dancing and peeped through her hair. Gwen sat back, slowly withdrawing her hand. "Maurice and I think you can go far if you are given the chance and that is what we do; we give young artists a chance." She took Janice's hand in hers and squeezed it ever so lightly but enough to make Janice's heart skip a beat.

"Darling, we are not wealthy, but we have the estate and we have some rental holdings in the city. Perhaps we can make some arrangement. After all, we do what we can to support our struggling artists. Let me discuss it with Maurice, it does seem he has had a very good day with the ponies."

"I'm sorry?"

"He flutters on horse racing and does very well with it, too. Sadly, he usually leaves most of his winnings behind the bar. But he has been very supportive of the Press: there are always handouts to poets and painters, until they get noticed."

With firelight dancing with flickering shadows around her head, Gwen looked like a face Janice had seen in a painting. "I couldn't ask you to do that for me."

"Darling, Maurice and I would be honoured to help but are you certain this is what you want to do?" Gwen touched her face. Her hand was cold despite the fire that smoldered between them. Her eyes shimmered like stars behind lace curtains. Janice wanted them to be closer, but they were interrupted by the noise from the bar. Aidan held his glass in a most predictable manner: his Brendan Behan pose. He clutched his drink in one hand and pushed his fluttering shirttails back inside his pants. He grunted twice and farted once. "Ah! Musical accompaniment!" Maurice chuckled until he started to cough and splutter.

"Shush!" Gwen admonished as Aidan stepped to the middle of the room and cleared his sinuses with exaggerated energy. He raised his eyes to the ceiling and began to sing:

> *On Raglan Road, on an autumn day*
> *I met her first and knew*
> *That her dark hair would weave a snare*
> *That I might one day rue;*
> *I saw the danger, yet I walked*
> *Along the enchanted way,*
> *And I said, let grief*
> *Be a fallen leaf*
> *At the dawning of the day.*

He sang it as Luke Kelly had done, not with the jangling rhyme of a waltz. Aidan sang with the sorrow of the poet who had fallen for false love.

> *On Grafton Street in November*
> *we tripped lightly along the ledge*
> *Of the deep ravine where can be seen*
> *the worth of passion's pledge,*

The Queen of Hearts still making tarts
and I not making hay —
O I loved too much and by such and such
is happiness thrown away.

Gwen closed her eyes, lost in the ancient melody. Janice, too, was moved. She reached out and took Gwen's hand in hers.

I gave her gifts of the mind, I gave her
The secret sign that's known
To the artists who have known the true
Gods of sound and stone
And word and tint. I did not stint
For I gave her poems to say
With her own name there
And her own dark hair
Like clouds over fields of May

Aidan closed his eyes. In his heart, he was singing to Janice, even as shadows gathered around them.

On a quiet street where old ghosts meet
I see her walking now
Away from me so hurriedly
My reason must allow
That I had wooed not as I should
A creature made of clay —
When the angel woos the clay he'd lose
his wings at the dawn of day.

And when he opened his eyes, Janice was leaning forward to hear what Gwen was saying.

Outside, ragged clouds rode beneath the moon. The main street was empty of sprites and goblins, but just beyond, in the shadows, a gentle breeze moved among the trees where branches shed their last withered leaves. The wind moved down the valley to an old circle of stones that lay forgotten, beyond the broken bones of cells and grass-covered memories of walls and graves that littered the glade near the old round tower. Shadows gathered as they had done for eons, beneath the moon and the twinkling of a million stars, like a gathering of forgotten deities.

Sinead rode the bus in a habit and veil. She was going to a party and couldn't go as a ghost: she'd have to uncover her head every time she drank and she wanted to drop into Grogan's first, just to see who was there. The habit had pockets, too, but the cross that hung from her belt banged her thighs when she walked and settled between them when she sat. But it was Hallowe'en, and she was just one of many nuns roaming the bars.

Grogan's was hopping: the regulars lingered in sorry state as the weekend crowd jostled around them, sloshing beer and filling the place with loud smoky laughter. Most of them talked too much and talked without listening. She stepped to the bar in the small space between Jimmy Neil and the wall.

"How are ya, Sinead?"

"Great, Jimmy, and you?"

"Sean, give Sinead a drink. Will ya?" He paused to look her up and down. "John, the twenty-third, must be rolling in his grave. Vatican Two will be the end of the world."

"Ah, it's not that bad, Jimmy. It's one of those progressive orders, you know? We get a night out every so often. So what's the crack?"

"This fuckin' capitalist lapdog is talking shite again."

"How are you, Sinead?" the lapdog asked.

"I'm fine, Tony. Why are you arguing with the Kamikaze Socialist?"

"Ah, sure you know how it is in here on a Saturday night."

"Well, Sinead's here so you can go fuck yourself."

"Go fuck yourself, Jimmy. Just ask her, she'll agree with me."

"What am I agreeing to?" Sinead looked around: there was no harm in hoping.

"That Ireland's moving toward a very promising future. This old relic of the class wars can't see what's more than obvious to the rest of us."

"What? Ya think that not taxing the multinationals will boost the economy. It will be Potez all over again."

"Nay, Jimmy, we're getting it right this time. I mean, look at all the stuff that's happening."

"Like what?"

"Well, what about free education?"

"I'm all for that," Jimmy snarled. "When all the young ones graduate, they can toddle off to work as civil servants in Brussels."

Sinead wasn't sure. If only Aidan would show up. She would be cool with him, of course.

"It's not going to be like that." Tony argued with all the conviction he could muster. Arguing with Jimmy was a lost cause; he knew better, but he couldn't help it. "We're producing great university graduates nowadays. We're creating a whole generation of skilled workers. No more shipping navvies off to Britain."

"So where the fuck are ya gonna ship them?"

It wasn't like she was still carrying a torch. She was more concerned for Janice, she wasn't right for Aidan; anybody could see that. Then, again, if they were together, she better just accept it and get on with life.

"Closure, Jimmy. We're going to have closure on emigration."

"Ya wee daft twit, the only closure we're gonna see is more factories closing. Take that back and write it into the next report you vomit up for the Propaganda Ministry."

"Who works for the Propaganda Ministry?" Gerry emerged from the crowd. "I thought that Tony worked for the Industrial Development Agency, and when Sinead finishes being a nun, she can work there, too. With her charm, she'll have every big company in the world lining up to be let in."

Sinead smiled, but she wasn't really listening.

"Give us three pints and whatever the Sister is having." Gerry smiled as he reached inside his jacket. He frowned and reached for the other side. He repeated the shuffle until Tony intervened: "I'll get those, it's my round, anyway."

"Fair play to you, anyway, Gerry."

"Thanks, Jimmy, I just wanted to buy you all a drink, but I must have left my money at home."

"I meant you still got the Macarena down pat."

"Jimmy," Sinead pulled herself away from her reflections. "Leave him alone. Go back to picking on the lapdog."

"Thanks, Sinead."

"You're welcome, Tony."

That was it; she had to get on with her own life. Aidan wasn't for her. She knew that all along so there was no point in stewing over it. "It's the only way forward all right."

"What is?"

"Bringing in foreign investment; every country in the world is going to have to compete for investment."

"Great, now we can get fucked by foreign capitalists."

"Don't be talking like that in front of the nun."

"Sorry, Sinead, it's just a bad habit."

"Listen, gents," she batted her eyes, in case they knew what she was thinking. "I'm tired of standing."

"You go on, I've to get home." Tony patted his pockets for his car keys. "C'mon, ya big daft Teuchtar, I'll give you a ride." Jimmy thought about it for a moment, but it was time to leave; he'd been drinking all day.

Gerry and Sinead settled around their table with their backs to the wall, looking out at the teeming crowd.

"This is like a date," Gerry beamed at her, "except I've never been out with a nun before."

"When's the last time you were out on a date?"

"Not since I was in England. I was one of the navvies we exported back in the fifties. We were shipped off like cattle. We'd no work here and there was lots of work rebuilding England after the war."

He paused to draw on his pint and to light a Woodbine. "Lots of work, but no life. You couldn't even get a decent place to live. 'No Dogs or Irish' the signs used to say. We worked like dogs all right, but we lived like pigs – gangs of us to a room, taking turns sleeping on the beds or floors when we were lucky enough to find a place. The only people who'd take us in were our own.

"Our own? Those fuckers sucked every penny out of us for dirty rooms and food that pigs would have turned their noses up at. We were just a bunch of lads from the villages and the farms. Most of us had never seen a city before. Can you imagine that, a bunch of Paddies wandering the streets of London full of drink? We were a drunken pack of dogs all right, snapping and snarling over everything."

"It must have been awful for you," Sinead fidgeted with the crucifix. She shouldn't have asked to sit down. "But you managed to get home?"

"I did Sinead. After twenty years, I'd enough and I came home. My old mother was unwell and she needed me. So I packed in the work and tried to make a go of the farm. But my mother died so I sold up and moved to the city. I like to think of myself as a retired farmer now, and that's a lot better than those I left in London. They're probably under the bridges by now with brown paper bagged bottles as the only comfort the world can offer. I did better than most."

For an unguarded moment, Sinead glimpsed it again, the anguished face she'd seen at the back of the church, the face of a man tormented by sin. She wanted to ask. "Gerry?" But she couldn't pry and searched for something else. "Have you seen Aidan recently?"

"The Bard? I heard that he went down the country for the weekend. I think he brought someone with him, too. A foreign student from what I hear. I suppose that you and him are no longer stepping out together."

"No Gerry. I stopped seeing him when I joined the order."

But he wasn't really listening. "It's a shame. You're the best thing that ever happened him. He looked like a young lad in love when he was with you."

Sinead bought him another drink and left.

The night was full of drunken fools, howling at the moon and creating a nuisance of themselves: offering to help her out of her habit. She dismissed them with her head down. She didn't feel like going to the party, anymore, but she did stop in an off-license to get a bottle of Blue Nun. It was all she could afford. She finished it alone in her bedroom as the clouds jumped over the moon as the wind was changing.

It turned at the top of the valley and whistled through the village, past the big house with the stones pheasants, where Gwen, Maurice and Aidan all slept, each to their own bed, but Janice walked a crooked path in an old dark forest.

She knew she would.

Hooves clip-clopped along behind her and red hooded eyes watched her pass.

Wolves, she decided, trying to be brave. They followed apace, unnerving her. She quickened but they did, too, moving silently and effortlessly along, always but a few paces behind. She tried to run, but it was impossible. Her shawl caught in the low branches and her skirt snagged on rambling thorns and briars. She crumpled by a tree trunk and lay akimbo as shapes emerged from all sides, closing in on her.

The Huntress nudged her horse closer as the hounds circled. Their eyes glowed like embers and held Janice transfixed as she approached.

Chapter 7

Dawn peeped over the hills and the night shriveled down the valley, whispering like penance. It was the price that had to be paid on All Saints' Day. They'd all been a little drunk after all. The old house was quiet so she rolled into the hollow of the sagging mattress and lay on her back tracing the ribs of the candlewick spread. In time, she heard someone stir and creak down the stairs. She waited for a while before following.

"Coffee, darling? It is from Bewley's."

"Thank you. What a lovely view, but where is your lake?"

"Lake darling?"

"Aidan told me you have a lake."

Gwen laughed like a wind chime. She wiped her hands and walked to the window. "We have a duck pond, but I suppose to a poet . . ."

They stood together and when Janice turned, they almost brushed cheeks.

"Gwen? Would you think it very strange if I asked for a hug?"

Gwen reached and coaxed Janice to her. "Has it all been a little too strange for you?"

"Not at all, Gwen, I have had a wonderful time."

They smiled and steadied themselves in each other's gaze until Gwen went back to slicing large pulpy tomatoes and laying them in rows beside the flaccid slices of rasher thick with rind and spouting a few stubby hairs. "Maurice insists on a large country breakfast," she explained to Janice's curiosity as she laid the bacon on the sizzling pan.

Janice savoured her coffee. They were relaxed with each other, standing close as she tried to help. Gwen didn't mind, though, sometimes, her breathing quickened when they touched. The kitchen grew warm and smelled deliciously, but when Aidan came down, he was sullen. Maurice, however, was delighted and showered them with compliments as he tucked a napkin under his jowls and beamed at them all, even Aidan.

"What's the matter with you? You are looking a little dour this morning."

Gwen didn't turn. She knew what Aidan could be like. Anything might ignite his smoldering fuses and set the whole day ablaze with acrimony so she busied herself with the frying pan that bubbled and spat every time she raised the lid. "Now, Gentlemen," she turned like a Lakshmi bearing plates of sizzling bacon with wobbly yellow eggs and red tomatoes nestled among the black and white blood pudding. "Please, don't get cranky, breakfast is ready. Maurice, sit down and eat before you do something silly, and Aidan, try to be civil. You can be very ill-tempered in the mornings. Oh! Excuse my clumsiness, Janice." She skipped like she had tripped on something. "I nearly delivered your eggs into your lap."

"Not at all, Gwen," Janice's smile froze for a moment but began to thaw as she put the pieces together. "I just don't know how you manage it all." But Gwen acted like she hadn't heard. "There, shall we all sit down and eat a pleasant breakfast?"

Maurice chuckled. "Ladies, please ignore the Bard. Perhaps his dissolute lifestyle has finally caught up with him."

"Today is going to be a fine day, Janice," Gwen soothed as she poured hot brown tea for them all. "You and Aidan should visit Clonmacnoise. It simply must be seen, especially by a painter. The ruins are spectacular and the light is so varied. I can't believe that you have been in Ireland for months and he hasn't taken you to see it. Aidan! You should be ashamed of yourself."

Aidan muttered about it being half-way across the country and about time and money.

"That is silly. You have a motorcar and it is Sunday, Maurice?"

He reached into his pocket and handed Aidan a few more banknotes. He was still ahead on the weekend, if only by a nose. He was sure Aidan's new book would sell – that it would allow him to break even and perhaps, with translations, raise a small profit. "Cheers, Bard!"

"An' what about my arse?" Aidan muttered as he stuffed the money into his pocket, wincing slightly as he balanced on one hip.

"Perhaps," Maurice muttered as he inspected the piece of pudding on his fork, "you should take that up with my wife." He hadn't mentioned it, yet: he had pulled a few strings to have Aidan included in an upcoming cultural exposé across the Continent. Sometimes, life smiled on him.

"How do you feel about taking their money?" Janice asked after the protracted goodbyes, as Maurice and Gwen became so small in the side mirror.

"Their money? And besides, it makes 'em happy. They're still Horse-Protestants, ya know?"

"I don't see what that has to do with taking their money."

"Ya know, Janice, we can act all artsy, but at the back of it all, we just want someone to look out for us until our work is out there and everybody's clamorin' and treatin' us like we're special. And besides, it's what patrons are supposed to do. Ya know back when . . ."

"Aidan, why does it feel like we're just using them?"

"Trust me, Janice, we're the ones bein' used. It's just business to them, ya know?"

"And what does that make us?"

"C'mon, Janice, you know what's goin' on here."

"Do you think for one second that I would . . .?"

"You're tryin' to get them to peddle yer paintin's?"

She folded her arms and stared through the grimy windshield as he struggled with the gears, lit another cigar and turned the cassette. It's one of the things he hated about women, acting like brassers one minute and then acting all defiled. He smiled at her, but she wasn't ready. He understood. She'd blame him until she got used to the idea. Women didn't like to face reality, especially his. They were brave enough when he was plying them with drink and showering them with compliments, but when the morning came, they shriveled up like shrews. They were all the same. It was like they always needed reassurance or something.

But he wanted things to be different with Janice.

By the fourth time he looked over, she almost smiled.

She was still angry, but there was some truth in what he said. Everybody had a price: it was the way the world worked. As long as the price was right, as long as they were discrete about it, even with themselves. Aidan and Gwen had a past and she and Aidan had a future. It was better to let things lie; Maurice and Gwen had accepted her. It was a little messy, but they were beyond the pale of petty mores.

They drove in silent truce as the car jigged and reeled through scruffy little villages where dingy men gathered on corners, waiting for pubs to open. She absorbed passing details and scratched with her charcoal, capturing as much as she could as they passed fields of contented cattle poking their heads through hedgerows. The Audi sputtered toward the river that ran past Clonmacnoise and down to Limerick where it meandered through stifling mudflats to mingle and merge with foamy tides that rolled in, all the way from Newfoundland where she had once been with her father.

'Over there is Europe.' He pointed out to sea, past an iceberg that calved and drifted aimlessly to its demise. 'You must visit it someday. Perhaps you'll become a famous painter there.'

But by the broken monastery, the Shannon was wide between rushy banks where reeds bowed and swayed to the ancient winds. The sun danced with clouds and breezes cast eddies across the water, combing reeds and long grasses around mossy tombstones that ringed the roofless walls and bric-a-brac of antiquity, silent but for the songs of plovers and bitterns, the bawling of calves disconcerted by shadows and the staccato of a barking dog. But in her mind's eye she saw a medieval monastery where pilgrims and peddlers, the sick and the poor, the pious and the powerful flocked. Beneath the vigilant tower where monks had cowered from the fury of Norsemen who rode the river seeking plunder.

"Ya know, when the rest of Europe was declinin' into feudal ignorance, the monks kept the flame of learnin' alive in places like this. For a while we were the 'True Church' an' had to be gotten rid of so the English Pope gave us to the Normans. We called it the time of 'The Saints and Scholars'. In fact, if it weren't for the Irish, a lot of stuff would have been lost in the Dark Ages. The monks used to spend their time transcribin' Gospels an' all that stuff, ya know? Like the Book of Kells an' stuff like that. And we made Christians out of the Vikings so they would stop killin' everyone. Nobody remembers that anymore."

"I know, Aidan. That's what I came to study."

"Well, excuse me for forgettin' my place."

"That's okay, you've been doing it all weekend."

He almost flinched for a moment. "C'mon in here a minute, I want to show you somethin'."

She followed him into the little house that squatted beyond the walls, now converted into an information kiosk. Its whitewashed walls sparkled in the sunshine under a grey slate roof. The doorway was low and the floors were flagstone. A counter ran through the parlour. The old fireplace still stood and cradled the smoky embers of a few sods of turf: a deliberate touch on a day that was still warm for that time of the year.

"Can I help you?" a pretty face with too much make up inquired. She smiled at Janice, but she batted her eyes at Aidan who stood far too close.

"I know this house. It used to belong to Miss O' Connell. She was my teacher years ago. Did you know her?" he asked the pretty young woman.

"I can't say that I did. She died when I was very young."

Good for you, thought Janice. *That should put Casanova back in his place*

"She brought me here once," he continued regardless, "durin' the summer holidays, the year my mother died. This was where we had tea an' scones, served on brown willow-pattern. Ya don't see them anymore, do ya?"

"No," the pretty young face replied as she stepped back a little. "I didn't know much about her except that she was a teacher and left the house to the government."

"She's the reason I started to write, ya know. She's the one who encouraged me."

"Oh! Are you a writer then?" She flashed her perfect smile and batted her beautiful blue eyes.

"He is," interrupted Janice, "He writes beautiful poetry about young girls who fall in love with wayward men who love and leave them. You should try reading them, they are very insightful." She turned and walked outside into the patchwork of sun and shade as the breeze blew on her flushed cheeks. She walked past ancient headstones and weather-worn stone crosses.

"Celtic crosses," he pointed out after he'd caught up with her, "real ones!"

"Don't you think I know that?"

"What's the matter now? Ah c'mon Janice, she's just being friendly. It's part of her job, ya know, to make tourist feel welcome."

"Really!"

"Ya, really, an' ya know somethin' else? I think you're jealous."

"Of what, a whore like you?"

"That's exactly what I mean. You're just jealous 'cause I'm better at it."

"That's only because you have had far more practice."

"So you're admittin' it then?"

"Admitting what? That you throw yourself at every woman who crosses your path?"

"Are you sayin' it's okay to throw yourself at someone for the sake of art but it's not okay to go around bein' nice? I'm a poet of the people. I need to interact with them. And besides, you were happy enough to throw yourself at the Fitzwilliams."

"Aidan, please, stop talking before you say something we'll regret."

"Like what, a bit of truth now an' then?"

She wanted to walk away from him, but she couldn't. How would she get back to the city?

"I don't think it's jealousy to object to your flirting. How the hell do you think it makes me feel to have to watch that?" He looked confused for a moment so she continued. "Am I not enough for you?"

"Do you really think that one person can be enough for someone? Can we really be expected to satisfy all of each other's needs?"

"Aidan, that is a wonderful rational but it is typical for a man."

"That's right Janice, that's the way real men are supposed to be. We're not supposed to settle down. We're supposed to wander around like hunters an' spread our seed an' all."

"Cut the bullshit, Aidan. Just shut up and tell me one thing. Have you been sleeping with Gwen?"

"What? Why would you even ask such a thing?"

"Because her husband shot you!"

Aidan looked trapped for a moment and took out his lighter again. He lit his slumbering cigar with exaggerated care and inhaled deeply before blowing the smoke out across his shoulder. "I won't lie to you. Yes, I have. But there's somethin' you should know. I had to. But I'm tryin' to end it now. Look, Janice. I'd been seein' her since before you came along and I want to change that now. But I have to handle it carefully. Listen, I'm sorry. What else can I say?"

She stared past him. Her impulse was to rage and, after he had dropped her off in Rathmines, close her door to him forever. But she had to stop and think for a moment: she didn't want to close the door on Gwen, and she couldn't see how she could keep in contact on her own, it was absurd: *Excuse me Gwen, Aidan and I have broken up because of you, but I was wondering, are you still offering to help me?*

"Aidan. Cut the bullshit and tell me one thing. Do you love her?"

"Of course, I don't. I love you. Why do you think I brought you to see them?"

"To rub my face in it." But she regretted it even as the words passed her lips. "I'm sorry, Aidan, that was petty of me. Tell me?"

"I wanted Gwen to know that we're together so she'll let me go."

"Why can't you just leave her?"

"Ah Janice, it's far more complicated than that."

Gwen had met him at the front door: she had come out to pay the taxi. She kissed him quickly as they rushed up the steps into the warm house full of glitterati and literati: he was making his debut. As he tried to swallow his second drink, he was called to read before them all. He didn't put it down in case he needed to wash away his rising bile. He wanted to seem nonchalant, as Behan might have done, but he wasn't prepared as the room hushed and turned to look at him. At first, his voiced wavered. Words that had looked so strong on the page, which ran through his mind like music, now shriveled in the air around him. He even skipped two lines as he stumbled to the end that was lost as he raised his glass and drained it in awkward silence. He didn't wait; he went outside and lit a Woodbine as his shoulders rose around his face.

In moments, Gwen was there, close but not too close, and waited for him to speak.

He was defiant, like he had been challenged on the street, like someone had called him out. "So?"

"They loved it, darling."

"They did like shite. They were all starin' at me like I was a dead cat in the gutter."

"Not at all, darling; they were enthralled by you, just like I said they would be."

"Don't give me that fuckin' crap. I could see for myself. They all think I'm some kind of fuckin' fraud."

"Darling, you are as real as they come, never doubt that. This is why I brought you here, to show these people what I know – that, someday, you will be considered among the great. Now I will leave you alone to smoke, but do join us soon."

When he returned to the boozy gathering, they accepted him each in their own way, some with deference and some with mock disdain – the language of Dublin, while all the time, Gwen smiled at him from across the room.

"I can't just leave her, Janice, not after all she has done for me. But you'll see. She'll do the right thing when she realises that we're in love."

"In love, Aidan?" And despite herself, Janice felt a tiny flutter inside. Besides, they had their art to consider, delicate threads of aspiration that needed protection and support for a while yet. And how long would she stay with him? She could go with the flow as long as it carried her to where she wanted to be.

"Okay, Aidan, but from now on, we should only see her to-gether – so she gets the message. Okay?"

"You and me and her?"

"No! You and me – meeting with her."

"Sure. But would you ever consider – ya know."

"Never"

"What if the price was right?"

"I'm not a whore like you."

"Don't give me that shite. We're all tryin' to sell somethin'."

Janice might have reacted but decided not to, not now, not yet. Instead, she walked among the crosses and the whimsy of long dead monks and the battering of time and weather: small details clamouring for attention. She sat against a broken chapel and let the memory of the place seep in. In time, he came and lay on the grass beside her with his hands cradling the back of his head and his dark glasses between him and the ever-changing sky.

"Janice?"

"What?"

"I'm sorry about all that. I never wanted it to come between us and I never meant to upset you or anythin'."

"Is that the best a poet can do?"

"Ya, that an' the fact that you're the prettiest. I mean it. I think you're the finest lookin' girl in all of Ireland. Gwen thinks so, too. She says that you have the looks and the talent to become a great painter."

Janice wanted to know more about what Gwen thought, but she couldn't let him off that easily. "What have looks got to do with talent?"

"Painters can be good-lookin', too."

"What about Picasso?"

"He was a man."

"And Frieda?"

"Never heard of her, was she beautiful?"

"Not really, she had one eyebrow."

They huddled by the wall, staying out of the wind until he had to stretch his legs and be alone with his thoughts. Janice watched him leave and reached for her sketchpad. The breezes teased her hair as she scratched. The old place called to her, voices coming up from the ground: pious voices of those who laboured in the anonymity of the darker centuries for the glory of the one God. But she could hear an older voice, too. It spoke of power and guile. It whispered in her ear and brought a subtle smile to her face. She drew the pretty young girl with the made-up face spread-eagle between marble pillars to which her hands and feet were bound with black satin cords. She strained and pleaded with Janice. She was helpless: she would become whatever Janice decided. She reached down to the front of the young woman's shirt and tore it, exposing breasts and a soft white belly. She stripped her and left her stand in the wind that tossed and teased her hair and the tattered rags that clung to her feet and ankles.

"I like that," he surprised her before she could close the pad, "I like the way you did her body."

"Do you only see the physical?"

"What else is there?"

"Well, it could be about a great many things, like constraints, like relationships, like falling in love with the wrong person, but you can't see past her breasts, can you?"

"What can I tell ya? It's the way I am. I mean, we're conditioned to respond to how things look."

"My goodness, Aidan, you should put that in a poem and write it on bathroom walls."

"Look, I love the image of a sexy young woman in restraints, it's very primitive an' none of it needs explanation, at least not to people who know the truth and try to figure things out for themselves. That's why there's so much opposition to books an' art, ya know, all the stuff that reminds people of what they're really about.

Even the monks who worked here wanted to hide behind some veneer of piety, like the only way to overcome weaknesses was to not let them happen. It's pretty stupid when you think about it: that the only way to avoid the bad side of ourselves is through restraint. What we should be doin' is embracin' all passions an' vices and choosing right from wrong from there."

"Are you are overcoming your demons by having sex with every woman you meet?"

"Men are wired to have sex with women who attract them, but for women, there has to be intimacy an' assurance. It's like you don't want to be honest that you're just fuckin'."

"In your case, it is beyond argument. You're just one big walking, talking penis who gets hard at the sight of big breasts. What's with that? Have you no control? I don't know why women bother. We should just give you naked pictures of ourselves and have you jerk-off into specimen jars."

"You'd do that for me?"

"I'm sure you'd like that: no emotional involvement, just sheer fantasy, big tits and sultry lips, spread-eagle and panting with desire. Men are idiots."

"That's because men are drawn to women who're young an' ready, ya know? Women who're in season already without hours of datin' an' foreplay an' all. It's all about the visuals. It's about stimulation not intimacy."

"And what visuals do you have when you are with me?"

Aidan blushed; he wasn't ready for that question.

"Aidan? Don't start getting all Irish-Catholic on me."

"Well. Sometimes, when I'm at it, I like to think about doin' it with more than one woman, at the same time, ya know?"

"How original, but tell me one thing. Who have you being sharing me with? It's Gwen, isn't it? Is that how you get your rocks off? What happens? Do we bring each other to wild orgasms as we take turns with your penis?"

Aidan knew enough to stop and think. He'd said far too much already. He lit another cigar and tried to find a way out. "Janice, I'm lookin' for the truth in everythin' an' I find a lot of it hidden behind taboos an' things like that. You know what I'm talkin' about. You're the same or you wouldn't be able to paint as good as you do."

"Greeley. You're so full of shit."

"C'mon, Janice, you know what I mean. It's like all that stuff about succubuses."

"Succubi."

"Ya them, monks had fantasies about them comin' and seducin' them an' all. I mean, it wasn't like they couldn't get off or anythin', what with all the other horny monks around. Maybe they did it for god. I mean, they did everythin' else for god, but my point is that even these guys had sexual images that got them goin', ya know?"

"Did they think about succubi while they were with each other or was it the other way around?"

"It doesn't really matter. Does it?"

"It would matter to me, and don't ask. I would rather you were with her and thinking about me."

"Really?"

"Yes. I guess it's the foolish romantic in me, but you see, I don't think that sex is my Muse."

"What's holdin' you back then?"

She made a fist behind her back as he continued. "Anyway, you can make fun of me if you like. But that's what I feel like after I do it, ya know. It's like one of those rituals you read about, ya know? And afterward, I want to write an' then what I write is like somethin' outside of me. It's like someone else speakin' through me."

"Oh! And what do you feel like after you do it with me?"

He almost skidded as he reached for the right thing to say. "Doing it again."

It worked, she looked softer so he reached for her and she let him touch her edges.

"That all sounds wonderful, but you got one little part wrong. The succubi tried to prevent the monks from writing. That was the point of the myth."

"Myth! Is that what you think? But okay, even if they were myths, think about it. The monks were spreadin' the word of the new god. The Succubi knew what would happen if the new belief spread."

"Aidan, that's ridiculous."

"Is it? Gods become myths when people stop believin' in them. The succubi were just actin' in self-defense." He stopped and looked at her for a while and she knew that look. If she didn't say anything, he just might reveal another part of himself. It worked.

"Ya might think I'm fucked in the head, but I think Gwen's a Lenanshee or somethin'."

"A Lenanshee?"

"Ya, because instead of stealin' my creativity – she adds to it."

"Do you really expect me to believe that?"

"It's not about what you fuckin' believe. I don't give a fuck what you or anyone . . ."

He never got to finish. She slapped his face and stood back in amazement as the shape of her hand grew red across his face. She glared at him until she noticed he had tears in his eyes. He mumbled that he was sorry that he spoke like that. It was because his whole life was one big fuck-up and she was the only decent thing that had ever happened to him.

She didn't answer. She didn't know what to believe.

"Janice, you have to believe this, if nothin' else. The only time I feel like I'm real is when I'm with you. The rest of the time, I feel like I'm a shadow, ya know, like the ones that live in dark caves an' stuff. Don't let me sink back in there, please?"

"Drive me home, Aidan, and let me sort things out for a while."

She waited in the coffee shop as the steam hissed and the cups clattered and everyone else came and went. Sinead had a class that morning, but she would come by soon, she always did.

"How was your weekend?"

"We lost on Saturday, but we'd a good night afterwards. How was your trip?"

"Does anything happen around here that you don't know about?"

"I don't know!"

"I met with Gwen Fitzwilliams. Do you know her?"

"I've heard about her."

"Aidan's been having an affair with her."

"What makes you think that?"

"He admitted it to me."

"Do you believe everything he says?"

"I'm serious. But he wants to end it now, but he's afraid she'll turn against him. What should I do?"

"I don't know."

"What would you do? I mean, he thinks she's the reason he's getting somewhere. Do you think that any of it is true?"

"Not really."

"Sinead, what do you think of muses?"

"What?"

"Aidan feels that Gwen might be his."

"We all draw inspiration from somewhere, and men think with their dicks. It makes sense when you think about."

Sinead watched her cross the street. Janice was such a lost lamb, but she brought some colour to the grey days. Ronan wasn't working again. She was beginning to think he might be avoiding her.

That wouldn't be too bad. At least it would mean that he knew I existed.

"Very well, Bridey, I will call Pimples, but are you sure? You haven't seen her work yet?"

"Trust me, Maurice. I have a feeling about her. She is exactly what I have been looking for. Of course, I will go and see her work, and I know we will be delighted; trust me."

"Always have, Bridey, always have. But what about the Bard?

"Darling, once Janice gets a taste of our world, she will quickly tire of Dublin and everything in it. Trust me, darling."

"Always, Bridey."

Chapter 8

Glasses gleamed and pumps shone like hope. The barman was welcoming but not intrusive, smiling like a curate as he fished out the bubbles, waited for it to settle, filled the last few inches and skimmed the top. He placed it on a fresh bar-mat and returned to wiping and restocking. The lower part was a good clean black, the type that glowed red against the light. The rest was darkening, too, as brown bubbles formed a Roman collar. Aidan lit a cigar and downed about a third. His upper lip crusted, but he smiled even as he shivered. He raised the glass a few more times until he almost reached the end. Only then did he start to uncoil. He nodded to Sean who acknowledged but pulled the second pint casually.

Aidan unfolded the 'Times.' He didn't want to have to think about anything for a while. He'd wanted the day to himself, to sort things out. As he ordered another, he rehearsed it in his mind. He and Janice had something good; something that actually meant something but that didn't mean he had to stop seeing Gwen. It's just that it would look better, she was married after all: this way people wouldn't suspect. It all made sense so he finished his drink and tucked his newspaper under his arm and cut through Powerscourt to avoid the rain.

"Does she know about us?" Her black satin robe was tied at the waist but opened like an hourglass, revealing more as time passed.

He might have to make his decision some other time. "How did she take it?" "Well, she was a bit shocked at first, but I explained that it was goin' on before an' now it's goin' to end."

"Is it going to end?"

"Well, she never said that I couldn't go on seein' you." He knew that he was sowing the seeds of his own destruction.

"So Janice has agreed to accept things just the way they are?"

"Are you sure?" He looked confused.

"Darling, how long have I been looking out for you? Of course that is what it means; women speak a different language. That is why men can never understand us. Come, let me help you out of that coat, you must be so hot in there."

He resisted a little as Gwen stood before him, as her robe revealed more, as she wrestled him out of his coat and his shirt. Her fingers were cold and thrilled his skin but her lips were warm and moist. She ran her fingers down his sides, meeting at his stomach and converging on his belt buckle. He lay back: there was no point in struggling. It was Fate after all. He just had to let it do with him as it pleased. Her hands clasped him and pulled him free of his pants. She straddled him, and as she rode the cresting waves, her satin robe floated behind her, collapsing around them when they came.

The sun crossed the floor and slid beneath the window. The streets grew noisier but couldn't drown out his conscience; he needed drink for that. Jimmy and the lads would be in Grogan's by now. He wished he had listened to them.

"What is the matter, darling? You are very restless." She placed her head on his chest where she could listen to his heart. She knew he loved the feeling of her hair on his naked skin. It was golden, not blond, soft and smelled of hawthorns, but he began to stir even as they grew warm together.

"I gotta see one of the lads; I owe him money."

"Do you have any?"

"I don't, as a matter of fact. I was just wondering – ya know – if you'd advance me a few quid."

"You are not considering dumping me, are you, darling? After all, one wouldn't want to tempt the Fates." She was struggling to keep calm. This was not the way things were supposed to be. He was not supposed to leave her: it had never happened before. She would have to be careful, at least until she was finished with him but he looked determined as he stood before her and struggled to find the right words.

"I don't think we should do this again, at least not for a while. I think we should cool things off a little, ya know, not see each other so much." His words raked her heart, almost tearing it from her. She couldn't let that happen. "Darling, don't be rash, let's talk about this."

He took the forty Pounds that fluttered between them, but he held on to his convictions. "I really am thinkin' about goin' to another press, too, ya know. It'd be better that way."

Gwen smiled as she watched her money disappear into his pocket. "Are you sure she loves you darling?" He hovered over the comment so she continued. "Can you trust her?"

"Ah c'mon, Gwen, why are you sayin' all of this?"

"She is not one of us, Aidan; she is just passing through. She is having a little blue period right now: a troubled search for the soul."

Aidan wanted to be firm, but his voice was unsure. "Don't talk about her like that. And besides, maybe I want to go to Paris with her. All the great writers go there, sooner or later."

"Aidan. She will go back to Toronto one day."

"Ya, well, maybe I'll go there with her too."

She laughed and reached for his hand. "Can you really see yourself sitting down to dinner with her mother in some dull little house in a cold, grey city? She will think you are from the IRA."

As she laughed, her shoulder emerged from the sheet revealing the top of her warm soft breast. She smiled as his eyes darted

back to her face. "Think about it, darling. That is all that I want you
to do, just think about it."

The sheet slipped from her head and her hair shone in the soft
light. She touched his hand lightly, a delicate touch that might have
been accidental if it wasn't so intimate.

"I still think we shouldn't see each other, at least not for a
while, and I'm goin' to start looking for another publisher, too. It's
better that way; it's less complicated."

"Aidan, we are bound to each other, don't forget that."

As the door closed behind him, Gwen wrapped herself against
the chill and fumbled through her bag until she found it. She
thumbed through the pages and began to dial the number.

She stared at her reflection in the mirror as the room darkened. In the cold light, her face was changing. Her cheeks seemed
to collapse until her bones might poke through. Her lips shriveled
and her teeth were exposed. Her eyes were dark pools and her hair
looked like straw. She snapped her fingers. *Doesn't anybody hear this
phone?*

Janice was getting frustrated: the round tower wasn't right.

It looks like the leaning tower of Pisa; she almost laughed. It needed to be more austere – more of an intrusion on the soft vista behind, the bend in the river and the rushy green spaces beyond. And
the monk didn't look startled enough; there was a naked woman in
front of him. He looked like he was smirking; he almost looked like
Aidan. She should change that, but she couldn't; there was something about the expression on his face.

The woman was perfect, though, well-proportioned and the
colour was just right. She was pale, almost luminous and her hair
was bright. Her left leg was a little twisted but that added something whimsical to her stance. She wouldn't change that, either.

She needed to take a break, to stand back and look again from
a distance. The next time the phone rang she didn't hesitate.

"Janice darling, I am in town for a few days and was hoping we could find the time for lunch." Her voice was soft and cautious.

"I'd love to but," Janice didn't want to seem too eager, "I'm very busy right now. I have so much schoolwork and I started a new painting. It's in that critical stage. I would be afraid to leave it?" She hoped it was plausible and not rude. She didn't want to offend Gwen, but she did want to register a touch of reserve, after all.

"Darling, I was just talking to someone about you and I really must see your work. I think things could be about to happen for you. We could meet tomorrow, in Bewley's. What time would be good for you, darling?"

Janice returned to her canvass with a bottle of French wine. She replayed their conversation all evening, twisting it and turning it until she settled in for the night.

Grafton Street teemed with the comings and goings of lunch-time crowds. Office friends skipped through puddles and smatter-ings of rain. Young women danced by, heels hard on the sidewalks, clutching shopping bags from Arnott's and Brown Thomas, while men went to O'Neill's and other pubs renowned for lunch. Be-wley's Oriental Cafe had seen it all for centuries, stoic behind its Chinese box façade: an exotic echo in the dowdy grey but a hint of complot lingered, wafting from the warren of cafes and cafeterias to the more reserved tearooms upstairs. She passed into the merry maelstrom of hissing and rattling, waitresses' sing-songing to the counter staff and the continuous mumble of a thousand conversa-tions of old friends, mothers and daughters, and a few shaggy post-graduate students.

Gwen waved from her table. She was wearing a smart tweed skirt and a stiff white blouse with her pearl necklace. She suited the décor; palm fronds, embossed red wallpaper, eastern carpets and a hundred marble-topped tables. "Is this your first time here, darling?"

Janice flustered as it all came flooding back: the day she first saw Gwen. She was unsure and mumbled something about it being quaint.

"Yes, it is very quaint, but I am afraid it has seen better days. It is a piece of Dublin history. The founder broke ranks with the East Indian Trading Company and imported tea and coffee directly, totally scandalous at the time: very seditious. Over the years, it has seen an assortment of rogues and rascals – artists mostly. But, somehow, it managed to blend all of that with a reasonable price for tea and crumpets for reasonable, respectable people, as well as those who couldn't afford it but came anyway, for sticky buns. I see you brought your work. May I take a look?"

Janice handed over the old leather map case. Her father had found it in a garage sale. He believed it was from the Hudson's Bay Company. "It's just a few sketches and some old paintings."

Gwen swiveled her hips beneath the table, crossed her legs and opened the case across her lap. Her hair streamed forward and her necklace swung back and forth enticingly as a delicate perfume rose from between her breasts.

"They are good, darling." She hummed and hawed through the loose sheets and small pieces of canvas. They almost fluttered to the floor when the waitress came by.

The waitress came back to see if everything was okay but still Janice waited until finally Gwen closed the case and beamed at her. "There is some wonderful work in here. I realise that they are rough, but they speak to me. I must see some of your larger pieces. You have real talent, darling. We just have to introduce you to the right people."

Janice had ordered a salad; it was awful, but she poked at it any way. She needed something to focus on, but her heart was soaring up the winding staircase. Gwen was enthused, too, almost gushing.

"Darling, I am so pleased. You are just what I have been look-ing for. Painters are few in this country; we are more suited to writing. I suppose it is because ours was an oral tradition. We do have some beautiful works of sculpture, but we do not seem to produce enough painters. We have had people like Jack Yeats, of course. Have you seen his work?"

Janice nodded and searched for the right thing to say, something that was more than a paraphrasing of all that she had read. Gwen smiled like she knew, so Janice remained silent.

"I suppose, darling, that it is time to clear the air about Aidan and me." She drank from her coffee cup and composed herself. "I must beg forgiveness for my impropriety in the past. Aidan and I were lovers but that must end now that I have met you."

She shook her head solemnly, eyes hard like diamonds, examining Janice's face. "I want to assure you that I will respect your relationship with Aidan without reservation."

She waited for Janice to absorb it all. "But I do ask that you seriously consider allowing me to help. See it as a gesture to correct any wrong I have done. I admit that I still have fondness for Aidan, but I would never dream of coming between the two of you. It is obvious that you truly love each other. Please allow me to love both of you, as friends and artists. Please, allow me to do that, darling."

There were so many things Janice wanted to say but didn't. Instead, she just sat there staring at the map case, afraid that it might blow away.

"Of course, I will never intrude on the two of you again, darling. You know I would never do that."

When Gwen paid the bill she took Janice in one arm and the map case in the other, ushering them out on to Grafton Street as a shower passed like a parade. "I will get these back to you, don't worry. And you must let me see the bigger pieces as soon as you can, darling. There is so much we can do together, and thank you for your understanding. You are as gracious as you are talented."

She had to flutter off somewhere, to meet someone about something, but Janice didn't mind. She wanted to be alone. She wanted to walk through the Green, to have some time alone with her thoughts, time to try to sort through her jumbled feelings. And later, after she crossed the canal, she stopped for a couple of bottles of wine.

"I'm sorry, but how could I know that it's your bath night, it's not even Saturday." She had run off after she let him in. She had been sitting on the couch. Her drawing pad was on the table, alongside a freshly opened bottle of wine. He put his bottle on the counter to let it breathe.

"Pour yourself a glass while I take my curlers out."

"I don't mind curlers. I grew up with them. When I was young, I used to think that every time my sisters had their 'time-of-the-month' they grew horns on their heads."

She had to stick her head around the door. "How did you arrive at that?"

"They always said that it was the curse, for takin' the apple. An' ya know, with curlers under their scarves, it looked like God put the horns of the Devil on them, too."

"Makes sense," Janice agreed as she emerged in leotards under a large shapeless sweater that hung low on her hips. She usually did her laundry on the weekends, and she hadn't had a chance to catch up. Her hair was still wet and straggled around her face.

"It makes you look Latin, ya know, real sultry an' all."

"I was going for something a little more Gallic. So? What couldn't wait?"

"I had to tell you, I saw Gwen yesterday, an' I told her that I was endin' it with her an' I also told her I wasn't goin' to have her work on my poetry anymore. I think that it's better if we don't have anythin' to do with her for a while."

Janice drained her wine and refilled their glasses as he bounded around like a spring uncoiled.

"So! You are going to avoid temptations?" She settled on the couch and patted the seat beside her.

"What? Oh, yea. I am. I want to prove that this really means somethin' to me."

"So how come you said 'for a while?'"

He sat beside her and started to fidget with his pockets. "Because you're goin' to leave one day. You will probably go to France an' become a famous painter, an' then you'll go back to Canada."

"Is that what you really think?"

"I don't know an' I don't care. I just want a chance at makin' things right for a while. No worryin' about the future an' all that stuff, I just want us to spend now together."

She decided to go along with it all for now, she could return to the matter of Gwen later. "So, what shall we do now, talk?"

"Sure. Tell me, what's Canada like then? I hear it'll be great when it's finished."

She giggled and sat closer to him, under his outstretched arm resting behind her head. She felt good after the hours she had spent alone, in front of her canvas. She needed to learn to stop once in a while and enjoy life before it passed in a blur.

"Canada isn't like other countries. It's like the blind guys who go to 'see' an elephant. One says it's like a wall and another says it's a forest and another says it's like a snake. You get the point?"

"It's a white elephant?"

"That's far more apt than you know. My mother's family used to see it as a very British place, while my father liked to think of it as a confederation. Of course, not everyone agreed. My mother's family disapproved of him because he was French, and his family would never speak to me in English, but we always laughed at that. He said the greatest thing our country produced was ice hockey and kids like me. Of course, I assumed it was personal."

"I'm sure it was."

She turned to kiss his hand that was stroking her cheek and flirting with her shoulder where it emerged from the loose neck of her sweater. "Go ahead and smoke if you want, I don't mind. I don't want you to get up, I might get cold."

But he did get up, to fetch his cigars and the other bottle of wine and she shivered until he got back.

"We had two solitudes, you know, the victorious English and the vanquished French, but we needed both to fill the open spaces so the Americans wouldn't take them. Of course, nobody stopped to consider the natives; they were just a part of the landscape. We had to form some type of confederation, and in time, we tried to make it more multicultural. One of the men behind that was Irish, Thomas D'Arcy McGee."

"He was one of the leaders of the 'Young Irelanders'."

She had his attention now. She could play him along and get him to change his mind, if she had to. Her meeting with Gwen had gone very well. She should tell him about it, but not just yet.

"Well, D'Arcy McGee came to Canada and was elected to Parliament. He believed the French should be a part of what was happening."

"To a good man."

"To a good man," she agreed as he topped up their glasses. "Sadly, he was shot by a Fenian: he had opposed their invasion of Canada."

"You know a lot of fuckin' stuff."

"I do study once in a while. Anyway, that was the start of it, and as more immigrants poured in, we had to learn how to get along with each other. We started having all these cultural festivals. They were awful, lots of speeches by politicians and hours of ethnic dancers. That's when I first saw Irish dancing."

"That stuff isn't real; we don't really dance like that."

"I know Aidan, that's my point. My mother used to say they should dance for us; after all, we had let them come and live with us. But there was one thing I liked about it all: ethnic food. I think that's why it all started to work."

"Your whole country is held together by food?"

"Well, yours is held together by drink."

"True."

"God, I really miss pizza."

"They're very flat, don't ya think?"

"They go great with wine. If we were in Canada right now, we could order one. They would deliver it right away."

"There's a place just down in Rathgar. I could . . ."

"No. I've tried it. Anyway, the older people didn't really like what was happening. My father says it all changed when Trudeau came along."

"I remember him. He was so fuckin' cool."

She loved the reaction Trudeau evoked. She felt warm and proud at the same time. She felt so . . . Canadian.

"In Canada, you can still be proud of the old country and help build a new one."

"How's that working out?'

She shrugged as she held her glass in front of her. They had started on the second bottle.

"Sometimes, people only bring the worst parts of their culture with them or to be fair, retreat into them when they were afraid and unsure. I can understand that – leaving everything you know to move to a new country where everything is different. But they retreat into xenophobia and close themselves off like ghettos."

She was slurring a bit but was impassioned. Canadians didn't blow their own horns enough.

"But their children break through. Of course, their parents don't like that. They call us cake-eaters and stuff like that, like we're second class citizens in our own country."

"It's like that here, too . . ."

"But it does work. It takes a generation or two, but it does and that makes us stronger."

"That sounds like a great place all right."

"Yea, it is for the most part. Why? Are you thinking of going?"

"You never know, I might one of these days. What's the weather like? I hear it's very cold."

"Oh, Aidan, it gets so cold sometimes, but we have to go out in it anyway. Everybody has to go out and ride toboggans and ski, it's the law."

"Really?"

"Of course, but you get to like winter, especially when it snows at Christmas. It gets really crisp and cold and you can see your breath – even before you go outside. But, by the end of February everybody has enough and prays that it all goes away."

Janice was enjoying herself. Her hands weaved and fluttered like snowflakes. She stared into his eyes, but he was watching her mouth, savouring every word that passed her lips. She almost melted in his attention.

"And just when you've had enough and go mad chasing moose around the house – they come in for the winter, you know? Then the spring springs. One day, it's winter and a few days later, it is summer, perfect weather for drinking ice-cold beer on the deck. But my favourite time is the fall.

"Oh, Aidan, you have to see Canada in the fall. The colours cannot be described. Even you couldn't find enough words to describe it. Will you come with me, someday, when we're both famous?"

"I don't know. Does it ever rain?"

"Only at night, after everyone has gone to bed."

"It sounds like the Garden of Eden."

He reached forward and kissed her, tracing her lips with his tongue and running his fingers through her hair.

She sat up as quickly as her wine haze would allow. "Aidan. I think you should leave."

"But why, we're havin' a really nice time. I'm just gettin' to know the real you, and besides, it's gettin' late and I'm drunk, who knows what kind of trouble I'd get into."

She didn't really want him to leave. She just felt she should say it, but she wanted him to stay beside her all night. "Eden, eh?"

"Ya, where we can be together without shame or guilt, free like animals are supposed to be."

"Animals again, Aidan, have you been with sheep?"

"Me, never, it's just the Irish in me. We're really a very passionate, uninhibited people."

Janice almost choked on her wine.

"No. I'm serious – deep down inside."

"It must be very deep."

"Ya, we had to hide it years ago. But before the Christians, we were a lot more open about sex an' all.

"Look at Maeve, the Queen of Connaught. She was celebrated for her hospitality.

"She shared herself with her guests, an' her husband couldn't object. Under our old laws, a woman wasn't a part of a man. She could own her own cattle an' everythin', she could've her own army an' she had total control of her body,

"The Christians suppressed that an' tried to ban sex, at least outside of marriage. Then we'd all that English shite to deal with, ya know, stiff upper lip an' all.

"Then, after the Rebellion, after Connolly was shot, the Church took over, an' they frown on women havin' sex, unless it's to bring more Catholics into the world. Then they're okay with it, as long as you don't enjoy it. I guess they're still afraid of succubuses."

"Succubi"

"Ya, but we weren't really like that. We love singin' an' dancin' an' drinkin' an' courtin'. It only makes sense that we were more comfortable with doin' the business, like the way we did when we all lived in Eden."

"So what was the apple then?"

"They say it was shame, but I think it was comparin' ourselves. I mean think about it. Older women look down on younger, more appealin' women an' any woman who admits to likin' sex is a whore or a tramp. And men are even worse. They all want to be with loose women, but they don't want to know about her seein' other men. I guess they're afraid she might compare them.

"No, it's not ridiculous. I mean, have you ever seen a statue of a man with a big dick?"

This time, Janice couldn't contain herself and as she laughed, wine trickled from her mouth. He traced the spills with his finger, gathering the rivulets before sucking his fingers. His other hand had reached her breast and turned her. He lowered his hand and settled on her hip, holding it tight.

She wanted to but not just yet. She wanted to tease him some more. She curled her legs beneath her and faced him. "So, tell me. Why do Irishmen call it 'doin'-the-business'?"

"I suppose it's mostly embarrassment an' shame. I mean, we're told that it's wrong, an' then we're told that we're stealin' somethin' from women, ya know, that we ruined them or that we took advantage of them. We're told women don't enjoy sex – that they only do it because they feel they have to."

"You don't really believe any of that, do you?"

"Well, it's different with you. You're not like the girls around here."

She pulled him on top of her and stripped him to the waist and melted into his warmth.

He picked her gently from the couch and lurched toward her bedroom where he lay her on her bed. She wriggled from her clothes and held his face for a moment. "Women don't really like sex? Well, let me show you."

They were drunk and loose, pleasuring each other furiously until they crumpled into each other's arms.

"Aidan, are you sure about changing publishers? I mean, you're established, and despite everything, Gwen does look out for you."

"Nay, it's the right thing to do. We don't need her anymore. It's like you said. I'm established now, an' they'll be linin' up once they hear I'm free, and besides, I don't want anythin' else to come between us."

He fell asleep as she watched him for a while. In time, she turned away and his words echoed in the darkness. She wasn't concerned; in fact, she was delighted. He was willing to give up everything for her: it was very flattering.

Later, she would talk to him about the Press; she could get him to change his mind. She didn't want anything to upset things now that Gwen had promised not to interfere.

That must have been hard for her to do.

For a moment, she saw Gwen's face in the dark. Tears streamed down her face.

But Gwen wasn't crying. She smiled at her reflection in the mirror as she brushed her hair again. She was calm and composed. She had packed already: she would go home in the morning. There was nothing else to do in the city, for now.

The winter was coming. Soon, they would all celebrate their own distorted versions of Christmas, after the shops had been stripped bare, when the entire city flocked to the bars with the same tried and true rational.

"Christmas comes but once a year."

Chapter 9

"But, Da, don't you think the Guards would've been involved?"

"Where do you think they get their orders from?"

"Ah, c'mon, Da."

"C'mon nothing, the Parish Priest and the Sergeant paid Joe a visit the other night, and they weren't there to toast the season. They told him that it'd be taken care of and not to make a fuss. They're all hand-in-glove, you know."

Sinead had hoped to relax over the holidays, but it wasn't going to happen. She'd have to coax them so, at least, they could have Christmas. Her sisters weren't coming again this year; they were working the holiday shift. She understood; they needed the money, but she resented it, too.

"And who'd you hear that from?" Her mother had to say something.

"Fitzer."

"Was he there?"

"He lives right next door."

"Were they shouting at each other?"

"It doesn't matter if he'd a glass up against the wall. We all agreed to keep an eye on Joe in case anybody tried to do anything to him."

"Tell him, Sinead, that no one believes him."

"I'm not going to tell anybody anything. You're both acting ridiculous."

"That's right, daughter. You tell him."

Her father was exasperated, too, and turned his back. "I'm going for a pint."

"You'd rather be anywhere but at home with your family at Christmas."

"Well, Sinead, are you coming at least?" They had planned to celebrate the end of her exams.

"Maybe in a little while, Da, let me just talk to Ma for a while and then I'll join you?"

They waited as he closed the door.

"Ma, I think there's some truth to it. You've known Joe and Nuala all your life. You know they'd never make this up."

"Joe and Nuala are just trying to be good parents but that young brat of theirs – he's the devil himself."

"He's only ten."

"Ah, Sinead, the world is full of evil and sometimes, it uses children too."

Sinead knew there was no point; her mother needed her Church to be a force for Good.

Flurries fell around the lights that twinkled on the bare tree outside. Robert had decorated it over cups of eggnog with generous sprinklings of cinnamon. "It only comes once a year," he agreed and besides, Janice was coming home. Her mother insisted he join them on Christmas Eve, too.

Janice was polite; it was the least that was expected of her, but it was a challenge. Her mother fussed on, pretending not to notice, but Robert did. After coffee, he excused himself. He waved when he got to the sidewalk and looked more forlorn when Janice hardly waved back. She couldn't be bothered anymore. She just wanted to sit in the window and watch the snow fall, slowly covering his footprints.

"Why are you so distant, dear?"

"Mother, why did you have Robert over? It was so awkward. I told you, it's over between us. And I wished you'd given me a bit more notice so I could've prepared myself."

Her mother looked startled. Janice had never been so curt; it must be the way they behave in Dublin. "I did, dear. I told you to expect a very special visitor."

She did have a point. It was Christmas after all, the time to go back and connect with things that had never really existed; to put aside all that happened and to pretend they were a family. "I thought you meant Santa Claus."

They both seized the lifeline and laughed until the chill between them thawed. "Oh, dear, forgive me. I promised that I wouldn't let my emotions get the better of me. Perhaps we should have a glass of sherry, to celebrate the season?"

"Mother, you never cease to amaze me," Janice called after her as she pottered into the kitchen where the cupboards were stuffed with things that would never be used again. She returned with the bottle and two delicate glasses.

The bottle had been well hidden; Janice hadn't been able to find it when she prowled around for something to fill that abscess that was growing inside. She was fine when she left Dublin, but all that she'd been there began to wither as soon as the plane took off. She felt like she'd shrivel up in her seat and clutched the thin blanket. She ordered a scotch to warm the chill in her stomach, but it could just be that time of the month.

She really had to sort out their birth control issue. Aidan never would, and as she thought of him, she realised that she resented him for that. She ordered another Scotch as the stewardess passed. 'I'm a nervous flier.'

'Yes, of course. Can I get you anything else, another blanket or a pillow?'

'No, thanks, just a scotch. I'll be fine then.'

She reached out from her blanket when the fresh drink arrived and swallowed a mouthful. She hated that they were parted, but there was no way that she could have brought him. He was willing to come. In fact, he looked a little hurt when she tried to explain it to him. She hoped he understood. He said he did, but she didn't believe him. She kissed him quickly and turned before she could change her mind but saw him again through several panes of glass. She couldn't be sure, but he looked like he was grinning from ear to ear. For a moment, she stopped as he smiled and turned to go. But what could she do?

She ordered another scotch. 'Just one more and I'll be out like a light.'

'I'll say,' the stewardess smiled and was gone.

Bitch, Janice glared after her. It wasn't just him: she was leaving the she that she'd become. She'd have to shrink a little to fit back into the her that her mother expected. The very thought of it made her cold. Even the third scotch didn't change that, but she couldn't ask for another.

She woke with popping ears. Her head was throbbing and her hair was a mess. She rushed to the washroom and realised, as she watched herself in the mirror, leaning forward so she didn't touch the seat, it was more than all of that: it was that time of the month.

She shuffled through long corridors, snaking back and forth before standing in line for the lethargic official to allow her into her own country. He eyed her coldly as he flicked through the pages of her passport. She squirmed a little, trying to hold the wedge of tissues between her thighs. She was angry with herself. She should have been prepared.

She grew more nauseous as the carousel went around and luckier passengers retrieved their bags and left.

'You look pale,' her mother insisted as the taxi pulled away from the busy curb where much happier people were still hugging each other and piling suitcases into cars. 'I'm fine mother. I'm just very tired.'

She caught the cabbie glancing at her in the mirror, but he looked away as traffic snarled before them. He turned the radio up to hear that the '401' was heavy in both directions along the top of the city, from the '427' to the 'Parkway.' The radio politely warned them to expect delays as it faded into another jingle-jangle. She stared through salty windows at all that had been familiar: great illuminated boxes and of course, the CN Tower, lit up like a Christmas tree.

Her mother was annoyed when they pulled into the driveway; she meant to turn the lights on too, to make it festive for when Janice returned. The driver wasn't happy, either. She gave him a fifty cent tip.

'My dear I can't believe how pale and thin you have become. Are you sure you are not unwell?'

'Mother,' Janice panted as she wrestled her suitcase through the doorway. 'I'm fine. It's just that time of the month and I was caught a little unprepared.'

Later, as she lay warm and refreshed in her childhood bed, she wished she could do it all over. She wished she'd been nicer. It wasn't the first time she had lain there among regrets, but it felt so different now. She was feeling very sorry for herself and could find no comfort in all that should have been warm and familiar. It had grown cold to her.

In time, her mother tapped and waited before struggling with the handle. She brought French onion soup, from a packet, but that wasn't the point. It was a treat Janice had often shared with her father. She rose from her covers with tears in her eyes as her mother placed the tray across her lap.

'I miss him, too, dear. I would take him back if I could.'

Janice didn't respond. She sniffled a few times as they struggled on. They had to observe Christmas together, they were all they had now.

After they poured the sherry, Janice was ready. It was the time for goodwill and for family.

"Mother, I'm sorry for the way I've been behaving. I was really looking forward to this because," she paused for effect, "I've really missed you. In fact I'm sorry now that I ever left. You were right; Dublin is too far away. But what can I do now? I must go back and finish as quickly as I can." She turned toward the window and squeezed out a few salty tears.

Her mother came over like a whisper, faintly caressing her elbow as she stood close, looking up at her like a child. "We cannot show Father sad eyes at Christmas."

Janice forced herself to smile as they clinked glasses and settled, side by side, on the prim settee as the 'CBC' proudly presented 'A Christmas Carol.' And each time a new ghost arrived, they poured another sherry.

"God bless us every one," they giggled when they finally headed for bed. Her childhood bedroom was warmer as she tumbled under the covers and turned off the bedside lamp. She was at peace with the emptiness. It was how things had always been, but soon, she could leave it all behind again.

Rain spattered the empty streets. It was Saint Stephen's Day, a day for families and Aidan was delighted to have something to do. He'd spent Christmas alone with a bottle of Jameson and two flagons of Bulmers, but Gwen was coming to town. She'd called on

Christmas Eve, to wish him Happy Christmas and to see if he'd like to get together.

Maurice had gone to England for the racing and to catch up with some old school friends. He would be gone for a few days, and when he returned, he would be renewed, full of plans and schemes and other ways to make money. He might even win some on the horses.

She had her usual room, one of the more stately the Shelbourne still offered. She had surprised the staff at the desk, checking in so early in the day so she told them that she had been flying all night and that the airline had lost her bags – she just needed to rest for a bit – to see if they would show up. But as soon as she got to her room and peeled down to her carefully selected underthings, she sat by the mirror arranging the details that had to be perfect. He would be here soon, 'no later than eleven,' he promised. It was quarter past; he wouldn't be much longer. She brought whiskey: a bottle tucked into her overnight bag, carefully wrapped in her negligee and her long black stocking. She sprayed scent between her and the mirror and leaned forward to catch the falling dew between her breasts.

He noticed and paused to inhale. "Jazus, but you smell wicked."

"Wicked," she laughed as she guided him inside, sliding up and down as they both moaned and groaned. He tried to hurry, but she rode to a canter: a plodding deliberation that she could enjoy. She plunged down and her breath misted around his face. His breathing was heavy, too, surging up like a tide, higher and higher until she crested and crashed down beside him.

"So?" she asked as he lay on his back and searched for the end of cigar with the intrusive flare of a match. "How was it for you, darling?"

"Fuckin' great."

"The best you ever had?"

"The very fuckin' best."

She raised herself on the crook of her arm and ran her fingers along his chest, searching for those parts that were more sensitive. When she touched them, his breathing quickened and she inhaled deeply.

"Better than Janice?"

He hesitated for a moment but decided to just barge through.

"Why don't we all do it together and you can decide for yourself?"

"Aidan, you are a devil. A black-hearted devil."

"But isn't that what you love about me?"

She wanted to scratch his chest, to carve her name as a warning to others. She wanted to delve in and pull his heart out. She would keep it somewhere safe where only she could find it. She leaned over and traced around his nipple. He didn't react at first, but as she continued, he stubbed his cigar and tried to sit up.

"No, don't move."

She moved so she could feast on his breath and reached down and fondled him with her cool hand.

He liked that. He squirmed, but she stayed in place, stroking him where he was most sensitive. She quickened a few times and slowed again. She wanted him to know: she was in control. She stopped long enough to straddle him as he lay like a bride, and took him in her hand again, holding him against her belly, like his was hers.

"Look at me," she commanded. "Let me see your eyes."

She slowly ran her hand, up and down, until he obliged. "You know," she hissed as she leaned toward him while her hand pumped. "If you really were a devil, you would know the depths of evil I could release on you if you ever left me." She clenched his climax and sprayed his chest.

She rose from the bed, naked but for her sheer black robe that drifted along behind her, disappearing as she closed the bathroom door, leaving him alone in the dark.

"I'm fucked now." he gasped as he struggled to sit up, as his own sticky mess dribbled down his belly. He grabbed a pillow to wipe himself off. He didn't care; he wasn't going to stay anyway. How could he?

When she came, out he shuffled past, but he didn't look at her face. How could he?

"Fuck it," he berated his own image that watched him dress. "Let's get out of here and try to figure this out."

"I'm right behind you," his other self agreed as he went back.

Gwen still sat before her mirror, softly brushing her hair. She looked more beautiful than ever. Her face was soft and young. He thought about taking her in his arms. He even walked to her, but when she looked up at him through the mirror, he knew there was no point. A deal was a deal.

"Would ya mind if I went to the pub?"

"Not at all, darling, I was just getting ready to leave anyway."

"You could come with me, if you wanted."

"Darling, I think we need some time to think about things. Perhaps, as you have suggested, we should take a break until you decide what it is you really want. You cannot expect me to tolerate this for much longer. Go to your pub and while you are there, you can make up your mind. It has come to that, Aidan. You have to de-cide between Janice and me."

She turned back to the mirror like he was no longer there. She puckered her lips a little and picked out the right colour; it was a dark red, and it made her lips look so much bigger. She smiled to herself as the door clicked behind him. He had nowhere to go. She had driven the wedge between them.

But, she flicked at her lashes with a small curved brush, *what if he chooses Janice?*

Then he will be destroyed.

And what about Janice?

She smirked at the mirror, it was all so perfect.

The wind met him as he stopped to light a cigar. He'd walk for a while, to try to find somewhere to figure it all out. The Green was almost empty, but his mind was crowded. He hardly noticed the ducks, even when they followed him forlornly as he kicked stones into the pond. He was on his way to the Yeats' monument to sit among the cold grey stones. Fate would have to listen to him there.

I know I made a deal an' all, but now I want to get out of it.

The whole city was silent for a moment. The wind stopped teasing the willow wands. Even the ducks and geese grew silent as he strained to hear a response.

"Amn't I delighted to see a friendly face. There's no one around. I guess they're all on holidays. Even Scots Corner has gone home for the Hogmanay. And how're things with you? I'm surprised that you're not off in Canada?" Gerry licked his lips. His nostrils were wide like he was on the scent.

"I had to stay. I'd some business to look after, ya know?"

"Some business, you say. And did it go well for you?"

"C'mon," Aidan laughed as he slapped the old man on the back. "I'm buying."

"Jazus lad, be careful. You don't know the strength you have. You nearly broke my back."

"C'mon then and I'll get ya a whiskey, too, then we'll be all square."

"Right enough," Gerry laughed as he hopped into step.

"We could try O'Donoghues."

Gerry liked to drop in when things were tight but only when he'd enough for the first drink. They wouldn't give him any slate, but it was still a good place to go, especially on a wet Saturday afternoon in the summer. It would be full of fine young American women spending a weekend in Dublin before they took the bus to Shannon.

They would linger by the counter, trying to recapture all that had been swirling around them the night before when they bought drinks for handsome young Irishmen who were so into them, fascinated by every little detail they foolishly shared. Some of the young men, those who acted more subtly, even went to the bother of scribbling down the woman's address on the inside of their cigarette packages and promised to look them up the next time they were in the States. That always made Gerry laugh: like the young bucks would even have the same pack when they woke up.

The poor jilted women would linger by the counter and, in time, start to complain.

That was his chance; he could sidle into the conversation. He would slather their wounds with the corniest Irish commiserations he could come up with.

If they were a bit older, they might even let him get close enough, as long as he didn't touch them. He would sit on his hands and rock back and forth like a little bird on his perch, reaching out every now and then for his pint. He could get two, maybe three out of most them, and by the time they were ready to go, they would hug him, too, pressing up against him as he smelled their hair, their skin and whatever perfumes they used.

"Ah for fuck's sake, Gerry, I want a quiet pint without having to talk about Leprechauns an' all."

"Let me just take a look, will ya?" But he knew better: no one came over in the winter.

"C'mon. Let's try this place instead."

"Have you ever been there before?'

"No and neither have you so there's a good chance that they'll serve us."

Aidan held the door as Gerry sidled into the crowd.

"Grab those two stools by the wall, and I'll get the drink."

"Christ, Gerry, take this will ya?" Aidan emerged from the crowd clutching the glasses in his white fists. "Thank Fuck!" He declared as he downed a mouthful. He stared at Gerry, like he'd just seen him. "Come here to me," he beckoned with his finger. "Do you know anythin' about Lenanshees?"

"Are you havin' me on or what?"

"I was just fuckin' askin'. I'm workin' on a poem, that's all. You know after a poet's been with her an' all, can he change his mind and go with someone else?"

Gerry nodded. "I seem to remember the old people saying something about that. Let me see if I can remember it now." He drained his drinks and stared at the empty glasses and waited for it to fall into place.

"I'll just get us another round then," Aidan said softly, so as not to break his concentration.

"Good man yourself," Gerry called after him in a distracted voice.

Sinead brushed her hair away from her face. The coffee shop was busier than she expected; mostly shoppers resting from the sales. She tried to compose herself as he left to get her coffee. She had slipped up again. He had wanted to hug her when he wished her 'Happy Christmas,' but she didn't react in time. She'd be ready when he came back.

"I'm a little surprised to see you today." He lingered as she sprinkled brown sugar on the foam.

"I was just passing, you know? I had to get out of the house for a while. You know how it is!"

But she couldn't face him as she spoke. She looked to the window and raised the mug to her face, dipping her lips through the foam as she watched his reflection through her fringe.

Feck, feck, fuck and shite! It was scalding.

"I know exactly what you mean. But I got lucky this year. My parents went away."

"For good?"

"I wish," he laughed as he pulled the other chair back, swung a leg over it and sat opposite her. "No, they have gone skiing in the Alps."

"And why aren't you off there instead of sloughing coffees here?"

"It's a job. I don't want my parents to help me any more than they have already."

He checked on the other patrons, but everybody was content and Sinead was delighted.

"I know what you mean. That's why I had to get away from mine, too."

"Do you know what I have been meaning to ask you for a while?" He smiled at her shyly.

This is what she'd really wanted for Christmas. She'd been so good. She'd even managed a truce between her parents. She had to plead with her mother and beg her father, but she managed. Her mother demanded a public act of contrition: her father would have to join her at midnight mass for everyone to see. It was that or the ten-in-the-morning and that meant the Parish Priest, and he'd go on forever.

'Ah Jazus, Sinead, she can't expect me to accept that.'

'What if we were to spend the whole evening, down in the pub, getting you ready for it?'

'That's the true Irish way to do it,' he declared as her mother tried to hurry them home. She had to get the bird in the oven by four, so that it'd be just right. She could have a lie-down then but only a short one. She had to get the vegetables ready too. She looked back at her husband and daughter. He was lurching, and she was a little unsteady too. She could expect little help from them. They'd be up half the night having a 'discussion.'

'A High Mass, with incense and all, and singing, too; there's nothing better after a few pints.'

'I thought you were against all that?'

'Ah, but it's Christmas. We celebrated that long before any of those fuckers came, and we'll go on doing it, too, even after we have driven the whole lot of them back to Rome.'

'Hush, the two of you,' her mother hissed back at them. 'The neighbours will be listening.'

But Sinead and her father just laughed and wobbled through a verse of Silent Night.

"Could you tell me the name of the American girl who comes in with you all the time?"

As she reshuffled her emotions, the door rattled. An old woman shook the rain from her umbrella and closed it as she stood by the counter, tapping the glass with the strange handle.

"What do you have to do to get a cup of tea in this place? Do I have to make an appointment with someone?" she called into the back room.

"I got to go" Ronan blushed as he rose. His eyes pleaded with her for a moment, but the tapping got louder. "I'll be right back."

But he wasn't. It took him an age to negotiate with the old woman, but finally, he settled her with a steaming pot of tea, a small jug of white milk and a bowl of sugar cubes. And he had to check the back room; he was sure they had some digestive biscuits there.

Sinead made a run for it while he was busy, but she should've known better. He came out as she got to the door.

"Her name is Janice, and she's Canadian. And she has a boy-friend: Aidan Greeley. I hear that they're moving to Paris." She left with as much dignity as she could muster: her mascara had begun to run.

"Sinead," he tugged at her arm. "Stop a minute. I'm really sorry. I should've realised."

But that didn't make her feel better.

He gently held her arm and turned her around. "Look, I'm really sorry. Maybe we could go back inside and talk for a while." He was shivering in the cold rain, and his shirt was plastered to his chest. "I'm so sorry," he called after her as she scuttled around the corner.

"Ah, the pains of love," the old woman cackled as he stepped back behind the counter. "Did you ever find some biscuits for me?"

You're damn right you're sorry. What you should've done was grabbed me in your arms and swept me off the ground. Instead, you just cut me off at the ankles.

But, she consoled her passing reflections in the front windows of Duke Street; *I just might be able to give him another chance. Off in the future, of course, after he has some time to suffer, at least for a while.*

After next year, God willing, if everything went right for her, she might take up skiing.

One day, she'd find him, crumpled against a tree. She'd always carry a little flask of brandy for just such an occasion. And, after she'd saved him, after he'd fallen in love with her, his parents would insist on a great big wedding with pictures in all the papers and all. She'd have to get her mother something really nice to wear. She was nervous about her father: he'd be sure to say something that would upset everybody, but she had to smile.

Dublin looked particularly dull and grey – Toronto had sparkled under cold blue skies. Dublin was much softer and seemed to sag.

Aidan stood back from the gate where people hung over the fence, waiting on friends and relatives. There were more at the departure gates and the mood there was far more somber. The happier crowd parted to let her through. She could see his face above them all, and she could smell his cigar and see he had one hand behind his back. *I hope it's not another shrubbery;* she laughed as she dropped her cases and ran to him. She jumped into his arms as he dropped the roses to the floor, but she didn't care. She kissed him, letting loose all that was pent up inside her as he spun her around, crushing the flowers, but she didn't care. He would let her down gently.

"Janice," he whispered into her ear. "Everybody is lookin'; let's get to fuck out of here."

"It's great to have you back", he muttered as he put another cigar between his lips.

The fog was bejeweling her hair with tiny crystals, like a halo shining through the haze he'd been lost in. He caught a taxi and piled her bags into the trunk. He held the door for her before nestling in beside her. "It's great to be back," she gasped as she kissed him a few more times.

"Janice," he implored, nodding at the driver. "Your man is listenin'." But the driver only smiled and turned the radio up.

'We have frost warnings for the North and West of the country and other higher areas. And in the South, we can expect more rain. For much of the East, it will remain dry with scattered showers developing through the morning. And here in the city, we will have fog patches overnight, but what can you expect for this time of the year?'

She was back in the land of shadows and light, of Aidan's smoky bars and ancient creatures that lingered even though the future loomed. But she had a place and a purpose here; she knew that now, but she would have to settle down and catch up with her studies. Aidan agreed and promised to give her the time and space she needed; he had work to do, too. The Twilight Press was planning to release his book in April; he would be busy for a while.

Chapter 10

Everyone began to dash for cover with newspapers over their heads: men teetering forward, holding their ties against their stomachs and women scuttling with knees together, heels flailing out behind them. Janice made it to the doorway as the tip-tap gave way to insistent spattering that drenched in moments. She forced her way under the arch among the wet and bedraggled looking skyward like a congregation. She'd get wet crossing Parliament Square, but it wasn't far to the Reading Room: she'd arranged to meet Sinead under the portico.

"So? What's so urgent that I had to cut out on my study group?"
"Well, I haven't seen you since the holidays."
"Yea, I've been busy, sorry about that."
"It almost felt like you're avoiding me and I had to talk to you. It's about Aidan and me. I hope you don't mind. I am beginning to think I might actually be in love with him. I realised it when I was at home. I felt so empty without him."

Raindrops dripped from Sinead's hair, caught on her eyelashes, streaked her cheeks and trickled beneath her collar. She curled her damp toes and her jeans were stained, almost to her calves. When her mother told her that Janice left a message, she assumed it was something serious. She'd been avoiding the coffee shop, too.

"Janice! Why are you telling me this?"

"I thought we could go for coffee and talk, just like we used to." Janice smiled a brittle smile, but Sinead looked horrified. "You'd like that, wouldn't you?"

"What's the matter, Sinead?"

"Janice! I don't have time for this right now."

"But, Sinead, I need to talk to someone about it. I still think about the whole thing with Gwen. I know he has stopped seeing her, but it still makes me wonder. What if she is a Lenanshee?"

"Janice, I don't have time for all this bullshit anymore and another thing, face up to it. He was probably doing it with Gwen because he had to: his poems aren't that good."

She stomped off under the arch and through the gates. She didn't wait for the lights and raced for the other side as a bus skidded and shuddered.

"Are you crazy?" the driver roared.

"That's the funny thing; I'm the only sane one left."

"I don't know about that, Sinead," someone reached and hauled her to the sidewalk as a bright yellow car slashed through the rain where she'd been standing. "You're a tough young woman, but I doubt you can take on a whole bus. What's got you so worked up anyway?" He paused to look back at where she came from. "No good ever comes out of that place."

"What place?"

"Trinity. Why don't you go to U.C.D? It's the place for the likes of us."

"Really, Gerry, do you think we are so alike?"

"Well, I do and I don't, but what do you think of getting in out of the rain until you calm down a bit? I'm buying, too; I'd a horse come in."

Sinead didn't respond, but she was like that sometimes.

"C'mon, there's a nice little place around the corner. We can have a quiet drink, and you can tell me what the matter is."

She said nothing and sipped the whiskey Gerry had insisted would warm her.

"So what's the matter? What's got you all fired up?"

"Ah Gerry, I'm sorry. It's nothing. I'm just getting sick and tired of all the feckin' bullshit I have to put up with. Everyone I know is going feckin' mad, and they're trying to take me with them."

"Ah, you shouldn't pay it any mind, this is Dublin after all."

He raised his pint and closed his eyes. His mouth danced along the rim as his lip foamed with froth. "Ah! That's my first today; now tell me what's got you so upset?"

"Gerry, you wouldn't believe the conversation I just had with Janice."

"Is that the young Canadian that Aidan is dating?" his face widened as he said it. "I'm sorry, Sinead. You're too good for the likes of him."

"You don't need to tell me." But she was glad he did.

"She seems a bit dizzy, that one, not that I know her, I've only talked to her once or twice."

"She's not dizzy, she's totally feckin' daft. She thinks Aidan's been having it off with a Lenanshee. I swear to God. She just told me."

Gerry almost spilled his pint. "Ah, now, Sinead, don't make me laugh while I'm trying to have a drink. I nearly fell in. Where did she come up with that?"

"The Bard of Bullshit told her."

"Why's she telling you all of this?"

"I know. I told her to stop bringing all her feckin' nonsense to me."

"Sinead, I don't know if it's my place or not, but I need to say something."

"What?"

"Did you think that you might be a bit mad at her?"

"Over what?"

"Aidan, of course."

"No way, Gerry, I'm over him."

"Are you sure?"

"Of course I'm feckin' sure. What? You think I still carry a torch for him?"

"Well. I certainly think that you're carrying a torch for someone, and you're afraid to tell them."

"Are you out of your feckin' mind?"

"Well, I was just saying . . ."

"You're saying a load of shite, Gerry. That's what you're saying. And you know what I got to say to that: feck you, too, Gerry. You're just like the rest of them. What do you know about anything?"

She grabbed her things and stormed out as the afternoon darkened and the rain gave way to a soft drizzle.

The rain eased and the wind came from the east, chilling the gathering gloom. Janice wandered along Grafton Street as the shops closed. She drifted by the Green and up Harcourt Street, passing warm windows of old hotels and guesthouses where fireplaces flickered and guests sat in armchairs, oblivious to the coming of the night.

She stopped and picked up two bottles of wine. She would start with the Italian, warm and reassuring. Later, she would open the French.

She poured her first as she stood by the table, as her coat dripped on the linoleum floor. Her bag tumbled as she tried to use her arm. Tears ran down her face and into her glass, making the sweet wine sour. Sinead had no right to talk to her like that.

She flopped on her couch in her rumpled coat, tugging to be free of her bag. She cried until her heart shriveled up and grew cold and stared at her empty glass for a long time. How could anyone think such things about her and Aidan? Sure, they were a little bohemian, they were artists after all, but Sinead had no right. Perhaps she really was jealous. Perhaps, she should call her up and . . .

But, there was no point. She peeled her coat off and brought the bottle from the table and poured another glass. She was finished with crying.

To hell with them all: she'd prove them wrong, but how?

Gwen will help; she said she would.

But if it was true, what would she have to give?

It wouldn't be like Dr. Faustus?

So what, we go dancing, we get drunk and then . . . well, we do things. At least I get something out of it, not like with Sinead. At least Gwen will look out for me. At least there is that.

She rose and sauntered toward her paints. Clonmacnoise was almost done; it needed some touches, but she wasn't going to work on it tonight, she had something else in mind and flicked through her drawing pad until she found it.

She would paint the alabaster-skinned girl with her wrists and ankles bound by black satin to white marble pillars, standing spread-eagle with her dark hair falling across one shoulder, her white flesh red where the hands of a man had furrowed.

He would be seen from the back so as not to take away from the expression on her face.

Her lips would be full and spread apart. This side of her breast would glisten and her torn red shirt would drape between her wide-spread legs. They would stand against a thunder sky, beside a Gothic Cathedral, and her eyes would be a green or a blue, a colour that you might see when the tide turns.

She opened the French and began with broad generous strokes: the pillars and the sky. Layers of detail followed with each glass until the bottle was empty.

She smiled laconically, it was coming together as her brush stokes became confused, but she smeared with abandon until she was satisfied. By then she was tired and yawned as she cleaned her brushes and navigated the passage to her bed. The covers were cold against her bare legs. She wrapped herself in her father's shirt and curled up in a ball. She fell asleep as the rain started again: the only sound in the slumbering city.

The mist parted as the cowled figure led her to the clearing. She couldn't see the face, but she knew it was Gwen. Cool hands peeled her clothes away and raised her arms, fastening them with satin knots against the old stone pillars, but she didn't struggle. Lips rippled along her skin like the breeze on the long grass around the monastery. Janice couldn't help herself and moaned as she thrust toward them.

She woke with a headache and wrapped herself in her warmest robe. She squinted around at the empty bottles and the easel. She went to it and carefully touched the soft texture of drying paint, tracing its curves as her dream lingered. It was crazy, fueled by wine.

"I have to watch my drinking," she said to the street outside as she sat in her perch with a hot cup of tea. "Soon, I will be as bad as Aidan. I'm even starting to think like he does. Not what kind of future is that?"

She looked across old rooftops where, here and there, modern buildings rose so rudely between her and the distant mountains. She remembered her walk to the ruined monastery of Glendalough where ancient monks had laboured in the flickering light of bees-wax candles to record the lives of saints and the annals of their times. It was where the fires of change were tended until they burst forth denouncing the shadows and darkness of the Christ-less cen-turies. Denouncing, but never extinguishing, the pagan fires that burned in the hearts of the Irish.

But she was neither pagan nor Irish. She could flirt along the edges without getting involved. She could watch it all unfold and capture it on canvas. She had come to study the past, to find where fact ended and where fancy began, but she couldn't find the demarcation line.

'Perhaps such a line never existed,' her Professor challenged them one sleepy afternoon as the sun slanted through the window and everyone was a thousand miles away.

'Or perhaps the line exists in us, the poor bastard children of the Reformation and its offspring – the Age of Enlightenment. The Ancients didn't burden themselves with the onus of proof. They simply accepted what made sense and ascribed the rest to the fickleness of the gods.

'We are not so fortunate. We try to prove what cannot be proven,' he added as he scanned his students for some flicker of attention and settled on Janice, who was watching him intently.

'Perhaps it was, for those who were governed by what we now call myth, a fact as indubitable as gravity. We accept what Newton gave us because it makes sense, but we reject what the Ancients held dear because we have been conditioned to believe that we're beyond such primitiveness. Once, we feared the unexplained forces that preyed upon us and developed rites and rituals to appease them. Now we have created "Science" and "Reason" and hold fast to absurd notions that anything that can't be explained doesn't exist. Perhaps in our enlightenment we have become very ignorant.

'Perhaps, that is why we suffer anxiety and alienation at levels never before seen.

'Perhaps without the comforting cloak of mythology, we are now very alone and afraid. We seek assurances in things that are fleeting, and like addicts, we become more dependent and less satisfied.

'We reject spirituality for pragmatic belief, and we become vessels of what we believe in – emptiness.'

She rose from her perch and got ready to leave. She found the note Aidan left under her door. He had also left a single yellow rose. He wanted her to go to Howth with him on Saturday, 'if she wasn't doing anything else and if she would like to spend the day with him.'

Saturday was Saint Valentine's Day. She wasn't sure if he remembered that.

When they met, she was shocked: he was pale and drawn and looked almost aged. He was moody and skittish; he had gone on a bit of a drinking spree with some old friends. But when they were seated on the bus, he began to talk.

"Out there," he pointed to the flat strand, "is Clontarf. That's where Brian Boru defeated the Vikings. He broke their hold on Ireland an' weakened them forever an' all of Europe was soon rid of the 'Norse Terror.' Sadly, the victory cost his life."

The bus stopped in the old fishing village on the north side of the headland, hiding from the city and facing the open sea. A half a mile out, breaking the surface like a whale, she saw what he pointed toward.

"That's Lambay. There used to be a monastery there, too, but back in seven ninety-five the monks woke to the terror of the first Vikin' raid."

"Were they alone or were they entertaining Night-Visitors?"

He lowered his finger and looked at her before slowly looking back to the sea.

"Sometimes, you don't make any sense, ya know that. You seem a bit different this mornin', is everythin' all right?"

"Everything's fine. I've had some time to sort a few things out, and I feel good about me; I'm still not sure about you, but what the hell."

"I know there's been a lot of shite goin' on but that's all goin' to change. From now on, things are goin' to be different, you'll see. I brought you here because it's a very special place. I love being able to stand by the sea and look across the waves. Sometimes, I think it understands me. I feel that I can talk to the old ways through the sea." He stopped and looked at her. "Does that make any sense?"

"No, but don't worry, sense is overrated. From now on, I want to live through my emotions. I want to know the world through them so I can feel what I paint."

"You're goin' to love it here then."

The headland towered behind them, connected to the city by a narrow strip, so easy to defend in times past, and even now, as the suburbs spread along the coast, Howth was a place apart. Clouds scurried by changing everything. One moment, it was like a Grecian Isle as sun-dappled water rippled between brightly coloured boats below the stony-brown harbour wall.

But when the sun hid, the wind rose, and the sea and sky greyed like in the Hebrides where men set out to wrest a living from the unforgiving depths. It was a very hard but beautiful place.

"How do I put it all on canvas?"

"By closin' your eyes an' breathin' it all in an' listenin' to everythin' that's goin' on around you. Then, you can open your eyes, and you'll see it as it really is and that's what you have to paint."

She closed her eyes and sensed the warmth of the air and the gentle swish of the tides as the waves rippled into the harbour, rising a little higher each time, lifting creaking boats and stretching their moorings.

Off to the side, raucous birds clung to life on sheer cliffs, waves breaking far below and slurping through little gullies they had quarried over eons.

She opened her eyes. It was a stark place: worn to bare essence, the domain of men of the sea.

Three of them sat against a whitewashed stone shed, so out of place against the fiery granite stretching into the sea. Their idle boats rocked gently atop swelling tides and their drying nets hung like cobwebs, shuddering like skin caressed. She reached for Aidan's hand and stepped into her own picture.

They passed the fishermen, who doffed their caps and smiled, but she felt apart and, while not quite naked, her clothes felt flimsy, that a sudden breeze might reach out and tear them away.

The fishermen smoked pipes as their berry-brown faces followed them, she felt warm in their eyes. When she looked back, they didn't turn away but grinned: one even winked. They were not attractive men, but they were vibrant and alive. She didn't dislike their attention, but she pulled Aidan toward her and held him tight.

They walked along the top of the seawall, letting their bodies bump gently together. The sunshine warmed her hair and blushed her cheeks while breezes played an Irish lament – squeezed out of the popping chanter against the intermittent regulators, above the continuity of the drones.

When he spoke, his cadence in time with the murmur of the tide, he talked about Death and Life like they were interchangeable – that Life and Death were inevitable and had to be considered as that – the happenstance of existence. And when Janice looked to the water, where Death lurked in the depths, devouring Life in endless cycles, she knew what he meant.

He stood close and she could smell whiskey on his breath mingled with tobacco, the seeds of his own destruction – the spoils of another day of victory against all that lurked in the night. His cheeks were less lifeless and his hands were steady and only trembled when the breeze reached inside his loose shirt and caressed his chest. He was coming back to her, back to the world of the living.

By the lighthouse, she leaned against the seaward side of the lichen-stained harbour and watched him scramble out past the tide pools, out onto limpeted rocks, where waves broke into spray and straggled off among tangled tresses of kelp.

Near the edge, he seemed more agile and invigorated. The wind and waves reached out to him and she was torn between wanting to rush over to draw him back and the desire to just stand there and watch him.

But what if he falls in? she asked herself.

Then he will surely drown, she answered with a fatalism that was new.

He crouched and held his palm, inches above the water. He was humming and his voice was carried back on the spray:

"I have laboured by the cromlech,

"The grey cairn on the hills of dawn.

"I weary of the world's empires and bow to you,

"Gods of the still stars and the deep."

The wind rose and tossed a wave toward her. Clouds blew in before ebbing back and a thousand sunbeams fell around her. She stood enthralled by all that she could see and hear and by all the images that formed in her mind and in her heart.

And when it all began to swirl, when it rose and threatened to sweep her away, she looked at him, a fixed point on the rocky shore that she could steer by. This turbulent man was the only constant she could find as the cliffs and the pier rode the tossing waves.

The sun grew hot on her face and across her breasts. Her heart began to race, and she was more aware than she could remember. She was aware of the confusion that was understanding: the uselessness of the mind in the world of spirits.

She closed her eyes again and listened. The noises of the harbour and the distant village drifted through pauses in the incessant tides and the cries of the gulls. The piping of the wind was joined by the timpani of boats lapping on the leeward side, huddled in the harbour and bobbing on the ripples. The gulls hung in the air like the ragged notes of a sawing fiddle, not at all like a violin!

This is where he belongs, she told herself, *out by the side of things. But where do I belong?*

When she opened her eyes, he was standing in the water, on the side of slippery rocks with his head low to the gentle waves where a seal broke the surface a few feet before him. He didn't move as the seal floated, and Janice knew they were sharing thoughts.

As he bent nearer the creature's head, she saw a face like a woman's turn and look into her heart. In those eyes, Janice was insignificantly young, while this placid had the beauty of eons in her limpid face.

Janice felt rebuked for her human inadequacy and mortal deceit. She was measured and found wanting and there was something else: she was where she wasn't wanted.

He would give up his gift for you? A creature of aging flesh that will rot and cease to appeal. You don't belong here. You are dabbling in that which you don't understand. Go while you can, you shouldn't have come.

The words cut like an old stone knife, shredding her to a thousand little pieces that the wind might scatter, and in the grip of that terrible feeling, she turned to go. She stumbled a little and the noise she made startled him. He turned from the disappearing seal and smiled.

"There's no need to be afraid. It's just other lives and other thoughts; you know we share the sun with all things."

She wanted to run, but where? She was three thousand miles from everything she knew and thought she understood, castaway on this beguiling island of incongruity where the night walked brazenly through the day. She felt grotesque and misshapen. She wanted to run, but where?

When he held her close, she buried her face in his neck and clung to him. If he let go the wind would blow her out to sea. She would float down into the grey-blue depths to hidden valleys where sea creatures would gather to mock her, where her lungs would burst, where . . .

"Hush now," he whispered into the shell of her ear, "it's nothin' but old memories and images of the past. The sea remembers them all."

"But . . . the seal?"

"Ah, it's nothin', forget it."

Without letting her go, he turned from the water and back toward the village. As they walked by, the fishermen pretended to be busy with their nets, but she could sense rebuke. The stern village echoed and the great hill joined in. The whole world roared around her and in the wind, and in the waves, and in the cry of the birds, she could hear it: she should not have come here!

They lay entwined in her bed that evening, wrapped together because she was still afraid and she was still cold and she cried like a child. She couldn't stop and tears ran along her cheek to his chest. She had been exposed, debased and derided: a mediocre talent and a child of comfort and ease – she had no business at the edge of the world. She didn't belong here with him. She had tried to attach herself to his star, but they both knew he was theirs. He was a part of the old ways, and he wasn't for her. She had been shown the portal to that world, but they would never let her enter.

He placed a finger in the growing pool of tears and tasted her sadness. He held her closer and let her cry: she didn't want to stop. He held her as sleep washed over them and they swam off in different directions.

Janice stood on the edge of a cliff. Behind her was all she once thought she wanted to be. Before her was the sea, calling to her. The sea had always drawn her into its noise and motion; it was magnetic and could draw the moon close each month.

But there was something in this sea that had never called to her before, something that was so familiar and something that was so frightening. The old ways were coming to claim her soul so she spread her arms and closed her eyes and tumbled forward.

She tossed and turned in turmoil until he woke and held her.

"What's the matter?" he asked as he scratched his chin on his shoulder. "There's nothin' to worry about. Everythin' will be fine. Just lie back and don't worry."

"What about the seal?" she asked through tears that seeped up as she woke.

"What about it," he answered. "It's only an old pet of a thing. It's used to people feedin' it and the likes – you know, from bein' around the harbour an' all. They can be as friendly as dogs."

She wanted to believe him and was grateful that he tried. He was so at ease with it all.

"I don't think I can do this, Aidan."

"Do what? What are you talkin' about?"

"I don't think I can make it here."

"Of course you can. You have me, remember. I know it's tough tryin' to be yourself when everybody is givin' you a hard time about things, but ya got to remember somethin': we're artists; we're different." He held her close to his chest and stroked her hair.

"I don't know, Aidan. I just got so frightened."

"Of course you would. But ya have to remember that we live and die at the whim of Fate."

"But I'm not like you. You'd gamble your life for a laugh or a dare."

"We're just used to hard times here, and when we get a chance to have a bit of a lark, we don't stop to think about it. Why would we?" He gently placed his fingers against her lips. They smelled of cigars and they smelled of the sea. "In Dublin, every night's a celebration for havin' survived another day. It's how we accept the happenstance of the Fates, just like how we accept the weather. "

"Aidan, sometimes, you really surprise me." She grew warmer in his arms and in his assurance. But it was the old beliefs that had called to her at the harbour. The Silkie: the seals that were human once. Or was it the other way around? "But she looked like a woman," Janice protested, and as they words left her mouth, she realised how absurd they sounded.

"That's right, they do. Old tales tell of fishermen and sailors fallin' in love an' jumpin' into the water, only to drown. They're seals all right, but they play tricks with your eyes. They're very playful animals."

She lay with her head on his chest and listened to his breathing, and in that soothing rhythm, her fears subsided. In time, she rose and wrapped herself in a blanket.

Above the sleeping city, the moon was full and hollow and moved through ragged clouds. Church spires pointed like hands frozen in prayer and a thousand stars kept vigil. In the soft light of delicate moonbeams, she saw the paper he'd carried. She knew she shouldn't read it.

His eyes twitched as she struck a match and brought a little glowing warmth into her room. The paper was wrinkled and stained, but she could read through the corrections. It had a title, but it had been scratched out. It had read 'My Night Visitor:'

> *Come and take what I offer.*
> *She can have my place*
> *By the sea and everything in it.*
> *When the sun chases mists into the ground*
> *I will spend my days at the corner of the street*
> *Singing a Silkie's song.*

And in the candlelight of the ancient Celtic night, it all began to make sense. She knew of the Silkie, and she knew what a Night-Visitor was. She just had no idea how she could have found her way into their world. She laid her head upon the table, and as she fell asleep, her breath played with the corner of his page.

"What time is it, Bridey?" Maurice grumbled from beneath his pillow.

"It is almost dawn."

He sat up and rubbed his face. "Is there something wrong?"

"Not at all, darling – go back to sleep now. I just got up to go for a brisk walk."

"Humph!"

Gwen walked as the morning winds scattered the low clouds. It would all be clear soon and she might get to see the sun for a while. They would have showers too, but what could you expect for this time of the year?

Chapter 11

Gerry hated going to Werburgh Street and shuffling along for doleful pittances. He never got used to it. He was a working man at heart even if he'd no work for years. One of these days, he'd lead the muttering grumbling masses to Leinster House, to demand the striped-shirted Seamuses, give up at least, a tithe from their thievery – they'd all that European money flowing in, and in Dublin, all monies passed through the same greasy hands. But the masses knew no other way. Their remittance begrudged through barred wickets; all revolution bred out of them; they lingered at the mercy of remote corporations and Public representatives for aggrandisement. No one cared about them: never had and never would. He signed his cards and queued again for his few Pounds at the other end of the hall.

"Have you been looking for work, Mr. Morrison?" the woman asked with disdain.

"I have indeed, but no one wants to hire old fellas like me. It's a young man's . . ."

"Have you considered getting retrained?"

"I have, but I'm a bit old for that."

"You'll never get anywhere with an attitude like that."

They were giving everybody a hard time. It was how they got them to fuck-off to England; there was always work in England. "And where is it that I should be getting to?"

He lit another Woodbine as Sean coaxed the fermenting stream down the side of the tilted glass and whistled. It would take a while to settle. He always pulled a perfect pint: a matter of professional pride, as well as tradition.

"Is Tommy about?"

"He'll not be in for a while. Did you need anything?"

"I just want to settle something."

Sean understood. Gerry had his dole. "There you are now, Mr. Morrison."

"That's a fine pint. Gimme twenty Afton, too."

Sean smiled as he turned. *Sweet Afton*, Gerry would be skint again by evening. "Are you right there, Aidan?"

He wobbled and held on to the wall, glaring at empty stools and low tables. He focused on the bar, and readied himself to lurch forward. "I'm fine, Sean. Thanks for askin' though." But he wasn't convincing, wavering as he tried to regroup. "How ya Gerry?"

"Grand, Aidan, how's yourself?"

"I was down in the markets, ya know?"

"Sit down then, like a good man. Will you have something?"

Aidan didn't answer, leaning against the pillar, measuring the distance to the bar. He wanted to reach for his pocket, but the room was spinning. Gerry winked at Sean who turned his back. The market bars opened at six. Some of Grogan's crowd, like John Jordan, began their day there. He was more coherent then, before his mind outraced his deliberate enunciation, before his words became intermittent.

Sean turned and placed coffee on the counter. "Start with that and we'll see how you get on?"

Aidan raised the cup and sniffed the coaly coffee. He teetered, spilling it across the bar. "Gimme a pint for fuck's sake."

"Sit down and I'll bring it over." Sean nodded to Gerry, who steered Aidan to a seat.

"Gerry, have you seen my cigars?"

"Here, have one of these."

Aidan reached for his mouth with the unfiltered cigarette as Gerry waited with a flaming match. "So? What are you celebrating?"

"Everythin' is all fucked up, just like it's supposed to be."

"Don't be talkin' like that – a young fella with your whole life before you."

"I'm a lowlife piece of shite that's not worth pissin' on."

"What's got you like this?"

"I did it, Gerry, just like you said. Only now I feel like I betrayed her, just like Judas"

"I always thought poor old Judas got a raw deal. I never really understood that story."

"What they fuck are you talkin' about Judas for?"

"You brought him up."

"Did I? Well, never mind that . . . What was I sayin'? Oh, ya, I sold her out just like you told me."

"What are you on about? You're not making any sense."

"I let them take Janice. Why the fuck did you make me do that?

"Because you had to, it's the way Lenanshees work. Even If you don't fall in love; she's still bound to you, and you can't break free, either. The only way's to have someone take your place."

"I never loved her. I mean I fucked her an' all, but anybody would do that. And then when Janice found out – she made me decide. Then Gwen said I'd to choose, too. Are you sure we did the right thing?"

"Sure of course we did. The bitch would've taken all your poetry and then where'd you be?"

"But what happens Janice now?"

"She'll be fine as long as she doesn't fall in love with her."

"But what happens if she does."

"Sure why'd she do a thing like that when she has you and all? You do love the girl, don't ya?"

"Of course I do. But what if it did happen?"

"Then poor Janice would be proper fucked." He sipped his drink as the enormity of it spread across the floor in front of him. "She'd probably get used against her will. The bitch would probably use the riding crop on her, too. But sure, it won't happen. Why would it?"

Aidan grimaced as he swallowed tepid coffee. "Ya know what! I'm gonna go an' tell her to change things back. I'm gonna tell her that she can have me, as long as she lets Janice go?"

"And do you think she'll go for that?"

"Why wouldn't she?"

"True for you."

Sean arrived with another coffee and a fresh pint for Gerry. "I've yours coming, Aidan. Just have this while you're waiting."

"I don't want coffee."

"Go on now, it's that or nothing."

Aidan drained the coffee and pleaded with Sean once more.

"Get this into you and then we'll see." Sean placed toasted cheese sandwiches on the table, along with another coffee. "You'll be all right soon enough."

Aidan stared forlornly at the coffee but devoured the sandwich and wiped his mouth with his hand.

"Gerry? Did you ever stop and think about who God really is?"

"Jesus Christ! Sure don't you see his picture in every house in the country? Of course, you see a lot of pictures of his Mother too."

"That's what I am askin'. We don't pray directly to God. We pray to his Ma, ya know, to put in a good word for us, unworthy fuckin' sinners that we are? Why do you think that is?"

"I suppose it's the way we're brought up by the nuns."

"The mickey-dodgers have fuck all to do with it. It's from the old days when we believed in the Goddess."

"I never really thought about that, I must confess."

"That's the problem with the way things are goin'. Nobody thinks for themselves anymore. We all want to be refined these days. What the fuck do we wanna be eatin' snails and snot like that for?"

"It's because of Europe and all," Gerry offered. He wasn't sure what else to say.

"Fuck Europe. We're still fuckin' Celts at heart. Deep down inside, we still have their blood runnin' through us, and now I gotta take a piss. That coffee's gone right through me."

A piece of paper fluttered from his pocket and Gerry couldn't help himself. He unfolded it and read.

Is love enough?
In the courtyard and the clutter
Nameless, faceless and unknown.
A fallen star.

He folded the paper and lit another cigarette. It would work out just fine: it had to. But he stopped to consider Janice for a moment. Of course she'd be fine; too, something would turn up.

She hated Dublin in the spring when buildings were damp and clothes gave off a little steam. The days were growing longer as the sun came north, but it never got to Ireland. She'd have to go elsewhere for that – to places where reason ruled.

She missed Sinead: they hadn't spoken since that day. They saw each other around the square, and Sinead stared through her like she wasn't there. Janice tried talking to her and had her heart broken; Sinead walked away as if she hadn't heard. And Aidan wasn't any help. He was either drinking or working. She hadn't seen him since Howth and that was a week and a half ago.

She was lonely and longed for comforting: something she hoped to find in the hiss of coffee machines and the ceaseless chatter that came and went. They all knew: she was sure of it. For all their efforts to become a part of Europe, the Irish were Pagans who lived at the edge of the world. They knew what lingered in the mists.

She had spent the last few days reading everything she could find on the Silkie. But while she accepted that they might have happened in the past – they couldn't be happening still?

But she knew that she had seen something else. She had been granted a glimpse of the Old Ways as they surged along below the surface and they had seen her. It made no sense, but that didn't matter. She had come to study the Celts and became wrapped up in the world they had left behind, a world that slumbered lightly and was now restless. Even in the midst of the bustling capital, old voices called to her, pleading to be included in the faceless crowds she would paint. She had stumbled on the bones of the pre-Christian world, the world that had inspired O'Casey, Synge and Yeats, whose brother Jack painted what he captured in simple verse. The same past was posing for her.

She had to get a grip. She was walking in shadows and believing in old stories and nursery rhymes. She thought about her father. He would have found this funny. He was always ready to believe in the old ways. She missed him more than anything else.

In her last year of high school, she had a dream in which the sky filled with ravens circling around the tall trees that separated the fields near Picton. She heard the owl as it searched for something in the spreading darkness. Janice's wings were translucent, like delicately painted rice paper. She flew low over the bridge where the large truck lay on its side, crushing the grill of a much-traveled Pontiac. The ravens scattered as the snow fell in tiny flecks tinged in red.

The phone woke Janice and the hall light streamed into her room around her mother's trembling shoulders.

"Would you mind if I sat here?"

She blinked into the wrinkled face of an old woman in a large floral hat dripping raindrops. She flopped into the chair and began to tap on the table with the strange bird-like handle of her umbrella. "I must get a cup of tea into me. Who do you have to talk with to get a cup of tea around here?" the old woman repeated into the space behind her shoulder and, turning to Janice, added, "I'm parched and it's raining so much outside."

She found this amusing and cackled. She continued to wave until someone brought her a teapot, a cup and saucer, milk and a bowl of sugar. She splashed tea across the table and into her cup. She fumbled with bony hands deep within her massive handbag until she found her pills. She rolled two of them onto her spoon, tipped it onto her tongue and swallowed a mouthful of hot tea. She burped silently and implored Janice's pardon. She smiled between the cup and the spoon, still raised to her face that was impish despite the lines of age and lines of doubt and fear.

Janice was becoming interested, but for the longest time, the old woman sat there, tilting forward every now and then to take another sip of tea.

Time passed and the old woman sat in the euphoria of her tea, turning at times to comment on the weather. At first, Janice thought she was trying to converse, but no matter what she said, the old woman didn't reply. Janice returned to her diary, but the old woman showed no sign of noticing. She continued to sip her tea and mutter about the weather. Janice smiled up at her every now and then, just to be polite, and as she was about to leave, the old woman raised her eyes and stared at her.

"What has you so frightened?"

Janice might have lied, but there was no point. "Too many strange things have happened since I came here."

"Oh! That sounds exciting."

Janice had to smile. Reluctantly at first, she began to speak, but as the words unfolded, she found comfort in her odd companion's attention and, with a growing sense of release, told the whole story of her outing to Howth.

As the old woman listened, she started to nod her head and Janice felt more encouraged. She tried to make it sound whimsical, like she was more curious than alarmed. When she finished, she waited for the old woman to comment, but she was hunched forward, as if she was still listening.

"So?" She regretted saying so much. Now that it was out there, it sounded like madness.

"I see," the old woman finally answered and returned to pottering among her thoughts.

"What do you see?" Janice blurted as impatience got the better of her. "Isn't that the strangest thing you have ever heard?"

"Oh, no, not at all, the very same thing happened to me."

"What do you mean?"

"The very same thing happened to me a long time ago, when I was a young woman. I was walking with my young man, just along from the very same pier. We used to like to walk along the cliffs, too, because, back then, we didn't go to the cinema that often, and of course, there was no television, either. Not that I am a big fan of television, mind you. I prefer reading a nice bit of poetry every now and then. Do you like poetry, my dear?"

Janice nodded; she didn't want to break the silky threads that held the old woman's gossamer thoughts together.

"Isn't it wonderful when someone can write a poem that takes you somewhere, even if it's only for a moment or two? And I prefer the old style of poetry because it makes more sense. I can't understand why modern poets don't learn to rhyme better, don't you agree? But then again, you're young and you might like modern poetry, especially if it's written by a handsome young man who wants to take you for walks along Howth Head and wants to try to steal a kiss when nobody is looking."

Janice nodded and wondered how much this crazy old woman could read from her face.

"You mustn't let them do that, you know!"

"Do what?"

"You mustn't let the young men kiss you. They're only after the one thing, even the good ones. But they're the ones who'll wait until you're married and appreciate you all the more for making them wait."

The old woman lowered her head to her raised teacup and looked inside. "That's what I don't like about television. People meet and start kissing each other all over the face and then start to take their clothes off, right there in front of everybody. I never watch after that because I don't want to see people committing sins. You're not like those people, are you? Are you?"

"Oh, no, of course not," Janice answered, trying not to think of the night on all fours in her room. "I do like to kiss and cuddle a bit, but you're right, they appreciate it more when you make them wait. But tell me more about what happened to you at Howth."

"Oh, yes, my dear, I was just about to tell you about that. It was very strange. It was like one of those things you read about in the poems by those English poets – you know the ones that took all that opium – like the fellow who wrote about Kubla Khan."

"Coleridge."

"Who, my dear?"

"Coleridge," Janice repeated.

"Oh! No! I think that it was Coleridge who wrote that poem. But I'm often wrong. Sometimes I wonder if reading all about them and their adventures didn't addle my brain a little. Have you ever tried opium?"

"No!"

"Good for you and neither have I. But I've heard of girls who have and then can't get enough and go running off to places like Constantinople and become white slaves to the Sultan. They take off all of their clothes, too, and let the Sultan use them carnally, if you can believe it – and all for opium. It's a shame. Someone should try to do something about it, don't you think?"

"Yes, yes it's a terrible thing, but you were telling me about Howth. You used to walk there with your young man. Did he marry you?"

"Oh, no, he died years ago."

She returned to her teacup as the settling sun hopscotched through holes in the clouds and through the fogged-up window. In the place between them, above the tea-stained table, dust and smoke particles gathered in the beams and were gone when the café moved beneath the clouds, but her silence remained.

"How did he die," Janice asked as delicately as her curiosity would allow.

"Who died, my dear?"

"The young man you were telling me about."

"Oh, yes, I must be getting addled. Well, let me tell you, he was walking along the cliffs one night and jumped into the sea and was never seen again." She nodded in agreement with her own lingering statement and raised her cup again but didn't drink. "It was terrible, but I suppose in some ways it wasn't so bad. He used to have seals come up to him, too, so I'm sure that they are good company for him now – but that might have been because he used to cut up fish."

"Cut up fish?"

"Yes, dear, he worked in the fishmongers. He always brought a nice bit of plaice for my father when he called around. He used to bring mackerel, too. I'm very fond of mackerel."

"You were saying that he jumped in?"

"Yes, he went mad for something or other and jumped in. He was mad surely because he was out walking alone on a bitter night in January. Perhaps he was taking opium." And for a moment, the old woman nodded at the plausibility. "Of course, I had stopped seeing him before this on account of his going mad and all, but I heard stories from the other young women of the time. They told me that he went mad and jumped – right into the sea. I'm surprised he wasn't broken open on the rocks on the way down, somebody was looking out for him that night."

"But he did die?"

"Oh, yes, of course he died, he jumped off the cliff! But he died in one piece, and he was a fine handsome man. It would have been a shame if he had died all broken into pieces. There are some that say that he can still be seen out at Howth in January, but what kind of person would go out there then; they would have to be touched in the head, if you know what I mean. They never found his body, either. I think the seals took him down into their place under the water."

"And why do you think they did that?"

"Because he smelled of fish, were you not listening to me at all?"

Janice sat back in her chair and looked this old woman over. Her hat was decorated with freshly plucked stems of fledgling flowers and her eye shadow was kingfisher-blue and her cheeks a smudged red. It would have made her look whorish if she wasn't so old. She wore a slender silver chain around her neck, dangling a white gold cross on which hung the dying Jesus. She had her handbag on her lap and had folded her arms on top of it. She was about to ask for more tea when a middle-aged couple whispered together for a moment before walking straight to their table. He took the old woman by the hand and gently helped her to stand up. "Come on now, Aunt Joan, it's time to get you back to the home."

"Who are you and what do you want with me? Are you one of the Sultan's eunuchs?"

"C'mon now, Joan," he took her elbow firmly, but gently. "Let's get you back to the home before the night."

As they struggled to move her away the younger woman turned to Janice, "I hope she wasn't bothering you, she's my husband's aunt, and she gets a bit scattered sometimes. She forgets herself and gets a bit confused. I hope she wasn't bothering you."

"Oh, no," Janice reassured her. "No, actually she was lovely company." And for reasons she didn't understand, Janice added, "She was just telling me about Howth."

The other woman's face changed and she exchanged a glance with her husband before she stepped closer to Janice and spoke softly. "Did she tell you what happened that poor young man? That's when her mind snapped, watching him fall right before her eyes. Anyway, thanks, and I hope she wasn't a bother."

They ushered the old woman out the door to the waiting car and drove off as the rain started again, hesitantly at first, until it gained the courage to pelt the streets and windowpanes. The wind tore at overcoats and twisted passing umbrellas inside out.

Janice sat and stared at the street as the car rounded a corner.

What was that all about? Am I crazy — is she crazy — or is all of Dublin crazy?

She closed her journal and left as the evening rush began. The buses were crowded and crawled along, squealing and shuddering. She decided to walk and raised her umbrella against the teasing winds that rushed out from the passing side streets. She headed toward the Green. It was where the gentry strolled when they came to town for the season. She would find peace and collect herself among the whisperings of spring before the gates were locked.

Since the English departed, the Irish had raised statues among the trees and shrubs. But they weren't the trumpeting statues of heroes who had risen in resistance. These statues celebrated the poets and playwrights who had kept the spirit alive, writers who blended myth and martyrdom, fact and fancy, and even after a half-century of church-dominated self-rule, their words still hovered.

She stopped by the Yeats' monument. Henry Moore had really got it right. She would have to paint it, the half-man, half-cross before a senate of mythology. When she squinted a little, it looked like one of the faces from Easter Island.

From another side, it looked like a Spanish dancer, but from the front it was plain, the cross on a restless grave.

She tugged at her journal and settled down on the cold damp stone. She flicked through the first few pages. She had done a sketch, somewhere at the beginning, one of her early ones.

Ah, she found it. She had captured it and added a few notes. But there was something else, something she hadn't remembered writing;

Until she came into the Land of Fairie,
Where nobody gets old and godly and grave,
Where nobody gets old and crafty and wise,
Where nobody gets old and bitter of tongue.
And she is still there, busied with a dance
Deep in the dewy shadow of a wood,
Or where stars walk upon a mountain-top.

She leafed through a few mores pages with notes she never remembered writing. Maybe she added them while she was drinking, but the handwriting was firm and deliberate. She shivered and looked around, but everything was as it always was, calm as the city bustled by. It would soon be night and all that had been benign and quaint would become menacing as the shadows grew.

Since Howth, her perceptions had changed. It was as if everything that had once been so comforting was now rising up against her. She was frightened and alone and wished Aidan could take her in his arms, to stand between her and the fears that rose from the stones around her. But, as she considered, he was the reason she was in this mess!

And, besides, she was getting a bit carried away, too. Maybe Sinead had a point. Maybe she was a little flighty, she was an artist after all, but that was the price she paid for her imagination and her inspiration. *This is it, my painful, messy rebirth.*

She flicked through her pages again and reconsidered. She must have written them, it looked like her writing, only it leaned the other way. The last page read:

> *It may be truth we do not know*
> *The limit of those powers*
> *God has permitted to the evil spirits*
> *For some mysterious end.*

She snapped the pad shut and shoved it back into her bag and strode from the Green, back into the busy wet streets. She needed to get away. Dublin was a little too Dublin, and sometimes, she wished she'd never come. Maybe, when Aidan went to the Continent; she could go with him. She needed to visit other places. She needed to feel the sun on her skin and wade in warm oceans free of cold clammy kelp and seals. She needed to sit in cafes as the sun slid lower in warm evenings, free of rain and clouds of doubt.

It is not so bad here, she decided as she stepped out of her shower and fumbled into flannel pajamas and her dad's hockey shirt.

She topped up her glass and brought the bottle with her. She stood in front of her canvas and tried to remember where she had left off.

In her painting, there were three old fishermen sitting on a bench in brilliant sunshine, smoking pipes with hats pulled down low. But you could tell where they were looking – out to the harbour, where a woman swam. She was shorter and more round, but what surprised her now, as she cast herself osmotically, was this woman's flesh was covered in a shiny black skin like vinyl.

She raised a clean brush and ran it slowly across her forehead, mesmerizing herself, tantalizing herself back into that mood. She wanted to get back to that feeling; she wanted to get back to that naked day when she stepped through the veil.

She had made a decision; she would try to do what Yeats had done.

But she would have to overcome all fears and confusions if she was going to paint what she'd seen.

Perhaps it is madness, but I choose to be a mad painter rather than a scattered old woman. I will not become a victim of Fate — I will capture it and smear its essence on canvas.

She began again, adding features and details; it was how she painted her people. One of the old men, although you could barely see his face, was Aidan. He said he was busy with his book, but she couldn't help feeling that he might be trying to avoid her.

But that was silly. He was probably just taking the space he needed. She could understand. Perhaps if they had a bigger place, they could work without getting in each other's way. They could live together and still have space. It would be the best of all possible worlds. The phone in the hall jangled again and again and again.

"Janice darling, sorry for calling so late, but I just had to share some good news with you. We have had a vacancy arise, just around the corner, on Belgrave Square."

"Oh, Gwen, that sounds so exciting. Please, tell me more."

"It is very roomy and even has a space you can use as a studio. You will have so much more room to spread yourself about."

"Well, I don't know what to say Gwen; thank you so much. Would it be all right with you if I invited Aidan to share it with me?"

"Of course, darling, but now I have to dash. I will call you back with more details."

"Are you sure about this, Bridey?"

"Of course I am, darling. After all, we wouldn't want young Janice to get lonely and leave, would we?"

"Bridey, you never cease to amaze me. You think of everything."

Chapter 12

"Well, what do you think?" Gwen spun around in the emptiness. "And there is a sunroom that would be perfect for painting."

"It is perfect, thank you." Janice kissed her, flustering her a little.

"Oh, darling, please, it is the least we can do, and Maurice has the most wonderful news. Maurice?"

"What? Oh, yes, I had a chat with an old school chum. He suggested that Bridey pick out a few of your better pieces. He has an 'in' with some galleries, and they are always looking for new works."

"Isn't that wonderful, darling? And you must go for the opening."

Janice couldn't contain herself and kissed Maurice, too.

"Yes, yes. You are welcome. Now let's not get too carried away, shall we?" He stepped back to readjust himself. "Are you planning on accompanying the Bard to Brussels?"

"Darling, you must go. Maurice will cover the arrangements, of course."

They both smiled as they watched her decide. They were getting more involved in her life. At first, they just offered advice on art but now they offered opinions on everything. She didn't mind: it felt familial.

Her parents were arguing again and her mother was tense. "It's just a few bad apples, that's all."

"Bad apples? Well, then you throw them out before they spoil the others. You don't spread the rot all over the country."

"Would you ever stop going on about it. I'll never believe the lies you're bringing home."

"Face it, woman, the Church is rotten to the core."

"Ah, Sinead, I didn't see you there."

"If you two don't stop, I'll walk out this door forever."

She excused herself while they stood staring at each other. She didn't even stop for tea. She'd have to stop at the coffee shop; it couldn't be helped. He might be there, and she might bump into Janice, too.

He wasn't, but Janice was. She hadn't showered and had paint smudged across her forehead.

"Janice. How've you been?" It was breezy enough, just what Sinead wanted.

They settled into awkward silence, savouring their coffees and passing small comments until Janice broke down. "Sinead, I've missed you, and I've so much to tell you." So much that she didn't stop to notice if Sinead was interested. "I'm off to London, to see the Queen."

"That's wonderful. I'm sure you'll be a big hit."

"Do you really think so?" Janice shivered a little, she was tired. She slept so little lately. Her dreams were labyrinths of jumbled confusion. She wanted to believe Sinead. Maurice and Gwen had seemed in earnest, too, but . . .

"Anyway, I gotta go, my lecture is starting. I'll see you around."

"Janice?"

Sometimes she regretted giving him a key. "In here."

"It's a great day, isn't?"

"Is it?" She'd been painting all night and hadn't noticed the morning creep up.

"Fuck, is it ever. I got my cheque and I got our tickets to Brussels."

"Is there any mention of the hotel?"

"There has to be. They can't expect a Bard of Ireland to sleep on the street."

"Most of you do, but perhaps you can pick up some pretty Belgian girl and go home with her."

"Well, I'm up for that?"

"So why are you taking me?"

"Because you're my one and only, my main squeeze, my . . ."

"I get the picture, Aidan." She smiled like it was his idea, but she was flattered that he made the effort. Sometimes, she became a little jaded with him, and besides, he couldn't come to London with her. He'd surely make a scene.

"Well? Wanna go shoppin' and stop in at Grogan's."

"Why don't you put it in a bank account, for a rainy day?"

"Every day is rainy and besides, only rich people use banks." But he agreed to think about it when her exasperation showed. For now, he'd cash it in Grogan's, to settle his debts. "I owe Jimmy a twenty and Joe, at least fifteen. Tony? I think it was . . ."

She wiped her hands and pulled the sheet over her unfinished work. She regretted his intrusion, but she needed to step back and reflect. "Did you say shopping? For what?"

"Somethin' classy to wear in Belgium."

He was generous; she had to admit that as she twirled around in front of a mirror in one of the little shops in Powerscourt. He'd bought her a Claddagh ring, too. "It's a token, ya know, 'bout how ya make me feel." he muttered when she put it on. It was too big. "Well, maybe you can grow into it."

"Are you saying that my fingers are getting fat?"

"Love has to grow, ya know? It starts out small an' has to be looked after until it gets big."

"Aidan, don't get all mushy on me. I wouldn't know how to deal with it."

"I was just talkin', that's all. I mean, a guy has feelings, ya know. I just wanted you to know what you meant to me, that's all." He looked a little defiant, like someone had called him out.

"I saw Gwen yesterday," she mentioned causally as he returned from the bar. He hesitated and placed their drinks on the low table with exaggerated care. "Did she ask about me?"

"Not really. Maurice arranged to show a few of my pieces in London. They want me to go over, too, in the summer."

"We could have tea with the Queen."

"Actually, I think they want me to make a bit of a splash on my own. You understand, darling?" She tilted her head so that she could look at him through her hair. He looked a little unhappy.

"So, you're blowin' me off?"

"Of course not, darling I was going to ask you to move in with me?"

"Yer kiddin', right?"

"No, Gwen just told me. They had a vacancy arise. They said we could move in a few weeks."

"We'd be livin' in sin."

"Are you saying that we aren't ready for this?"

"Of course not, it'll be grand, and we can be together while we work."

"But what about things like money, we need to discuss stuff like that."

"Everythin' will be fine. I'm gonna be sellin' loads of books, and you'll start sellin' your paintin's, too." He paused for a moment as he considered what he said. "And that's great. I'm really happy for you."

They spent the evening surrounded by friends and shopping bags. He was basking in new fame; his work had been mentioned in the 'Times' again. It was a matter for discussion around the bar.

"Ya made the papers again, Aidan. They're sayin' that you're the voice of Ireland's conscience."

"He's just an illiterate little bollocks that got lucky."

"Fuck you'se, yer all fuckin' jealous. That's your problem."

"The only fuckin' thing of yours I'd want is your girlfriend; she's far too good for the likes of you."

"She's gonna be a great painter and I'm gonna be a great poet. We're made for each other."

"Ya but, you're gonna fuck it up."

"Kiss my arse, yer all fuckin' jealous."

They left the pub early; Janice had grown tired of the rancorous banter, but as they walked to Rathmines, she knew what was really bothering her. Her mother had asked her to come home for the summer, at least for a visit, and Janice was running out of excuses. She was tempted; she needed a break from Dublin, but she couldn't face the tiny existence that waited there. She felt constrained just thinking about it. She felt a tightening in her chest every time she opened her mother's weekly letters, full of news that was of no importance anymore. The Baillie's dog was dead and Mrs. Paterson had her hip replaced, the Liberals were destroying everything Ontario stood for, and Robert was seeing someone new. She seemed nice enough, but she just wasn't right for Robert. She reread the letter when they got home, as Aidan watched her intently. "Everythin' okay?"

"Yes, everything's fine. It's just my past is moving on without me."

"We could go over for a few weeks, if you want."

Janice tried to imagine Aidan and her mother sitting in the front room, drinking tea as they leafed through family albums. It almost made her laugh. She poured some wine and joined him on the couch. She liked when they left the pub early, when he left his friends to be with her. He was changing. Perhaps the times she was jaded with him were just her own resistance to the changes that love demanded.

"Aidan. Why do you think Gwen and Maurice are being so helpful?"

"It's their station in life, an' you can bet they're makin' loads of money off us, too."

Janice eyed him through the dark red filter of her glass. He looked more poetic in the candle light. "What about the other stuff you said about her being a Lenanshee?"

"Did she say anythin' to you about that?"

"Of course she did. It was the first thing we talked about."

"Yer kiddin', right?" He swallowed his wine and held his glass up for more.

"Why do you think she is getting so involved with my work?"

"Maybe she fancies you."

"Down boy, you'll upset the table with your enthusiasm. Have some more wine instead."

"Are you tryin' to get me drunk?"

"You've never needed my help before, and no, I'm trying to get myself drunk." She raised her glass to her face; her eye looked huge as it watched him. "Life is so much clearer through rose-coloured glasses. I think that's your problem – you look at the world through pints of black stout."

"How many have you had?"

"This is my first of the day, if you don't count the bottle that kept me company all night. But it doesn't count if you never go to sleep, right? And we can't count those at the pub; that was social. None of that brooding stuff, eh, Aidan? None of that."

"Has she ever . . . ya know?"

"What? Has she ever come on to me?"

"No. Of course I'm not askin' that but now that you mention it."

Janice smiled. She teased her hair close to her face. "You'd like to see us drinking wine from each other's lips." She ran her hand across the opening of her shirt, forcing buttons apart, exposing herself as she leaned forward. He was entranced as she ran her tongue along her lips. "We'd take turns caressing each other while we moaned and groaned." She paused to moisten her lips. "Then we'd press our naked bodies together."

His lips curled between a smile and a leer and his eyes glazed. She laughed and poured her wine over his head.

"What the fuck. What did you do that for?"

"Forget it; it doesn't happen in real life." She rose and refilled her glass. "I'm going to bed."

He watched her leave as the wine trickled through his hair. They just needed to get away for a little while, and the trip to Brussels would be perfect.

But he got drunk on the plane: one of the attendants had read his poems. She brought extra pillows and a blanket and hovered, never far away.

"Very well," Janice smiled as the pretty young blonde brought him another free drink.

"What was that?" the made-upped face inquired without taking her eyes off Aidan.

"I said 'very well,' bring me a Scotch."

"I'll have to charge you."

"Bring it."

"Ah, Janice, what's the matter with you now? She's just bein' friendly."

He slurred and swayed as the lights broiled him. She stood at the back of the room, and her heart ached. She wanted to lead him somewhere dark and cool, but the crowd thought it was part of the act. They were mostly ex-pats and those who worked so hard to be seen as culturally aware.

They rose to their feet as he stumbled through his last reading. It was a very clever debate between an up-and-coming businessman, a country priest who was Saint Patrick reincarnate and a Dublin docker who was clearly Aidan. They discussed the European Union in mystical and symbolic terms. It was the best piece he'd written, and she wished he was sober, to do it justice. But he wasn't, and when he muffed the last and most important lines, he looked up and blinked into the warm glow of applause. He gripped the lectern, looking for the right thing to say, but he couldn't find it.

She went backstage and found him lighting a cigar in a circle of ribboned ringlets and embroidered set dancers. The girls were jigging and giggling as she approached. "Aidan, are you taking up dancing now?"

"I could do a fair old step in my day." He jammed his two arms stiffly by his sides, raised himself on his toes and kicked his right leg into air. He had poise and grace until gravity reacted and he fell in among the Tara brooches and a cascade of arms, legs and ribbons. His cigar was burning a hole in someone's cape.

"Ah, for fuck's sake, Janice, gimme a hand."

"Let's go for a walk darling?"

"Can we get somethin' to drink?"

"Sure, let's just walk until we find a nice little pub where we can be alone." She took the green ribbon that had gotten caught between his shirt and his pants and let it flutter to the ground. "Come on, let's go."

As time passed, he was able to walk without staggering and speak without slurring, but he was getting cranky. "For fuck's sake, Janice, there has to be a pub somewhere."

"There's one just up ahead, darling, they even have Stella Artois."

"Who's she?"

"She's a blonde, with great breasts and lots of make-up."

"Jazus, Janice. That sounds great. Are ya up for a three-way?"

"Sure! Let's make it a foursome, you, me and two Stellas."

"You're all right Janice, ya know that?" He tried to kiss her, but she nudged him with her elbow, almost knocking him over as they stepped onto the patio.

"Due-os Stellas Artwas, sil-vous-play," Aidan smiled at the waiter whose disdain was totally wasted, "et mercy-bow-coo."

"Why was givin' me a funny look?" he added as the waiter shrugged and stomped off.

"Perhaps he's a Walloon."

"What?"

"Never mind."

"What's the matter now?"

"Nothing."

As they waited, he lit another cigar and Janice looked at the night. The air was warm, hinting of summer when everything would change. If the year went the way Maurice and Gwen seemed to think, she and Aidan would go somewhere warm and bright before the winter returned. If they had a really good year, they could think about moving to Paris. He could drink coffee all day, in the café on the street below her loft, like a great big guard dog. She had to get him away from Dublin before he drank himself to death. Why did she ever get involved with a poet?

But he was and they'd find their way like all those lovers who fled through the woods, making great sacrifices and finding true love on the other side. The stories always glossed over the bad parts when fears and doubts tore at them. If only he didn't . . .

"Grey facades, all around the Square.

"Buildings tall and Flemish

"Somber and brooding

"At the crossroads of Europe.

"The epicenter of Europe."

It was far from his best, but what could she expect?

He knew she was disapproving of something; he just wasn't sure what; there was always something. She was probably getting tired of him; they all did sooner or later. He had hoped it'd be different with her. She was an artist, too, and shouldn't get hung up on all the shitty little things. She was going to be the one to lead him away from the darkness but he knew that he'd fuck it up. "What's the name of this place anyway?"

"It is called the Grote Market."

"What the fuck is a Gruet?"

"It's a type of three-legged goat. They were sold at the market here, for satanic sacrifice." She smothered her smile as he gazed at her in admiration.

"How the fuck do you know that?"

"Because I'm a lot smarter than you."

"If you're so fuckin' smart then whatcha ya doin' with me," he reasoned as he drained his glass and gestured to the waiter. "Due-os Stellas, encore et merci-buckets." The waiter frowned at Janice as he left.

"Killing time until the waiter gets off work." She looked into his eyes like he was no longer there, just a glazed imitation with a round foolish face.

"Ah, Jazus Janice, yer all right, ya know that? I mean you're so fuckin' talented an' all, an' you put up with me. You're the best! Let's go back an' have an old shag for ourselves. Do ya have any idea where the hotel is?"

"It's a few blocks that way." She pointed past his head.

"Jazus, Janice, ya have great tits." He had lolled into her lap.

"Oh, Aidan, you'll have my panties off in a moment."

"There are two things that I don't like about what you just said," he confided to her navel. "The first is that I don't know what the fuck a block is — an' they're not panties, puffters wear panties. Over here, girls wear knickers. Second thing was . . ."

She should get him home while he could still walk. He would want to have sex, but that wouldn't be a problem. He would fall asleep as soon as he lay down, while she stayed in the bathroom. She sipped her beer and stroked his hair, twisting curls and letting them spring free. He reeked of beer and tobacco. He was trapped in the boozy personality he'd created. His calculated drunkenness had gained him enough notoriety but now trapped him in caricature. It was sad and predictable and worst of all — she needed him for a while yet. She wasn't ready to do it on her own. She'd need someone to talk to at night, someone who understood her and the thousand and one thoughts that flashed across her mind.

But Aidan was wandering down the paths that had led him here. He'd gone to see Gwen in the Garden of Remembrance, just before they left. He'd been there the day it opened, too, back in nineteen-sixty six. His father held him on his shoulders so he could see the President.

'That's Dev himself. He's the man who sent the Brits packin'.'

'He did fuck all,' Uncle Tadhg added from beside Aidan's knee.

'Would you ever go and shite, you and Collins and all the fuckin' Free Staters, you'se gave away the North.'

'Ah now,' said the man in front of them, 'don't be bringing that up. Today we're here to remember all that died for Ireland.'

'Who the fuck asked you, ya gobshite?' the two brothers asked in unison. 'Mind your own fuckin' business before I give you a dig.'

'Two of them,' Uncle Tadhg added from beside Aidan's knee.

"How delightful to see you, Aidan, how are you?" She seemed relaxed as they walked by the cruciform pool where images of ancient weapons lay submerged in the hope of appeasing the gods that enticed men to war.

"I think you know."

"Aidan, let's not have any unpleasantness."

"I want you to take me back."

"Just like that?"

"Ya and I want you to stay away from Janice, too. She's no idea about any of this."

"Aidan, there was a time when your drunken ramblings amused me, but you ended it, remember?"

"I know and I'm sorry about that." He reached for her, but she turned and climbed the steps to where the wall curved and caught the sun behind the bronze sculpture: the children of Lir, released from a wicked spell, free of the enchantment that had held them for nine hundred years, free to falter into old age.

"Aidan, darling, let us leave it at that. We have enjoyed a wonderful time together, but you ended it. I was hurt, Aidan, by that, but I respected your wishes and now I would ask that you respect mine."

"Well, if that's the case, I'd ask that you stay the fuck away from Janice, too."

"What do you think I am? And besides, what's done is done; you know how these things are. Look at this," she pointed to the four aged people descending into dotage as swans strained toward the heavens. "They were changed back, just as they wished."

"Look, it wasn't my fault. I made a mistake for fuck's sake. It was all old Gerry's idea anyway."

Gwen turned on her heel and clattered down the steps. She might have to do something about that. She couldn't have the dregs of Grogan's spoiling things for her now. But she wasn't concerned; it was only a matter of time before Aidan ruined himself anyway.

She trailed her hand in the pool as she passed, leaving a long ambiguous ripple. She would have to find someone else for Janice, too, she didn't want her to get lonely and leave.

He raised his head from her lap and swallowed some beer. He blinked at the night and lowered his head again. "I'm fucked now; ya know that, right fucked."

"What's the matter?"

"I'm finished with the 'Twilight,' this is my last gig. Maurice told me that I had to sign for another two books before we left. The bastard must have known that I was holding back on them," he glanced at Janice, "that's almost all of the work I hadn't told them about." He drained his glass with resignation. "Anyway, he told me that if I didn't, he'd have me removed from the tour when we get back."

"And what did you say?" His smoke drifted around her like a conspiracy.

"I told him, 'You can stuff your fuckin' Press up your arse,' that's what I told him. But what I should've said was that he can stuff his fuckin' wife, too, 'cos I'm tired shaggin' her."

"But you didn't?"

"No, but I should've rubbed his smug little face in his own shit. I mean, I'm fucked anyway."

"You don't think he's really going to ruin you?" She patted his head until it was back on her lap where she could hold it for a little while.

"You don't know Dublin, do ya? If Maurice and Gwen say you're finished, then you're fucked altogether."

She ran her fingers through his hair. She needed to change the mood. "Why don't you go to London and talk to some people there."

"Ah, Janice, I'd an emotional bond with the Twilight. It meant somethin' gettin' published by them. It's part of Dublin, just like me."

"Oh, Aidan, you're a drunken fool."

"Of course, I'm drunk, and you'd be, too, if you lost your Muse."

She was afraid something would come along and shatter everything, but she didn't expect it here. He was falling apart and she couldn't despise him for that. He'd done it for her. It was like one of those epic sacrifices you read about. Only, in those stories, you never get to read about what happens in the happy ever after. "I suppose this is what happens when the angel woos the clay."

She had never asked him to stop seeing Gwen, at least not on a professional level. It had nothing to do with her. It was between him and Gwen and Maurice.

"Huh. What are you sayin'?"

"I was saying you shouldn't worry, everything will work out just fine."

In time, she had to rouse his head from her lap. She took his arm as they headed off into the night.

"Bon Swar, Bon Swar my bon barman."

"Janice."

"What now?"

"That sound's makin' me wanna piss."

"What sound? Oh! Now I can hear it."

The narrow street broadened as they approached the crossroads and saw where the sound was coming from. A small stone boy was pissing into the fountain.

"It's the Manneken Pis. I'd forgotten it was here."

She stepped back to get a better view in the uneven glow of the streetlights and could just make out a proud little smile between two full cheeks. He was leaning back with his knees bent, enjoying his eternal release. Aidan, too, was leaning back with bent knees and dueled with the fountain.

"Oh, for Christ's sake, Aidan; sometimes, you can be disgusting."

"I was just sendin' Stella off home, before we go to bed, ya know."

"You shouldn't have done that, Genius. Now you're going to have to sleep alone."

"Ah, bollocks, Stella? Stella? STELLA!"

Janice struggled into her apartment, wrestling her baggage through the doorway. She picked up the pile of letters as she glanced through the hallway, marched to her bedroom and fell on her bed. She wanted to claim it before he did. It had all unraveled again in the taxi from the airport.

'Menstruatin', is that still allowed?'

'You have no idea what I'm talking about, do you?'

'Course I do, I just don't wanna talk about, all right?'

'That is because you can't decide if it's thinking, chewing or wanking.'

'Janice, c'mon, yer man's listenin',' he nodded toward the driver.

She just smiled, but it withered when he got out with her, she had hoped to have some time alone.

As long as she stayed in her room, she would be fine. She ran her hand through her hair and felt the letter she'd dropped on her pillow. She tore the side off the envelope and looked inside. There, among the carefully folded sheets, were a thousand sleeping words. They seemed harmless, but Janice knew better. If she unfolded the creased pages, those words would buzz around her head and fill her ears with noise and subtle condemnations. It was such a small package for such great incessantness. But it was magnetic.

Her mother hoped she was happy with the way things had turned out. Robert was getting married.

'*Dear, you know I love you. And you know I have always tried to give you the best because I believed in my little girl. I believed she would grow up to be a fine young woman who would always choose right from wrong. I never believed I would live to see such a selfish act.*'

Janice stopped reading and let the letter fall to the floor. It wasn't really news, she had read about it since Robert got engaged. But a part of her was smarting: he wasn't supposed to move on, at least not until she had. A door had closed; there was no going back. She had to move along a path that would never lead to where she came from. She could only move forward to whatever the future might hold. She just needed a few moments to let it all settle.

"Janice, are ya decent in there? I'm after cuttin' my hand. Can ya come out and get me a bandage?"

"And I gave up Robert for you?"

"Robert? Did he write ya? Did he send us any money?"

"Not this time, sweetie. The letter was from my mother."

"And how is the old darlin'? Did she ask about me? Did she Janice?"

Chapter 13

It was the main floor of an old townhouse with huge windows and high ceilings: a stoic redbrick of fading elegance with a Georgian door, obscured by a century of paint, between ornately carved pillars, crowned by a fanlight and centered by a speckled-greened brass knocker: the face of a river god with a ring through his ears. They spent a sunny afternoon buffing until it was no longer green.

"That's the same face as the old tenner," he repeated until she proved him wrong. She loved to show him how much she knew about 'his' Dublin.

"Fair enough," he muttered. "Are ya happy now?"

"Come on, god's face is clean enough. I'll buy you a pint," she offered in truce.

But when it came to decorating, she didn't compromise. He'd wanted to bring his things, but she preferred the furnishings Gwen and Maurice offered, including the old, hand-carved, four-poster that had been in his family for years.

The drawing-room had ornate moldings and a large fireplace. Aidan's armchair looked great in the corner where he had plenty of space for books, if only he'd put them back. Sliding doors opened to their bedroom that looked out on the sunroom, abutting the large but poorly equipped kitchen, a part of which had been sectioned off as a modern bathroom. It was brightly painted and Janice added innumerable plants that withered within days.

"It's like pissin' in the jungle in there."

"Well, try not to piss on the vegetation and lower the seat when you're done," but she smiled sweetly. He was struggling to reform himself. He had started to go for walks like Austin Clarke, but sometimes, she smelled beer on his breath when he returned. She wanted to call him on that but he was making an effort, and besides, she did not want him underfoot all the time.

"I gotta go out. Do you need anythin'?"

"Milk and bread, more cheese and wine."

When the phone rang she thought it was him. He'd probably met someone and would be late.

"Janice, darling, we are in the neighbourhood." She wanted to make sure Aidan wasn't there. "We don't want the two bulls to lock horns again."

"No," Janice replied. "He'll be out all day." She waited by the window until they arrived. Maurice tumbled out first and bustled to the passenger side and held the door as Gwen emerged with such elegance that Janice had to smile.

"We haven't seen you since Brussels."

Janice almost blushed in her gaze until Maurice bustled by, separating them. "I trust that damn ingrate will not intrude."

"Now, Maurice, Janice had nothing to do with that. Did you, darling?" she added as she linked arms. "How are you managing?"

"Oh, Gwen, I love the place; it's perfect, but we haven't discussed rent." Aidan had suggested she bring it up, just to be sure.

"Let us not discuss money, darling, it is such a common vulgar thing. And, besides, you and Aidan can help to keep an eye on the place. Maybe even help with the upkeep?"

"Can we get the cover and get out before he shows up?" Maurice grumbled from Aidan's chair.

"Maurice, you are being rude."

"Humph!"

Janice smiled and handed over the print for Aidan's cover; a plain charcoal of the Yeats monument from the back before an assorted gathering of vague shapes. She wanted to discuss a fee but that would have been a common vulgar thing to do. Maurice was impressed and moved to the window to examine it in better light. "Capitol, Janice, capitol."

"Aidan really liked it, too."

Gwen's smile froze and beckoned Janice to the kitchen.

"Darling, avoid mentioning Aidan's name. The damn thug threatened Maurice."

"Gwen, I am sorry, but I don't want things to go badly for him. Isn't there anything we can do?"

Gwen smiled, even as her eyes narrowed. "Let us wait until after London and then I will talk to Maurice. I am sure it will all blow over. But right now, we need to concentrate on you, darling. And besides, let Aidan wander in the wilderness for a while, it will do wonders for his poetry, and his humility." She led her back to the drawing room. "Come on, Maurice. I am sure Janice has work to do."

They kissed the air between them again as Maurice grunted from the armchair.

Outside, he started to grumble, but Gwen was ready. "Darling, let us observe Janice's wishes. After all, we should indulge her while she is working – you know what artists are like."

"Of course, Bridey, forgive me."

She smiled as she had often done before, that please-do-not-intrude smile; it was really very charming. But behind it all, she had a lot to think about.

Maurice looked over as he nudged the car though traffic. She was getting damn skittish again, and he couldn't wait to get out of the city. Perhaps they could stop for a drink when they got to the mountains.

"They only came by to pick up the cover."

"Did they offer to pay for it?"

"Is that all they are to you?"

"They're Horse-Protestants, Janice."

They had been flirting with an argument since they woke, simmering in careless moments when casual disregard could be seen as contempt – off-handed moments that were of so little consequences in hindsight. It all boiled over when she made coffee; it was too mild for his 'refined Irish palette.' He had asked for maple syrup to give it some body, because 'Americans know nothing about coffee.'

She stood before him with her hands on her hips.

"You know, you are smothering me with your cultural imperialism. I am interested, but I don't wish to be drowned in the vulgar collection of anecdotes that you call history. That's why I'm studying at Trinity – the University that does not accept people like you." The cultural imperialist comment had been designed to cut deeply and the 'anecdotes' was the salt in the wound, but he smiled and held up the dime he had found in her jacket pocket. He carried it as a talisman ever since.

"This is the Bluenose, the champion of the Cod fleet that was never defeated in a hundred races."

It was a concession – not a personal one, but it would do. She wanted to kiss him, but as she leaned forward, he continued. "It was sold as a coal scow and lost in a storm off the Caribbean, so much for Canadian cultural pride!"

"Fuck you, darling." Janice left him in the drawing room and went to her sanctuary.

Clouds were piled on top of each other. He turned up his collar and lit his cigar as he walked down the garden path. The children played in Belgrave Square under the watchful eye of their nannies, eyes that followed him when he walked too close.

He strolled toward Rathmines Road and stopped to look at the house where Joyce had lived before he gave up and moved to France. It was just across the road from Walter Osborne's house, something Janice loved to point out. Sometimes, when they walked that way, they walked on different sides of the street.

That tells you all you need to know, a little voice reminded him. He'd stop in at Madigan's and settle himself.

Over the first, he'd consider both points of view. He was difficult to get along with. It was his moods; he'd so little control over them. Every little thing that happened got stuck inside like niggling sand. And it happened a lot lately. Janice was an ever-changing enigma – when he thought he'd figured her out, she would do the unexpected again.

By the second, he would be less impartial; emotions would rise, obscuring clarity.

By the fourth, he would be impassioned. *That's the way with women*, he would remind himself. *They never go for the man they really want. Instead, they find some poor fucker and try to turn him into that.*

He would chew on that for a while until the little voice rose again: he wasn't what he pretended to be, either.

He shook his head and turned toward the city. He couldn't get drunk today: he had to see the reporter from the 'Hot Press' and had to stay out of the pub for a while, but even as he walked, the whispers started again, following in his wake, taunting him like children. He jumped on a passing bus and rode to the city centre. He'd wait in the Green until his mind was clear.

Ah, c'mon, one or two never did any harm.

He smiled at himself. It was so seductive, but a few drinks had a habit of stretching through the night or a blur of hazy days.

It was starting to catch up with him.

Some mornings, he would sit and stare at his first: a pool of reflection with a stiff white collar; bitterness that caused him to grimace. He'd force himself past that, swallowing as much as he dared until it settled his queasy stomach and the cold sweats passed.

The first took a while now, warming in the glass, and the last few swigs were always tepid. The second was the new hope that calmed his jangling nerves and settled his resolve. He'd just have one more.

"Fine," Janice decided as the door closed behind him. She poured a glass of French, it was early in the day, but it was okay. "I will work all day," she promised as she took her glass and bottle into the sunroom. It was bright but the garden was a sad mess of neglected roses and a stunted apple tree, bole-deep in dandelions.

We just never seem to be in sync.

She thought of her father searching for moments of peace in the endless fuss that was life with her mother. 'You can be in love with someone and still have difficulty getting along,' he once confided to her after a petty dispute with her mother. 'I guess the trick is to remember the good things when things are not so good, eh, Princess?'

"You're so right, Dad," she said to the canvas in front of her.

It was the painting she'd wanted to start for years – a painting for her father. But she couldn't decide how to paint him. Aidan stumbled on the key to that as they lay in bed one night. 'Just paint him as he appears in your mind. Don't be worryin' if he'd like it an' all that stuff ya do. Just paint him as he was to you.'

And she did but not as he was when they were together. The man in this painting was in his early twenties; hair slicked back and curled out at the ends. He wore blue jeans with a three-inch turn up at the hems. His t-shirt was tight across his chest and a cigarette hung from his lips. He leaned against the fins of a large black and white car, cleaning his hands with a rag, gazing steadily as a woman walked past.

She was tall and slender in a kingfisher blue skirt and her blonde hair held back with a turquoise scarf that hung down across her shoulder. Her waist was narrow and white belted. Her white blouse was loose and showed a peep of cleavage.

"That's yer old man?"

She hadn't noticed him standing behind her. "You're back early. Did they run out of beer, or did you run out of money?"

"Nay, the guy wants to meet later so I thought I'd take it easy for a while."

"Aidan, be careful, you're in danger of becoming temperate." She smiled more kindly than she had intended. The bottle was almost empty and she was feeling warm and forgiving. "Yes, that's my father as I think he was before he met my mother."

"Is that your Ma?"

"I don't think so."

"She's pretty hot; in a way she reminds me of you."

Janice smiled at her father; she wasn't ready to turn around. He came home to offer a truce, but she would make him wait a little. 'Reminds me of you' still floated in the cool air between them. She could reach out and savour it – when she was ready.

Sorry, Dad, I'll get back to you, she nodded to her father as she turned and smiled.

"C'mon," Janice smiled, accepting his olive branch. "I won't bite."

He shuffled in, contrite and uncertain and absentmindedly re-arranged her pots and paints. "I know I can be a pain in the arse to live with an' all, but ya gotta remember that I'm not very good at this livin' together stuff. After all, I've been on my own since my Ma died."

He gets me with that every time, Janice wrapped her arms around his waist and hugged him against her belly where she could feel him start to stir. She hated that part of her could grow cold to him. She snuggled into his chest and remembered her father and those times when she bored all the way to his heart. Aidan's heart was much harder to find. It was there, she could hear it in the pulse of his verse. She could feel it when he held her in the early morning or the times when she grew sad. She assumed it moved around because sometimes, when she needed it most, she couldn't find it.

Love, she reminded herself, *is good times and bad times, but it is the coming together again that makes it all worthwhile.*

He relaxed in her arms, like he had stepped out of the suit of armour that he wore against the world. They had got lost in the forest again. They would stay in the small open glade for now.

"I do love you, Aidan. You know that?"

"Yea, I know ya do, and I love ya, too, only I'm not as good at it as you are."

She knew him well enough by now. He just needed to be held. Something was bothering him, something that he wasn't ready to talk about. But she knew how to get him talking.

"Let's go to Grogan's, eh?"

"Ya, sure, I gotta meet yer man from 'Hot Press' there at seven. What time is it now?"

She knew he would relax in the bar, surrounded by friends and pints, charming and engaging as she nestled into his side, coy and assured like a sphinx on a Pharaoh's lap.

"Come on, we can come home early if you like," she said as they separated but she was careful to let her hand stray across his hip and over his pelvis. "If you like," she repeated.

They stepped from the drizzle into the smoky pub that was loud with full-moon madness.

Scots Corner was in full swing, arguing about everything and enjoying every moment of it. There were a few literary types at the bar, too, planning books they would never write as they drank another evening away. Aidan elbowed his way among them to get the barman's attention as Janice secured two stools by a table in the corner. She shook back her rain-beaded hair and peeled her jacket off. She crossed her legs and waited. Aidan was in conversation with someone at the bar – there was always someone! He did, however, find the time to bring her a drink and leave a couple of his small black cigars. "I'll be right back, I need to talk with this guy, ya know?"

"No problem, I'll be right here," she smiled up at him. "Sitting right here waiting to talk to you," she added under her breath.

"Ah, the price of being famous. Can I keep ya company until the Bard returns?"

"I don't know, Gerry; you know how I feel about you. I might have to make love to you, right here on the table, and then Aidan will come back and there will be such a row."

"Ah, now, Janice, I'm too old for shaggin' on table tops, but I'll take my chances and besides, it'll teach your man not to leave you alone. One of these nights, some smart young Dick, from Barcelona or Paris, is gonna walk in here and steal you right out from under his nose."

"I don't care for Spaniards but I might go for a Frenchman, my father was French-Canadian."

"Is that a fact? Now isn't that amazin'?"

Janice was at ease in the old man's company. He was as whimsical as the rest of the crowd but he was, as he said himself, past shagging on table tops. She could talk with him without any of the complications that rose when she talked with other, younger, men.

"How's the studyin' comin' along? Ya must be very wise by now."

Janice fumbled with one of Aidan's cigars; she hadn't been to school in a few weeks. There were too many things clamouring for her attention, pleading with her to be painted. Her professors had been as accommodating as they could. She had told them her mother was unwell and that she had to return to Canada for a few weeks but that lie couldn't last forever.

"Wisdom doesn't come from learning, Gerry."

"Well, it sure doesn't come with age."

"I don't know. You seem pretty wise to me."

"Ah, sure, darlin', that's awful nice of you, but if I'm wise then it's only because the whole country is goin' daft. It's like they've all been with the Lenanshee."

Janice studied him for a moment. She lit a cigar and let the smoke drift slowly from her mouth, through her dark red lips. "What do you mean, Gerry?" she asked without turning her face.

"Well, in these parts, we used to believe in the Lenanshee. She used to be a kind of a muse that bestowed great artistic talents on those that took up with her, or so the old people used to say. Those that gave their love to her were rewarded with sheer brilliance, but only for a while, like she only give 'em the loan of it. Then they would die young."

Janice stared past him at the ambiguity that hovered in the smoke.

"I'm not very familiar with that myth. I have read a little about it, of course."

"Ah, but ya see, readin' is only a part of learnin'. Ya can learn more on a night in here than in hours of listenin' to them professors down at that university of yours. Some of them want to drink in here, but Paddy finds a way to get them to move on, unless, of course, they have a bit of character. This bar has a great reputation for the characters that drink here and we have to keep that standard up. John Jordan has a lot of character and he comes in here all of the time; he's a poet, too, and he's a literary critic, ya know?"

"Yes, I've met John, a very interesting character," she tested the seat she sat on.

She had tried to talk with him once, but it was impossible. By early evening, he had moved into the nether world of dear, departed friends. There he would engage in animated conversations, his face lightening and darkening but only half of his words came out.

'Who's that strange person?' she had asked Aidan. 'And why is he talking to the wall?'

'Ah! That's John, he's harmless.'

'Who is he talking with?'

'Probably Behan and Kavanagh.'

'But they're dead.'

'Not a problem for John, when he gets to this state. But be careful where you sit.'

"Tell me more about the Lenanshee."

"Ah, sure, she used to be all over the place, years ago now, and every poet would have a go at her but she didn't seem to mind. If ya ask me, I think she was a lusty old thing."

"Oh really, the paintings I've seen all show her as a beautiful and ageless woman."

"Ah, sure, isn't that what the monks down in the old monasteries did with her."

"Really?"

"Sure of course they did. They spent all of their time taming our old pagan ways and makin' them clean and civilised for the good pious Christian world they forced on us. "At least that was what they did when they weren't buggerin' the arses off themselves. The old people used to say that the love between the poet and the Shee was a pure love with no lust at all. Well, knowing what I do about poets, a horny lot if ever there was, I can tell you that none of them would be satisfied with holding hands, not unless they got to put their peckers in and have her give it an old shake. Even then they'd want to . . ."

He stopped and stared at Janice in horror.

"What is it, Gerry. What's the matter?"

"Ah Christ, can ya ever forgive me for talking like that in front of you like you're a brasser or somethin', and I don't mean that 'cos of the way you're dressed or anything."

He stopped again and turned a deep crimson until Janice was sure he would die, but what could she say? Part of her was shocked, but most of her wanted to laugh, right in the old man's face, but she did tug at her short skirt and straightened her shoulders.

"It's okay, Gerry, relax. Tell me why you think it seems like everyone is seeing her?"

"Who's seeing who?"

"You were saying that it's like the whole country had been with the Lenanshee."

"Ah, sure, I was just thinking aloud. I didn't really mean anythin' by it."

"I don't know, Gerry, I think that's when we speak the truth, but if you want to think to yourself I can always join Aidan at the bar!"

Gerry blushed again. He never touched her, but every time she moved, he inhaled deeply like he was trying to gather her essence, something to take back to his lonely room in a dark house on a dank street on the Northside of the river.

"Gerry?"

"Ah, sure now, if ya really want to know then I may's well tell ya. I was thinking on all of this European money that is starting to pour in and all the local lads passing themselves off as businessman, and they're getting away with it too. Jazus, if only I was younger I'd show them how it's done."

"How does that fit with the Lenanshee?"

"Ah, sure, don't ya see darlin'? The Common Market is like the Lenanshee, and if we hop into bed with her, we'll get paid for it."

"Did the Lenanshee only inspire men?"

He stared at her as he lit another Woodbine. "I don't know."

He paused to consider before he continued. "It's hard to say really. I suppose it's possible. I mean, everything we know about her is from men. I suppose that back before, when women had their own say, I mean, I suppose it's possible. But why do you ask such a question?"

"Oh, it's nothing. I just wonder about things like that. There never seems to be much about women as poets and such." Janice's voiced trailed away as Gerry looked uneasy.

"If you really want to know more you should ask Aidan."

"Why do you say that?"

"No reason, it's just that he's a poet and all. Don't ya think that he might know something about that? I mean Sinead was telling me . . ."

He stopped abruptly and reached for his glass. Sometimes, he said far more than he meant to.

"Oh! And what did she have to say?"

"Oh, nothing really."

"Gerry?"

"Ah, it's nothing, girl. It's just something she mentioned a long time ago."

"What was it?"

"Oh, I can't remember now. I think it was something about his poetry being so good and all that he must be inspired or something."

They sat together in silence as they searched for something else to say. Gerry lit another cigarette from the shriveled end of the last. He coughed and beat his chest before emptying his glass. "It's just talk, ya know. It's like Beanshees and Leprechauns and all."

"Don't you think it must have some basis in fact?"

"Ah, sure, I wouldn't know about that. I'm not a scholar like you."

There was something hovering over him, something he would never share with her.

"Ya know, it doesn't really matter what you believe in," he decided as the cigarette dangled on his lip. "As long as you believe in something. I mean, it's all mythology when you think about it. Not I'm saying that the Church is wrong or anything like that, but it's no different than what we believed in before. Look at Saint Brigid: now she's a good Christian Saint, but before she was the goddess of poetry and the bards adored her. It was how they got us to believe in the new religion; they dressed her up as a nun and made her all Christian. It was easier that way."

It made sense to Janice, too.

"Ya see, Janice, this is a very backward country, and it's getting worse every day. But long ago, it was different, back when we had our own ways of doing things. We had Druids and Bards and Brehons; they were our judges, and we had good laws to keep the peace when the rest of the world was still clubbing each other and all.

"But that's all forgotten now. The English made shite of the old ways. But we got rid of them, too, and now we have all this European money to play with, but mark my words, a day will come when all this wonderful wealth, and all that it can buy, will shrivel up. And then what'll we do? We'll be a people with neither a past nor a future."

"That's a sad thought," Janice agreed as she finished her drink. She needed to get away; he was becoming a little morbid. "Well, good night, I'm going to join Aidan at the bar, we're going to have an early night."

"And you should, too; you're both young and healthy,"

Gerry lowered his head and stared at his empty glass. He would have an early night, too, he had no money left and she hadn't offered to buy him a drink.

"You'd think," he muttered to himself, "that with all of her learning that she'd know enough to buy an old man a drink for his company."

But, he added on reflection, *she has a grand arse on her. A fella could write great poetry after riding that all night, but I may's well get myself off home. There's no point in sitting here looking at my empty glass.*

He raised his collar around his face and pattered off in the soft rain and headed for the river. He stopped on the Ha'penny Bridge and looked down at the lights jigging on the dark water.

"I'm sorry," Aidan repeated as they left the bar, as Janice walked in silence, deep within herself. "I just had to talk to your man, it was important, it was about my book, and then we just got talkin' and the time flew by."

"It's okay, Aidan; it's just that I got stuck with old Gerry."

"Look, I'm sorry, it couldn't be helped and besides, he's all right."

"I suppose, but he wasn't making any sense tonight. He was rambling on about Lenanshees and things like that." Janice was walking with her head down, in the soft rain and didn't notice as he paused before falling in step with her again.

"What was he sayin'?"

"He was saying that the people of Ireland have become infatuated with a Lenanshee who will bestow great wealth on them if they adore her. And that it will all come to nothing in the end. He's not the most optimistic, is he?"

"Ah, Gerry, no, no one could ever accuse him of being too rosy. But which Lenanshee, or did he say?"

"Oh, yes, she's the European Union! I think Gerry is the maddest man in Ireland. They should hold competitions – you know, like a 'King of Fools' pageant. There should be an award for the winner, eh?"

"There is."

"Oh! And what's that?"

"The maddest man in Ireland gets to fall in love with a beautiful Canadian painter an' they live happily ever after."

"Ah, gee, Aidan, I wasn't going to stay for the happily ever after, I'm just here for the sex."

"Ya know, Janice, after you sell a few more paintings an' I publish a few more books, we should get a place on the West Coast, ya know? Somewhere where you can paint an' I can write in peace. We could sit an' listen to the ocean at night, an' the world could go an' fuck itself."

"Ah, Aidan, that is so sweet, a cottage by the sea."

Chapter 14

She put down her coffee and added watercolours: a white blob cottage thatched with a yellow smear and a blue smudged cove wrinkling to the slopes of the purple mountains. They could be happy there where the fresh winds from the Atlantic blew the mists away. And when August storms bore in, tearing at the eaves and tossing waves into the cove, they could sit close to the fire as the crackle of burning driftwood drowned out the world. She wanted them to be in love, even if only for a while. But, as she painted, the paper wrinkled and become soggy.

Since Howth, things were clearer. She understood what happened that day and why she felt she was intruding. Mythology was filled with stories of jealous gods and he had taken her there to declare his love before all that mattered. He'd taken her into his world, and even though their time together mightn't be forever, it would be fuller than anything she had known so far.

Everything had new meaning since Howth: everything, including his feelings for her. She could see herself in his eyes: a dark and smoldering Lorelie inspiring him with sprinklings of Neruda. He pored over her father's copy for weeks, leaving it all around the flat.

Life with him was haphazard: sometimes, they did the craziest things. Once, he arranged a midnight picnic on Dollymount Strand. But it might have been better suited to the Caribbean or a Greek island. Irish beaches were cold and damp at night and when they made love, she stayed on top of him. He didn't seem to mind, even when the cold tide reached for his ankles.

Then there was the time when he carried her brushes and paints up a mountain: she wanted to paint his naked body and have him pose as an ancient Celtic warrior.

'Are you sure they used blue paint? Maybe they were all just fuckin' freezin'?'

It was embarrassing and silly at first, but she found herself being drawn into it – until a passing car stopped and a gaggle of children and dogs came bounding toward them. Janice couldn't help but laugh as Aidan's freshly coloured bottom scurried for cover under a gorse bush. She spent the whole evening washing the paint from his scratched and bruised body. The gorse bush stood at the edge of a fifteen-foot drop to a stony riverbank. He still wasn't ready to laugh about that, but at least he no longer got mad when she re-enacted the scene for him.

'And this is you running for cover,' she pretended to run before flopping on the bed.

'And this is you at the bottom.' She lay distorted, like a swastika.

But dark clouds were gathering, too; he had to go to London to find a publisher.

And there was something else, something that often happened since Howth, happening more and more. They would be talking when he would trail off somewhere, away from her. At first, she would call him, and he'd return with a frown, like he didn't know where he had been. She wanted him to see a doctor, but he assured her that it was tiredness or that he was thinking of his writing. She didn't believe him and pushed a few more times.

'Ya know that even when I'm starin' out the window, I'm still workin'.'

She knew she'd pushed him and he was pushing back. She knew the pattern from the first few weeks when their polished personae began to come apart at the seams. So she didn't mention the doctor again: she would go to her room and paint.

When he followed, he'd say he'd been sleeping.

And sometimes, he was still where she had left him, and when he woke, he wore a scowl, like he had returned from somewhere he'd have rather stayed.

She'd almost finished packing when he came back. He'd gone to see somebody about something but he remembered to drop by the off-license. She'd made pasta, and they were out of wine.

"I got Mouton Cadet; they were out of the officers."

"Just two, oh, dear, I guess we have to make it an early night. Come here, taste this. Why are you opening both?"

"We can have one while the other is breathin'."

"I'm impressed by your logic."

"Your sauce is pretty good, too, for an American."

He carried the bottles and glasses to the table and returned for the bread. "How come there are no knives?"

"We're having spaghetti."

"Oh!"

"You like spaghetti."

"It's all right, I suppose."

She smiled as he chased strands of pasta around his plate. He cranked his wrist a few more times before he thought to watch her. Slyly, he raised his glass between them.

"To my Canadian Darlin'," he lowered his glass and raised his spoon with a dexterity he had learned on the street.

"To a very successful trip," she raised her glass before her eye.

"You look like Sauron when you do that."

"You look like a . . . actually, you look really good in red."

By the time he woke, his taxi was waiting, but he took the time to kiss her before he left.

By the time she rose, he was trekking around London trying to sell himself. She didn't want to think about that. The world was such a harsh place, especially for those who walked the forest alone.

She shivered like she did when the whispering of the past swirled around her. Since Howth, they often spoke of doubt and deception, and when the wind played with the windows of her studio, they cackled. They were alone in the woods, and now, when she thought of being secure, she thought of Gwen. But Aidan wasn't happy that she was spending so much time with her. It was almost like they were pulling her in different directions.

She picked up whiskey to welcome him back – and some cheese and a few bottles of wine. She wished he had called. It felt like he had been away for days. But, she decided as she finished the first glass, she would work. It was all she could do while Fate sorted itself out.

She sipped her glass and studied her canvas: she couldn't get the face right but the rest was getting there, a red and black bedroom with Gothic lace and a solid four-poster. His head was thrown back on dark satin sheets.

She added the women during the first bottle and cleaned her brushes before opening the second.

His eyes should be staring more, but when she lowered her glass, she was smiling.

He lay with hands above his head, wrists crossed as though they were bound. A green glow hovered above him. His body was drenched in sweat and his hips arched toward the vague but obvious shape.

Janice sat back on the couch to get a different view and placed the bottle within reach.

I need to make her more transparent. But she was happy and filled her glass again.

It was almost time; he should be getting on the plane soon.

She left the wheel of Brie in the wrapper, between the crackers and the kitchen knife and the long tapered candles. She curled her legs beneath her and wrapped herself in a blanket. It was ugly, but it was warm and still smelled a little like Aidan. He would be home soon, but she could catch a brief nap. Her hair would be a mess, but sometimes, that made her look sexy. She closed her eyes and drifted off to where her paintings were a reality.

To where he lay naked on their bed as a green glow hovered above him. Janice wanted to cover him with her body but couldn't move and had to watch as the phantasm stretched along his body. He groaned and thrust up to meet it. His skin glistened with sweat, and his eyes were glazed. Green hands stroked his skin, causing it to shudder until the Shee rose like a Godiva and plunged its fingers into his chest. It tore out his heart and held it aloft while screaming a shrill silent noise.

He stood in the drawing room with the evening's mist beading on his coat. His hair was plastered to his head. He hadn't shaved and smelled of whiskey. She was about to take him in her arms, to cover his heart with hers but paused; there was something wrong.

He slumped into the chair opposite her and poured a large whiskey.

"How was London?"

"Fuckin' great, I'd have been better tryin' to sell myself in a convent."

He didn't want to talk, but he knew she would keep asking. "Well, ya may's well hear it from me. London was a total fuckin' waste of time. Maurice got to everybody there, too."

"What do you mean?"

She sat up and reached for him but he recoiled.

"I mean the filthy little bugger fucked me. He told everybody that I took money for a book that I won't deliver. Now nobody will touch me. Fuckin' West Brits, I should get a few of the lads an' go down and burn the bastards out. That would fuckin' show them that they can't mess with me."

"Aidan. I'm so sorry." She rose and tried to take him in her arms, but he pushed her back.

"Don't. I don't want to be touched."

"But, Aidan, you need to calm down. Let me get you some coffee."

"I don't fuckin' want coffee."

"What about some cheese?" She cut a small slice from the wheel and raised it between him and his glass.

"I don't want fuckin' cheese."

"Aidan. Please let me get you something."

"I don't want any fuckin' cheese or coffee. Why buy this shite anyway? It's like eating sperm an' snot mixed together."

"Aidan! Why are you taking this out on me?"

He poured another whiskey and glared at her.

"What the fuck are you on about? I'm the one who is gettin' shafted here, as if you didn't know."

"Know what, Aidan? What are you talking about?"

"You know fine fuckin' well what I'm talkin' about. You an' that bitch, that's what I'm talkin' about. I know you have been seein' her behind my back. I know the two of you have been havin' a great laugh at my expense. That's why she is doin' all of these things for you? It's just so they can get back at me."

"Aidan, it's not like that."

"Shut the fuck up an' leave me alone, will ya?"

She wanted to touch his face to stop him talking, but there was a crazed look in his eyes that said: Keep Out. She slumped back on the couch and watched him for a while.

"I am tired of you locking me out."

"What the fuck are ya on about now, who the fuck locked you out?"

"You do, you bastard. Every time we argue, a wall goes up."

She knew he was lost in the forest. It was no use calling out to him. He would stay silent and retreat to a bower within. She should let it lie, but she had to know what else was in there with him. "Why won't you let me in?"

"Cos I can do just fuckin' fine on my own."

"Really, well, I don't think that is quite true. I think you're afraid of what's in there with you."

"In fuckin' where?"

"In the forest."

"What fuckin' forest are ya on about. Talk sense, woman!"

"You're frightened, Aidan. Face it, we both are. We have wandered too far into the woods, and now we're lost. It's like you once said to me, we give anything to be known but we never consider the price we have to pay. We've surrendered everything we were for our art. We sold our souls to Gwen and Maurice. They hold our destinies in their hands. We just have to accept that."

"Is that what you think, ya fuckin' Princess? Well, let me tell ya somethin'. I still write poems for my people, ya know? Not spoiled little college girls who think they're artists because some fuckin' Horse-Protestant tells them that. Do you know why they say that? Well, I will tell ya."

He tore her hands away from her ears. "Ya'll wanna hear this, Princess. Look at me when I am talkin' to ya. Look at me, ya bitch!"

Janice's eyes glazed as the pain splashed across her face and she slumped to the floor.

He knelt before her and carefully took her chin in his hand. His breath was acrid and his face was twisted with hatred. "They tell ya that because it gets whores like you to drop your knickers, it's cheaper than getting' it on the streets. That's why they do it."

She lay on the floor and watched his shoes turn and leave for the door. They stepped from view as it closed with a finality that rattled the bookshelves and pounded in her ears, but she didn't move.

She could almost see herself from above as if she was someone else, like the person she had once been before she gave a huge part of herself to him.

He had no right to hit you — you can't stay with a man who does that, you know better.

I do know better, I know that I should've let it lie. I shouldn't have pushed it so far.

How much of yourself are you going to give?

Everything I have to.

She hauled herself to the couch and pulled the phone toward her. She sobbed as she explained and cried as she put the handset down. Gwen said she would be right over.

The cold wet cloth stung her cheek and she cried against Gwen's shoulder, her tears dampening the crisp whiteness of her shirt, making it saggy and grey. "I'm sorry, Gwen. I'm so sorry."

"Hush, darling," Gwen refolded the cloth to a cool side and wiped her face again, wiping away the warm tears that had trickled down her throbbing cheek. Gwen was trembling, but her face was calm as her cool fingers combed Janice's hair back from her face. "Let's get you warm, darling," she added as she wrapped Janice in the ugly blanket. "Stay here while I make some tea."

"I would rather have wine," Janice sobbed as she reached for the bottle.

"In time, darling, but first, let me make you some tea, it will relax you."

"Here, drink this now."

Janice sat up and took the hot cup in her trembling hands. The tea was dark and bitter and left a green tang on her tongue. She grimaced at the taste.

"It is herbal, darling; it will help you to relax. Come on, drink a little more."

"It tastes like dandelions," Janice slobbered through her tears.

"Of course it does, darling. It is from my garden. Drink some more, please."

Janice felt the warm tea inside her, a comforting feeling that spread through numbness and pain. She sat back against the couch, pulling her knees to her chin and rocked back and forth. Little ripples of comfort trickled through her, and now, when she replayed the moment he hit her, she didn't shudder. Now she just blinked in disbelieve.

"I can't believe it. I can't . . ."

"Hush, darling," Gwen lit candles, lifted bottles from the floor, wrapped Janice in another blanket – one of her blankets and poured herself a glass of wine. "Have a little more tea, and do not be afraid. I will be here with you."

Janice blinked as she held her cup up for more. Gwen's face glowed from the gloom, smiling Cheshirely, calm and warm in the dancing glow of candlelight that dueled with the dark shadows that danced around the walls, shapes like men and women, shapes like horses with wind combed manes galloping on dancing seas, shapes that confused her.

"You are safe, now darling." Gwen's voice seemed to come from those shadows. "Have a little more tea, it will help you." Her eyes sparkled in the flickering light, like a lake through lace curtains, and Janice felt a little more secure.

"Ah, Gwen, I know you tried to warn me, but I didn't listen. Please, come and sit beside me. I need someone to hold me right now."

Gwen rose like a willow, with her lake-laced eyes, but her smile was warm. She sat beside her and took her in her arms. She stroked Janice's hair and coaxed her head against her shoulder and rocked gently back and forth. "Sometimes, we are the victims of Fate, darling. We think we are steering our own course when really we are just small boats on the tide."

Her pearls reflected the candlelight: little orbs of red and yellow, peeping through the folds of her shirt, open to the third button, a crisp white shirt with a grey damp stain on one shoulder. Janice had never realised how beautiful she was. Her skin was clear and perfect, almost like, and it caused a flutter when she realised it, alabaster! And now her eyes were different, too, more like veils parting, revealing a long crystal tunnel to somewhere red and yellow and flecked with a dark green.

"Gwen?"

"Yes, darling," Gwen ran her fingers across Janice's brow and touched her temple for a moment.

"Is it true? Is the stuff about you being a Lenanshee really true?"

"What?" Gwen laughed as she tussled Janice's hair. "What on earth has Aidan being telling you about me?"

She laughed with her head back and Janice's head slipped from her shoulder, toward her breast. Her long cool fingers stroked Janice's hair for a moment before they lifted her face. Gwen's lace-veiled eyes were billowing outward, almost into Janice's soul.

"He said you were his Muse, that you inspired him and in return . . ."

But she never got to finish. Gwen wrapped her palm against her mouth, her other arm snared her waist, drawing the two of them together, almost lip to lip. Janice's eyes darted back and forth and her pupils were huge. Gwen smiled as Janice's breathing increased, drawing air through the scented hand and then her breathing grew shallow. It was just a little way to go now.

She surrendered meekly, her hair tumbling out as Gwen rose from the couch and carried her to her bed. She giggled as Gwen leaned over and tried to undress her, pearls glowing with dull warmth in the dark bedroom.

"Gwen, I want you to be my . . ."

"Hush, hush, hush."

Gwen kissed her brow and held her until she was calm. She tugged on the covers, pulling them over the uplifted arm and the soft breast that had spilled through open buttons. She pulled the covers to Janice's chin and reached forward again with her lips searching in the dark and the dim red and yellow lights that had followed them from the other room. Janice was calm and drifting, slower and slower.

"Sleep now, darling," she ran her hand through Janice's hair, smoothing it back from her face. "Sleep now. We can talk tomorrow." She rose from the bed and walked toward the door, "I will be in the other room if you need anything. Good night, darling."

But Gwen never went to sleep. She sat on the couch, drinking wine and poking the flickering flames with long needles of wax she had peeled from the candles.

As the light flared, she saw the soft watercolour: the white cottage, yellow thatched, in a sheltered blue cove by the edge of the ocean that wrinkled where it met the slopes of the purple mountain. She twisted the paper into a long taper and touched the end to the candle. It burned slowly, filling the room with acrid smoke.

Janice woke late as sunlight filtered through her drapes.

Gwen was tapping on the door, with a steaming mug of coffee in her hand.

"Are you awake, darling?" She hesitated as Janice rose, as her exposed breasts rose above the covers.

Gwen placed the coffee on the bedside table and went to the closet. She grabbed a plain powder blue shirt and wrapped Janice's shoulders, coaxing her arms into the sleeves and fumbled with the buttons.

"How are you feeling?"

Janice flopped back on her pillows, her hair cascading out behind her, her half-buttoned shirt drawing back like curtains, her eyes clouding a little as they widened.

She was about to rise again when Gwen sat on the edge of the bed. She stroked Janice's hair and looked deep into her eyes. They were clearer now, clear but with a hint of shadow that hadn't been there before, a shadow that swirled and could become dark thoughts that might lurk for years.

But Janice was okay. Her face was red and a little yellow. It would bruise but she could hide it with makeup and dark glasses. Gwen wanted to take her in her arms, but she couldn't. What comfort could there be?

She had spent the night with it, poking at it from every angle, but there was no way around it. She was as governed by the Fates as anyone. She was bound to accept love, but this was a woman's, delicate and enduring but brittle around the edges.

"Gwen, I feel so strange. What was in the tea?"

"Nothing, darling, just some herbs to help you sleep."

"Well, it certainly did that. I think I must have passed out."

She looked down at the powder blue shirt and frowned.

"Gwen? Did we do anything last night?"

Gwen just smiled, like she expected the question. "Janice, what on earth has Aidan been saying about me?"

She showered until the water grew cold and her skin turned white, except for the angry red blotches. She had scrubbed until it hurt, but she still felt shame.

She stared at the angry mark on her reflected face. She almost wished Sinead was there: she would know what to say. She always knew what to say to make things right again. Gwen didn't do that. With Gwen, she felt she was always being tested or something.

She combed her hair tight against her head, away from her pale and bruised face and wrapped herself in her warm fluffy robe, the white one that made her feel like the Faerie Queen. That almost made her smile.

Gwen sat by the kitchen table, drinking coffee and smoking one of Aidan's cigars, hurriedly stubbing it out. "Sorry, darling, I just needed to smoke and I found it by his desk. I am sorry, it was very gauche."

Janice smiled as she sat across from her. "You know that shirt you wrapped me in? It was one of Aidan's, now that was gauche."

"I am sorry, darling; I just didn't want you to get cold. More coffee? Darling, we do need to talk about what happened between you and Aidan."

She held Janice's hand and looked deep into her eyes, drawing out the horror and shame, the indignation and the revulsion as Janice sobbed and cried and blurted out every detail until she shuddered and shriveled up inside her robe.

"Aidan had no right, you know that, darling, don't you? This is his shame. Never forget that. This is not something for you to let into your heart. It could grow inside you until its poison spreads and destroys you slowly, unnoticed at first. You end up misshapen by his distortion, passed on like a plague. Hurt people hurt people."

"Gwen?"

"Forgive me, darling, it's just that I am in some way responsible for all of this. I did spread a bit of a stink about him. It was petty of me, but I was hurt. I felt that he owed us something after all that we had given him. It was vindictive, but I never meant for it to turn out like this. I am so sorry that you paid the price."

"Gwen. Aidan did this, not you."

"I know, darling, but I provoked him."

"I am okay, Gwen. I just have to take it easy for a few days, until I calm down inside, but I'll be fine."

She would. She just needed time and she would need love. She had blurted it out before, but she still needed to ask, just to be sure. "Gwen, did I do anything last night; anything I shouldn't have done?"

"Don't be silly, darling."

"Gwen. I wanted to."

Gwen hesitated as she gathered her composure and smiled.

"Janice, you have been through a horrible ordeal. You are confused right now. Over the next few days, you may find things are like a roller-coaster. You may find yourself having very confused thoughts and feelings or saying things that otherwise might not be said. I am concerned about that. Are you going to be all right here alone?"

"Alone?" It hadn't occurred to Janice. He wasn't coming back. She wondered if she would ever miss him again.

"Is there anybody who could come and stay with you, even for a few days?"

"Can you stay with me?"

"No, darling. But, if it makes you feel better, I will drop in and see you, every time I am in the city."

Sinead agreed to come over and could be there by the early evening. She had a few things to do but, as she assured Gwen, 'it really wasn't a bother,' she was more than happy to help. Her voice was crisp and Gwen knew she was the right choice. But Janice was unsure if she wanted Sinead to see her like this. She sipped her tea and huddled deep within her robe until Gwen insisted she go back to bed while she tidied up.

As Janice lay back, Gwen moved around in the other room, packing things together and making little piles. She came into the bedroom, to go through closets and drawers, taking everything that was his as Janice drifted off to gentle and forgiving sleep. She didn't hear Aidan come for his things. She didn't hear the hissing back and forth as he and Gwen whispered angrily. Instead, she rode on the waves by the harbour wall, rolling among the long tresses of kelp draped around her belly and down between her legs.

The sea embraced her, welcoming her, wringing out her pain and sadness and soothing her with each gentle rise. Seabirds took up the song, decrying him and all that made him bitter. Breezes whispered as waves rippled, as the sun settled low. The night would come to the ocean and all that happened would be forgotten in time.

She wouldn't cling to umbrage; it was of no value here where waves went on forever, sometimes grey and angry when winds from the moon came close and, sometimes, soft as the sun rippled, as birds straddled rising breezes near the cliffs.

She would do something else with her anger and shame. She would tend them like a sacred fire inside to banish fear and doubt. She would become all she aspired to. She would become renowned so that everywhere he went, he would know of her and all that he had lost.

He would wander, like Cain, with the fanfare of her success ringing in his ears.

"Darling, are you awake?"

Gwen stood in the doorway and waited for Janice to answer.

"Your friend called, she will be here in a little while. Is there anything else you need before I go?"

"No, Gwen. But thank you. I couldn't have managed without you."

"Think nothing of it, darling. Are you sure there is nothing else I can do for you?"

"Gwen? There is one thing. Can you destroy Aidan?"

"Do you really want that, darling?"

"I guess not. Maybe you could just make him miserable for the rest of his days?"

"Janice, you must promise me that you will not allow him back into your life."

Gwen smiled at the sky and stepped down to the street. All things were unfolding according to plan, like they had done for eons.

But this time there was a wrinkle, like a ripple on a pond.

That was all it was. She would find her way through that, too.

Yet, she wasn't happy; she knew someday Fate would come and collect its price. Someday, she might have to pay with her own existence, that was how it worked, but that day was a long way off. Before then, she could watch Aidan bleed to death while she stroked his truelove's heart.

Chapter 15

"Mairead?" He held his cap like he was wringing the words from it. She didn't turn, but Sinead could tell her mother was listening. "I'm not good at saying things, but I'm trying to tell you that I love you."

Sinead needed them to be able to talk again: life was so empty without their banter. "And I hate when life lets you down. I can't stand that look you get." Her mother had to respond to that.

"Then come back to Church with me this Sunday?"

He looked like the tide was carrying her away. "Mairead, how can you ask me to do that?"

"Because I still love you too; even after everything."

"Let's drop it then. It'll be like it never happened."

Sinead was happy to get away: they needed to sort it out without her.

She hugged Janice carefully; she didn't want to squeeze anything that hurt and avoided looking at the red mark. All acrimony and resentment withered as she led her to the couch and stroked her cheek and wrapped her in a soft white blanket, rocking back and forth like an old woman until the crying abated. "Can I get you anything?"

"Yes, a tissue," Janice stopped crying, "and a glass of wine."

"Are you sure? Gwen said she gave you something to calm you down."

"She gave me homemade tea," Janice sobbed. "I've spent all day running to the washroom."

"Well, you look good," Sinead laughed. "I guess it's all the exercise. Where's the wine?"

There was no wine and they were dubious about whiskey. "We could have tea. Put the kettle on and I'll get the cups."

"Gwen's being awfully friendly."

"I think it's herbal, or would you prefer regular?"

"No, Gwen's tea is fine and don't answer me."

"What? Sometimes, I think we're on completely different wavelengths. But," she took time to look into Sinead's eyes, "I don't know how I managed without you. Let's promise to never allow anything to come between us again? Eh, promise?"

She reached out and waited to be hugged and Sinead couldn't say no; even if she wanted to, even if Janice was smiling that smile she used whenever she was about to get her own way. Sinead didn't really mind; it was the least that she could do. "I promise."

Janice smiled until her cheek hurt. She made a point of touching it before she continued. "So what were you saying about Gwen?"

"Never mind, what's in this tea? It smells like opium."

"I'll have you know that this tea was very popular with the Sultans in Constantinople."

"Really?" Sinead raised her eyebrows, sipped from her cup and grimaced a little. "Don't worry, it's safe, it just tastes like cat piss."

"You've no idea what cat piss tastes like, do you, darling?"

"No. You're right. It tastes like dandelions that a cat's pissed on. Would you mind if I put some whiskey in mine?"

By the time Sinead lit a candle, they were giggling at everything, but at least Janice hadn't cried in awhile. They'd made another pot of tea and placed it beside the bottle of Jameson and the shrinking wheel of Brie.

"Do you think the cheese tastes like sperm?"

"Janice! For Christ's sake, I just put some in my mouth."

Janice looked like she might cry. "It was something Aidan said."

"How'd he know what it tastes like?" But Janice didn't laugh so Sinead carried on. "Why do you keep holding the cup to your face, doesn't the heat bother it?"

"I've learned to look at the world through what I'm drinking; it's given me a whole new perspective."

"It's a cup; you're supposed to look in and read the leaves when you're finished."

"Well, that might explain why everything looks so dark. What's in this tea?"

"Whiskey."

"No, besides that, it had the same effect last night when . . ." but she never finished.

"What's the matter with you now?"

"I can't believe I'm telling you this."

"You haven't told me anything yet."

"I made a pass at Gwen last night."

"You did what?"

"I tried to. But we didn't."

"You're kidding, right?"

Janice sat back and ran her hand through her hair. "No. I'm not, oh, my God!"

"Well, that might explain why she's being so nice," Sinead muttered into her cup, trying to hide her smile. This was so Janice, flirting from disaster to drama. "Well, at least you're getting over Aidan."

Janice stiffened at the sound of his name. "What's that supposed to mean?"

"Relax, Janice, I was just joking, I mean . . . ah, forget it." Sinead poured more tea, but Janice's eyes never left her face.

"And what about you? I've been so absorbed that I haven't even asked about you?"

"Ah, sure you know me, Janice, same old shite."

"What? No stories of love and conquest?"

"Are you kidding? More?" She held the whiskey between them, but Janice moved it aside. "Sinead?"

"Well, if you must know, there's this really cute . . . Ah, never mind. It didn't work out."

"Does he have a name?"

"Yes, Ronan: the guy who works at the coffee shop?"

"Did he turn you down?"

"Actually, he asked me out, but he's not really my type. And besides, I've so much to do right now." She considered a diversion – asking Janice about her studies. She hadn't seen her around the college in a while but she wasn't sure. She might get upset again.

"Sinead, why didn't you go out with him?"

"I heard he's interested in someone else."

"Oh, darling, you should go with him."

"I don't know. I'd spend the whole evening just wondering if he was thinking about her."

"That's ridiculous, darling."

"Maybe, but it's just the way I am, you know? I'd feel a little sleazy."

"So how do you feel about what I just told you, about Gwen and me, now that's sleazy?"

Sinead was relieved: the spotlight had moved on. "No, Janice, that's repulsive."

"Sinead! Are you homophobic?"

Sinead paused to sip her tea. She wasn't really shocked; it was Janice after all. It was understandable, too, given all that she'd been through. "It's just, well, it's not like I'm against it or anything. Each to their own and all of that but . . ."

"It's okay, darling. I wasn't terribly serious. I was in shock and we do the strangest things when we're like that."

"Of course: who wouldn't? Would you like another splash of whiskey? I think the tea is making me thirsty. I read somewhere that drugs make you dry in the mouth. Do you think she might have been trying to get you high?"

"Who, darling?"

"Gwen, of course. Then she'd carry you off somewhere and have her way with you." She wanted it to be something they could laugh about, but because there might be more to it, she had to ask. "You know what you were telling me before, about Gwen being a Lenanshee and all; do you still think about that?"

"Gwen looked after me when," and she fanned a few tears, "I needed her. I know what everyone thinks about Horse-Protestants and all, but Sinead, they're my friends. They know what it feels like to be cut off."

"Cut off from what?"

"Oh, darling, you of all people know what I mean." Janice was getting angry: the whiskey and tea were beginning to take their toll. "And they are going to help me with my art. Do you have any idea what that means?" Sinead just nodded but that seemed to irritate Janice. "Of course, you don't. How could you?"

Be nice now. "Shut up, Janice; you're drunk."

"Maybe I am, but at least, I'm not repressed."

Be feckin' nice now! "What's wrong with having a few principles, not that I'm judging you or anything?"

Janice was beginning to slur her words and her eyes were glazed. "Really, darling? Well, I think you are."

"And I think you should go to bed now and get some sleep, you must be very tired."

"Tired? Yes, Sinead. I'm tired of watching you shying away from life. I have courage, darling, something you seem to lack." She tried to rise but gave up and slumped back.

Be nice! Ah, feck it. "And look where it got you."

Janice froze for a moment before melting into a pool of tears. Sinead moved to the couch and stroked her hair until the sobbing abated into soft shallow breathing. She covered her with the blanket and rose to draw the curtains. Things would be better in the morning. Janice would be a mess, but she wouldn't remember half of what had been said. She whistled softly as she checked doors and windows. She was nervous in the studio where faces loomed up from the darkness and strange eyes followed her. The streetlight flickered across the easel where the young girl strained against her bonds. Green hands caressed her and slithered down to her hips as a soft breeze drifted through the open window. A green cape drifted around them as they stood entwined, writhing against each other in the red and yellow and orange light. Sinead found it a little disturbing.

She poured herself a drink. The raw whiskey made her shiver, but she needed to settle herself again. Despite all that Janice said, she had a lot to be happy about. At least, the future held promise if she could just get through the muck and the mire. It wasn't just Janice; it was her parents, too, tearing at themselves.

She brought tea and toast with thin shavings of Brie topped with a hint of marmalade. Janice looked terrible, but Sinead smiled like she didn't notice. "I take it you're not up for going to school?"

Janice shivered back under her covers, "No, darling. I couldn't face that today."

"You're probably better off here anyway; it's been pissing all morning." She pushed the curtains aside. "Will you be okay until I get back?" She was worried. She didn't want Janice to do something that she might regret. She didn't think she should get too close to

Gwen, either: not that she believed all that stuff; that was all Aidan's doing, filling her head with nonsense.

Janice stayed on the couch as the sunshine broke through the clouds. She was empty and alone again. Aidan was gone: all traces of him erased except for the slight hint of cigar smoke that lingered near the chair. She rose and walked to her studio and stood among her paintings. She fought the urge to pick up a brush, but she caressed her stiff dry canvases. She could draw strength from them, and in time she would rise like a phoenix. She would go on to that idyllic cottage by the sea, but it wouldn't be in Ireland; it would be somewhere warm and sunny.

She wandered back and opened the bedroom door. In many ways, it looked the same, but there were spaces and gaps. All that he'd brought had been expunged and it was painful, like hearts pulled apart.

How could you, Aidan? She sobbed as another shower of salty tears ran down her cheeks and dripped onto the bed. She sobbed until sleep rose to carry her away from her pool of tears.

The woman sat with her shawl around her face. She was facing the sea and, as Janice approached, she turned. "Why have you come back?"

"I didn't know where else to go."

"Have you not found the Truth and Love you sought?"

"They turned against me."

The woman laughed and pointed past Janice. "Then you must take your heart back from him."

Janice turned to where she pointed; Aidan had followed her along the path.

"I knew I'd find you here. I had to come and see you were all right."

Janice stepped back. They were standing over the most pre-cipitous cliff on the headland: the one she imagined the crazy old lady's boyfriend had jumped from, all those years ago. *Did he jump or did she push him*, she considered and measured the distance between them, but Aidan read that look.

"Look, I'm sorrier about hittin' you than anythin' else I've ever been sorry for. You gotta believe me, Janice. I got fucked up, again."

"Is that all that you have to say for yourself?"

"Ya know I'm all fucked up an' you got Gwen now an' I'm on the outside. You two will go off an' enjoy yourselves, an' I'll be like some old ghost, hoverin' around inside your head. Look, Janice, before you came along, Gwen an' I were together, but there were no ties – I wouldn't have gone out with you if there were. An' then you made me fall in love with you, an' you know I know nothin' about love."

"I think you have proven that point."

"That's what I'm tryin' to tell you. I didn't have to be in love with her. I mean, she was beautiful an' desirable an' all. But I knew what she was. I had read about her an' then I got a chance to be with her. Can you imagine what that is like? I felt like I was adored."

"I wouldn't know because I was so busy adoring you that I never noticed you didn't give a shit about me."

"Ah, Janice, that's not how it was; I mean, she's a Lenanshee but you're the real woman I love. I mean I love you like no one else. It's just . . . Well, it just sort of like . . . You know! Don't ya?"

"Know what, Aidan? That, even after you hit me, you make some bullshit excuse about how you're jealous your girlfriend and your Muse have dumped you and gone off together. You're so far up your own ass you don't even know what you lost. Shit, Aidan! I've never been like this with anybody else. I loved you like I never loved anyone. And what do you do with this? You throw it all over and beat me because of some Myth from Ireland's great bog of a past." And even as she said it, she couldn't deny that, from one side, it was funny in a very twisted way. Aidan sensed the change in her mood and reached out to take her in his arms, but Janice wasn't ready. "Wait!" she said loudly and raised her arms. He lost his footing and slid feet first over the side, stopping briefly as he clung to the edge. She leaned down and took his chin in her hand: "She is my Muse now."

Without a sound, he let go and tumbled down, bouncing like a rag-doll on the larger rocks and rousing the birds that hovered like angels as he dropped into the waves that rose up to take him and then receded.

Maurice eyed his single boiled egg, standing defiantly where his large plate of rashers and eggs, black and white pudding and thick slices of fried bread normally sat. Gwen was staring out the window with her coffee cup poised.

"Maurice, darling, the pond is running low again. We really must get someone in." She couldn't ask him. The last time he broke the bank, allowing the pond to drain to the great annoyance of the ducks and geese.

Maurice sighed and cracked his egg, removing the top in one stroke. He held it between his thumb and forefinger, it was almost hard-boiled and he preferred them runny. He poked it with a finger of toast and humphed a few more times, but Gwen didn't turn.

"Is everything okay, Bridey?"

"What? Oh, yes, darling, thank you for asking. Perhaps I should lie down."

"Yes, do it right away. Should I bring you anything?"

"No, darling. It's just a woman's problem."

"Whatever you say, my dear, I am not one to pry." He examined her face for a clue. "Are you sure? I have never seen you like this before."

"Yes, yes. Please don't fuss, darling, I will be fine."

She hadn't been right since her last trip to the city. He humphed a few more times, to dispel any lingering doubt and delved into the morning paper. He began with the business page and smiled. At least the investments were untroubled.

Gwen stared through the curtains that breezed into her room, fresh warm air tinged by young green leafs and fresh grass. She thought of Janice again; she hadn't been able to clear her from her mind. She was so delicate, but she was very confused, too. Gwen had seen it in her eyes: fears and doubts that could cause her to say or do anything. After all, she had been through a terrible ordeal. Gwen had been careless with her spite and Janice had paid the price. Every time she closed her eyes, she saw Janice's face and remembered the taste of her tears. She rose and walked to the window. Far off, beyond the leafy trees, she could see the tower in the old glade. It stared back at her. She had to go back and accept what Fate had offered.

"What is this?" Maurice's rheumy eyes narrowed.

"Breakfast for lunch, darling, consider it Bohemian."

"Are you not eating?"

"Not right now, darling, I am just going to enjoy a cup of tea."

"I take it that you are feeling better."

"Yes, darling. In fact, I think I am well enough to go back to the city. I should look in on Janice."

"I should go with you. Someone should give that gutter poet a good horse-whipping, eh, what?"

"I have no doubt that you would be the best person for that, but I will go on my own. We don't want to embarrass young Janice. She needs discretion until she gets over her humiliation."

"She has nothing to be ashamed of. Tell her I said that and that he is a mangy mongrel that should be horsewhipped. And tell her I would be delighted to oblige."

"Of course, darling, I will take the afternoon bus."

"Very well, Bridey, I have a few things to keep me busy anyway. I need to have the vet take a look at the old mare. She is not right, off her feed. Damn skittish, if you ask me."

He walked from Gratton Bridge to Inchicore and back again before his mind began to clear. He rested his elbows on the parapet as the river glissaded toward the sea. Later on, after the city woke, the tide would turn and whales of grey silt would rise, tattooed by shopping carts and old rubber tires. It rose in the mountains where the marginalized clung to the earth until the Famine scoured them away, down to the city and out to the sea. He'd have to follow them now. There was nothing here for him anymore. The Old Ways had turned against him. It was the darkest night of his life.

The churches pealed their matins, angels spreading the dawn, but Aidan was deaf to all of that. He'd heard all that he wanted to hear. It was six in the morning – the market bars were open. He crossed to the Northside while the red hand flashed. Capel Street was dark and narrow between jostled houses frowning down on him as he turned at Mary's Abbey. The streets rumbled with diesel engines resting after hauling fruits and vegetables from Spain and other places to the south. Forklift trucks scuttled back and forth, growling as skids groaned against the slick cobblestones. He ducked inside the first open doorway. It was warm and smoky inside.

"And how are you doing this morning; the usual?"

"Ya! Good man and gimme a whiskey, too."

He lit a small cigar and looked around the bar, but no one looked back. They were busy with their realities, rationalizing or denying them, lingering over fresh pints, hoping that today would be a better day. At any moment, a Ganger might stick his head in and pick out a lucky few to unload trucks. On a good day they might get three or four: good cash money that left no trace when they reached out for their weekly dole.

Others drank with their backs to the door to block out the day even as it started. Their days were already full of disappointments. They had given up all pretense of normalcy; it was just too hard to do anymore. They shivered in doubt and despair. It would take too many drinks to wash all of that away: a luxury that few of them could afford. It was the bitter end of the street, but for a little while, it was warm; they could rest and those with any resources left could regroup.

Aidan looked at himself in the mirror behind the bar. *What else do you think about when you are drinking before the day begins?* he asked his reflection.

"Did you say something, Sir?"

He had to go and see her, to tell her he was sorry, to see if there was any way they could move past what had happened. But first, he would have another drink. He needed whiskey to fight the numbing cold that had spread inside him like a great storm of melancholic longings.

Gwen ordered coffee and a toasted ham, smeared it with mustard and let it cool as she folded her newspaper and found something to read. The lounge was empty, but someone was talking in the bar.

It was Gerry, trying to remain cheerful, but it was a quiet morning. He'd have to nurse his pint and stick to Woodbines. He'd only four left, but he wasn't concerned, someone would show up soon, someone who'd lend him a few Pounds. He'd enough for one more drink, but he'd wait a while and see what Fate might have in store.

His prayers were answered when Aidan staggered in. He held the door jamb as he reached for the bar. It wasn't far, but he waited until the room stopped swaying.

"Ah, Jazus, how ya, Aidan?"

"Fuck you, ya old curmudgeon. Are you well?"

"Better than some and worse than others."

Aidan pulled himself along the bar, barging through the neat line of empty stools and pulling an ashtray along for ballast. "Gimme a pint and a Jameson," he announced as he fumbled in his pocket. "And give Gerry one, too."

"Ah, good man yourself. Sit down now, while you can." Gerry watched him through the mirror, while acknowledging the look on Paddy's face.

"Would you like a sandwich with that?"

"Ah, good man, Paddy, I'll have a toasted ham with mine, with a bit of mustard, too, if it's not too much bother."

Aidan raised himself on his elbows and farted from the emptiness inside him. "Ya, gimme one of them, too."

They ate in silence as Aidan struggled with his fisted sandwich. He farted a few more times and emptied his whiskey in one go. "Paddy, gimme another."

Paddy smiled, "Of course, right away," but he turned and put another sandwich in the toaster.

"Did you have an early morning?"

"Ah, sure, ya know yourself, Gerry. It was a long night."

"Were you writing at least?"

He looked around before leaning close to Gerry. "I got nothin' left to write."

"Now that's very sad, and how did that happen?"

"You know fine fuckin' well how it happened, Gerry. I should've known better than to listen to you. But I suppose that it wasn't all your fault. I let myself get sucked in to believin' that life wasn't a bucket of shite, and ya know what happens when you do that! Life gives you the biggest kick in the bollocks. And then, when you are fallin', it gives you another kick, right in the teeth."

Paddy removed the plates and empty glasses and wiped the counter in front of them. His cheeks were ruddy, but his face was troubled. "That's awfully fatalistic there, Aidan. That's the high road to sheer madness, that's what that is. And, I must remind you: in this establishment we encourage more positive, creative forms of insanity. Isn't that right, Mr. Morrison?"

"True for you, Paddy," Gerry agreed, "that's just what I was about to say."

Aidan glared at him. "What have you got to be so happy about, sittin' around all day waitin' for someone to buy you a drink?"

"Now, Aidan," Paddy admonished, "leave Mr. Morrison alone. You could learn something from old fellas like us, if you had half a mind to."

Aidan glowered into his empty glass. They were right, they always were. He should've listened to them all along. He nodded and placed his glass on the counter. "I'm goin' home before the two of you to start singin' the Sound-of-Fuckin'-Music."

"Ah, good man yourself. Go and have a rest for yourself and when you get back we'll still be here, dispensing food and drink and good cheer to all men of good will."

Paddy was relieved; he didn't want to have to ask him to leave. He prided himself on the way he handled his customers. He'd been doing it since his days in McDaid's, stroking the ruffled feathers of genius and steering them off home when the storms inside of them threatened to upset the delicate scales they all teetered on. If they resisted, he'd remain pleasantly forceful and, if he had to, he'd bar them, at least for a while. "He'll be all right after a bit of sleep."

"I don't know, Paddy; I think he's got himself into woman trouble."

"Is that all? Sure that's no trouble at all. You just have to learn to do as you're told and everything works out just fine." He fussed behind the bar as he watched Aidan walk into the lounge. "Oh! Hold that thought. Now he's talking to Mrs. Fitzwilliams. I'll just make sure he's not bothering her."

Gwen smiled as Paddy approached. "Bring us two coffees, Paddy, please."

"I don't want coffee." Aidan sat on the low stool. Gwen sat higher on the bench.

"Two coffees coming right up."

"I said I don't want coffee."

"What you want is no longer a concern of mine."

Aidan was about to argue, but he could see that look in her eye. He lowered his head and never raised it while she continued.

"Aidan. Janice told me what happened. What you did was unacceptable, and I will not waste time talking about it. But I will say that you must leave her alone. You must move to London and never contact her again."

"You'd like that, wouldn't you?" But he spoke to the floor; he didn't dare to look at her.

She reached into her purse and took out ten crisp new bank notes. "There is five hundred Pound here. That should cover your travel expenses and enough to find some place to live. Take it and leave or I will."

"Look, Gwen. I never meant for . . ."

"Take it and leave."

As Gwen left by the front door, Aidan lurched through the bar, cursing and swearing as he went. Gerry watched it all dolefully.

"Paddy, I'm goin' to have to owe you for these. Himself ordered them and had to take off before he paid, but ya know me, I'm good for it, and maybe, you'd give me another, to bring it up to a nice even number, and twenty Sweet Afton, too, if you wouldn't mind."

Gerry sat over his fresh pint and lit another cigarette; he was having a good day. Any day that wasn't spent alone, shunned and forsaken in his closet of a flat, was a good day.

"Sinead, tell me what to do about your mother. It's driving me to drink."

"C'mon, Da, don't be getting me involved, and besides, you know all that I've to teach you." But he didn't even crack a smile; he was really down. "What's the matter, have you gone and lost that famous sense of humour?"

"I don't know what to do with her anymore, and now that I'm about to be made redundant, I don't even know what to do with myself." He watched himself tumble in his daughter's eyes, falling from the meager heights that were the culmination of his life's efforts. It was all so empty and hollow now. His entire existence had been filled with the distractions of those around him but now, as they wandered off on their own, he felt stripped to the bare bones of futility.

"I'm sorry. I shouldn't have brought it up. Forget I ever said it. Are you up for another pint? Sure of course you are. You know, Sinead, you're like the son I never had. Not that I'm complaining about you being my daughter or anything because you're the happiest part of my whole life."

"I'll get these, Da."

"You will not. I'll not have anybody giving me charity."

"But it's my round."

"Oh! Go on then, I'll have another and twenty Woodbine, too, if it isn't a bother."

Chapter 16

Janice missed their smoky nights in the pub when reality and myth mingled, where everyone jostled to oblivion and where shadowy men smoldered in private anguish – the backdrop to her portrait of the artist as a young woman, colourful and vibrant against all that was dark and dowdy. She had been working on a few sketches, but Gwen was dismissive as she leafed through them. 'Don't waste anymore of your time on him.' They had dropped by to pick up some more paintings. She suggested that she stay away from Grogan's, too, for a while. She felt the natives might be getting restless: 'now that their bard was in exile.' Janice almost resented her comments, but moments later, her heart fluttered as Gwen stopped to look at another piece and smiled. "Now this, darling, this is a Tremblay."

She waved again from the car as Maurice struggled with the canvases. Janice felt a pang as she watched, a postpartum moment that almost made her run out to take her paintings back. Instead, she poured a glass of Medoc and settled into her perch as doubt settled around her. She really should go home for the holidays, but she couldn't. How could she explain that she had dropped her studies to pursue art? It would cause a shock that would be felt as far away as Picton.

She was changing, and while she was becoming all that she had wanted to be, she would have to sever ties with all that had been.

She understood that now, and it made her feel a little cold inside. Maybe later, with the help of another bottle of wine, she would write a long, breezy letter about her coming show and all that she had to do to be ready.

Gwen dropped by again that evening without calling. It put Janice on edge at first and they reached for each other and paused.

"We didn't really get a chance to talk earlier, and I brought you some more tea. I hope I am not interrupting." She studied Janice for a moment before forging her way in and throwing her jacket on the couch, sweeping the room with her eyes as she turned. "You can hardly see the mark anymore, in fact, you look positively gorgeous."

"I feel a little addled and bedraggled." She meant it to sound whimsical, but it sounded whiny.

"Tea?" Gwen brushed so close as she squeezed past and filled the kettle. Janice was still tingling as she placed it on the blue and yellow flame that spat a few times.

By the time the tea had brewed, they were settled on opposite ends of the couch with their feet up, almost touching. Janice wanted them to be closer, but Gwen seemed remote, like she was wrestling with something.

"Gwen? Do you really believe in my work?"

"Of course, darling."

"I am so unsure, about so many things."

"Don't worry; your path will unfold before you."

"Can't you show me the way?" Janice turned and her hair fell across her face.

Her eyes peeped through the veil and her breathing was short and sweet. But there was something coy about it all – almost like she was unaware of what she was doing. Gwen couldn't be sure and leaned forward a little and inhaled to clear her mind.

"Janice, Janice." Gwen reached out and took her by the wrist, feeling warm young blood as it pulsed between her fingers. Their breath misted between them. She could lean forward and taste the soft red lips, they were so close, but she didn't. "Darling, you must not be afraid anymore. Forget about Aidan; he is a part of your past; you must move on."

"I know, I know."

Janice wished they had some wine: that always made her more at ease, free of the inhibitions and taboos she had inherited. It would be so bohemian to love another woman, especially a woman like Gwen. Janice gazed into her eyes where the mists of lace parted for a moment. She leaned forward again so their lips could meet; feeling like she did on her first dates with Robert, wanting to be anything other than the gawky, gangly girl on the edge, peeping over but afraid to take that leap.

Gwen moved back a little so she could look in her eyes. She ran her fingers through Janice's hair and down to her neck where they were met with a shiver.

"It is getting late, and I should leave." She cupped Janice's chin in her hands and looked into her eyes. "Will you be all right, darling?" She didn't wait for an answer and kissed her gently before she rose and draped her jacket across her shoulders.

"Are you sure, Gwen? Are you sure you don't want to stay?"

Gwen paused at the bottom of the stone steps and looked up at her. "You are very pretty, darling, standing there between the pillars."

Janice was flustered, but Gwen just smiled. "Good night, darling, I will talk with you soon."

"You really are very pretty." The young woman behind the counter smiled carefully and held up a mirror. "You just need the right makeup. Your eyes are sparkling, too, look."

She did look good and her eyes were sparkling, but she didn't look like herself anymore. *Christ, she has turned me into one of Janice's paintings.* But she smiled up through her wayward fringe. The young woman whisked the mirror away. "So, will it be the whole set then?"

Sinead nodded and fumbled in her large shoulder bag. One of these days, she would buy a new one, something like the one Janice had, only she wouldn't get it in red. That would be too much.

She headed toward College Green to gauge everyone's reaction. If it was too much, she would stop somewhere and wash it all off, but it seemed to be working. She was getting a lot of second glances and even a few roving eyes from men. She stopped to look at herself again. She felt a little stupid, too, but she had to go through with it. She wanted to show Janice.

She would have to wear make-up when she went skiing in the Alps so, when she gave him the kiss of life, her red lips would mark him as hers forever. And when they got married, she would ask Janice to be her bridesmaid, only Janice would probably start flirting with his best man and create a scene and when it was time for the bride and groom to kiss, nobody would notice.

Ronan noticed right away – he did a double-take but recovered quickly and smiled.

She ordered a cappuccino without thinking; she'd have to be careful with her lipstick.

She settled by the window and searched for her book. She wanted to seem so casual. It was starting to drizzle again; she had got in just in time. When he returned with her coffee, she looked up and smiled a careful smile, afraid her face might crack; it felt so tight. They were just about to speak when the door rattled again. Janice smiled from the doorway, her hair billowing around her like a cloud, sparkling where tiny beads of moisture clung to her curls. Ronan placed Sinead's coffee on the table and went back behind the counter without another word.

"Sinead, Sinead, Sinead!"

"Yes, Janice, it's me. Don't make such a big deal, will you."

"Sinead, I've never seeing you look so beautiful before. What's going on?"

"Nothing."

"Oh, please, darling."

"I'm waiting to go out on a date. Are you happy now?"

"Here you go now." He placed the coffee before Janice without taking his eyes off Sinead.

"I could have come over to get it," Janice looked up through her hair

"No problem. I had to come over this way anyhow."

"Why?"

"Why what?"

Sinead giggled a little, but Janice just smiled and flicked her hair. "Well, I'm so glad you did. Sinead was just about to tell me who her mystery date is. It must be serious. Look at her. She is sparkling."

But Sinead lowered her head and stared into her cup as the foam began to collapse. Ronan was still looking at her, but his smile was a little forced. "Well, I'll leave the two of you to get on with it then. Have a great evening, Sinead," he added as he turned to go, back among the forest of stools and small round tables, back behind the counter where he disappeared into the backroom.

"Darling, be careful. You've smudged your lipstick. You don't want to look like a clown, do you?"

Sinead smiled, but her eyes hardened. "Speaking of clowns; have you heard about Aidan?"

"I don't think I want to hear about Aidan."

"No, it's good news. He left for England last night; I just thought that you'd be happy to hear that."

Janice's lips looked like a gash across her face as Sinead glanced at her watch. "I have to run Janice, you know, got my date waiting and all."

She cried along Duke Street, but it didn't matter, there was no one around to see her. She was hot and bothered and her face was getting itchy – she shouldn't have done that to Janice, even if she was being a bitch. She snuck into Davey Byrne's to clean her face and felt much better. She was even tempted to stop for a drink, but that place intimidated her. But that was all going to change; her professor had just told her. His wife was some high-up in the I.D.A. and was heading up a new group to work with foreign investors. He had recommended Sinead. All she had to do was apply formally, and the job was hers.

"So? Is Sinead gone?"

"Yes and we were going to spend the evening together, and now I'm left high and dry."

"But you were going out with that poet, weren't you?"

"It didn't work out." Janice casually turned and brushed her hair back from the bruised side of her face. It was growing fainter now, but it was still noticeable. Ronan noticed it immediately.

"That's too bad."

He was hooked and almost looked like he was gasping for air. It took him forever to ask. "Would you like to go for something to eat later? Nothing formal, you know, just a friend thing."

"You really know how to sweep a girl of her feet."

"So is that a yes?"

"Maybe."

"I get off work in an hour. Do you want to wait or go and get ready?"

"Ready for what? I thought this was going to be casual."

He looked embarrassed. "It's just . . . I'm going to go and start clearing off a few tables. See you in an hour, okay?"

She smiled as the dust settled, as the sunbeams slanted through the clouds and brightened the entire length of Dawson Street until someone stopped by her table.

"I am sorry to have to bother you. Do you remember me by any chance?"

"No!" Janice hesitated, but there was something familiar.

"We met, very briefly, a few months ago, in here. You'd been talking with my husband's mother – the old lady in the hat, you know, the one who talked to you about Howth."

"Oh, yes." Janice answered cautiously. "I'm sorry; would you like to sit down?"

"Actually, it's Aunt Joan that wants to talk with you; she's outside in the car. She's been pestering us for weeks to bring her back here. We had to move her into a new home, you know; she was really starting to wander. But she kept insisting that she had to talk with you again. Of course we said no – at least we did the first few dozen times. But she's so stubborn, when she gets something in her mind . . ."

"Where is she? I would love to see her," Janice interrupted; she didn't want the bobbing, nervous woman to explode in front of her.

"Are you sure? That's awful nice of you. She's outside in the car. I'll just run and get her. We didn't want to bring her in without talking with you first. Are you sure it is all right, are you sure you're not just being nice now?"

Janice smiled as her husband began to coax the older woman out of the back of the car but was beaten back by the umbrella with the strange handle. The old woman was screeching about eunuchs and harems to the astonishment of the bystanders. Janice was tempted to offer help, but the old woman had conceded and was being led to the door so she ordered a pot of tea.

"Hello, my dear. Are you well and isn't a fine day, when it's not raining?"

"But it's been raining for most of the day."

"True enough, but it's still a fine day – other than that. Listen, any day I get out of that old people's place they have me in, I'm happy. And you, my dear, how have you been?"

"Oh, me, I've been fine."

"Why don't you just tell me the truth, my dear, I can see it on your face. That's how you go mad, you know, trying to hold everything inside when it keeps bursting out. Then you have to pretend that it isn't, and you have to start inventing reasons for why your face gets all twisted. You are better off just telling the truth."

Janice was a little unsure, but she smiled and waited for the old woman to take her pills and sip her tea.

"There's a crazy old woman in the home that I'm in. She thinks she's at a hotel on the Costa del Sol, no less. I was just sitting by the window, before I came out, and her complaining to me about the Spanish weather. Says she, 'it's no better than the weather in Dublin,' and us sitting there all along."

"Why does she think she is in the Costa del Sol?"

"She was there once on holidays, and she thinks she knows me from then."

"Poor thing."

"Not really, my dear. She's better off thinking she's on holidays instead of knowing that she was thrown in there by the family she scrimped and saved to raise, only for them to cast her off when her old mind started to go."

"I see. I would never have thought of it that way."

"That's only because you don't know what's real and what's made up, anymore."

"What do you mean?"

"She came between you and your fella, didn't she?"

"What are you talking about?"

"That woman, the green hussy, she came between you and your fella and turned him against you, didn't she? She's the Lenanshee all right; I knew that this would happen when you told me about the seals."

"And you couldn't have warned me?"

"Ah sure, you'd never believe me. You'd have thought that I was mad or something. The seals knew, too. That's why they came to him. They carry messages back and forth to the Old Ways."

"How do you know all of this?"

"She came between me and my young man, too, a long time ago." She paused as she shivered. "She turned him away from me, too. She made him go mad, whispering her spells into his ear. That's what she did to you, too, I can tell."

Janice wanted to remain impassive, but she couldn't. There were seeds of truth in the dazed ramblings. "Did you ever see her?"

"Oh God no, it's bad luck to see her. They say that sometimes she goes after young girls, too, if you can believe such a thing. They say that if she touches you that you will always feel the cold of her touch – it's the cold of longing, of unfulfilled heart's desire, or so they say. The girls that she touches would be better off with the Sultan of Constantinople, even taking opium. You know," she paused to raise her tea cup to her puckering lips, "I never thought of it before, but I'm sure that's what happens them, you know, that she lures them off the path."

"She touched you, didn't she?" Janice asked as the dawning realization almost made her smile.

"How can you say such things and me a respectable woman that has never been touched by anyone."

"So what cracked you then, and don't tell me you aren't."

The old woman didn't answer, and for a moment, Janice saw her own face under the hat, years from now. "Look. I'm sorry. I shouldn't have said that. I'm sorry."

"Sorry for what, my dear," the old woman pursed her smile, but her eyes were deep with sadness.

Outside, clouds gathered on the shoulders of the mountains. The fingers of the sun reached down and touched the table between them as Janice gathered granules of salt and sugar, anything to buy time until she found something else to say as the sky grew darker.

"It was very good of you to come and see me, and all."

"Oh, my dear, I love coming here. They have the best tea in the Costa del Sol."

Joan's cracked old smile was warm and infectious for a moment. "Ah, damn it all, can I not have a moment of peace."

"Sorry?"

"Oh! Please excuse me, my dear, but there's my nephew and his giant tic of a wife and they've come to take me back to the home. They just can't wait to get me back there."

"Wait, wait, Joan. You have to leave me a number or an address – so that I can come and visit you."

"You would come to see, my dear. That's so kind and thoughtful of you. You don't find too much of that these days."

"Of course I will, Joan. We're like sisters, you know, touched by similar tragedy."

"I never let that hussy touch me, mind you. I never let her touch me," she repeated as she was ushered out of the shop and into the back of the car. She waved from the side window, like the queen staring straight ahead.

Thanks, Joan, Janice mouthed after her. *Thanks for the warning. I will never let that happen to me. I won't end up like you, Joan, but I will never forget you and your hat.*

"Is everything okay?"

"Yes, yes, of course. Why? Were you afraid that I had changed my mind?"

"Not really. But, for a moment there, I thought that you might go with her, you know, to the Harem."

"Do all men . . ." But she stopped. How much had he heard?

"So how is Old Joan then?"

"Do you know her?"

"Know her? We used to go out together. Only as friends though." He held her jacket as she reached back with her arms, stepping back a little as he pulled it over her shoulders.

He insisted on seeing her home, too. "It's not a bother; I can grab a taxi from there." But he didn't look at her eyes as they spoke, as they strolled casually past the Green, he was looking at her cheek.

"Yes," he continued as they headed toward Harcourt Street. "I'll be glad when it is over. I enjoyed it, don't get me wrong, but I'm tired of living as a student. I'm hoping to work abroad, too, at least for a few years. Dublin is a little small for me. I want some place bigger."

But Janice wasn't really listening. She was very conflicted, strolling toward Rathmines and the purple hills beyond, darkening with every step as the sun settled over the midlands. She was playing a high risk game; she knew that, but it would be worth it. It had worked out very well for Aidan, until he fucked it all up. She would never make that mistake.

"Could I tempt you with another glass of wine?" she asked as they passed the off-license.

He smiled as he stole a glance at the clock tower. "Well, maybe one."

She bought two bottles. She had so much to think about and smiled as she stepped back out on the street where he waited. It was all starting to make perfect sense: Aidan, Gwen and Maurice, Old Joan and all that happened. "I like to keep wine around the house, for when I'm working," she explained as they turned and walked together.

And there was the whole issue of actually doing it with Gwen — she had to admit it: she was very conflicted about that part. She wished she could talk to someone about it. "Are you sure you are Irish?"

"Yes, no doubt about it, only we're not all caricatures, you know."

She was infatuated. She craved Gwen's attention and her approval, and sometimes, she just wanted to reach out and touch some part of her, just to make contact. She wanted Gwen to take her heart and keep it somewhere safe, somewhere where the world could not scratch and bruise it. She wanted them to kiss, too, long and passionately, running fingers through each other's hair. But Gwen would have to be the one to make the first move.

"I live up this way," she pointed when they got to the corner of Castlewood Avenue. "I'm just around the corner. You don't have to come, and there are taxis just over there."

"I thought I was going to get a glass of wine, for being so gallant and all."

Yes, she could force Gwen to make her move. When she saw her with Ronan, she would have to react. It would be better this way. "Just the one, I don't want the neighbours talking."

She wanted to make Gwen suffer a little, too; it would be good for her soul if she had one.

In time, she would let Gwen take her. But she would have to seduce her, sensuously and seductively.

He offered to help, but she couldn't accept.

"No, darling, I can manage my own house, but please make yourself comfortable. I'm just going to pop into the kitchen for a moment. If you really want to do something, you could light the candles."

"I would be delighted," he smiled as he stooped to pick the matches from the coffee table. "All of them?"

"Use your imagination."

"Sure. And do you mind if I look through these?" He pointed at the canvases against the wall.

"Oh! Are you interested in art?"

"My father is a collector."

Janice felt her face getting flushed. She wanted to squeal, but she couldn't. She had to be someone else right now. "Really, well, please feel free – I'd like to hear what you think of them."

She had to rinse a few glasses, but she really wanted to check herself in the mirror, in the washroom, at the side of the kitchen where the plants were thriving.

Sinead looked back at her for a moment, but she brushed her aside as she touched up her lips and teased her hair away from her face. The mark of the hand was faint, but she had seen him looking at it and that subtle little charm that bewitched men. She stood erect and leaned forward. Four buttons was too much. She could pull off the three-button look as long as she leaned forward a little. No, that was too much, now she looked like a Harpie. And not that much either; she looked like a flat-chested dryad or the Virgin.

There! Perfect.

"These are amazing."

His eyes were wide. She could feel his warm breath on her arm as she stood as close as she could. "I'm so glad you like them. Would you like to see more?"

He had really fine cheekbones. His skin was clear and tight, warm in the candlelight and his breath was sweet. "You sit there and I will just kneel here and we can look at them one at a time."

He looked down as she sat back on her heels with her hips and thighs stretching denim, her throat and breasts framed in the wide neck of her shirt that was slipping from one shoulder. She raised her glass toward the painting he held and smiled. "This is one of the first ones I did when I came here."

"Voyageur, right?"

"Very good."

He carefully placed it back against the wall and lifted another. "Christchurch! But it's almost reminiscent of Notre Dame, too, or the one in Milan."

"This one," Janice pulled at a canvas just beyond her reach. They were almost face to face and smiled as they both recoiled slowly. "Is very dark: one of my more tormented moments."

"So tell me, what happened with you and the poet?"

"He came home drunk one night and beat me."

"I'm sorry, Janice. I shouldn't have asked."

"No. It's okay. I need to talk about it." She drew herself up and rested her arm across his knees. She raised her glass between them, candles dancing in the depths, and dipped her lips for a moment. "Ronan?"

"Yes?"

"Would you think less of me if I asked you to stay? You could sleep on the couch. It's just that I don't want to be alone tonight." She leaned back on her haunches and pushed her hair back from her cheek. "I am still afraid, sometimes."

He did think of Sinead for a moment. But it was obvious she had moved on. "I know, Janice."

"But you never said anything."

"I figured that you weren't ready to talk about it yet."

She rested on his knees as candlelight flickered in the red depths. He reached forward and brushed her hair away as he gently stroked her ear.

"Would you like to sit up here with me?" He shifted until there was enough room on the armrest.

"That's from my disturbed erotica collection. They're just themes I'm working out."

"They're very sensual."

"Just sensual?"

"Well," he hesitated as he tried not to talk to her breasts. "I didn't want to say something else."

"Like what?"

"Well. . ."

"Ronan, don't tell me that you're repressed, too."

"Well, it's like you use erotica as an invitation to an entirely different world. I mean, look at the monk. You can see he's thinking about it. He knows that she's from another world and he doesn't care, he is going for it. And even this one," he lifted the painting of the girl tied to the pillars. "This reminds me of the one by Guido Reni. You know, the one of the brilliant white Christ and he is already nailed to the cross. But he's not all bloody. He is looking up to Heaven like he is assured. It's like you're trying to show us some kind of spiritual transformation."

She leaned forward and kissed his lips that tasted so sweet. Slowly, she sat back and took another sip of wine.

"Is that the Castle Lounge?"

"No, it's Grogan's."

He smiled again, and this time, he reached around with his lips, looking for her mouth.

He held her against his bare chest where she could listen to his heart as his breathing slowed.

She wet her lips and drew a heart on the side of his chest. She wet it again before she drew the arrow. There was nothing in the night that could harm her here against his chest, but in time, he moved. He rolled over and pulled the covers to his shoulders. A cold breeze reached underneath and chilled her breasts. It was soothing after their exertions and she lay there watching his side rise and fall with each breath.

It took forever to remove her makeup. She heard her father as he fumbled with his front door key. She waited, ready to intervene.

She heard her mother as she came out to meet him. "Look at me, Colum."

She couldn't remember the last time she heard her mother call him by his name.

"I want to tell you how sorry I am about all that has been going on. I talked with Nuala today, and she told me the whole story; they're leaving for Australia next month."

She looked like she had seen her own death so he waited for her to continue.

"I was wrong not to believe you. In all our years together, you have never lied to me and I forgot all about that. I'm sorry, and I will understand if you can never forgive me."

"Forgive you? Sure what harm have you ever done anybody? You're always the one to see some good in everybody. If it was up to me, the whole world would be an even worse mess than it already is. We need people like you around. I need you. We all do. How could the world go on if you weren't in it?"

She let him hug her because she was lost and frightened, and despite herself, Sinead cried, too.

Chapter 17

The hotel was a reminder of more gracious times, palm fronds in the lobby, comfortable chairs strategically placed for the solitary enjoyment of the 'Times' or 'Observer' under elegant wall-mounts poking through thick embossed paper. Turner-like prints hung in gilt-edged frames: pastoral scenes of pot-bellied gentry on quarter-horses, rustics threshing and gleaning and barges gliding through fields dotted with elms and oaks. It was a museum of times past. The lobby smelled of pipe-smoke and old money and the bar smelled of gin. She didn't have a room with a view, but it didn't matter; she was in one of those parts of London that survived the Blitz and now huddled in the shadows of commercial fortresses: the new lairs of the Trading Companies that had once pillaged the world for fame and fortune and the glory of the Empire.

She wore black leather pants with a stiff white shirt, not unlike the type Gwen wore. She spent forever on her hair so it would shine as she turned her head in the warm glow of the lights.

"There, that's perfection," but her reflection was distracted. She'd heard Aidan was living low in the East End, drinking hard and writing dissipated poetry in a shabby room near Upton Park, across the street from a pub called 'The Green Man.' She wanted to see him so he could watch her bask in success. Of course she would have nothing to do with him and that would crush him, but her reflection didn't agree; she never wanted to see him again. *Be careful*, it cautioned as she touched up her lipstick. *Don't spoil it all now, eh, Princess?*

But Janice hardly heard as she gathered her things and left, gliding down the red-carpeted staircase to the lobby where she would step out into a thunderstorm of flashing cameras and surging media.

The street was empty except for the doorman who furtively enjoyed a cigarette.

He stubbed it out and called a taxi for the docklands, a forgotten part of the city for years, dilapidated warehouses and dingy dwellings near the river. But revival had blown through and filled the streets with the smell of potential. But it was still off the beaten track. However, her cabbie knew it well.

The gallery was predictable, pot lights and newly dry-walled on one side with track lighting and exposed brick on the other. Old wooden floors shone as the catering staff scurried back and forth, disappearing through the blue curtains behind the white-clothed tables. Janice had arrived too early. Her work hung on the dry-walled side, including the one she did after Howth. It was one of her better pieces, a blend of Dadaism for everything that changed that day.

It was a 'Collection of New Contemporary Art.' Janice smiled at the additional qualification – almost, but not quite there. 'But it will lead to greater things,' Gwen assured her. They hadn't traveled together as Gwen had matters to attend to and felt Janice would benefit from absorbing the experience alone so Janice wandered, pausing to admire the work of others, lingering with anticipation, expecting to be announced or something. A small group stood in front of her work when she passed. She sidled up behind them and held her breath.

"Very pretentious, I think Tremblay has talent but no direction what-so-ever. Let us move on, there is a young sculptor from Cornwall over there, he does wonderful work in bronze."

They passed and didn't notice; their casually discarded words had squeezed tears from her heart.

And not just tears of sorrow; the essence of her being, naively exposed in hope of praise, had been wrung through the cruel vice of disregard. And for a moment, her crushed delusions seeped through dappled canvas as hope melted and dribbled down the drywall and across the burnished floors.

She grabbed her things and ran into the streets, empty but for the ghosts of those who had once passed this way, bound for transportation to Botany Bay where they could labour like slaves to redeem their souls.

The damp night cooled her flustered cheeks but her humiliation lingered. She thought she heard Aidan's voice following along behind her. She turned a couple of times, but the night stayed just beyond the pools of streetlight and followed when she started to walk again. She grew angry as the very thought of him galvinised her. She couldn't let the sneering voices of scorn deflect her. She had poured everything into her work, too much to have it derided by casual indifference.

She wrapped herself in that assurance and walked among her thoughts until she had no idea where she was. She needed to reshape herself in a gentle place where her injured pride could heal. She needed comfort and understanding, something the streets of Wapping couldn't provide, and she needed to rest.

A cab was parked up ahead, in front of a pub. They'd have a phone, and maybe, the driver might be inside. She should have turned when she saw him, but it was too late; he'd seen her.

"Ah Jazus, if it isn't the world famous painter herself. Will ya have a drink with an old pal who knew you before you became famous an' all?"

She decided to act like he meant nothing to her anymore. "I came to find the driver of that cab outside." She was mad at herself; it sounded like an explanation.

"He's takin' a break," he grinned as he lit a cigar.

That was how she'd paint him, standing at a bar smoking and drinking. She paused for a moment: they were in a public place, with people all around and she was tired. She needed to gather in the scattered pieces of herself. "And how would you know that?"

"'Cos it's my cab, darlin'." He had that quizzical look she gave the monk by the round tower, the one who should have been startled by the succubus.

She struggled to stay calm and speak in a dispassionate manner, the way she imagined Gwen would. "Oh, God, you're the very last person I wanted to see."

He paused to regroup and raised his glass between them but he didn't drink. "All I can do is tell you that I'm sorry." His shoulders rose around his ears and his eyes grew softer. "Can I get you a drink?"

He actually sounded contrite, but she'd never forgive him. However, she did need to rest and find her bearings, and they were in a public place with plenty of people around so she sat on the bar stool next to his. She did, however, move it back a bit.

"I'll say it again, Janice. I'm so fuckin' sorry."

"It's not something that I'll ever forgive: you hit me."

"Oh, yea, I'm sorry about that, too."

She was about to drain her glass when his words reached her. "What were you apologising for?"

"Nothin', listen, are you ready for another drink?"

"No, Aidan, but I do want an explanation."

He ordered another round of drinks and lit another cigar, exhaling a long stream of smoke to the yellow ceiling. "So, how's Gwen?"

"Why don't you ask her yourself? She's here in London right now."

"I'm sure she is?"

"What do you mean by that?"

"Oh, nothin', I just figured she wouldn't miss this trip, ya know – a chance to spend some time with you."

He raised his cigar without taking his eyes off her face. The old Janice might have flinched.

"Aidan. Don't start that nonsense again." She raised her voice, and everyone along the bar stopped to stare at her and glare at him.

"She's gonna try an' make you fall in love with her an' then you'll be fucked. If you fall in love with her, you're goin' to get your couple years of fame an' all. Then you gotta die young."

"Aidan, that is nonsense." She was quieter this time and a little curious, too.

"Nonsense? C'mon Janice, you know better than that. Nothin' ever makes sense. Everythin' . . ."

"Ya, ya, Aidan. Everything gets all fucked up. I've heard it all before." She wanted to shut him out for a while, until she thought about what he'd said. "But, if what you're saying is true, how come you're still alive?"

"'Cos she fell in love with me. She was bound to me, but I was free."

"The only way you could get out was by having someone take your place."

He ordered more drinks as the reality settled around them.

"You cruel hearted bastard."

"Look, I'm sorry. I was only tryin' to do somethin' good for you. How was I to know that you and her were gonna be all friend-ly like? I expected the two of you to hate each other like normal women would."

"You bastard, are you telling me that you gave me to her, to take your place?"

"Ah, now, Janice, it wasn't really like that." He looked away, but everyone along the bar was glaring at him so he turned to his reflection in the mirror. "I didn't know what would happen."

"You lying, cheating bastard." Janice rose and threw her drink in his face but should have held on to the glass. It hit him on the nose as the vodka stung his eyes.

"Ah for fuck's sake, what the fuck are you doin', ya fuckin' cunt ya?"

"Now, pets," the barmaid said as she rested her large breasts on the counter between them. "My name is Sal and I run this place, and I'm going to ask you to leave. The sailors and the whores in the back room are complaining about your language.

"Relax Ladies and Gentlemen," she soothed the rest of the bar. "She's American and he's Irish, vulgarity is the only language they have in common. But they were just leaving, weren't you, pets?"

As they stood outside, Aidan held some ice to his nose. It was a parting gift from Sal if they left quietly. She also advised him to stick with local girls. Janice could almost see the funny side but she was still furious at him.

"Well, it was so nice to catch up, Aidan. You've helped me re-alise that everyone was right about you. I just wish I had realised it earlier. Now, if you could excuse me, I must go and please remem-ber this: I never want to see you again."

"C'mon Janice, don't be like that. I told you I'm sorry. Let me give ya a ride to your hotel."

"Aidan, I wouldn't get in that cab with you if it was the last cab on earth."

"That's too bad because you're too lost to find your hotel."

She looked around at the empty streets and the mist billowing around the corners. "Okay, just drop me off at the subway."

"Listen, Janice, there's somethin' I have to explain."

"Just drive," she snorted as she slumped into the back seat, "and try not to get us killed."

"Janice, as long as you don't fall in love with her, you will be okay."

She lurched forward for the door handle. "I've heard enough. Let me out."

"But ya don't understand. I can't let you out here; we're in the middle of nowhere. You'll never find your hotel and I won't say anymore. I just had to warn you. Now it's up to you."

She settled back and watched the damp streets sparkle as they passed. She would just ignore him; he was pathetic. She wanted to lean forward and tell him that she knew it was all a plot to drive a wedge between her and all that was happening for her but what was the point?

So they drove in silence as she watched unknown streets and alleys slip by.

"Aren't ya gonna ask?"

"Ask what?"

"Why I'm drivin' a cab."

"I assume it is because you like to take people for rides."

"Janice, gimme a break, I know I was an arsehole an' I know ya'll never forgive me, but let's just be civil, at least 'til I find your hotel and then ya can go off and forget all about me."

So he'd set it all in motion. Old Gerry was probably involved, too, Aidan couldn't have come up with this on his own, but what about Gwen? She must have known what was happening. *Why didn't she do something to stop it?*

It all made sense now and presented her with an opportunity. This was how she'd crush him.

She'd sleep with Gwen: she had to. She'd give her body freely, knowing that the very idea of it would tear his heart out but she'd withhold her love, and when she didn't need her anymore, she'd pass her on, just like Aidan did.

She felt warm after the numbing cold of the gallery, but she'd need a few drinks first.

"So why are you driving cab?" Janice asked as the silence grew tedious.

"Well, Princess, after I left you, things were never the same. I haven't been able to write and no one wants any part of me anymore."

"That's so sad," Janice said as they stopped in front of her hotel. "But in a way, it makes me happy."

"And why's that, Princess?"

"Because now you know what it's like to get fucked, you bastard. And another thing, don't ever call me Princess again. And you know something else? You're absolutely right, you're an arsehole, and you know what happens arseholes like you – they get fucked Aidan. Goodnight and goodbye."

Gwen's taxi found its way through the docks as she fidgeted with the clasp of her beaded black purse; it had been in the family for years and complimented her black suit and pearl necklace. She wanted to look into her tiny compact mirror but what was the point? She knew she looked like an old fresco. But the hunt was on. Her cheeks grew ruddy at the very thought of it. Her heart was racing as the cab stopped by the gallery door.

She sauntered through the crowd, smiling at those who knew her. She couldn't find Janice but her paintings were drawing a crowd. Pimples' people were in place, creating a 'bit of a buzz.' It was so easy to do. People just needed to be told what was 'in' and what was 'hot.'

She saw him in the midst of a crowd with a younger man in tow.

"Pierce, darling." She leaned forward to kiss the air between them. "I can't find Janice anywhere. You haven't done something terrible to her, have you?"

"Gwen Fitzwilliams, how wonderful to see you again," he hesitated as the younger man stood a little closer, waiting to be introduced.

"Darling," Pimples smiled as he moved her away. "I'm afraid that it was too much for your protégé. I believe one of these troglodytes was unkind and she overheard. She was last seen running for the exits. Are you sure about this one, darling?"

Gwen was delighted but couldn't let it show. "Oh, she will be fine. Maurice and I have every confidence in her."

"And how is old Maurice then? I haven't seen him since the races. I must say, Gwen, he has the most remarkable fortune with the ponies. Is he so lucky elsewhere in life?"

Gwen knew what Pimples was asking. He had never really forgiven her, but it was not her doing. Maurice made his choice long ago. "Oh, darling, you know Maurice. His contentment is his good fortune."

"Indeed." He stepped back a little to look into her eyes. "But we must discuss Janice. There's only so much that I can do. Let's be honest, darling, she has no direction whatsoever. She flits from one style to the next. She needs to narrow her focus. It might seem that she's distracted."

Gwen was anxious to get away; she didn't want to leave Janice on her own for too long. That would be tempting Fate.

"Perhaps," Pimples hesitated as he tried to read her face. "You might consider moving her to Paris. I can recommend someone who could help with that. A delightful young man, a regular ladies man," he added as his young companion joined them looking a little miffed and Gwen seized the chance to excuse herself.

"I should go to her, darling. I am sure she is crying her eyes out."

She kissed they air between them and offered a limp cold hand to his young companion.

She settled into the back of the cab and examined her reflection. She snapped the case shut and dropped it into her purse and fastened the clasp. It wouldn't be much longer and she had some time to think about what 'Pimples' had said. He was actually jealous of her. That still made her feel so good.

She first met Maurice at a hunt; he'd been in England for years and his mother told her mother that it was time he settled down. She knew what he was and his mother had told her mother that it was time for him to find a wife, somebody fitting for him.

Later, he asked her to dance as the hunt feasted the evening away, as horses stood in their stalls, as hounds slept in kennels dreaming of fields of foxes. He held her close but his breath was cold, but that didn't matter. All she had to do was to tell her mother to tell his mother that she was interested.

"Bridey? Now that is a wonderful name."

"It is, and I am wonderful, too."

He twirled her around before holding her close. His mother was smiling and nodding.

They announced their engagement in the spring. It was a very good arrangement. They both understood the deal: he loved art and she loved artists.

"Bridey, you need to know that my work takes me to London, regularly."

"Of course, darling."

"But I think I might have found something to keep you busy, after all, we wouldn't want you to sit around alone."

He bought the Press; the previous owner owed him money. She smiled demurely and batted her eyes. "Darling, I might have to spend some nights in the city, after openings and readings, you understand."

He just smiled and she was happy. She didn't want to seem like a common whore.

Whore? That word didn't apply to her. She laboured in a changing world, tending the spirit of the old ways. Her mother had warned her that she would never find peace. It was not their lot in life. She had a purpose appointed by Fate, but she preferred to think of it as a series of 'love affairs' with very talented but tormented souls. She offered comfort and consolation. She granted validation and in return, inhaled the vapours of lust until love shriveled up and was no more, something that could still tear at her heart.

It had never been easy, even with Aidan, even though poets accepted her arrangement like it was the foregone conclusion to a problem that evaded them for years. But she made a mistake with him, she began to care for him, and by the time she realised, she no longer cared; she was in love with him.

She paid the cabbie and stood for a moment, looking up at Janice's windows; the lights were on and the front desk confirmed that she'd picked up her key.

Janice wiped the steam from the mirror. She teased her hair and paused for her reflection's reaction; she wasn't so sure anymore. Gwen had called; she was on her way. Perhaps if she had a few more drinks. She struggled with the champagne cork until it popped and bubbled for a moment. She didn't want to get too tipsy. She just needed the right amount and would keep sipping until she found it.

It was the right thing to do. She needed someone and she needed that someone to be Gwen. She refilled her glass with total conviction and slipped between the sheets. She sat back against her pile of pillows and bolsters, allowing her robe to fall away. She wanted to look perfect.

As she raised her glass, a few cold beads fell and trickled along her skin. She watched a quiver ripple across her stomach and struggled to stay awake as winds rose on the river, dispelling the mist and revealing the cold hard stars.

After the third ring, she rolled across her wide empty bed.

"Darling, would you care to join me for breakfast?"

Gwen sounded so pleased. "I was hoping to have something light before we left for the airport, and I just spoke with Maurice's friend; all three pieces sold last night and there is considerable interest in the rest of your work. Janice, your new life begins today."

But Janice said nothing. She could almost feel Gwen's lips through the phone. She could almost feel cold white fingers trail across her skin.

"Darling, is everything okay?"

Janice struggled. She knew that her life depended on it.

She had to do what Aidan had done, but she had to be careful.

They met in the dining room, swirling with stiff white waiters and delicious aromas of tea, coffee and sizzled bacon. The carpet was red with browns and greens, and the tables and chairs had stiff slender legs. Gwen waited behind green fronds, like a tiger. Her smile was calm, but her fingers twitched amongst her pearls and her eyes fluttered for a moment. She rose and held Janice far too close.

Janice had to undo what had been done and grabbed the first thing she could think of to pry them apart. "I saw Aidan last night."

It became a little cooler as they parted, and Gwen held her in her stony gaze until she continued.

"He told me a lot of nonsense about you. He warned me not to get involved with you. He said it would cost me my life."

"And did you believe him?"

"No, nothing he says is true."

Gwen was smiling again.

"And besides," Janice smiled back as they settled on the edges of their chairs, as Janice fumbled among her personae. "I'm sure that Aidan was just trying to come between us. He doesn't want me to be successful."

Gwen stroked her cheek as she lowered her head again and waited for Gwen to respond. "What else is the matter with you?"

Janice looked up through her hair. "Oh, Gwen, I know that I'm being silly, but I don't know what to believe anymore. I guess that seeing him again just raised all these fears and doubts. Sometimes, I think I might have become infected by Aidan's past."

"And this is bothering you this morning?"

"I guess it was because I saw him again; I'm not sure what is real anymore."

Gwen sat back in her chair and nestled against the cushion. She rearranged herself, legs carefully folded and fingers clasped below her knee.

"Darling, Aidan made a living evoking the ghosts of the past. But he was a drunken fool and became ensnared in his own mythologies." She flashed her warmest smile and offered Janice a long slender cigarette. "You are not going to make the same mistake?" She blew a long stream of smoke toward the ceiling.

Janice blew her smoke over her shoulder. "Aidan told me that if I fall in love with you that I'll have a brief life of fame and then I'll die young. He insists you're a Lenanshee." She paused for a moment to inhale again.

Gwen stifled a spluttering smoky laugh. She leaned her head to one side and her pearls began to trickle through the buttons of her dark red shirt. "Do you believe it is true?"

"Not at all, I just wonder, though. I mean, you were involved with him, and he did very well for a while." Janice peeped up through her hair, but Gwen remained impassive.

"Darling, my involvement with Aidan was a mistake; I was lonely. But his fame and good fortune were the results of the efforts Maurice and I made on his behalf."

"I'm sorry, Gwen; it was silly of me to even think it. I guess I have been in Dublin too long. I think I might even be becoming one of them."

"Darling, every culture has mythologies in which Gods come down and influence people, and the Irish are no different. They would rather believe in the whims of Fate than recognise that achievement is more likely the result of great effort. It is an excuse for their indolence."

"Gwen?"

"Yes, darling?"

"I need to talk about last night. I don't really know how to say this."

"Darling, please. You know that you can say anything to me."

"Gwen, I'm sorry. I'm not sure if I'm ready for this." She sobbed a little and hid behind the tissue Gwen offered.

"Well, that is a little disappointing, darling," Gwen smiled as Janice reemerged.

"I'm so sorry, Gwen. I have all these doubts this morning."

"Was it so bad?"

"No, not at all, Gwen, it's just that I . . . Well, I guess I'm not ready for this. I'm still dealing with all these issues with Aidan and all, you understand?"

Gwen leaned forward and her pearls peeped out again. "What is it that you are asking me to understand?"

"Oh, Gwen, I'm so sorry, and now you're going to hate me."

She shrank back behind the tissue but continued. "I really do love you, but I'm not ready for this. You must understand that . . . after all that happened . . . between Aidan and me." She waited for Gwen to say something.

"Perhaps, darling, we should give it a little time. We both need time to stop and think about things, don't you agree? Who knows? Perhaps, in time, you will feel differently." They both fell silent. For a moment Gwen looked like her heart was broken, but she pulled herself together and smiled.

Ronan surprised them at the airport, still entwined in their awkwardness.

"So, ladies, how was the show?"

"Simply marvelous, darling," Gwen gushed forward as Janice hesitated. "Janice was very well received and sold all three." She was surprised to see him: she hadn't given him a lot of thought and now she would have to deal with that. Perhaps she would have to consider what 'Pimples' had suggested.

"Janice, that's great news." He reached for her, but she recoiled a little.

"Yes," Gwen replied as she stood back to watch them.

"Sorry I am late," Maurice puffed in among them. "I ran into a few old chums and couldn't get away."

"Ah," Gwen inhaled as he kissed the air by her cheeks, "a few of your Scotch friends?"

"Yes, darling. I do admit it. I'm not without my vices. And how are you, young lady?" He beamed at Janice. "I hear wonderful things from London. We should celebrate, eh, Bridey?"

Janice was about to explain that she was feeling tired, but Gwen edged in before her. "Maurice darling, what a capital idea."

"So? How was it really?" Ronan asked as they drove off.

"I don't want to talk about it."

"That bad, eh?"

She had to be careful. "Far worse than you can believe."

She nestled into his side, her head against his shoulder and her hand resting on his thigh. "I think I might be falling in love with you." She kissed his lips as he struggled to watch the road.

"What brought that on?"

"Oh, nothing, I just felt so alone without you." She sat back as the car lurched forward, as impatient traffic crawled through plastic pylons where men in hard hats stood around like they were waiting for her to continue. She couldn't risk having anything come between them. She reached for him again.

"C'mon, Janice, let me get this car home before you start having your way with me. Then I'm all yours."

She laughed; she couldn't help it. She had to be in love with him. She couldn't risk feeling any other way.

Despite his persistent efforts, Janice couldn't find release; it just wasn't going to happen. She rose and led him toward the mirror.

"Is this something new you learned in London?"

She winced as he forced her forward, pressing her against the glass, cold against her skin, trapping her as Gwen's face rose before her and smiled: "We will be lovers until the end."

In time, she moaned and crumpled, leaving snail-trails with her lips.

Ronan tossed and turned until he gave up trying to sleep. He lay on his back, looking at the ceiling.

He turned to his left and stared into silence, to his right, into Janice's sleeping face and back to stare at the ceiling. He was taking a job abroad.

I should've told her. Ah fuck it; I'll do it in the morning.

Chapter 18

"I believed them, Sinead. I believed all the lies, and now I don't know what to believe anymore." Her mother looked worried. She feared for their Holy Catholic identity: when that was gone, what would they have?

"Can't you go on believing in the good parts?"

"Ah, daughter, nothing ever dulls your skies, does it?" Her father smiled from the doorway. He'd been to the Employment Centre, but it hadn't gone well. He was too old for the future despite all that European Funds promised so he clung to his sense of humour and flashed his old smile. "We should've joined the Soviet Union instead."

"God almighty, will you listen to him, Comrade Hennessy himself." Her mother blessed herself and rolled her eyes to the ceiling. "Father, forgive him, he's no idea what he's prattling on about."

"Shush, woman! Remember, I've an uncle dead in Spain from fighting Franco and Hitler. And where were O'Duffy's fellas? Shooting at the Canaries before they were packed off to sun themselves. At least that's what they were doing when they weren't vomiting all over the Spaniards."

Her mother took the bait without thinking; "And what were your crowd up to? Shooting priests and nuns. That's all Communists know: shooting anybody who disagrees with them. I don't know how you can go along with such people."

But he just laughed and puffed himself up as he sang:

There's a Valley in Spain called Jarama,
It's a place that we all know so well,
It is there that we gave of our manhood,
And so many of our brave comrades fell.

"Have you been drinking already, or are you still drunk from yesterday? Hush now or the neighbours will be talking – singing at this hour of the day. He's on the road to sheer madness, Sinead, and he wants me to keep him company."

"James Connolly was right," her father continued as he struggled to contain his smile, "when he told the boys to hold on to their guns after the fighting at the G.P.O. He knew that the real fighting would begin after the British left."

"There! Do you see what I've to put up with?"

Sinead pushed her plate aside. "I have to get back to the library."

"Ah, darling, you'll wear a hole in your brains."

"Jazus, woman, will you ever give her space to grow up in; you'll smother her with all your fussing. Are you all right for money, Sinead?"

"No, I'm fine."

"Don't forget your sandwiches."

They watched her walk down the street. "Well, if this country is ever going to be worth a damn, it'll take the likes of that girl." He lit his pipe and watched the sky as the sun peeped out through the clouds. "She takes after my side, you know?"

"And since when did your side ever have an ounce of brains?"

Sinead threw the last few breadcrumbs at the gulls that had intruded on her lunch with the ducks and geese that now hovered at a safer distance looking doleful. *Feeding the ducks is an art I declare . . .*

She hadn't been to Grogan's in weeks. She was putting more space between her worlds for when everything changed. She might even start trying the nice new restaurants that she'd read about, if they were still there. What the hell was taking so long? She was perfect for the job. Christ! What if she didn't get it?

Maurice had clipped and forwarded the reviews from London, but it still felt a little hollow.

'It's funny,' Ronan tried to assure her. 'We only remember the criticism.' Janice had been careful about what she told him. She hadn't actually lied, just withheld some details and let him assume what he wanted. She was becoming a little Aidan-like!

Since London, she felt differently about him, too. She understood what he'd been offered and how bitter it must have been to have it all taken away. She had been avoiding Gwen, too, but she dropped in while Janice was cleaning her brushes and flipped through the canvases against the wall.

"I see you have been working, I was beginning to think that you were avoiding me."

The doorbell chimed, cracking the frozen moment, and Janice rushed from the room. Gwen eyes narrowed when she recognised Ronan's voice. "Good evening Ronan, darling. It is delightful to see you again. I was just checking on my protégée. I hope that you haven't been monopolising all of her time."

"Ah, Gwen, as a matter of fact, she's no time for me, either. Perhaps we should start dating instead."

Gwen laughed, but it was awkward; standing like a part of a Pentacle, Janice didn't look up. She knew that they expected her to say something but she just wished they'd go away.

"Oh Ronan, how risqué, but I should leave. And Janice, I will be in touch soon."

"That was awkward," he tried to be casual as the front door closed.

"Well?" she inquired. "Did you talk with your father?" She wasn't going to make the same mistake as Aidan.

"Not yet, but I'm working on it."

She stood over him with her hands on her hips. "How hard would it be to do this one favour?"

He fingered his options on the back of the couch. They weren't going to be long term, they knew that from the beginning, but he wanted whatever they had to be something they could enjoy. But she was preoccupied with what she wanted from life, something that wouldn't change so he reached for his jacket.

"What's the matter, darling? Where are you going?"

"Home, I can see you're busy, and I've things to do too."

"But why?"

"I think we both need a little time to think."

"And what do I have to think about?"

He smiled, but he looked resigned. He still hadn't told her about the job; he was waiting for the right time.

Grogan's is long and rectangular with a counter on one side divided into a 'bar' and a 'lounge' by a wooden partition, jokingly referred to as 'the Berlin Wall.' Drinks were a few pennies more expensive in the lounge, enough to persuade the less entitled to stay in the bar, leaving the more genteel to enjoy the better seating on the other side. 'It's the kind of place where decorum is enforced with respect for humanity, despite its condition,' Aidan had told Janice one of the nights they closed the place, back when they first got together. 'Ya know, Paddy served the Dublin literati of the nineteen-fifties, Behan, Kavanagh an' the others over in McDaid's. When he moved, they all followed – the livin' an' the dead.'

Aidan also told her of a character who evoked the wrath of the bar staff and was subsequently barred from the lounge, 'to let the decent people drink in peace. But Joe O'Brien just stood on the seats an' talked over the partition. However, he fucked up again an' was barred from the premises, but he could sit on the front steps and enjoy his favourite wine from a brown paper bag. If you wanted to talk with him, you could do it through the open door.'

Janice nestled into the corner of the lounge reading a collection of short stories. She'd never found the time to read it before. But now, since she quit school, she spent part of her mornings pouring over every page, rereading and reinterpreting every story and making notes and observations in her dog-eared journal.

"Excuse me, Janice, but the phone is for you. Someone with a French accent, too."

It had to be a prank.

"Am I speaking with Janice Tremblay, the artist?"

"Yes, who is this?"

"My name is Thierry Demarais."

"And?"

"I am visiting from Paris."

"That's nice."

"I am arranging a show and was told that I must see your work while I am in Dublin."

"Really, and who told you that?"

"I beg your pardon . . . Did I catch you in an inopportune moment?"

"What? Are you for real?"

She wasn't fully convinced, even as she hung up the phone. It was almost too good to be true, and for now, she could happily overlook that he'd found her through Ronan's father. She settled back with her book. It was her little island of Canada in the stormy seas of Dublin.

'I read on, sharing Caesar's admiration for a people who would not submit but chose to fight and see glory in their wounds. I misread it all and bent it until I was satisfied. I reasoned the way I had to, for my sake, for my father's. What was he but a man dishonoured by faceless foes? His instincts could not help but prevail, and like his ancestors, in the end, on that one day, what could he do but make the shadows real, and fight to be free of them?'

"Are you all right there, Janice?" Tommy was concerned and hesitated before putting his hand on her shoulder. "What's the matter?"

She hauled herself back from the Manitoba border and the sad, dusty existence poor 'Dutchie' had found himself in and the sad reality that his son had come to grips with. "Oh, Tommy, I'm all right. I just finished reading some beautiful short stories from Canada, and they made me a little homesick."

"Who's the author," Tommy asked with relief.

"Guy Vanderhaeghe."

"Never heard of him."

"He's new. He won the Governor General's Award."

"Is that a blessing or a curse?" Tommy inquired with a touch of disdain as his glasses wrinkled. "It says here," he added as he took off his glasses to examine the cover, "that it was published in nineteen-eighty two."

"It takes a few years for new things to reach Ireland." She smiled her sweetest smile. She loved jousting with Tommy. She loved to tell him that the Irish were a people whose time had passed.

"It's not that, Janice; we're full of writers over here. If we take in any more, the whole island might sink, and if you know anything about Saint Malachi, you'll know that he foretold that Ireland would be under water just before the end of the world. So ya see! We're still keeping civilization afloat."

"Cultural Imperialist."

"It's not like that, now c'mon. Listen. If this Vanderfella' ever comes in here, I'll be very nice to him. How's that? And, if he turns out to be a decent fella', I'll buy his books, and if he can write as good as you say, I'll recommend them to all that come in here. Will that make you happy?"

"Thanks, Tommy, you are such a sweetheart."

"Not a bother, not a bother," he offered over his shoulder as he returned to his post. "By the way," he added as he turned to close the hatch behind him, "you might want to go to the ladies room and adjust your make-up; it's after moving around a bit.

"Lads, lads, there's something important I want to say to you all," he called all attention to himself as Janice flittered through the pillars that ran down the center of the bar, passing unnoticed, like a raccoon in the bushes at the back of her father's house, overlooking the ravine, just off Don Mills Road.

The bar was in uproarious delight as she returned. Tommy has started a favourite discussion – Had Ireland done the right thing in joining the Common Market?

The small crowd was a mixed lot. There were those who had lost their jobs when the 'obsolete' Irish factories closed. The others were those who were young enough, or adaptable enough, to take advantage of the wide range of opportunities that change presented.

She paused to light another cigarette and looked at the cover of her journal. She wanted to sketch the way her countryman had made her feel: almost forgiven.

"Are you writin' a book about us all?" Gerry asked as Janice quickly closed her journal. She hadn't noticed him arrive.

"You never know, I might."

"Would ya do me a favour and make me interesting?"

"Actually, Gerry, it's a journal. I make notes and sketches for my painting."

"Ya can paint me if you like – ya know, a colourful bit of local character." He pushed through the swinging door giving Janice a brief view of the men at the bar: Jimmy Neil, the snarling socialist; Shuggie Murray, an eternal fountain of hope; and wee Joe McPeak, an old soul wandering the world again. They were celebrating another self-declared 'Scottish Bank Holiday,' observed on arbitrarily selected Mondays after particularly hard weekends. "I don't know, lads; I mean, it'll be tough for a while. That's only to be expected."

"Tough?" Jimmy settled in as he lit a foul smelling cigarette. "It's only the beginning," Jimmy laughed. "Mark my fucking words. All the big ones will start eating the little ones until they're all gone. Then they will turn on themselves."

Shuggie's eyes grew like an owl's as he smiled at wee Joe, who looked like a mouse. "You'll be the first to go."

Joe tore himself from his reflections. "What are you talking about now, ya big draft man?"

"When we get to start eating each other; Jimmy was just explaining it."

Janice stifled a laugh as she put down her journal and looked at the cover of her book. She smiled at the title, 'Man Descending.' *Mr. Vanderhaeghe, do you have any idea how low they can go?* But the conversation on the other side of the partition was too good to ignore. It was just getting raucous.

"So what do they expect us to live on then?" Wee Joe complained as he nodded to Tommy. "Three pints, please."

"Crumbs from the table – only they call it trickle-down economics."

"Ah! But look at all the investment that is pourin' in now. Everywhere you go, they're building new roads – funded by the 'European Development' thing – German Marks, every penny of it."

"Autobahns," snarled Jimmy. "Hitler built them so his fuckin' Panzers could roll across Europe."

"But the Germans are okay now, they're helping us."

"It's still a fuckin' capitalist invasion. Welcome to the future. It's going to be great for a while."

"Great? I think we should take their money and build a big fuckin' wall around ourselves to keep all you'se fuckin' foreigners out," Caulfield muttered. He didn't like the Scots.

Tommy stood to the taps, eying each one of them in turn, in a casual sort of way, but he didn't speak.

"You're right there, Jimmy. I'm tellin' you'se. This man could have been a genius if he wasn't born in the Gorbals: too much lead in the pipes." Shuggie beamed at them all though his ridiculously thick glasses, but he didn't divert the mood.

"Fuck you, ya Scottish Shite. Why don't ya join your 'squadies' and go shoot children on the Falls Road'."

Caulfield had gone too far. Any mention of the smoldering 'troubles' in Ulster put everyone on edge. The Irish Civil War had petered out, but its ghosts could still flare up in pubs across the country, even Grogan's – but only from time to time. Grogan's was where those who claimed allegiance to the 'Pinnies' or the 'Stickies', as the two sundered halves of the IRA were then known, could drink side-by-side, as long as the conversation stayed on safe ground. Tommy had to intercede: "Now, lads, decorum please. Young Janice the painter is in quiet contemplation on the other side."

"Maybe I should go in and keep her company?" asked Gerry with seemingly earnest innocence.

"Stay where you are, Mr. Morrison." Tommy commanded. "She's a business meeting with a fella about showing her work in Paris."

Janice felt warm inside; Tommy was such a knight in shining armour. *But how could he know that I had a meeting?* Ronan would have some explaining to do, but it would have to wait. An elegant man was standing over her table. His suit was a silvery charcoal and his shoes were grey; his briefcase was also grey but a much darker shade. He looked so out of place in Grogan's.

"I'm sorry," Janice offered along with her hand, "I was lost in the conversation."

Thierry was gallant and bowed at the waist to kiss her hand. *I like him! He is so French. What a refreshing change.* "Conversation?" he asked, looking around the empty lounge.

He is cute, too, and he smells good. "On the other side of the Berlin Wall," she nodded toward the partition where the conversation had changed – they were discussing the Spanish Civil War; someone had mentioned Franco.

"Ah! So you are not mad. One has to be so very careful with painters, you know? I suppose it is all the fumes." He sat on the stool opposite her and leaned forward a little, a casual but intimate gesture that caused her to smile.

Don't spoil it now, Princess. She plucked a Gauloises from the tight pack and offered it to Thierry.

"Real cigarettes, what a pleasant surprise. I don't smoke, but you go ahead, please."

"You speak English very well," Janice offered as she choked down the pungent smoke. She had never smoked French cigarettes before. She saw them behind the bar, Tommy kept a stock for Jimmy Neil, and it was all that he would smoke. 'It will add to my urbanity,' she had quipped. 'They'll make you as sick as a dog,' Tommy warned. 'Jimmy Neil used to be in the choir and now listen to him. He sounds like someone sawing through rusty old metal.'

"You mean, I don't say my words with a terr-ib-le accent?" Thierry continued. "Actually, I learned my English here in Dublin. I came over every summer and stayed with an Irish family."

Christ, he is perfect. He ordered drinks and shifted his stool a little closer. "So! How do you like living in Ireland?"

"Funny you should ask. I was just reading a book from Canada, and I started to cry, I don't know why; I just got homesick." She wished she hadn't said that. It was gangly, like adolescence, and not at all the way she wanted to be.

"You are not what I expected."

"Oh really?" Janice shifted on her seat and leaned forward enough for her belt to pull her shirt tighter as she flicked her dark curls back over her shoulders. Thierry watched the adjustment with amusement and interest. "I am so glad that we could meet. We have so much to discuss. I have heard so many wonderful things about you."

Of course, he was flirting with her, and he was good at it. It was something she had missed. It wasn't something that Irishmen excelled at. "So where did you hear about me?"

"Oh, how can one say where? Here and there, your name is being discussed in London."

Janice eyed him coldly. He hadn't lied, but he wasn't telling the truth. "That is so sweet of you to say. Very sweet and very charming," she added as her options opened in her mind. "So! How long are you in Dublin? We must arrange for you to see my work."

"I return to Paris tomorrow."

"Oh! You're leaving so soon."

"Yes, I am busy, but perhaps, we could find time to look over your work before I leave."

Janice moistened her lips. "I have a portfolio; I could bring it to your hotel."

They smiled at each other in a moment of knowing silence. He handed her his card, he had written the details on the back and bowed, allowing his warm breath to caress the back of her hand. "But now I must go. So! Until we meet again; Bon Soir."

"Bon Soir," Janice agreed, still holding her hand aloft as she watched his grey suit shimmer as he left.

"Did he hurt your paw?" asked Gerry's nose, which was protruding around the door.

Oh, shit! That goddamn old weasel was standing there since . . .

"Gerry, Leave young Janice alone," Tommy called from behind the bar. "Come and tell everyone what you were saying the other night about the Africans and all."

Gerry hovered for a moment.

"What the fuck would that old curmudgeon know about Africa?"

Gerry had to react; his honour was on the line. "Well now," he began as he returned to his stool. "Tommy and I were having a quiet chat, not at all what ruffians would appreciate, but I did have a few points that I would like to share with you all."

"Ya heard him, Tommy, five pints, please."

As Tommy rose to pour the pints, he winked at Gerry, "I still have your change. Remember?" he asked Gerry's blank face. "Ya gave me a twenty and I never gave you your change. I'll give it to you now, after I take out for these."

"Ah good man, Tommy, I'd almost forgotten. Here, gimme twenty Afton, too, like a good man?" Gerry was reinforced by his good fortune and perched on his stool. "As I was sayin' to this fine gentleman behind the bar, that with the way things are going a time will come when we won't have to go away for work. They'll all be comin' over here."

"Who? The Germans? They'll only be comin' to buy the place."

"Actually, I was talkin' about the people from the Third World," Gerry piped over the undercurrents.

"Mayo?"

"No! He's talkin' about Birmingham and Brixton, aren't ya, Gerry?"

"Actually gentlemen, I was talkin' about Africans. You know, big black fellas who'll be happy to come over here and work for half of what you'se make."

"It's been done Gerry, by the Cotton Barons in the Southern States."

"I know but that's not what I'm talkin' about. I think there's goin' to be a time when we'll be like that TV show. Ya know, the one where they're always drivin' around in space?"

"Star Wars?"

"Nay, he means Star Trek, don't ya, Gerry?"

"Yup, that's the one. Anyways we'll all be fancy and educated and we'll be so busy leadin' very important lives that we'll have to hire people to come and drive the taxis and the buses and the stuff we couldn't be bothered doing for ourselves anymore."

"Ya mean that all I have to do is to sit here, listenin' to the shite that comes outta yer mouth and them black fellas will come and drive me home? Jazus, Gerry, that doesn't sound too bad."

"Ah but ya don't understand. They'll come here just like the way we went out to America, ya know? They'll shovel shite and work really, really hard. And then they'll send their kids to school to do really, really well, and in time there'll be a black President of the Republic of Ireland."

"They'd elect a woman first."

"They'll do that, too."

"Listen, Gerry, explain to me why, outta of all the places in the world, would they come to a country that throws away its children?"

"Ah," Gerry lolled in the glow of their attention. "With all this European investment, there'll be jobs goin' empty for one thing. But there's another reason. Think about it, gentlemen, what's the first sign of civilization these Heathens saw?"

"A British Red Coat with his bayonet?"

"No! I mean after that, when it was time for them to get civilized and all, what did they see?" He paused and savoured their silence. "Well I'll tell ya then. They would've met a Missionary: an Irish Priest, or Brother, or even a Nun, and they'd have thought that Ireland must be like a Heaven, ya know, full of smilin' angels that only bring peace and happiness."

"That's why I came here from Glasgae!"

"That's my point, Jimmy; they're in for a real shock. They think they are comin' to the Ireland of a Thousand Welcomes, poor bastards, are they ever in for a nasty reception."

Ronan entered the lounge door and smiled sheepishly as Janice crossed her legs and lit another cigarette. It almost made her cough as she glared at him, but he was looking past her already, toward the bar where the voices were getting louder. "Ah! How ya, Janice. Can I get you a drink?"

"Sure, go check your lines with Tommy; I will be waiting here for an explanation."

On cue, Tommy's face appeared around the door. "I'm off duty now so I'll wish you a good evening now, and I'll see ya later.

"Good night, lads," Tommy grinned as he bustled through the bar and out the side door to the corner of South William Street and the cool evening rain. He had just given Gwen Fitzwilliams some information. She was looking for an Irish-owned company to put up some money for a show. She was surprised when he told her about Ronan's father and how they were all connected.

And poor Ronan, ah sure, I'll be able to help him explain it when she has cooled down a bit.

A bit high strung is our Janice, he reminded himself as he walked toward the decrepit streets around Temple Bar.

"Okay, start explaining," But it really didn't matter what he said – she was furious. Her art was a private matter and not grist for the mill around the bar.

"But you asked me to talk with my father, and I did."

"So why didn't you mention it before?"

"I wanted to make sure before I told you. And then the time was never right."

"So let me get this straight," she raised her pitch again as she stubbed her cigarette.

"Janice, the lads," he pleaded, nodding his head toward the partition.

"Oh, you're worried about what your friends might think? Well, let's ask them Ronan. Let's invite them into our little row as I'm sure they are all listening." She rose and opened the door to the bar and stood in the frame with her hands on her hips, speaking to her right, where Ronan sat, and then turning a stony stare on the cowering men. "Ronan arranged for a Frenchman to come and take my work to Paris!"

"Ah now, that was very decent of ya. Good man yourself Ronan."

She turned and stared at them all.

"It's not like that, Janice!" Ronan stammered before she continued.

"No! You're right. Gentlemen, I apologise," she tossed her hair again. "Ronan's father agreed to be a sponsor for an Art Exhibit in Paris and by sheer coincidence the Art Director flies over to see me."

"What a wonderful coincidence," Shuggie chortled until Janice's glare froze him.

"So you and your father are pimping me out, and what did Tommy have to do with it all?"

"It was all his idea. He was the one who knew about the show."

"Pimps, you are all goddamn pimps."

"Actually, Janice darlin', if they're paying him to . . ."

"Fuck off back to Scotland, you, I am out of here."

"Ah Janice, wait."

"You should've stuck with flowers, me boyo. You can never go wrong with flowers, unless she is allergic. But even then ya can get some nice fake ones and they last a lot a longer too."

"Thanks, Shuggie, but I'm not sure if that helps."

"Ach, nae worries! Gie o'er here and have a pint wi' uz. C'mon. She'll be all right. She just needs to git it outta her hair."

"That's what worries me."

"Ach c'mon, that's what you have mates for — to help ya sort out yer problems. Lads, we have a night's work with this one, call the wife and tell her that I won't be home 'til late."

"I thought she had left you?"

"She did, but her parents sent her back — said I was her lot in life, me, Shuggie Murray. I always knew that they liked me."

"Ah shite," thought Ronan. "Oh well, I may as well be hung for a sheep as a lamb. Five pints, please there, Sean!"

Chapter 19

A woman approached with a squeaky-wheeled trolley stuffed to overflowing. It would take at least ten minutes to ring it all in. Sinead wanted to say 'Hi' or something, but her customer didn't look so happy as she flicked her 'Di do' and rattled her bangles. *Fair enough, be a bitch, see if I care,* but she did run a few items through twice. *Christ, does she cook anything from scratch?* The woman looked up from her magazine before Sinead could look away. "Can I help you with something?"

It was almost half past; only another thirty minutes to go. She hated working there, but until she heard back from the Government, she had to work somewhere. Only why did it have to be with Valerie, a thin lipped, bag-faced woman who didn't like the fact that Sinead had gone to Trinity? She had taken the job for her father's sake. He knew the manager's father and was so proud of himself – being able to use his influence. She couldn't take that away from him, and each evening as they sat like a family again, she forced herself to smile when he asked: 'How was work?'

'It was fine, just work, you know.'

'Sure of course I do, didn't I spend the best years of my life . . . ?'

"I'm home!"

"I wanted to get you flowers, but I didn't know what type you liked so I got a bottle of wine instead," her father blushed as he placed the fiasco on the table and nodded to her mother. "Show her the letter."

Her mother removed the official looking letter from her apron and placed it on the table. "Go on; open it before we die of suspense. You've been waiting long enough."

"Would you ever leave her alone; she is opening it, only she's doing it careful so as nothing spills."

"But what if it's bad news? What will we do with the wine?"

"Ah sure if that were to happen, and it won't, we can drown our sorrows."

"Well, what does it say?" Her mother couldn't contain herself.

"They want me to start in two weeks."

But her mother hardly heard; she blessed herself and muttered to the ceiling as she slid to her knees. "Get down and give thanks to the Holy Mother of God. Hail Mary. Full of grace . . ." She prayed with her elbows on the table, looking like she could see and hear the Gods she spoke with. But Sinead stayed in her chair and sent her thanks to the other Mary, the one who had inspired her all the way.

Her mother daubed her eyes with a tea towel and flung her arms wide. "I always knew that you were something special. Come here to me until I squeeze the life out of you. I'm so proud of you. And look at your father; he'll be buying drinks for the whole pub."

"C'mon then, let's get the dinner in to us so we can go."

"Are you coming Ma?"

"I will be down after I clean up, but you go ahead before your father gets excited and starts piddling. And when he gets all mushy and starts promising things, would you ever ask him to redo the kitchen like he promised me last Christmas."

"Ah Jazus, Mairead, can you not give the girl her moment in the sun without sticking your oar in the water. And what's wrong with this kitchen, anyway?"

She got up early to phone Valerie: to tell her that she wouldn't be going to work.

Valerie thought she should have given her a little more notice.

"But I can't. The I.D.A. insists that I start this morning. They have some big crisis that only I can solve. You know how it is for those of us who went to Trinity, we're in great demand."

She was brimming and wanted to share her news with everyone. She called Janice, but no one answered. She'd have to walk over, but first, she'd go to the coffee shop and clear the air with Ronan.

She almost bumped into him as she walked on Grafton Street, before she'd finished rehearsing it all in her mind. But he looked like he wanted to avoid her. "Hey Sailor, want to buy a girl a drink?"

"Oh. How are ya, Sinead? I didn't see you there. Are you well?" *Christ, why did I have to bump into her, of all people.*

"I'm great and I'm serious about that drink." *He doesn't look too happy to see me.*

He looked at his watch. "I only have time for a coffee, will that do?"

Well feck him up the arse anyway. "Never mind then."

"I'm sorry, Sinead; I've a lot on my mind these days."

He looks so cute when he's sorry. "What's the matter?"

"Ah fuck it, I may as well tell you, you probably know already. C'mon then, let's go to Bewley's."

"Wow, Ronan, you really know how to sweep a girl off her feet."

They sat near the window, but he was lost inside of himself again. She could see he wasn't ready to talk so she watched him watch the crowds go by. It was awkward, but she couldn't just leave: it was pissing down with rain. She'd have to wait and finish her coffee. "So how's Janice?"

"What can I say, Sinead. It's over between us."

"Just like that?"

He leaned forward and looked directly at her. His eyes were misty, and his smile was a little wrinkled at the edges. He was clean-shaven; he was even wearing cologne. He had straight white teeth, too; she'd forgotten all of that. "She went off and screwed some guy from Paris."

"Oh God, I'm so sorry, Ronan. I didn't know."

"It's okay; I was thinking about leaving her anyway."

She reached out and placed her hand on his forearm, just up from his hands that were pressed against each other like they were trying to squash something. "Ah, Ronan, what am I going to do with you?"

He sat back like he had just noticed her. "I'm sorry, Sinead. I just never seem to be able to get it right with you. Here I am prattling on about my problems, and I never even asked how you have been?"

"I got the job!"

"That's brilliant, I'm so happy for you. Fair play to you, I know you worked harder than anybody I know – not that I'm saying you're not smart or anything . . . Ah fuck it. I'll just shut up now."

She took his hands in hers. They were warm and trembled at her touch. She squeezed them gently and looked in his eyes. "So what's your next mistake going to be?"

"I'm leaving, Sinead. My father bought a company in Belgium and wants me to go and work there, you know, to learn the business."

She put aside all that swirled inside and looked at him as they stood in the doorway. He was tall and, for a Dubliner, quite dapper. He looked brave, too, and determined, but for Sinead, it was just sad; he couldn't wait for the future.

"Well, good luck to you then," he hugged her tight. "I'll write you ever week."

"You'd better, or I'll track you down and beat the crap out of you."

He smiled and turned to walk away, almost knocking over an old woman.

"Ronan, leave that poor old woman alone." She held her arm for a moment, to steady her. "Are you okay there, Missus?"

"Is he a eunuch? They're always on the lookout for white women. You should get away while you can."

Sinead had never seen dock leaves in a hat before – with a proud antenna thistle. She stared until Ronan stepped in front of her. "Would you ever think about coming with me?"

That, as she remembered for years, almost put the heart across her, but she couldn't. The timing was all wrong, and besides, it would be like she was taking Janice's hand-me-downs. She'd let some time pass and in a few months she could casually arrange a trip to see him, as a friend, of course, at least for a while.

"I can't, Ronan. Think about it: me in a country made of chocolate. I'd lose my girlish figure in weeks and then you'd dump me for someone called 'Nicollette.' It just wouldn't work out. You can see that for yourself? Can't you?"

"Maybe you're right, I'm sorry I asked. Forget that I ever said it. But I promise I'll keep in touch with you. I'll write you, maybe not every week, but I'll write."

You should've grabbed him while you had the chance.

But what about my job and my career? And besides, there'll be a lot more chances to see him again.

I hope you're right.

It was all Janice's fault really. They could've had a few months together. They might even have been able to do the long distance thing.

That would've been so nice, leaving the office on Fridays with everybody knowing that she was going to Brussels to see her boyfriend. Of course they'd meet in the other cities, too, walking by the Seine at night, watching the sunset from the top of the Spanish Steps, or doing whatever Berliners did on that street with all the lindens. Feck Janice anyway!

She was getting angry and not just about Ronan; it was all the other stuff: Lenanshees and Muses and Fate; Faeries and Ghouls and Goblins, it was enough to drive a Saint mad! She needed a deflection and stopped for Chinese food.

Janice had so many things hanging on delicate threads, clamouring for attention. She had spent the last few days on 'The Lovers,' a fauvist effort of vividness and carefully smudged brush-strokes. It was worth it; the subjects were ridiculously bright against dark shadows. The older woman held the other's head against her shoulder, protecting her and watching over her. Their eyes were defiant! She loved their lips; they'd taken time, but they were perfect. It was propped against the wall where she could see it, even as she worked on another.

'The Night Out' was a much more accessible piece, a bar scene full of characters loosely based on faces she remembered from Grogan's. Scots Corner was there like a scene unto themselves.

She had used a palette knife and was delighted with the depth. It was noisy, like a rowdy night. A woman sat alone in the center of the canvas, on a low stool by a small table, dressed in an austere suit that parted to reveal a stiff white shirt with buttons undone to the waist; pulled tight against her breasts. Her skirt parted just above the knee, daring and daunting the men; keeping them at bay while enticing them to approach. They looked like gargoyles and the woman looked like Gwen. She stared out from the canvas, like she was waiting for an answer.

There were a few others, too, evocative and ethereal images she carried back from the mists her mind wandered in. Her apartment was full of faces crying for attention. Sometimes, their clamour almost drove her into the streets.

She would work on 'An old woman in a hat' next: a melancholy tribute to Old Joan. She'd already drawn the outlines with charcoal as her nose wrinkled: she'd promised to call, but what was the point? All she could do now was to leave her paintings, like a trail of breadcrumbs, a warning to others about was happening just beyond the edge where the old ways surged like undertows.

"Well, you'd better come in and, please, excuse the mess; I've had no time to tidy up."

She wasn't kidding and Sinead struggled to remain cheery as she scoured the littered kitchen for clean plates and cutlery. The air was heavy and the plants needed watering. She wanted to be buoyant and chattered away, but Janice hardly replied, like she was at a distance watching with bemusement.

They sat in silence as Janice poked at her food.

Sinead ate regardless, grinding on each mouthful, but her patience was wearing thin, despite her best intentions. "What's the matter with the food?"

"It's okay," Janice answered at last. "I'm just not very hungry."

"So what's new with you and Ronan?" Sinead poked at a small mushroom.

"Oh! Sinead," Janice sat back and ran her fingers through her hair. "Why must you ask such questions?"

"Tell me. You know I'll find out anyway."

"Very well then, he and I parted ways, a few days ago."

"Why?"

"You're being very intrusive."

"Maybe, but isn't that what you love about me?"

"He started to get too involved. I wasn't ready for that."

"That drives me nuts, too. It's enough to make you go looking for someone else. Was there someone else?"

"Well, yes, there was as a matter of fact, but that's his fault, too."

"And how did you arrive at that?"

"Sinead, what does it matter? I was angry at him."

"Who was it?"

"A Frenchman, the Director of the Paris show, to be exact."

"Nice," Sinead whistled softly. "How was it?"

"Some things you do for love, some for lust and some for other reasons."

"That bad?" Sinead was enjoying herself, and Janice had started to eat, a pick here and a peck there until finally she took an entire chicken ball in her fingers and popped it into her mouth.

"I just went to show him my portfolio. I never intended for anything to happen. You know what it's like."

Janice was happy that she had someone to tell, like it was such an everyday thing, the way that Gwen would have explained it. "It's just one of those things you do when you're young and full of Scotch," Janice nodded, agreeing with the plausibility of her own statement. She really had no choice; she had to be in love with somebody and he seemed interested, even intimating that he might take her to Paris as they danced around his hotel room. She could almost imagine it as he turned her toward the full length mirror, as he gently drew her shirt from her neck. She would spend her days in a studio on the left bank, and in the evening, they would dine in one of the better cafés. She smiled at herself as she emerged from her shirt that had tumbled to her waist, but the stiff cuffs held her wrists captive.

Her skirt and underwear were discarded in a pool around her long heels – he had left her stockings on. He pushed her forward, face-to-face with her own reflection. A small green mist appeared in the depths of her pupils. It flickered as if it might die, but then it grew with the urgency of his rhythm. She placed her hands on the mirror as her shirt stretched across her back. She arched her back and raised her breasts, shivering against the cold. Fingers, deliciously chilled, like water from a mountain spring, reached down across her belly and the front of her thighs. But she didn't mention that part to Sinead.

"And he left you because of that?"

"Really, I know. Can you believe it?"

"How did he find out?"

"I told him."

"And how did he take it? Did he get mad?"

"No! That was the worst part. He just accepted it all so calmly." She smiled into Sinead's tears. There was no point in dramatics; he had closed the door, gently but firmly. There was no point in him staying – she was never going to be allowed to love him.

Sinead rose and tidied away the plates without comment.

"I suppose you're frowning at me." Janice asked as she followed.

"Did you love him at least?"

"Oh, Sinead, what is Love, anyway?"

"Well, it's not something you'll find jumping in and out of other peoples' beds."

"That's very judgmental of you."

Sinead turned from the sink. The Chinese food came off easily, but there were wine encrusted glasses and others, stained forever with specks of paint. "Janice! You know what I'm trying to say. You can't just transfer Love that easily."

Janice tried to smile, even as her tears bubbled up. "Oh, Sinead, where can I ever find true love now?"

"Right here, Janice. I've always loved you, only you were too busy to notice. I've just been sitting back waiting for you to realise it." They held each other as the showers blew over Belgrave Square, but it was still a nice day. A little cold for that time of the year, but it would be September soon. They held each other and rocked back and forth. "Why don't you take a shower and I'll go get some wine and you and I'll spend the evening together, like we once did?"

"Oh, Sinead, I would love to, darling, but I can't. I have so much to do."

But Sinead was adamant, and deep down, Janice knew it was time to close her mind to the haunted faces and their incessant whispers. She couldn't paint them all. Her future was obvious to her now. She'd be successful; that was assured; she had paid the price with her heart. She was doomed to unfulfilled desires that she would try to sate with twisted and tormented affairs, alternatively moaning like a bitch and crying like a baby. She needed to spend a little time with all that had been before: warm candlelit evenings, drinking wine and laughing from her heart. "Okay, get wine if you must, but get a few and get some cheese, too."

"Right away, Princess," Sinead muttered as she left.

When she returned, Janice felt so much better and was in the mood to laugh a little, something she had almost forgotten how to do. "You look like an old woman struggling with your shopping bags."

"Would you ever go and shite! Here I am lugging bags around while you sit at home and get all dolled up. And by the way, why are wearing black underwear?"

"I'm having a date over."

"Well, I'll leave when they arrive."

"Typical, just when I am about to tell you how much you mean to me. Are you sure you weren't supposed to be a man?"

"Sorry, I was just getting confused."

"About what: that I love you?"

"Ah, Jeeze, Janice, don't be getting all maudlin, at least not until we're drunk. Go and finish getting ready."

"You're not comfortable with emotions, are you?" Janice called over her shoulder as she left to get dressed.

"They're over-rated." Sinead busied herself among her bags until Janice returned in black slacks and her loose black sweater, the one with the deep vee-neck that hung down around her shoulders. Her hair was still damp and ran in dark rivulets over her thick towel collar. Her fingers were clean and her nails were polished. She leaned against the doorway as she wrapped the towel around her hair. "What did you mean by that?"

"I mean that emotions are like the weather. I put out the cheese; it's in the other room."

They'd opened the Italian first; there were two more for later: French, for when their conversation was more delicate. They were celebrating as their new lives opened before them.

"You're not going to become a soulless bureaucrat, are you?"

"So what if I am? We can't all be artists, you know?"

Janice drained her glass and refilled it. She held the bottle toward Sinead. "Were you mad at me?"

"When?"

"When you first came over?"

"A little."

"Why?"

"I don't know, Janice."

"Sinead, since when did you start shying away from speaking your mind?"

"Feck-off, it's just that I don't know who you are any more. I thought I knew you, but you've changed and I understand that. I can understand the thing with Aidan would leave you a little reluctant with trust and all, but you had something good with Ronan." Janice recoiled a little but it was out there now, and Sinead just had to blunder on. "Couldn't you just be happy with that? Why did you have to go and fuck around on him? He's not the one you're mad at."

Janice topped up their glasses. Sinead always spoke her mind, and it was a valid enough denunciation, albeit embarrassing in front of the gallery of faces, now turned toward the wall but still pleading with the edges of her mind. She didn't want them to see her like this: so fallible. She needed to be omniscient to them. She would explain it to them later, that this was the cruel narrow little world she'd brought them into. She envied them, looking out but never getting involved. They were so unaffected.

She lit candles though the evening was still bright, but the sun had moved past the window and shadows were gathering.

She sat back down and drank in silence for a while.

She was a little ashamed of herself but that was because she was in Dublin: it was infested with guilt. "Sinead, do you really think there is such thing as happily-ever-after?"

"Not really."

"What about all those stories of lovers who struggle against all odds?"

"I don't know. You never really hear about what happens them after that. It's probably more like what happens our parents, you know."

"That's very sad."

"I don't think so. I think we make too much out of love when we are young. People change and we can't expect the love we had at the beginning to last, but how can you know who you're going to be in ten years? How can you know who the person you love is going to be?"

"You have never really forgiven me for Aidan, have you?"

"Something like that."

"So why are you here then?" Janice didn't mean it to sound like a challenge; she didn't want her friend to leave. She had stepped out of the mists and, for the first time in weeks, felt naked and afraid.

"Old time's sake." Sinead softened as she said it. She raised her glass and drank freely but looked a bit resigned. "Old habits, and besides, you need someone like me in your life to keep you grounded. And," she added as Janice topped up her glass, "this is the first date I have been on in weeks. So! Tell me, how's life as a scarlet woman?"

Janice might have sneered, but she didn't. She needed Sinead around. She loved her, despite everything. She was a good friend, even if she could never understand. "Oh, darling, don't be so provincial. I am not like other women."

"So from now on, you're going to do it with anyone who grabs your fancy?"

"Not at all, just those who can help me get to where I am going. Oh don't look so shocked, darling. I'm no different from any other woman. I'm just more honest about it."

"But can you really fall in love so easily?"

Janice shook her head and her hair tumbled around her face like the dark and brooding shadows that whispered in the corners of her room. Her lips were full and her cheeks were flushed, but her eyes were deep and dark.

"What is love, anyway? It is like you said – it's not supposed to last. That's just another lie we are told. We fall in love with images we conjure up and see only what we want to see. Then, when they fail, we say that love is a hollow, bitter thing – that love is nothing more than a lie. But that is not love, it's an emotional exchange, and when it fails, we call it false love. There really is no such thing, but we never admit to that. And, after our little bouts of self-delusion, we decide that the other person led us on, that they lied to us. Or we reach for the tired old classic – that they changed."

"When I was younger, I always wanted to believe in true love." Sinead didn't look up from her glass, now dark and cloudy except where the candlelight danced near the stem. "I used to think that there was someone just for me. I know it's silly, but I just wanted to believe in it."

Janice smiled at a passing thought; Sinead standing in front of the jeweler's window. "So what do you believe in now?"

Sinead drained her glass and poured another. "I suppose that now I believe that you just go about your life and let love come and find you. I don't think too much about it, anymore. I mean, I'll be starting a new job and all, and I won't have any time for it for a while, except, maybe, a regular shag with someone dreamy."

"That sounds like a plan," Janice opened another bottle. "Let's switch to French, darling; I've had enough Italian for now. It causes the emotions to gush."

"Janice, did you and Gwen . . ., you know?" Sinead asked after she had sipped the new wine, after they had sat in silence for a while. It was gauche and hung in the air between them. Sinead regretted saying it, but Janice just smiled.

"Why do you want to know?" She felt her sweater slip from her shoulder. Sinead's eyes followed it as she tasted her wine again.

"I'll tell you then." Sinead sat forward. "I was wondering why you did it with her and you never even tried with me."

"Would you like me to?"

"No! But that's not the point. I just want to know that you fancied me, that's all."

Janice took her in her arms as they both laughed; warm together; comforting and forgiving after all they'd been through, and Janice began to cry. "We have true love, Sinead, we'd never risk that."

"But you do fancy me, even though you know that I'd never . . ."

They snuggled into each other's warmth as the room flickered and the evening stretched toward the northwest sky. The silence settled around them, resting on matters resolved and matters forgiven. They were friends who loved each other dearly. They never wanted to move again.

"Sinead, I may not see you again, after I go to Paris."

"But, of course we'll see each other. What do you think, that I'd let my one true love, who's crazy about me, even though I won't do the business with . . .?"

"Seriously, Sinead, I've seen the whole picture of my life. It was a little shocking at first, but I've come to accept it. I'll die young. I know that now. And I'm okay with it because I'll leave a glorious legacy." She waved her arms around the room where canvasses lurked in the shadows, where shadowy faces pleaded against the walls. "I just wish I could get to enjoy it all a bit longer."

They sat together, holding each other as the future began to pull them apart. It wasn't what they wanted. They wanted to go on together for a while yet, but they were heading down different paths. They'd have to let go and let Fate send them where it decreed, and there was nothing they could do but smile at each other, a soft sad smile that almost brought tears to their eyes.

Sinead drained her glass and rose from the couch.

There was no point when Janice was like this. It was because she was artistic and she was probably nervous about the show in Paris, Sinead knew that she would be. She leaned forward and kissed her on the lips. "You'll write, won't you? If you don't, I'll track you down and . . ."

She hesitated for a moment as the door closed behind her. The fanlight was grimy and the pillars were dirty. The wide granite steps led down to the sad neglected patch of grass and forgotten flowers. A shadow flitted near the window, but Sinead paid it no attention. She was a little drunk and susceptible to the foolishness of twilight so she headed back toward her parent's house.

But the shadow waited and watched Janice as she refilled her glass. She changed back into her work clothes. She turned all of her paintings around and picked one and placed it on the easel. The shadow shed a silent tear. There was nothing that could be done now. It was the way things had to be. Fate demanded it.

Chapter 20

The Luas slithered around Peter's Place and along Adelaide Road. It reminded her of the day with her father, riding in the front of the upper deck of a 49A, one of the first things he wanted to do after the doctor had told him. They rode to Tallaght and back a few times. The conductor smirked the third time he took their fare: "Have you forgotten where you live?"

Her father eyed him coldly. "Can't a dying man have a chance to talk with his daughter alone?"

As the conductor scuttled away, he patted her hands. "He'll leave us alone now and we can ride for free. So, have you come up with how you're going to tell your mother?"

"Why am I the one who's going to tell her?"

"Ah, Sinead, you wouldn't ask a dying man to?"

He died a few months after she brought her baby to see him. He held her in his bony hands and studied his granddaughter until he tired and shriveled back into his tubes and wrinkled sheets.

After he died, her mother gave up and, for ten years, withered away. She was heartbroken without him, moaning and groaning as the doctors shook their heads. Mairead was offended by that, that they'd think there was something wrong with her sanity so she proved them wrong. Her heart gave out, and the doctors had to pronounce her dead by natural causes.

She almost fell into the aisle as the Luas lurched around Harcourt Street. Her reflection looked very tired. That wasn't surprising given all that had happened with Derek and the Markets. The whole world was trembling and everything that was built on nothing was collapsing. The Tiger had been and gone and Dublin was left shivering, but she looked good for her age. She would be forty-four soon, Maeve was almost fifteen, Roisin was twelve and Niall was nine. Her mother warned that it would all go by too fast. She also said the good times wouldn't last: that for all their pretending that the Golden Calf was now good; that Judgment Day would come, and it would hit them where it hurt the most.

She really missed them as the months became years and all that had been so warm and constant began to fade. Now, when she remembered her mother, she saw herself instead. Was she a good mother? Did her kids know she loved them? Even before Derek shattered it all, there had been days when she'd said things that could have been left unsaid, sharp words when her patience snapped, and that was something that waited by her bed each night. What if they all died that night? Sometimes, she dwelt on the thought as she rolled away from him: he always went to sleep so quickly as she stared at the wall.

The Luas slithered to a stop, but Sinead sat for a moment. She always thought of Janice near the Green.

She ducked beneath the Arch as the Green opened before her. It was habit and that made it so much easier to do when her heart wanted to get back on the Luas and ride it to the edge of the mountains where she could hide in her bed for days. But she was determined that they'd all be happy again. She stopped before O'Donovan Rossa. It was another habit, and it remained refreshingly hopeful, even if his message remained cryptic. It always made her shiver, sometimes for the passion and conviction and sometimes for the sad inevitability of it all.

The ducks and geese played hide-and-seek in the trailing willow fingers, just below Yeats' glade where she once thought she saw Janice's ghost, although she had been out drinking with the girls. *Girls?* They were a mob of bored women sprung from the isolation of the deepest suburbs, on the lam from designed urbaneness until the chains of marriage grew taut and hauled them home in a shared taxi where they purged themselves of every lewd and bawdy thought they'd repressed. Derek had always encouraged her to go, even when she didn't want to. That made sense now.

She passed the Three Fates: a gift from the grateful people of Germany before they started sending something more practical – the funds to feed the fledgling Tiger. Ireland had done well with it all. For a few years, it had been the 'Poster Boy' for Europe: a model for the Poles and Slavs to follow. But that was before the sky tumbled in, before Derek left and all they had built collapsed around her.

She couldn't dwell on that, she'd have to be brave in front of the Solicitors. They were waiting in an office on Leeson Street. It was all so formal, but at least, he wouldn't be there.

She handled it well; like it wasn't personal. She just wanted what was best for the kids. Of course he could have visitation rights – he'd never use them, but she wouldn't be the reason. Things would be hard enough and she'd take the higher road, at least for their sake. She couldn't allow herself to become bitter. She'd spent too many nights sipping wine after the kids had been settled. Some nights, she brought the bottle to her empty bed. But today, she would be happy. She was proud that she could be so positive. "I must be getting wiser."

She looked around, but no one had heard, except the mannequins in their glass cages, blushing in the united colours of global consumerism. They meant so little anymore. It was all empty and hollow. For a while, it was engrossing, clamouring up the social

ladder and holidaying on the continent, but she never took up skiing; she preferred something warmer, and then she became a mother so there really was no point.

She lived for her career for years before ceding to her mater-
nal instincts. She'd always said she wanted them, but when the time
came, when Derek's mother inquiries had lost all pretense at subtly,
she didn't want to interrupt her life. Even when everyone said that
it was no big deal, that it was only for a while and she could just pick
up where she had left off. After all, Mary did: both of them.

But it didn't turn out like that. Instead, her life faded, dangling
at their beck and call until everything moved on without her. After a
few years, she stopped going to office parties – she was far too busy,
and she stopped dropping by for lunch – she felt forgotten even by
those who remembered her, and in time, she started to have lunch
with her neighbours.

She had given up so much for Derek, but she couldn't be angry. Not about the kids; she could never resent them. She loved
them and the years of being bound to their lives. Sometimes, she'd
been happiest when she had no time for herself, not even enough to
notice that her husband was changing.

He had done very well with the Bank and pampered her, buying whatever caught her fancy, and she got lost in it, like the city
around her. But even that was not enough. They had to become
something else, too, looking down their noses at foreigners who
processed their purchases and smiled regardless of the rudeness of
the New and Improved Ireland.

But Bewley's was solid on its old Quaker foundations. She
dropped in from time to time and always left a tip for the young
girls who served her, blond Poles and dark, gypsy-looking girls
from Romania, Czechs and big-eyed girls from Africa who always
smiled, even on the greyest days when the Island of the Thousand
Welcomes was lost in the mists. She wanted to take them home and

fill the great hole that emigration created. The one the Irish had known so well but had forgotten. The Tiger had changed all that.

She was hurrying past Coppinger Row when he called to her. "Sinead, it's me, Ronan."

"I'm sorry; you have me confused with someone else."

She re-crossed the street to Mark's and Spencer's, they had a coffee shop and she could gather her composure there. She ordered her latte and took it to a stool by the window. He was still standing in the middle of the street. In time, he smiled and walked toward her. "Don't you remember me? I know it's been twenty years but . . ."

"I'm sorry, Ronan; I'm having the worst day of my life, why did you have to show up today of all days?"

"How was I supposed to know?"

"You could've written. Well? Are you just going to stand there and stare?"

Grogan's had changed too, but it changed at its own pace. Paddy O'Brian died a few years back and had died contented. But Tommy Smith was still holding the fort and rushed out to greet her with a smile and a slight limp. "Well, I thought you'd gone off and joined the convent."

"I did, but it's one of those very progressive orders."

"Well, it's fresh and well you're looking."

"Don't be getting any ideas, a night with me and you'd have to get the other hip replaced, and everyone says the last time the price of drink went through the roof."

"Ah, Sinead, still a mouth of honey, and Ronan, too. Jeeze, I haven't seen you in years."

They sat by the window as the sun lingered in the smokeless air and searched for the right words to bridge the span of years. "So, how've you been?"

"Ah sure you know, Sinead, just stumbling along with the best of them."

"Well it is great to see you again. You heard about Janice, didn't you?"

"I did, yeah. How long's it now?"

"At least fifteen years."

"You heard it was suicide?"

"I did. What did you hear?"

"The same; I heard it was an overdose."

Tommy placed their drinks on the table, wrinkling his nose to keep his glasses in place. "Do you know what I wanted to tell you, old Gerry was found dead in his bed a few months ago. He'd been there for a week or so, too."

"Did no one miss him?"

"Sure you know yourself. You only notice after it's been a while. I was just thinking of him when I heard."

"Didn't the neighbours notice?"

"They're all Africans. They didn't realise for a while and then they were afraid to call the Guards. I suppose they're afraid that they'd get blamed. It was sad, poor old Gerry deserved better. He was a decent old sort, but he had a very sad life. He used to send money back to his mother when he was over in London, to keep the farm up, but she drank it all. And she used to tell the neighbours that he never kept in touch with her at all. And then, when he went home for the funeral, everybody was very cool with him. The poor old soul, there was no badness in him at all, was there?"

"Not a shred of it."

"He was a clever sort, too. He used to say the strangest things. He told me once that Dublin would fill up with Africans, he was right about that and, may God forgive us, but he was right about the welcome they got too."

"Yeah, he'll be missed."

"Do you remember what else he said? That the E.U. was like a Lenanshee. Well, he was right there, too, and the poor old Celtic Tiger had a very short and spectacular life. And did you hear? Jimmy Neil died a few years back, too. He was coming out of a pub on Dorset Street and fell down dead on the street. Shuggie Murray was saying that he should have known better than to leave the pub early. And you heard about Janice, didn't you? That was very sad all right, and she was still so young. I was just reading that her paintings sold at an auction recently, and they went for big money, too." He retreated back behind the bar and closed the hatch behind him.

"I wondered what happened to them."

"I had them." Ronan didn't look up from his drink. "I collected them after she died."

"Really?"

"Sure. They were good investments but you know where things are going. In a few months, nobody will even remember the Credit Suisse thing."

"I know. I was just reading the paper before I came out. We're facing our first recession in over twenty years. Half of the country is too young to remember the last one. I suppose its long over-due. We've all been living beyond ourselves for years."

He jay-walked across Westmoreland Street, through the blur of BMW's and SUVs. They were in such a hurry now so he lit a cigar as he strolled past the Bank of Ireland. It housed Gratton's Parliament before they sold the country out, too. He spluttered and coughed a few times. He was getting old, and besides, the city was infested with shiny new cars that idled down narrow streets spewing invisible poisons – *and they banned fuckin' smokin'!*

'Seamuses in striped shirts,' he called them, affluent and arrogant and oblivious to everything around them. It wasn't their success he resented, it was their indifference to the past and all that had made them. "Bastard sons of a Strumpet," he growled as his chest heaved a little. He had a good night and still had a few Euros left: a few of his poems had been included in a new collection. He headed to Grogan's to see what the day might bring.

"Speak for yourself," he snorted as he joined them. "Not all of us are livin' in the elevated 'burbs.'"

Sinead hadn't seen him in years, but he looked the same, except for a few more lines in his face, and his cheeks were hollow, probably from gnawing at himself, and his hair was mostly grey. He'd look so much better if he cut it; it was flaring out behind his ears and over his collar. And he could use a tan; he was as white as a fish belly, but she rose and hugged him anyway. He shuffled as she held him and nodded at Ronan who nodded back. "So you're the famous Aidan Greeley that I've heard so much about?"

Aidan eyed his striped shirt and silky tie. "What the fuck is that supposed to mean?"

"It's just a question; I thought poets were supposed to be in the questioning business."

"We are and you can go-and-fuck-yourself for an answer."

"Now boys, let me introduce you formally. Aidan, this is Ronan, the guy that Janice dumped you for before she dumped him for some French Art Pimp. So both of you sit down and behave yourselves." She glared at both of them but softened when Tommy placed fresh drinks before them. The two men raised their pints in perfect synchronization, something that caused them to smile and nod to each other. Aidan lowered his glass with a wry smile and looked at Sinead. "So what's the fuckin' matter with ya? Is that husband of yours neglectin' you? Maybe he's found someone else, someone who lets him wear the pants once in a while."

Sinead struggled to find her composure and took a sip of her wine. "Please, excuse me, gents! I just found that my no-good feckin' husband's been cheating on me. Except the way he sees it, he's in love with a twenty-two-year-old someone else."

"What a fuckin' dick-weed. He'll never find another woman like you."

"I guess that's why he left me for a man." Sinead was still smiling but it was strained.

"Shit, Sinead, I am sorry."

"So? Did you fuckin' kill him or what?

"Well." She daubed her eyes and sipped more wine. "After he left the kids and me, he left the Bank in a hurry, too, and moved to the Algarve. Then his lawyer was on to me, to ask me to refer any queries to him. Of course, I was as nice as pie. But when the people from the Bank came, I let them have the run of his desk, where his computer was."

"Well, at least, he will be very fuckin' popular in prison."

She needed to create a diversion: "I know it sounds old but I still miss the fun we used to have in here."

"Fat lot of fuckin' good it did us."

"Ah c'mon Aidan, you got to admit they were great times."

"It all turned to fuckin' shite, just like I told ya it would."

"Don't waste your time on him, Sinead. He's one of those brooding poety types."

She continued regardless. "Back then, we had a bit of balance. We believed in the past and the future, and now we have nothing."

"That's what I've been tryin' to tell everyone for years and now we're fucked. Now all the great ones are gone: John Jordan, Paddy, Jimmy Neil. Ah fuck it. Here's to them all."

"Here's to them all and, especially, old Gerry," they raised their glasses again. "And here's to Janice."

"To Janice," they echoed and raised their glasses again.

"I still think of her, you know. I feel that there had to be a way to help her, only I missed it."

"There was nothing we could have done for her. Isn't that right, Aidan?"

But Aidan didn't answer. He didn't dare. He'd opened the door to the other world, a world she could never survive. He'd caused the pain that festered inside of her, driving her into the arms of the Fates where the air was heavy with ecstasy and despair, poisoning her until she couldn't take it anymore.

He remained scrunched and constricted as Tommy brought fresh drink.

"Ah for feck's sake, Aidan," Sinead pushed him with her shoulder. "Stop gnawing at yourself. Ronan's right. Let it go."

"I can't, it was all my fuckin' fault."

"How could that be? She left a note."

He raised his glass and eyed the two of them from the rim. "Ya didn't believe her about Gwen bein' a Lenanshee an' all, did ya?"

Sinead said nothing, but Ronan laughed. "What are you on about, Greeley?"

"Ah what's the fuckin' point; you'd never believe me."

"Believe what?" Sinead asked as casually as she could.

"Don't ya get it? Gwen took her and gave her fame in return, that's how it works."

"Greeley, you're drunk."

"You knew, Sinead. I know she told you."

"Come on, Aidan, you didn't really believe all of that, did you?" She paused to take a very measured sip. "I knew she had a thing for Gwen, but I don't think they ever got together or anything, at least not while she was here. I don't know what happened after she left for Paris. Except she did tell me something before she left; she told me that she saw what was going to happen to her. I didn't believe her, at the time."

"You're both crazy."

"What, you didn't know?"

"Know what? I was only with her for a few months, and without speaking ill of the dead, she was a bit full of herself and all." Ronan hesitated for a moment. "Was she really having it off with Gwen too?"

Sinead glanced at Aidan before she answered. "No, of course not. You remember what she was like, away with the faeries half of the time. I mean she did have a crush on Gwen, but I don't think anything ever came of it."

"She didn't fuckin' have to; all she had to do was fall in love."

"So how did you . . . ?"

"Am I missing something here?" Ronan asked the silence that grew between them.

"I never loved her," Aidan answered cautiously. "I mean I did it with her an' all, but I never fell in love with her. That's why I was able to get away."

"But that means you would have had to find someone to take . . ." Sinead never finished her sentence; she just stared at her drink.

"You're both mad." Ronan watched as they stared at their glasses, as memories danced with the dust in the sunbeams, as Tommy left more drink without comment.

"So? Ronan, what's been happening in your glamorous life? The last I heard, you were married to some gorgeous young Parisian. So how are things?"

"Fantastic, Sinead, thanks for asking. I'm just winding up a divorce."

Aidan finally laughed, "Why would you even think about gettin' married anyway? Everything turns to shite, just like I fuckin' told you."

"Show some feckin' compassion, can't you? I don't know what to say, Ronan. Was it awful?"

"You know how it is. For the first years, it was great. She was perfect, beautiful and cultured and all."

"And what was so bad with that? It sounds like a man's dream."

He answered without taking his eyes from Sinead. "It was never mine, and one day, she stopped in the middle of whatever we were doing and asked me what it was that would make me happy. I told her I was, but she knew me better than that. I tried, you know, but I couldn't hide it. Well, after a while, I stayed in Brussels and she stayed in Paris. I told everybody that work was so busy, and she went back to school, but after a few years, what was the point anymore?" He paused as he drained his glass.

"We should never have gotten involved with all those fuckin' Europeans." Aidan tried to change the mood. It did make them laugh. "Why the fuck didn't we opt out when we had a chance? I mean, what were we afraid of anyway, upsetting the Lisboners? Fuck them, too. We don't need any of them; we had a rich uncle in America. But, I suppose, that's all we became in the end, fuckin' Euro-Yanks."

Aidan was flushed and his eyes were glassy. "But it all turned to shite, just like I said, and now, even our uncle is broke. Jimmy Neil was right, ya know. He said the whole fuckin' system would devour everythin' and then devour itself. 'Crumbs from the table,' that's what he called it. Here's to Jimmy, the Kamikaze Socialist."

"To Jimmy," they rejoined in a discordance.

"You're right, Aidan. We didn't know when we were well off."

"What the fuck are you talkin' about? You were one of the first to run over there."

"Now kids," Sinead admonished. She wasn't too concerned, but Ronan was beginning to come apart at the seams. His tie was hanging low and his stomach peeped through an open button. He had to stop drinking while he still had the choice.

"Ah for fuck's sake, we're just getting started. That's what's wrong with fuckin' foreigners, you know? They don't understand social drinkin'. I mean they have wine an' all, but they don't understand what it's like to sit down an' have a few pints. This is as good as it gets, sittin' in Dublin, havin' a few drinks with old friends, but you, ya fuckin' fop, had to go and ruin the mood."

"Ah fuck it, Greeley, I just know my limit. Do you have a problem with that?"

"It's no fuckin' wonder Janice gave up on you."

"Fuck you Greeley. You're the one who did her head in. Don't try to pin it on me. Go back to the part where you were pondering your inner pools of piss. You know, the part where you were blaming yourself for selling her into black magic or whatever it was. In fact, no, skip it, and you don't need to write about it, either, it's not that interesting."

"And how would you fuckin' know what I write about?"

"I used to collect your books."

Sinead was a little surprised, too. "Investments?"

"No, they were always too toxic; even by today's standards."

"Fuck you, Ronan, you're a prick."

"Listen, Greeley, you bollocks . . ."

Tommy saw them to the door where they linked arms and rambled down the alley beside Powerscourt, past Saint Teresa's, past the old jewelry store and out to the bustle of Grafton Street. The night was full of languages, a smattering of French and some guttural German, the roly-poly of Italian, so similar to happy chatter of the Romanians who finished work and bade good night to their Polish friends. "We've become the tower of fuckin' Babel."

"You're right, it was okay for us to go over there, but no one agreed that they could come here. There's a reason we live on an island. Why the fuck can't they give us one little place to call our own."

"The Book of Invasions, you gobshite: it predetermined us."

"Shut up, the pair of you. It's the way things should be, you know one big happy family with no divides and no barriers."

"Well, there's a good side to all of this doom an' gloom. Soon all these fuckin' foreigners will be gone, and we can get back to the way things were."

"You're right there, Greeley, we can go back to being miserable, too, just like before. You never know, when we get really depressed, we might start reading poetry again, even yours."

"Fuck you, Ronan."

"I don't want to hear that shite," Sinead almost stumbled. "We, of all the people in the world, should know better. For years, we were the bottom of the ladder. Don't you remember old Gerry telling us about those signs, you know, 'the no dogs or Irish' ones. You should both be ashamed of yourselves. All we care about now is making money. We are as bad as Americans."

She still hadn't forgiven them for what Bush did to Mary Robinson.

"Remember, we were the champions of social justice: priests, nuns and revolutionaries. We were the backbone of trade unions and every respectable revolution. Remember what we used to stand for before we became seduced by the money they told us we had; back when we thought it would never end? And now they want to tell us that it was our fault. They were right, too, but how the hell did they think we would act? We're Irish, for Christ's sake. We do nothing in moderation."

"Go home Sinead, you're drunk. You are startin' to sound like me." Aidan wavered as he shook hands with Ronan and nearly fell on her as they hugged. He was too drunk to carry on. He left them near Trinity College, lighting a cigar as he wandered toward the river, toward his small flat somewhere on the Northside of the river, near Capel Street. *In the middle of the fuckin' Warsaw Ghetto.*

"Which way are you going?"

"To the Green – to catch the Luas."

"Can I walk with you?"

"Why? Are you lost?" She nudged him with her shoulder as they linked arms and strolled along Grafton Street, right past Bewley's as the evening waned and the warm summer night drifted in from the bay.

"Not anymore," he laughed as he let go her arm and stepped back into the street with his arms spread wide. "I always remembered you standing right here: the day we said goodbye. Do you remember that day, Sinead?"

"Never gave it a second thought, but tell me, how often did you think about it?'

"Often enough."

"Do you remember when you nearly knocked that old woman down? I still remember the hat she wore."

"One of Janice's paintings was of an old woman in a hat with weeds in it. I wonder if it was the same one."

"The woman or the hat?"

"Both, I suppose. You know, when you think about it, they both got immortality. I wonder if she is happy now. Do you really think there was anything in what Aidan was saying?"

"C'mon Ronan, not you, too. Janice was very artistic; it makes sense that she created a fantasy world around her. I mean she needed it because, God love her, this one was far more than she could handle."

"So you don't believe in any of that Lenanshee stuff, do you?"

"No. She was in awe of Gwen and even tried to become like her, but I don't think that made Gwen a muse or anything, even if they did get together. They were very alike in some ways, and Gwen was a very powerful friend, don't forget that. I mean, look at Aidan and how well he did when he was with her."

"I can understand Aidan; I mean, Gwen was a fine thing, but Janice? What would make her do something like that?"

"Ronan, Janice picked her own path through the world, just like you and I did; only hers was a lot shorter than it should've been, but I don't think she would've wanted to grow old."

"Sinead, how are we ever going to be able to make the world feel better again? You used to be the one that always had hope. Where do we find that now?"

"Ah feck it, Ronan, how the hell would I know? Everything that I believed in has been swept away, too, you know? But I think we all have to try a little more reasonableness."

"Is that even a real word?"

"I hope so." She reached out for him and linked their arms. "So what's your next mistake going to be?"

"What would you think of you and me, you know, after you get everything settled?"

"I might consider it, after the kids are dead."

"Well, could I date you until then?"

"We'll see; we'll see," she laughed as she took him by the hand and crossed to the Green.

"So how old are the kids?"

But Sinead didn't answer. She was staring across the street, at the foyer of the Fitzwilliam Hotel, where Gwen walked with a young man on her arm. She hadn't changed; it was remarkable, after all the years. In fact, she looked great. She must have had work done.

Almost as much as the corner where Rice's pub stood, recreated in a niche among the exposed frames of the new shopping center, built over the graves of the little shops where you could find the things you were really looking for. There were a few pawn shops and little bookstores, too, the type of place where you could find first impressions of long poems, bejeweled with original sketches and the fading watercolours of the old ways.

"Will you marry me, if they all emigrate?"

"We'll see; we'll see."